The Thin Red Line; And Blue Blood

by

Major Arthur Griffiths

The Thin Red Line; and Blue Blood
by Major Arthur Griffiths

ISBN: 978-93-67147-55-9

Published by

DOUBLE 9 BOOKS

2/13-B, Ansari Road
Daryaganj, New Delhi – 110002
info@double9books.com
www.double9books.com
Tel. 011-40042856

ABOUT THE AUTHOR

Arthur George Frederick Griffiths (1838-1908) become a British writer, journalist, and prison administrator acknowledged for his great contributions to the sphere of criminology and his keen interest in penal reform. Griffiths had a various career that blanketed serving as an army officer, a prison governor, and a prolific author on various subjects associated with crime and punishment. One of Griffiths' tremendous works is "Early French Prisons," posted within the overdue 19th century. This masterpiece delves into the historic evolution of prisons in France, offering a meticulous examination in their structures, situations, and the prevailing penal systems from medieval instances to the 18th century. Griffiths employed his firsthand experiences as a jail governor to offer insightful analyses of the social and institutional factors of French prisons. "Early French Prisons" stands out for its meticulous research, bright descriptions, and Griffiths' commitment to losing mild on the frequently harsh and inhumane situations of historical prison systems. The book now not simplest serves as a treasured historic record but also contributes to the wider discourse on penal reform. Arthur Griffiths' multidimensional profession, combining practical revel in with a literary flair, underscores his effect on shaping conversations about criminal justice and penology. His paintings remains relevant for scholars, historians, and those interested in the evolution of prison systems and the quest for humane and powerful approaches to criminal punishment.

CONTENTS

VOLUME I

CHAPTER I
THE COMMISSARY IS CALLED 9

CHAPTER II
ARREST AND INTERROGATION...14

CHAPTER III
THE MOUSETRAP 20

CHAPTER IV
A SPIDER'S WEB 26

CHAPTER V
THE WAR FEVER...32

CHAPTER VI
ON DANGEROUS GROUND 38

CHAPTER VII
AN OLD ACQUAINTANCE..44

CHAPTER VIII
A SOUTHERN PEARL 51

CHAPTER IX
OFF TO THE WARS 57

CHAPTER X
A GENERAL ACTION 65

CHAPTER XI
AFTER THE BATTLE 77

CHAPTER XII
CATCHING A TARTAR...83

CHAPTER XIII
"NOT WAR!" 90

CHAPTER XIV
THE GOLDEN HORN 102

CHAPTER XV
THE LAST OF LORD LYDSTONE 109

CHAPTER XVI
"HARD POUNDING" 116

CHAPTER XVII
A COSTLY VICTORY 124

CHAPTER XVIII
A NOVEMBER GALE 135

CHAPTER XIX
UNCLE AND NEPHEW 143

CHAPTER XX
RED TAPE 149

CHAPTER XXI
AGAIN ON THE ROCK 156

CHAPTER XXII
MR. HOBSON CALLS 163

CHAPTER XXIII
WAR TO THE KNIFE 168

CHAPTER XXIV
AT MOTHER CHARCOAL'S 174

VOLUME II

CHAPTER I
SECRET SERVICE 183

CHAPTER II
AMONG THE COSSACKS 189

CHAPTER III
A PURVEYOR OF NEWS 200

CHAPTER IV
IN WHITEHALL 207

CHAPTER V
MR. FAULKS TALKS 213

CHAPTER VI
MARIQUITA'S QUEST 220

CHAPTER VII
INSIDE THE FORTRESS 230

CHAPTER VIII
FROM THE DEAD 235

CHAPTER IX
IN PARIS 241

CHAPTER X
SUSPENSE 254

CHAPTER XI
AMONG FRIENDS AGAIN 260

CHAPTER XII
IN LINCOLN'S INN 267

CHAPTER XIII
HUSBAND AND WIFE..272

CHAPTER XIV
THE SCALES REMOVED 276

CHAPTER XV
L'ENVOI..281

BLUE BLOOD

CHAPTER I...284

CHAPTER II...290

CHAPTER III..294

CHAPTER IV 299

CHAPTER V..305

CHAPTER VI 310

VOLUME I

CHAPTER I
THE COMMISSARY IS CALLED

In the Paris of the first half of this century there was no darker, dingier, or more forbidding quarter than that which lay north of the Rue de Rivoli, round about the great central market, commonly called the Halles.

The worst part of it, perhaps, was the Rue Assiette d'Etain, or Tinplate Street. All day evil-looking loafers lounged about its doorways, nodding lazily to the passing workmen, who, blue-bloused, with silk cap on head, each with his loa under his arm, came to take their meals at the wine-shop at the corner; or gossiping with the porters, male and female, while the one followed closely his usual trade as a cobbler, and the other attended to her soup.

By day there was little traffic. Occasionally a long dray, on a gigantic pair of wheels, drawn by a long string of white Normandy horses in single file, with blue harness and jangling bells, filled up the roadway. Costermongers trundled their barrows along with strange, unmusical cries. Now and again an empty cab returning to its stable, with weary horse and semi-somnolent coachman, crawled through the street.

But at night it was otherwise. Many vehicles came dashing down Tinplate Street: carriages, public and private, of every variety, from the rattletrap cab hired off the stand, or the decent coach from the livery stable, to the smart spick-and-span brougham, with its well-appointed horses and servants in neat livery. They all set down at the same door, and took up from it at any hour between midnight and dawn, waiting patiently in file in the wide street round the corner, till the summons came as each carriage was required.

As seen in the daytime, there was nothing strange about the door, or the house to which it gave access. The place purported to be an hotel — a seedy, out-at-elbows, seemingly little-frequented hotel, rejoicing in the altogether inappropriate name of the Hôtel Paradis, or the Paradise Hotel. Its outward appearance was calculated to repel rather than invite customers; no one would be likely to lodge there who could go elsewhere. It had habitually a deserted look, with all its blinds and casements close shut, as though its lodgers slept through the day, or had gone away, never to return.

But this was only by day. At night the street-door stood wide open, and a porter was on duty at the foot of the staircase within. He was on the inner side of a stout oaken door, in which was a small window, opening with a trap. Through this he reconnoitred all arrivals, taking stock of their appearance, and only giving admission when satisfied as to what he saw.

The Hôtel Paradis, in plain English, was a gambling-house, largely patronised, yet with an evil reputation. It was well known to, and constantly watched by, the police, who were always at hand, although they seldom interfered with the hotel.

But when the porter's wife came shrieking into the street early one summer's morning, with wildest terror depicted in her face, and shaking like a jelly, the police felt bound to come to the front.

"Has madame seen a ghost?" asked a stern official in a cocked hat and sword, accosting her abruptly.

"No, no! Fetch the commissary, quick! A crime has been committed—a terrible crime!" she gasped.

This was business, and the police-officer knew what he had to do.

"Run, Jules," he said to a colleague. "You know where M. Bontoux lives. Tell him he is wanted at the Hôtel Paradis." Then, turning to the woman, he said, "Now, madame, explain yourself."

"It is a murder, I am afraid. A gentleman has been stabbed."

"What gentleman? Where?"

"In the drawing-room, upstairs. I don't know his name, but he came here frequently. My husband will perhaps be able to tell you; he is there."

"Lead on," said the police-officer; "take me to the place. I will see to it myself."

They passed into the hotel through the inner portal, and up the stairs to the first floor, where the principal rooms were situated—three of them furnished and decorated magnificently, altogether out of keeping with the miserable exterior of the house, having enormous mirrors from ceiling to floor, gilt cornices, damask hangings, marble console tables, and chairs and sofas in marqueterie and buhl. The first room evidently served for reception; there was a sideboard in one corner, on which were the remains of a succulent repast, and dozens of empty bottles. The second and third rooms were more especially devoted to the business of the establishment. Long tables, covered with green cloth, filled up the centre of each, and were strewed with cards, dice and their boxes, croupier's rakes, and other implements of gaming.

The third room had been the scene of the crime. There upon the floor lay the body of a man, a well-dressed man, wearing the white kerseymere trousers, the light waistcoat, and long-tailed green coat which were then in vogue. His clothes were all spotted and bedrabbled with gore; his shirt was torn open, and plainly revealed the great gaping wound from which his life's blood was quickly ebbing away.

The wounded man's head rested on the knee of the night porter, a personage wearing a kind of livery, a strongly built, truculent-looking villain, whose duties, no doubt, comprised the putting of people out as well as the letting them into the house.

"Oh, Anatole! my cherished one!" began the porter's wife. "Here are the police. Tell us then, how this occurred."

"I will tell all I know," replied her husband, looking at the police-officer. "This morning, when the clients had nearly all gone, and I was sitting half asleep in the lodge, I heard—"

"Stop," said the police-officer, "not another word. Keep all you have to say for the commissary. He is already on the stairs."

The next minute M. Bontoux entered, accompanied by his clerk and the official doctor of the quarter.

"A crime," said the commissary, slowly, and with as much dignity as was possible in a middle-aged gentleman pulled from his bed at daybreak, and compelled to dress in a hurry. "A crime," he repeated. "Of that there can be no doubt. But let us establish the fact formally. Where are the witnesses?"

The porter, having relinquished the care of the wounded man to the doctor, stood up slowly and saluted the commissary.

"Very well; tell us what you know. Sit down"—this to the clerk. "Produce your writing-materials and prepare the report."

"It must have been about four this morning, but I was very drowsy, and the gentlemen had nearly all gone," said the night porter, speaking fluently, "when I was disturbed by the noise of a quarrel, a fight, up here in the principal drawing-room. While I was still rubbing my eyes, for I was very drowsy, and fancied I was dreaming, I heard a scream, a second, and a third, followed by a heavy fall on the floor. I rushed upstairs then, and found this poor gentleman as you see him."

"Alone?"

"Quite alone."

"But there must have been other people here. Did they come down the stairs past you?"

"No, sir; they must have escaped by that window. It was open—"

The commissary looked at the police-officer, who nodded intelligently.

"I had already noticed it, Mr. Commissary. The window gives upon a low roof, which communicates with the back street. Escape would be quite easy from that side."

"Well," said the commissary, "and you found this gentleman? Do you know him? His name? Have you ever seen him before?"

"He is M. le Baron d'Enot; he is a constant visitor at the house. Very fortunate, I believe, and I heard he won largely last night."

"Ah!" said the commissary. This fact was important, as affording a reason for the crime. "And do you suspect any one? Have you any idea who was here at the last?"

"I scarcely noticed the gentlemen as they went away; it would be impossible for me, therefore, to say who remained."

"Then there is no clue—"

"Hush! Mr. Commissary." It was the doctor's exclamation. "The victim is still alive, and is trying, I think, to speak." Evidence given at the point of death has extreme value in every country, under every kind of law. The commissary therefore bent his head, closely attentive to catch any words the dying man might utter.

"Water! water!" he gasped out. "Revenge me; it was a foul and cowardly blow."

"Who struck you, can you tell us? Do you know him?" inquired the commissary, eagerly.

"Yes. I—know—" The voice grew visibly weaker; it sank into a whisper, and could speak only in monosyllables.

"His name—quick!"

"There—were—three—I had no chance—Gas—coigne—"

"Strange name—not French?"

The dying man shook his head.

"Gasc—tell—Engl—"

It was the last supreme effort. With a long, deep groan, the poor fellow fell back dead.

"How unfortunate!" cried the commissary, "to die just when he would have told us all. These few words will scarcely suffice to identify the murderers. Can any one help us?"

M. Bontoux looked round.

"The name he mentioned I know," said the night-porter, quickly. "This M. Gascoigne came here frequently. He is an Englishman."

"So I gathered from the dead man's words. Do you know his domicile in Paris?"

"Rue St. Honoré, Hôtel Versailles and St. Cloud. I have seen him enter it more than once, with his wife. He has lived there some months."

"We must, if possible, lay hands on him at once. You, Jules, hasten with another police-agent to the Rue St. Honoré; he may have gone straight to his hotel."

"And if we find him?"

"Arrest him and take him straight to the Préfecture. I will follow. There, there! lose no time."

"I am already gone," said the police-officer as he ran downstairs.

CHAPTER II
ARREST AND INTERROGATION

The Hôtel Versailles and St. Cloud was one of the best hotels of Paris at this time, a time long antecedent to the opening of such vast caravansaries as the Louvre, the Continental, the Athenée, or the Grand. It occupied four sides of a courtyard, to which access was had by the usual gateway. The porter's lodge was in the latter, and this functionary, in sabots and shirt-sleeves, was sweeping out the entrance when the police arrived in a cab, which they ordered to wait at the door.

"M. Gascoigne?" asked the agent.

"On the first floor, number forty-three," replied the porter, without looking up. "Monsieur has but just returned," he went on. "Knock gently, or you may disturb him in his first sleep."

"We shall disturb him in any case," said the police-officer, gruffly. "Justice cannot wait."

"The police!" cried the porter, now recognising his visitors for the first time. "What has happened, in Heaven's name?"

"Stand aside; we have no time to gossip," replied the agent, as he passed on.

The occupant of No. 43 upon the first floor was pacing his room with agitated steps—a young man with fair complexion and light curly hair; but his blue eyes were clouded, and his fresh, youthful face was drawn and haggard. His attire, too—English, like his aspect—was torn and dishevelled, his voluminous neckcloth was disarranged, his waistcoat had lost several buttons, and there were stains—dark purple stains—upon sleeves and smallclothes.

"What has become of her?" he was saying as he strode up and down; "she has not been here; she could not have come home when we parted at the door of the Vaudeville—the bed has not been slept in. Can she have gone? Is it possible that she has left me?"

He sank into a chair and hid his face in his hands.

"It was too horrible. To see him fall at my feet, struck down just when I—Who is there?" he cried suddenly, in answer to a knock at the door.

"Open, in the name of the law!"

"The police here already! What shall I do?"

"Open at once, or we shall force the door."

The young man slowly drew back the bolt and admitted the two police-agents.

"M. Gascoigne? You will not answer to your name? That is equal—we arrest you."

"On what charge?"

"It is not our place to explain. We act by authority: that is enough. Will you go with us quietly, or must we use force?"

"Of what am I accused?"

"You will hear in good time. Isidore, where is your rope?"

His colleague produced the long thin cord that serves instead of handcuffs in France.

"Must we tie you?"

"No, no! I am ready to submit, but under protest. You shall answer for this outrage. I am an Englishman. I will appeal to our ambassador."

"With all my heart! We are not afraid. But enough said. Come."

The three—police-agents and their prisoner—went out together. On the threshold of No. 43 the officer named Jules said—

"Your key, monsieur—the key of your room. I will take charge of it. Monsieur the Judge will no doubt make a searching perquisition, and no one must enter it till then."

The door was locked, M. Jules put the key in his pocket, and the party went down to the cab, which was driven off rapidly to the depôt of the Préfecture.

Here the usual formalities were gone through. Rupert Gascoigne, as the Englishman was called, was interrogated, searched, deprived of money, watch, penknife, and pencil-case; his description was noted down, and then he was asked whether he would go into the common prison, or pay for the accommodation of the *pistole* or private "side."

For sixteen sous daily they gave him a room to himself, with a little iron cot, a chair, and a table. Another franc or two got him his breakfast and dinner, and he was allowed to enjoy them with such appetite as he could command.

No one came near him till next morning, when he was roused from the heavy sleep that had only come to him after dawn by a summons to appear before the *Juge d'instruction*.

He was led by two policemen to a little room, barely furnished, with one great bureau, or desk, in the centre, at which sat the judge, his back to the window. On one side of him was a smaller desk for the clerk, and exactly opposite a chair for the accused, so arranged that the light beat full upon his face.

"Sit down," said the judge, abruptly.

He was a stern-looking man, dressed all in black, still young, with a cold and impassive face, the extreme pallor of which was heightened by his close-cut, coal-black hair, and his small, piercing, beady black eyes.

"Your name and nationality?"

"Rupert Gascoigne. I am an Englishman, and as such I must at once protest against the treatment I have received."

"You have been treated in accordance with the law—of France. You must abide by it, since you choose to live here. I do not owe you this explanation, but I give it to uphold the majesty of the law."

"I shall appeal to our ambassador."

The judge waved his hand, as though the threat did not affect him.

"I must ask you to keep silence. You are here to be interrogated; you will only speak in reply to my questions."

There was a pause, during which judge and accused looked hard at each other; the former seeking to read the other's inmost thoughts, the latter meeting the gaze with resolute and unflinching eyes.

"What is your age?"

"Twenty-six."

"Are you married?"

"Yes."

"But your wife has left you."

Gascoigne started in spite of himself.

"How do you know that?" he asked, nervously.

"It is for me to question. But I know it: that is enough. Your occupation and position in life?"

"I am a gentleman, living on my means."

"It is false." An angry flush rose to Gascoigne's face as the judge thus gave him the lie. "It is false—you are a professional gambler—a Greek—a sharper, with no ostensible means!"

"Pardon me, monsieur; you are quite misinformed. I could prove to you ----"

"It would be useless; the police have long known and watched you."

"Such espionage is below contempt," cried Gascoigne, indignantly.

"Silence! Do not dare to question the conduct of the authorities. It is the visit of persons of your stamp to Paris that renders such precautions necessary."

"If you believe all you hear from your low agents, with their lying, scandalous reports—"

"Be careful, prisoner; your demeanour will get you into trouble. Our information about you is accurate and trustworthy. Judge for yourself."

Gascoigne looked incredulous.

"Listen; you arrived in Paris three months ago, accompanied by a young demoiselle whom you had decoyed from her home."

"She was my wife."

"Yes; you married her after your arrival here. The official records of the 21st arrondisement prove that—married her without her parents' consent."

"That is not so. They approved."

"How could they? Your wife's father is French vice-consul at Gibraltar. Her mother is dead. Neither was present at your marriage; how, then, could they approve?"

Gascoigne did not answer.

"On your first arrival you were well provided with funds—the proceeds, no doubt, of some nefarious scheme; a run of luck at the tables; the plunder of some pigeon—"

"The price of my commission in the English Army."

"Bah! You never were in the English Army."

"I can prove it."

"I shall not believe you. Being in funds, I say, you lived riotously, stayed at one of the best hotels, kept a landau and pair, dined at the Trois Frères and the Rocher de Cancale, frequented the theatres; madame wore the most expensive toilettes. But you presently ran short of cash."

"It's not surprising. But I presume I was at liberty to do what I liked with my own."

"Coming to the end of your resources," went on the judge, coldly ignoring the sneer, "you tried the gaming-table again, with varying success. You went constantly to the Hôtel Paradis—"

"On the contrary, occasionally, not often."

"You were there last night; it is useless to deny it. We have the deposition of the proprietor, who is well known to the police—M. Hippolyte Ledantec; you shall be confronted with him."

"Is he in custody?" asked Gascoigne, eagerly.

"I tell you it is not your place to question."

"He ought to be. It was he who committed the murder."

"You know there was a murder, then? Curious. When the body was discovered by the porter there was no one present. How could you know of the crime unless you had a hand in it?"

"I saw it committed. I tried my best to save the Baron, but Ledantec stabbed him before I could interpose."

"An ingenious attempt to shift the guilt; but it will not serve. We know better."

"I am prepared to swear it was Ledantec. Why should I attack the Baron? I owed him no grudge."

"Why? I will tell you. For some time past, as I have reminded you, your funds have been running low, fortune has been against you at the tables, and you could not correct it at the Hôtel Paradis as you do with less clever players—"

"You are taking an unfair advantage of your position, Monsieur le Juge. Any one else who dared accuse me of cheating—"

"Bah! no heroics. You could not correct fortune, I say; yet money you must have. The hotel-keeper was pressing for his long-unpaid account. Madame, your smart wife, was dissatisfied; she made you scenes because you refused her money; in return, you ill-used her."

"It is false! My wife has always received proper consideration at my hands."

"You ill-used her, ill-treated her; we have it from herself."

"Do you know, then, where she is?" interrupted Gascoigne, with so much eagerness that it was plain he had taken his wife's defection greatly to heart. "Why has she left me? With whom? I have always suspected that villain Ledantec; he is an arch scoundrel, a very devil!"

"The reasons for your wife's disappearance are sufficiently explained by this letter."

"To me?" said Gascoigne, stretching out his hand for it.

"To you, but impounded by us. It was found, in our search of your apartments yesterday, placed in a prominent place upon your dressing-table."

"Give it me—it is mine!"

"No! but you shall hear what it says. Listen:—

"'I could have borne with resignation the miserable part you have imposed upon me. After luring me from my home with dazzling offers, after promising me a life of luxury and splendid ease, you rudely, cruelly dispelled the illusion, and made it plain to me that I had shared the lot of a pauper. All this I could have borne—poverty, however distasteful, but not the infamy, the degradation, of being the partner and associate of your evil deeds. Sooner than fall so low I prefer to leave you for ever. Do not seek for me. I have done with you. All is at an end between us!'"

CHAPTER III
THE MOUSETRAP

"Well," said the judge, when he had finished reading, "you see what your wife thinks of you. What do you say now?"

"There is not a word of truth in that letter. It is a tissue of misstatements from beginning to end. You must place no reliance upon it."

"There you must allow me to differ from you. This letter is, in my belief, perfectly genuine. It supplies a most important link in the chain of evidence, and I shall give it the weight it deserves. But enough—will you still deny your guilt?"

"It is Ledantec's doing," said Gascoigne, following out a line of thought of his own. "She was nothing loth, perhaps, for he has been instilling insidious poison into her ears for these weeks past. I had my suspicions, but could prove nothing; now I know. It was for this, to put money in his purse for her extravagance, that he first robbed, then struck down the baron."

"Why do you still persist in this shallow line of defence? You cannot deceive me; it would be far better to make a clean breast of it at once."

"I have already told you all I know. I repeat, I saw Ledantec strike the blow."

"Psha! this is puerile. I will be frank with you. We have the fullest and strongest evidence of your guilt—why, then, will you not confess it?"

"I have nothing to confess; I am perfectly innocent. I was the poor man's friend, not his murderer. I tried hard to save him, but, unhappily, I was too late."

"You will not confess?"

A flush of anger rose to Gascoigne's cheek; his eyes flashed with the indignation he felt at being thus bullied and browbeaten; his lips quivered, but still he made no reply.

"Come! you have played this comedy long enough," said the judge, his manner growing more insolent, his look more threatening. "Will you, or will you not, confess?"

Gascoigne met his gaze resolutely, but with a dogged, obstinate silence, the result of a firm determination not to utter a word.

"This is unbearable," said the judge, angrily, after having repeated his question several times without eliciting any reply. "Take him away! Let him be kept in complete isolation, in one of the separate cells of the Mousetrap — the Souricière."

At a signal from within the police entered, resumed charge of the prisoner, and escorted him, by many winding passages, down a steep staircase to an underground passage, ending in a dungeon-like room, badly lighted by one small, heavily-barred window, through which no glimpse of the sky was seen.

Here he was left alone, and for a long time utterly neglected. No one came near him till late in the day, when he was brought a basin of thin soup and a hunch of coarse ammunition bread. He spoke to his jailers, asking for more and better food, but obtained no reply. He asked them for paper, pens, and ink; he wished, he said, to make a full statement of his case to the British Embassy, and demand its protection. Still no reply. Maddened by this contemptuous treatment, and despairing almost of justice, he begged, entreated the warder to take pity on him, to tell him at least how long they meant to keep him there in such terrible solitude, cut off altogether from the advice and assistance of friends. The warder shook his head stolidly, and at length broke silence, but only to say, "It is by superior order," then left him.

Gascoigne passed a terrible night, the second night in durance, but far worse than the first. He was torn now with apprehensions as to his fate; circumstances seemed so much against him; the facts, as stated by the judge, might be grossly misrepresented; but how was he to dispute them? There was no justice in this miserable country, with such a partial and one-sided system of law. He began to fear that his life was in their hands; already he felt his head on the block, under the shadow of the awful guillotine.

Nor were his personal terrors the only nightmare that visited and oppressed him. He was harassed, tortured, by the shameless conduct of his wife; of the woman for whom he had sacrificed everything — profession, fortune, name, the affection of relatives, the respect of friends. With base, black-hearted perfidy, she had deserted him for another, had plotted against him, had helped to bring him into his present terrible straits.

Once again they awoke him, unrefreshed, from the deep sleep haunted by such hideous dreams. He was told to dress himself and come out. At the door of his cell the same escort — two police-agents — awaited him.

"Where are you taking me? Again before that hateful judge?"

"Monsieur had better speak more respectfully," replied one of them, in a warning voice.

"It is no use, I tell you, his interrogating me. I have nothing more to say."

"Silence!" cried the other, "and march."

They led him along the passage and upstairs, but not, as before, to the judge's cabinet. Turning aside, they passed on one side of it, and out into the open air. There was a cab drawn up close to the door, the prisoner was ordered to get in, one police-agent taking his seat alongside, the other mounting on the box. The glasses were drawn up, and the cab drove rapidly away.

"Where are you taking me?" asked Gascoigne.

"You will see," replied his conductor, coldly.

"To another prison?"

"Silence! A prisoner is not permitted to enter into conversation with his guard."

Thus rebuffed, Gascoigne resigned himself to gazing mournfully through the windows as the cab rattled along. He did not know this quarter of Paris well, but he could see that they were passing along one of the quays of the Ile de la Cité. He could see the houses on the opposite bank, and knew from the narrowness of the river that it was not the main stream of the Seine. It was still early morning; the streets were not as yet very crowded, but as the cab entered a wide square it came upon a throng issuing from the portals of a large church, the congregation that had been attending some celebration at Notre Dame. He recognised the church as he passed it, still driving, however, by the quays. Then they came to a low building, with a dirty, ill-kept, unpretentious doorway. The cab passed through into an inner court, stopped, and Gascoigne was ordered to alight.

The police-agents, one on each side of him, took him to a rather large but dirty, squalid-looking room, which might have been part of an old-clothes shop. All round, hanging from pegs, each neatly ticketed with its own number, were sets of garments, male and female, of every description: rags and velvets, a common blouse and good broadcloth, side by side.

At a small common table in the centre of the room sat Gascoigne's judge, with the same cold face, only darkened now by a frown.

"Once more," he said, abruptly—"will you confess your crime?"

Gascoigne looked at him contemptuously, but held his tongue.

"Do you still refuse? Do you still obstinately persist in remaining dumb? Very well, we shall see."

The judge got up from his chair, and disappeared through a side-door.

After a short pause, Gascoigne's escort bade him march, and the three followed through the same door.

They entered a second chamber, smaller than the first, the uses of which were at once obvious to Gascoigne, although he had never been there before. It was like a low shed or workroom, lighted from above, perfectly plain — even bald — in its decoration, but in the centre, occupying the greater part of the space, and leaving room only for a passage around, was a large flat slab of marble, something like that seen in fishmongers' shops. The similarity was maintained by the sound of water constantly flowing and falling upon the marble slab, as though to keep it and its burden always fresh and cool.

But that burden! Three corpses, stark naked but for a decent waistband, were laid out upon the marble table. One was that of a child who had been fished up from the Seine that morning; the second that of a stonemason who had fallen from a scaffolding and broken his neck and both legs; the third was the murdered man of the Hôtel Paradis, the Baron d'Enot, stripped of his well-made clothes, lying stark and stiff on his back, with the great knife-wound gaping red and festering in his breast.

"There!" cried the judge, triumphantly, leaning forward to scrutinise narrowly the effect of this hideous confrontation upon the prisoner.

To his bitter disappointment, this carefully prepared theatrical effect, so frequently practised and so often successful with French criminals, altogether failed with Gascoigne. The Englishman certainly had started at the first sight of the corpse, but it was a natural movement of horror which might have escaped any unconcerned spectator at being brought into the presence of death in such a hideous form. After betraying this first and not unnatural sign of emotion, Gascoigne remained perfectly cool, self-possessed, and unperturbed.

"You see your victim there; now will you confess?" cried the judge, almost passionately.

"Ledantec's victim, not mine," replied Gascoigne, quietly. Then, as if in apology to himself, he added, "I could not help speaking, but I shall say nothing more."

"He is very strong, extraordinarily strong!" cried the judge, his rage giving place to admiration at the obstinate fortitude of his prisoner. "In all my experience" — this was to the police and the chief custodian of the

Morgue—"I have never come across a more cold-blooded, cynical wretch; but he shall not beat me; he shall not outrage and set the law at defiance; we will bend his spirit yet. Take him back to the Mousetrap; he shall stay there until he chooses to speak."

With this unfair threat, which was tantamount to a sentence of unlimited imprisonment, the judge dismissed his prisoner.

Gascoigne was marched back to the cab; the police-agents ordered him to re-enter it; one of them took his seat by his side as before, the other remounted the box. Then the cab started on its journey back to the Préfecture.

Gascoigne, silent, pre-occupied, and outwardly calm, was yet inwardly consumed with a fierce though impotent rage. He was indignant at the shameful treatment he had received. To be arraigned as a criminal prematurely, his guilt taken for granted on the testimony of unseen witnesses whose evidence he had no chance of rebutting—all this, so intolerable to the spirit of British justice, revolted him and outraged his sense of fair play.

Yet what could he do? He was without redress. They had denied him his right of appeal to his ambassador; he was forbidden to communicate with his friends. There seemed no hope for him, no chance of justice, no loophole of escape.

Stay! Escape?

As the thought flashed quickly across his brain it lingered, taking practical shape. Surely it was worth his while to make an effort, to strike one bold blow for liberty now, before it was too late!

He quickly cast up the chances for and against. The cab was following the line of quays as before, but along the northern bank of the island, that bordering the main stream. It was going at little better than a foot's pace; the door next which he sat was on the side of the river. What if he knocked his guardian senseless, striking him a couple of British blows—one, two, straight from the shoulder—then, flinging open the door, spring out, and over the parapet into the swift-flowing Seine? He was an excellent swimmer; once in the water, surely he might trust to his luck!

These were the arguments in his favour. Against him were the chances that his companion might show fight; that he might check his prisoner's exit until his comrade on the box could come to the rescue; or that some officious bystander might act on the side of the law; or that a shot might drop him as he fled; or, finally, and most probably of all, that he might be drowned in the turbulent stream.

Gascoigne was not long in coming to a decision. "Nothing venture, nothing have," was his watchword. At this moment the cab was near the end of the Quai aux Fleurs, near the Pont d'Arcole. There was no time to be lost; at any moment it might turn down from the river, taking one of the cross streets. Setting his teeth firmly, and nerving himself for a supreme effort, Gascoigne sprang suddenly upon the police-agent, twisted his hands inside the stiff stock, and, having thus nearly throttled him, felled him with two tremendous blows.

With a groan, the man fell to the bottom of the cab; the next instant Gascoigne had opened the door and dropped into the roadway.

The escape was observed by one or two passers-by; but they were evidently people who owed the police no good-will, for, although they stood still to watch the fugitive, they did not give the alarm. This came first from the policeman who had been assaulted, who, recovering quickly from the attack, roared lustily to his fellow for help. The cab stopped, the officials alighted hurriedly, and looking to right and left caught sight of Gascoigne as he stood upon the parapet and made his plunge into the river. Both rushed to the spot, pistol in hand.

Down below was the figure of their escaped prisoner battling with the rapid stream. Both fired, almost simultaneously, and one at least must have hit the mark.

Gascoigne's body turned over and then sank, leaving a small crimson stain upon the water.

Was he killed? Drowned? That is what no one could tell; but it was certain that no corpse answering the Englishman's description was ever recovered from the river; nor, on the other hand, did the police, in spite of an active pursuit, lay hands on their prisoner again alive.

CHAPTER IV
A SPIDER'S WEB

Some half a dozen years after the occurrences just recorded there was a great gathering one night at Essendine House, a palatial mansion occupying the whole angle of a great London square. The reception-rooms upon the first floor, five of them, and all *en suite*, and gorgeously decorated in white and gold, were brilliantly lighted and thrown open to the best of London society. Lady Essendine was at home to her friends, and seemingly she had plenty of them, for the place was thronged.

The party was by way of being musical—that is to say, a famous pianist had been engaged to let off a lot of rockets from his finger-tips, and a buffo singer from the opera roared out his "Figaro la, Figaro quà," with all the strength of his brazen lungs; while one or two gifted amateurs sang glees in washed-out, apologetical accents, which were nearly lost in the din of the room.

But there was yet another singer, whose performance was attended with rather more display. It was preluded by a good deal of whispering and nodding of heads. Lady Essendine posed as a charitable person, always anxious to do good, and this singer was a *protégée* of hers—an interesting but unfortunate foreigner in very reduced circumstances, whom she had discovered by accident, and to whom she was most anxious to give a helping hand.

"A sweet creature," she had said quite audibly that evening, although the object of her remarks was at her elbow. "A most engaging person; poor thing, when I found her she was almost destitute. Wasn't it sad?"

"Quite pretty, too," her friends had remarked, also ignoring the near neighbourhood of the singer.

It did not seem to matter much. The stranger sat there calmly, proudly unconscious of all that was said about her. Pretty!—the epithet was well within the mark. Beautiful, rather—magnificently, splendidly beautiful, with a noble presence and almost queenly air. Her small, exquisitely-proportioned head, crowned with a coronet of deep chestnut hair, was well poised upon a long, slender neck; she had a refined, aristocratic face, with clear-cut features, a well-shaped, aquiline nose, with slender nostrils;

a perfect mouth, great lustrous dark eyes, with brows and lashes rather darker than her hair. Her teeth were perfect—perhaps she knew it, for her lower lip hung down a little, constantly displaying their pearly whiteness, and adding somewhat to the decided outline of the firm well-rounded chin.

Seated, her beauty claimed attention; but her appearance was still more attractive when she stood up and moved across the room, to take her seat at the piano. Her figure was tall and commanding, full, yet faultless in outline, as that of one in the prime of ripe, rich womanhood, and its perfect proportions were fully set off by her close-fitting but perfectly plain black dress.

A little hum of approval greeted her from this well-bred audience as she sat down and swept her fingers with a flourish over the keys. Then, without further prelude, she sang a little French song in a pleasing, musical voice, without much compass, but well trained; before the applause ended she broke into a Spanish ballad, tender and passionate, which gained her still greater success; and thus accepted and approved amidst continual cries of "Brava!" and "Encore!" she was not allowed to leave her seat until she had sung at least a dozen times.

When she arose from the piano Lady Essendine went up to her, patronising and gracious.

"Oh! thank you so much. I don't know when I have heard anything so charming."

Other ladies followed suit, and, amidst the general cries of approval, the beautiful singer was engaged a dozen deep to sing at other great houses in the town.

Presently they pressed her to perform again. Was she not paid for it? No one, Lady Essendine least of all, thought for one moment of her *protégée's* fatigue, and the poor singer might have worked on till she fainted from exhaustion had not the son of the house interposed.

"You must be tired, mademoiselle," said Lord Lydstone, coming up to the piano. "Surely you would like a little refreshment? Let me take you to the tea-room," and, offering his arm, he led her away, despite his mother's black looks and frowns of displeasure.

"Lydstone is so impulsive," she whispered to the first confidant she could find. It was Colonel Wilders, one of the family—a poor relation, in fact, commonly called by them "Cousin Bill"—a hale, hearty, middle-aged man, with grey hair he was not ashamed of, but erect and vigorous, with a soldierly air. "I wish he would not advertise himself with such a person in this way."

"A monstrously handsome person!" cried the blunt soldier, evidently cordially endorsing Lord Lydstone's taste.

"That's not the question, Colonel Wilders; it was not my son's place to take her to the tea-room, and I am much annoyed. Will you, to oblige me, go and tell Lydstone I want to speak to him?"

Cousin Bill, docile and obsequious, hurried off to execute her ladyship's commission. He found the pair chatting pleasantly together in a corner of the deserted tea-room, and delivered his message.

"Oh, bother!" cried Lord Lydstone undutifully. "What can mother want with me?"

"You had better go to her," said the colonel, who was a little afraid of his cousin, the female head of the house. "I will take your place here—that is to say, if mademoiselle will permit me."

"Madame," corrected Lord Lydstone, who had been already put right himself. "Let me introduce you. Madame Cyprienne—my cousin, Colonel Wilders, of the Royal Rangers. I hope we shall hear you sing again to-night, unless you are too tired."

"I shall do whatever *miladi* wishes," said Madame Cyprienne, in a deep but musical voice, with a slight foreign accent. "It is for her to command, me to obey. She has been very kind, you know," she went on to Colonel Wilders, who had taken Lydstone's seat by her side. "But for her I should have starved."

"Dear me! how sad," said the colonel. "Was it so bad as that? How did it happen. Was M. Cyprienne unlucky?"

She did not answer; and the colonel, wondering, looked up, to find her fine eyes filled with tears.

"How stupid of me! What an idiot I am! Of course, your husband is ----"

She pointed to her black dress, edged with crape, but said nothing.

"Yes, yes! I quite understand. Pray forgive me," stammered the colonel, and there followed an awkward pause.

"Mine is a sad story," she said at length, in a sorrowful tone. "I was left suddenly alone, unprotected, without resources, in this strange country—to fight my own battle, to earn a crust of bread by my own exertions, or starve."

"Dear, dear!" said the colonel, his sympathies fully aroused.

"I should have starved, but for Lady Essendine. She heard of me. I was trying to dispose of some lace—some very old Spanish point. You are a judge of lace, monsieur?"

"Of course, of course!" said the colonel, although, as a matter of fact, he did not know Spanish point from common *écru*.

"This was some lace that had been in our family for generations. You must understand we were not always as you see me—poor; we belong to the old nobility. My husband was highly born, but when he died I dropped the title and became Madame Cyprienne. It was better, don't you think?"

"Perhaps so; I am not sure," replied the colonel, hardly knowing what to say.

"It was. The idea of a countess a pauper, begging her bread!"

"What was your title, may I ask?" inquired the colonel, eagerly. These tender confidences, accompanied by an occasional encouraging glance from her bright eyes, were rapidly increasing the interest he took in her.

"I am the Countess de Saint Clair," replied Madame Cyprienne, proudly; "but I do not assume the title now. I do not choose it to be known that I live by singing, and by selling the remnants of our family lace."

"I hope Lady Essendine paid you a decent price," said the colonel, pleasantly.

Madame Cyprienne shook her head, with a little laugh—

"She has been very kind—exceedingly kind—but she knows how to drive a bargain: all women do."

"What a shame! And have you sold it all? You had better entrust me with the disposal of the rest."

"Oh! Colonel Wilders, I could not think of giving you so much trouble."

"But I will; I should like to. Send it to me. My chambers are in Ryder Street; or, better still, I will call for it if you will tell me where," said the colonel, artfully.

"I am lodging in a very poor place, not at all such as the Countess de Saint Clair should receive in. But I am not ashamed of it; it is in Frith Street, Soho, No. 29a; but I do not think you ought to come there."

"A most delightful part of the town," said the colonel, who at the moment would have approved of Whitechapel or the New Cut. "When shall I call?"

"In the afternoon. In the morning I am engaged in giving lessons. But come, we have lingered here long enough. *Miladi* will expect me to sing again."

Lady Essendine frowned at Cousin Bill when he brought back her singer; but whether it was at the length of the talk, or the withdrawal of her *protégée* from the duties for which she was paid, her ladyship did not condescend to explain. It was a little of both. She was pleased to have hindered her son from paying marked attention to a person in Madame Cyprienne's doubtful position. Now she found that person exercising her fascinations upon Colonel Wilders, and it annoyed her, although Cousin Bill was surely old enough to take care of himself. Already she was changing her opinion concerning the fair singer she had introduced into the London world. She could not fail to notice the admiration Madame Cyprienne generally received, especially from the men, and she doubted whether she had done wisely in taking her by the hand.

A few days later she had no doubt at all. To her disgust, all the old Spanish point-lace was gone; and Madame Cyprienne had told her plainly that it was her own fault for haggling over the price. Her ladyship's disgust was heightened when she found the best piece of all—a magnificent white mantilla—in the possession of a rival leader of fashion, who refused to say where she had got it, or how.

She set her emissaries at work, however—for every great London lady has a dozen devoted, unpaid *attachés*, ready to do any little commission of this kind—and the lace was traced back to Colonel Wilders.

"My dear," she said, one morning, to her lord, "I am afraid Colonel Wilders is very intimate with that Madame Cyprienne."

"Our eccentric Cousin Bill! You don't say so? Well, there's no fool like an old fool," said Lord Essendine, who was a very matter-of-fact, plain-spoken peer.

"I always thought she was an adventuress," cried Lady Essendine, angrily.

"Then why did you take her up so hotly? But for you, no one would ever have heard of the woman, least of all Cousin Bill."

"Well, I have done with her now. I shall drop her."

"The mischief's done. Unless I am much mistaken, she won't drop Cousin Bill."

Lord Essendine, who was, perhaps, behind the scenes, was not wrong in his estimate of the influence Madame Cyprienne exercised. Before six months were out, Colonel Wilders came, with rather a sheepish air, to the head of the house, and informed him of his approaching marriage to the Countess de Saint Clair.

"That's a new title to me, Bill. Foreign, I suppose?" Lord Essendine had the usual contempt of the respectable Briton for titles not mentioned in Debrett or Burke.

"It's French, I fancy; and for the moment it is in abeyance. Madame Cyprienne tells me—"

"Gracious powers, William Wilders! have you fallen into that woman's clutches?"

"I must ask you, Lord Essendine, to speak more respectfully of the lady I propose to make my wife."

"You had better not! I warn you while there is yet time."

"What do you know against her?" asked the colonel, hotly.

"What do you know of or for her?" replied the peer, quickly. "I tell you, man, it's a disgrace to the family. Lady Essendine will be furious. If I had any authority over you I would forbid the marriage. In any case," he went on, "do not look for any countenance or support from me."

"I hope we shall be able to get on without your assistance, Lord Essendine. I thought it my duty to inform you of my marriage, and I think I might have been better received."

"Stay, you idiot; don't go off in a huff. I don't like the match, I tell you frankly; but I don't want to quarrel. Is there anything I can do for you, except attending the wedding? I won't do that."

Colonel Wilders could not bring himself to ask any favours of his unsympathetic kinsman. Nevertheless, it was through Lord Essendine's interest that he obtained a snug staff appointment in one of the large garrison towns; and he did not return indignantly the very handsome cheque paid in by his cousin to his account as a wedding present.

He was still serving at Chatsmouth, his young and beautiful wife the life of the gay garrison, when the war-clouds gathered dark upon the horizon, and, thanks again to the Essendine interest, he found himself transferred, still on the staff, to the expeditionary army under orders for the East.

CHAPTER V
THE WAR FEVER

They were stirring times, those early days of '54. After half a century of peace the shadow of a great contest loomed dark and near. The whole British nation, sick and tired of Russian double-dealing, was eager to cut the knot of political difficulty with the sword. Everyone was mad to fight; only a few optimists, statesmen mostly, still relying on the sedative processes of diplomacy, had any hopes of averting war. A race reputed peace-loving, but most pugnacious when roused, was stirred now to its very depths. British hearts beat high throughout the length and breadth of the land, proudly mindful of their former prowess and manfully hopeful of emulating former glorious deeds.

It was the same wherever Englishmen gathered under the old flag; in every corner of the world peopled by offshoots from the old stock, most of all in those strongholds and dependencies beyond sea captured in the old wars, and still held by our arms.

It was so upon the great Rock, the commonly counted impregnable fortress, one of the ancient pillars of Hercules that still stands silently strong and watchful at the mouth of the Mediterranean Sea.

Nowhere did the war fever rage higher than at Gibraltar. Before everything, a garrison town, battlemented and fortified on every side, resonant from morning gunfire till watch-setting with martial sounds, its principal pageants military, with soldiers filling its streets, and sentinels at every corner, the prospect of active service was naturally the one theme and topic of the place.

As spring advanced, one of those balmy-scented Southern springs when flowers highly prized with us blossomed wild everywhere, even in the fissures of the rock—when the days are already long and bright, under ever-blue and cloudless skies, Gibraltar realised more fully that war was close at hand. Lying in the high road to the East, it saw daily the armed strength of England sweep proudly by. Now a squadron of men-of-war: not the hideous, shapeless ironclad of to-day, but the traditional three-decker, with its tiers of snarling teeth and its beauty of white-bellying canvas and majestic spar. Now a troopship with its consorts, two, or three, or more, tightly packed with their living cargo—whole regiments of red-coated soldiers on their way to Malta and beyond.

Such sights as these kept the garrison—friends and comrades of those bound eastward—in a state of constant high-pitched excitement. At first, forbidden by strict quarantine, there was no communication between the sea and the shore, but all day long there were crowds of idlers ready to line the sea-wall and greet every ship that came in close enough with hearty repeated cheers. When the vexatious health-rules were relaxed, and troopships landed some of their passengers, there was endless fraternisation, eager discussion of coming operations, and unlimited denunciation of the common foe.

Members of the garrison itself were, of course, frantically jealous of all who had the better luck to belong to the expeditionary force. That they were not under orders for the East was the daily burden of complaint in every barrack-room and guard-house upon the Rock. The British soldier is an inveterate grumbler; he quarrels perpetually with his quarters, his food, his clothing, and his general want of luck. Just now the bad luck of being refused a share in an arduous campaign, with its attendant chances of hardships, sufferings, perhaps a violent death, made every soldier condemned to remain in safety at Gibraltar discontented and sore at heart.

"No orders for us by the last mail, Hyde," said a young sergeant of the Royal Picts, as he walked briskly up to the entrance of the Waterport Guard.

A tall, well-grown, clean-limbed young fellow of twenty-four or five: one who prided himself on being a smart soldier, and fully deserved the name. He was admirably turned out; his coatee with wings, showing that he belonged to one of the flank companies, fitted him to perfection; the pale blue trousers, the hideous fashion of the day, for which Prince Albert was said to be responsible, were carefully cut; his white belts were beautifully pipe-clayed, and the use of pipe-clay was at that time an art; you could see your face in the polish of his boots. A smart soldier, and as fine-looking a young fellow as wore the Queen's uniform in 1854. He had an open, honest face, handsome withal; clear bright grey eyes, broad forehead, and a firm mouth and chin.

"Worrying yourself, as usual, for permission to have your throat cut. Can't you bide your time, Sergeant McKay?"

The answer came from another sergeant of the same regiment, an elder, sterner man—a veteran evidently, for he wore two medals for Indian campaigns, and his bronzed, weather-beaten face showed that he had seen service in many climes. As a soldier he was in no wise inferior to his comrade:

his uniform and appointments were as clean and correct, but he lacked the extra polish—the military dandyism, so to speak—of the younger man.

"War is our regular trade. Isn't it natural we should want to be at it?" said Sergeant McKay.

"You talk like a youngster who doesn't know what it's like," replied Sergeant Hyde. "I've seen something of campaigning, and it's rough work at the best, even in India, where soldiers are as well off as officers here."

"Officers!" said McKay, rather bitterly. "They have the best of it everywhere."

"Hush! don't be an insubordinate young idiot," interposed his comrade, hastily. "Here come two of them."

The sergeants sprang hastily to their feet, and, standing strictly to attention, saluted their superiors in proper military form.

"That's what I hate," went on McKay.

"Then you are no true soldier, and don't know what proper discipline means. They are as much bound to salute us as we them."

"Yes, but they don't."

"That's their want of manners; so much the worse for them. Besides, I am quite sure Mr. Wilders didn't mean it; he is far too good an officer— always civil-spoken, too, and considerate to the men."

"I object to saluting him more than any one else."

"Why, McKay! what's the matter with you? What particular fault have you to find with Mr. Wilders?"

"I am just as good as he is."

"In your own opinion, perhaps; not in that of this garrison—certainly not under the Mutiny Act and Articles of War."

"I am just as good. I am his cousin—"

Sergeant McKay stopped suddenly, bit his lip, and flushed very red.

"So you have let the cat out of the bag at last, my young friend," said Sergeant Hyde, quietly. "I always thought this—that you were a gentleman—"

"Superior to my station, in fact."

"By no means, Sergeant McKay. I should be sorry to admit that any man, however highly born, had lost his right to be deemed a gentleman because he is a sergeant in the Royal Picts."

"You, Hyde, are a gentleman too. I am sure of that."

"I am a sergeant in the Royal Picts. That is enough for me and for you."

"Why did you enlist?"

Hyde shook his head gravely.

"There are pages in every man's life," he said, "which he does not care to lift again when they are once turned down. I have not asked you for your secret; respect mine."

"But I have nothing to conceal," said McKay, quickly. "I am ready enough to tell you why I enlisted."

"As you please; but, mind, I have not asked you."

There was little encouragement in this speech; but McKay ignored it, and went on—

"I enlisted because I could not enter the army in any other way. My friends could not afford to purchase me a commission."

"Why were you so wild to become a soldier?"

"It was my father's profession. He was a captain in—"

"That should have given you a claim for an ensigncy, as an officer's son."

"But my father was not in the English service. He was only half an Englishman, really."

"Indeed! How so?"

"Although Scotch by extraction, as our name will tell you, my father was born in Poland. He was a Russian subject, and as such was compelled to serve in the Russian army."

"For long?"

"Until he was mixed in an unfortunate national movement, and only escaped execution by flight. He lived afterwards at Geneva. It was there he met my mother."

"Is it through him or her that you are related to the Wilders?"

"Through my mother. She was daughter of the Honourable Anastasius, son of the twelfth earl."

"And what might be the distinguishing numeral of the present Essendine potentate?"

"He is fourteenth earl."

"Then he and your mother are first cousins?"

"Quite so; and I am his first cousin once removed."

"Ah! that is very nice for you," said old Hyde, with a tinge of contempt in his tone. "They're not much use to you though, these fine relations. Surely Lord Essendine could have got you a commission by holding up his hand?"

"That's just what he would not do, and why I hate him and the whole of the Wilders family. Lord Essendine has never recognised us."

"Why? Is there any reason?"

"The Honourable Anastasius made a poor match, married against his father's wish, and was cut off with a shilling. His brother, the next earl, was disposed to make it up, but my grandfather died, and my grandmother married again—an honest sea-captain—and the noble peer cut her dead."

"And so you joined the Royal Picts. But I wonder you came to this regiment to serve with your cousin."

"I enlisted, you know, a couple of years before he was gazetted to the corps."

"Do they know you took the shilling?—that you are now a colour-sergeant in the Royal Picts?"

"I don't think they are aware of my existence even."

"Well, never mind. Don't be cast down. The time may come when they will be proud to recognise you. It all depends upon yourself?"

"I will do all I know to force them, you may be sure."

"And you will have your chance, in a great war like this which is coming. Everything is possible to a man whose heart is in the right place. You have pluck and spirit."

The young fellow's eyes flashed.

"Trust me, Hyde; I sha'n't flinch, if I only get the chance."

"You are well educated; you can draw; you have picked up Spanish since you have been here; and I suppose you inherit a taste for languages from your Polish father?"

"I don't know; at any rate, I can talk French fluently, and I speak Russian of course."

"Why, man! the game is positively in your own hands. You are bound to get on: mark my words."

"Not if we stay here, Hyde, keeping guard upon this old Rock and losing all the fun. Can you wonder why I am so anxious the regiment should get the route?"

"It will come, never fear. They will want every soldier that carries a musket before this war is over, or I'm a much-mistaken man. Only have patience."

"How can I? I am eating my heart out, Hyde."

"Was it to tell me this you came down here? What brings you to Waterport this morning? Only to gossip with me?"

"That, and something more. I am on duty, detailed as orderly sergeant to one of the Expeditionary Generals; he is just going to land from a yacht in the bay."

"Do you know his name?"

"Yes, Wilders—another of my fine cousins. You can understand now why I am so bitter against my relations to-day: there are too many of them about."

"I suppose that is what's brought our Mr. Wilders here to-day—to meet his cousin."

"And his brother; for they are on board Lord Lydstone's yacht."

"They! How many of them?"

"General Wilders has his wife with him, I believe, accompanying him to the East."

"Old idiot! Why couldn't he leave her at home? Women are in the way at these times. Soldiers have no business with wives."

"That's why you never married, I suppose?"

Hyde did not answer his question, but got up and left his comrade abruptly, to re-enter the guard-room.

CHAPTER VI
ON DANGEROUS GROUND

The *Arcadia*, Lord Lydstone's yacht, was a fine three-masted schooner of a couple of hundred tons. She was lying far out in the bay, amidst a crowd of shipping of every kind—coal-hulks, black and grimy; H.M.S. *Samarang*, receiving-ship, and home of the captain of the port; British vessels, steamers and sailing-ships, of every rig; foreign craft of every aspect native to its waters: zebecques, faluchas, and polaccas, with their curved spars and heavy lateen sails.

A fleet of small boats surrounded the yacht, native boats of curious build, and manned by dark-skinned natives of the Rock, in nondescript attire—a noisy, pushing, quarrelsome lot, eager to do business, gesticulating wildly, and jabbering loudly in many strange tongues. Here was a pure Spaniard, with a red sash round his waist, and a velvet cap, round as a cartwheel, on his head, with a boatful of vegetables and early fruit. There was a grave and sedate Moor, in green turban and white flowing robes, with an assortment of gold-braided slippers and large brass trays. Next a Maltese milk-seller, in scanty garments, nothing but short canvas trousers and a shirt, who had come with cans full of goats'-milk from the herds he kept on the barren slopes of the Rock. Not far off was the galley of the health-officer, with a crew of "scorpion" boatmen in neat white jackets and straw hats.

On the deck of the yacht, under an awning—for the spring sun already beat down hotly at noon—were the owner and his guests. Lord Lydstone, cigar in mouth, lounged lazily upon a heap of rugs and cushions at the feet of Mrs. Wilders, who took her ease luxuriantly in a comfortable cane arm-chair.

Blanche Cyprienne, Countess of St. Clair, had changed little since her marriage. Her beauty had gained rather than lost; her manner was more commanding, her look more haughty. Her fine eyes flashed insolently, or were veiled in lazy disdain, and her voice spoke scornfully or drawled with careless contempt, according to her mood.

"So that is the Rock—the great Rock of Gibraltar," she was saying. "What an extraordinary-looking place!"

"You will say so, Countess, when you get on shore," said Lord Lydstone.

"Is there anything really to see?" she asked. "Is it worth the trouble of landing?"

"Why, of course! I thought it was all settled. The general sent some hours ago to say he proposed to pay his respect to the Governor. You cannot help yourself now."

"Oh! the general," remarked Mrs. Wilders, as she was generally styled—the title Countess was only used by intimate friends—in a tone that implied she was not at all bound by her husband's plans.

"Where is the good man just now?" inquired Lord Lydstone, in much the same tone.

"There, forward," said Mrs. Wilders, pointing to the part of the deck beyond the awning. "Trying to get a sunstroke by walking about with his head bare."

"He does that on principle, Countess, don't you know. He wants to harden his cranium, in case he loses his hat some day in action."

"I hope he may never go into action. If he does, I should be sorry for his men."

"Not for him?"

"That may be taken for granted," she replied, in a matter-of-fact way.

"How fond you are of him! What devoted affection! It's lucky you have little to spare!"

"I keep it for the proper person."

"Is there none for his relatives?" asked Lydstone, with a meaning look.

"Do any of them deserve my affection?"

"I try very hard, Countess; and I should so value the smallest crumb."

"Don't be foolish, Lord Lydstone! you must not try to make love to me; it would be wrong. Besides, we are too nearly connected now."

"You never throw me a single kind word, Blanche."

"Certainly not. I won't have it on my conscience that I led you astray, poor innocent lamb! A fine thing! What would your people say? They're bitter enough against me as it is!"

The Essendines had never properly acknowledged Colonel Wilders's marriage, or treated his wife, the foreign countess, other than with the coldest contempt. Lord Lydstone knew this, and knew too that his mother was right; yet he could not defend her when this woman, whom he admired still—too much, indeed, for his peace of mind—resented her treatment.

"Your mother has behaved disgracefully to me—that you must admit, Lord Lydstone."

"She is an old-fashioned, old-world lady, with peculiar straitlaced notions of her own. But, if you please, we won't talk about her."

"Why not? You cannot pretend that she was right in ignoring me, flouting me, insulting me! Am I not your near relative's wife? Why, Bill is only four off the title now."

"One of them being your humble servant, who devoutly hopes that all four will long interpose between him and the succession," said Lord Lydstone, with a pleasant laugh.

"I don't wish you any harm, of course; still it is as I say, and my son—"

"Aged two, and at present in England at nurse."

"—May be the future Earl of Essendine."

"He shan't be, if I can prevent it!" cried Lord Lydstone, gaily; "you may rely on that. But, I say, here is a smart gig coming off from the shore. I believe the Governor has sent his own barge for you. Here, Bill! I say, Bill!"

General Wilders came aft.

"You had better put on your best clothes, general; they are coming to fetch you in state."

"I suppose, on this occasion only, you will wear a hat, Bill?" said Mrs. Wilders.

"I wish you would go down and get ready, my dear; we ought not to keep the gig," said the general, as he himself went below to dress.

"I am not so sure I shall go on shore at all," replied his wife.

"No!" cried Lord Lydstone. "Throw the general over, and stay on board with me."

"That would be too great penance," said Mrs. Wilders, as she moved towards the companion-ladder. "I've had enough of your lordship for one day."

Lydstone got up, looking rather vexed, and followed her across the deck. When he was quite close to her side he whispered with suppressed but manifest feeling—

"Why do you torture me so? Sometimes I think you care for me; sometimes that you hate and detest me. What am I think?"

"What you choose," she answered, in a low, quick voice, evidently much displeased. "I have given you no right to speak to me in this way. Let me pass, or I shall appeal to my lawful protector!"

Presently Mrs. Wilders reappeared, dressed to perfection in some cool light fabric, serene and smiling to everyone but Lord Lydstone. She was especially gracious to young Mr. Wilders, who had come off in the Governor's gig, and had been cordially welcomed by his brother.

"Another cousin," said the general, introducing him. He was now in uniform—the general—in uniform to suit his own fancy rather than the regulations. The only orthodox articles of apparel were his twisted general's scimitar and a forage-cap with a broad gold band. His coat and waistcoat were of white cloth; he had a wide crimson sash round his waist, and his lower limbs were encased in hunting-breeches and long boots. "Anastasius, one of the Royal Picts."

"All soldiers, you Wilders, all—except one." This was specially intended to annoy Lydstone. "The future head of the house is kept in cotton-wool; he is too precious, I suppose, to be risked."

"It is not my fault," began Lydstone. It was a sore point with him that he had not been permitted—in deference to his mother's fond protests—to enter the army.

"Are you not coming with us, Lydstone?" said his young brother, greatly disappointed. "I did want to show you our mess."

"I know Gibraltar by heart, and I have letters to write. I hope you will enjoy yourself, Countess," he added, sarcastically, as they went down the side.

"There's no fear of that, now we have left you behind," replied Mrs. Wilders, sharply.

"Why can't you and Lydstone keep better friends?" said General Wilders, a little shocked at this remark.

"It's his fault, not mine, and that's enough about it," replied Mrs. Wilders, rather petulantly. "Did you ever quarrel with your brother," she went on to Anastasius, "when you were boys?"

"I would not have dared. Not that I wanted to: we three brothers were always the best of friends."

"You are an affectionate family, Mr. Wilders; I have long been convinced of that," said Mrs. Wilders, who could not leave the subject alone.

But now the gig, impelled by six stout oarsmen, was nearing the Waterport Guard, and was already under the shadow of the frowning batteries of the Devil's Tongue. High above them rose the sheer straight wall of the rock, bristling with frowning fortifications, line above line, and countless embrasures armed with heavy artillery.

The wharf itself was crowded with the usual motley polyglot gathering—sailors of all nations, soldiers of the garrison, Spanish peasants from the neighbouring villages, native scorpions, policemen, and inspectors of strangers.

"How amusing! How interesting! It's like a scene in a play!" cried Mrs. Wilders, as she stepped ashore.

Escorted by her husband and cousin, they pushed their way through the crowd towards the Waterport gateway, and under it into the main ditch. As they approached there was a cry of "Guard, turn out!" and the Waterport Guard, under its officer, fell in with open ranks to give the general a salute. General Wilders acknowledged the compliment, and, while he stood there with two fingers to his hat, Sergeant McKay advanced and reported himself.

"Your orderly, sir."

"Eh! what?" said the general, a little surprised. "My orderly! Very considerate of Sir Thomas," he went on. "One of the Royal Picts, too, and a guard from the same regiment! Most attentive, I'm sure!"

The general went up at once to the front rank of the guard, and proceeded to inspect the men carefully. With his own hands he altered the hang of the knapsacks and the position of the belts; he measured in the regular way, with two fingers, the length of the pouch below the elbow, grumbling to himself as he went along.

"So you use harness-blacking for your pouches. I don't approve of that. And your pipe-clay; it's got too blue a tinge."

While he lingered thus fondly over the trifling details that, to his mind, summed up the whole duty of a general officer, his wife's voice was heard impatiently calling him to her side.

"Come, general, don't be all day! How can you waste time over such nonsense!"

"My dear," said her husband, gravely, as he rejoined her, "this regiment is to form part of my brigade"—McKay pricked up his ears—"it is the first time I have seen any of it. You must allow me—"

"I am going on into the town; inspecting guards doesn't amuse me," and the general discreetly abandoned his professional duties and walked on by her side.

The guard was dismissed by its commander; the men "lodged arms" and went back to the guard-room. Only Sergeant Hyde remained outside, watching the retreating figures of the Wilders' party.

"I should have known her voice again amongst a thousand," said the old sergeant, shaking his head; "and from the glimpse I caught of her she seemed but little changed. I wonder whether she saw me. Not that she would have recognised me; I am not what I was. No one here has made me out, although a dozen years ago I was well known all over the Rock. Besides, how could she see me? I was on the other flank, and, fortunately, she left the general to inspect us by himself. Poor man! I had rather be a sergeant—a private even—than stand in that general's shoes."

CHAPTER VII
AN OLD ACQUAINTANCE

The Wilders' party, after leaving the Waterport, passed through the Casemate Barrack Square and entered Waterport Street, the chief thoroughfare of the town. It was a narrow, unpretending street, very foreign in aspect; the houses tall and overhanging with balconies filled with flowers; the lattice-shutters gaily painted, having outside blinds of brilliantly striped stuffs.

The shop fronts were small, the wares common-place; the best show was at the drapers, where they sold British calicoes and piece-goods in flaunting colours, calculated to suit the local taste.

The street, both pavement and roadway, was crowded. In the former were long strings of pack-horses bringing in straw and charcoal from Spain; small stout donkeys laden with water-barrels; officers, some in undress uniform, many more in plain clothes, riding long-tailed barbs; occasionally a commissariat wagon drawn by a pair of sleek mules, or a high-hooded *calêche*, with its driver seated on the shafts, cut through the throng. Detachments of troops, too, marched by: recruits returning from drill upon the North Front, armed parties, guards coming off duty, and others going on fatigue—all these cleared the street before them. On the pavement the crowd was as diverse as might be expected, from the mixed population. Stately Moors rubbed elbows with stalwart British soldiers; Barbary Jews, dejected in mien, but with shrewd, cunning eyes, chaffered with the itinerant vendors of freshly caught sardines, or the newly-picked fruit of the prickly pear. Now and again, quite out of keeping with her surroundings, a rosy-cheeked British nursemaid passed by escorting her charges—the blue-eyed, flaxen-haired children of the dominant race.

General Wilders walked along with head erect, returning punctiliously the innumerable salutes he received, quite happy, and in his element in this essentially military post and stronghold. Mrs. Wilders seemed also to enjoy the busy, animated scene: it was all so new to her, so different from anything she had expected, as she was at great pains to explain. The sight of this foreign town held by British bayonets pleased her, she said; she was proud to think that she was now an Englishwoman.

"It is your first visit to Gibraltar, then?" said young Mr. Wilders, anxious to be civil.

"Oh, yes!" she replied; "that is why I am so interested—so amused by all I see."

Was this absolutely true? She seemed, as she led the way across the casemate square and up Waterport Street, to know the road without guidance, and once or twice a passer-by paused to look at her. Were they only paying tribute to her radiant beauty, or was her's not altogether an unfamiliar face?

It was evident that there were those at Gibraltar who knew her, or mistook her for some one else.

As the party reached the Commercial Square, and the main guard, like that at Waterport, turned out to do honour to the general, a man pushed forward from a little group that stood respectfully behind the party, and whispered hoarsely in Mrs. Wilders's ear—

"*Dios mio! Cypriana! Es usted?*" (Gracious Heavens! Cyprienne! Is it you?)

Mrs. Wilders stopped and looked round. At that moment, too, young Wilders turned angrily on the man—a black-muzzled, Spanish-looking fellow, dressed in a suit of coarse brown cloth, short jacket, knee-breeches, and leather gaiters—the dress, in fact, of a well-to-do Spanish peasant—and said, sharply, "How dare you speak to this lady? What did he say to you, Mrs. Wilders—anything rude?"

Mrs. Wilders had recovered herself sufficiently to reply in an unconcerned tone—

"I did not understand his jargon; but it does not matter in the least; don't make any fuss, I beg."

The incident had been unobserved by any but these two, and it must have been speedily forgotten by young Wilders, for he said nothing more. But Mrs. Wilders, as they passed on, and for the rest of their walk to the Convent, as the Governor's residence is still styled, looked anxiously behind to see if the man who had claimed acquaintance with her was still in sight.

Yes; he was following her. What did he mean?

Half an hour later, when the Wilders had made their bow to the Governor, and it had been arranged that the general should attend an inspection of troops upon the North Front, Mrs. Wilders declined to accept the seat in the carriage offered her. She preferred, she said, to explore the quaint old town. Mr. Wilders and one of the Governor's aides-de-camps eagerly volunteered to escort, but she declined.

"Many thanks, but I'd rather go alone. I shall be more independent."

"You'll lose your way; or be arrested by the garrison police and taken before the town major as a suspicious character, loitering too near the fortifications," said the Governor, who thought it a capital joke.

"No one will interfere with me, I think," she replied, quietly. "I am quite able to take care of myself."

She looked it just then, with her firm-set lips and flashing eyes.

"Mrs. Wilders will have her own way," said her husband. "It's best to give in to her. That's what I've found," he added, with a laugh, in which all joined.

When the horses were brought out for the parade, Mrs. Wilders, still persisting in her intention of walking alone, said, gaily—

"Well, gentlemen, while you are playing at soldiers I shall go off on my own devices. If I get tired, Bill, I shall go back to the yacht."

And with this Mrs. Wilders walked off.

"Here, sergeant!" cried the general to his orderly, McKay. "I don't want you; you may be of use to Mrs. Wilders. Go after her."

"Shall I report myself to her, sir?"

"I don't advise you, my man. She'd send you about your business double-quick. But you can keep your eye on her, and see she comes to no harm."

Sergeant McKay saluted and hastened out of the courtyard. Mrs. Wilders had already disappeared down Convent Lane, and was just turning into the main street. McKay followed quickly, keeping her in sight.

It was evident that the best part of Gibraltar had no charms for Mrs. Wilders; she did not want to look into the shop windows, such as they were; nor did she pause to admire the architectural beauties of the Garrison Library or other severely plain masterpieces of our military engineers. Her course was towards the upper town, and she pressed on with quick, unfaltering steps, as though she knew every inch of the ground.

Ten minutes' sharp walking, sometimes by steep lanes, sometimes up long flights of stone steps, brought her to the upper road leading to the Moorish castle. This was essentially a native quarter; Spanish was the only language heard from the children who swarmed about the doorways, or their slatternly mothers quarreling over their washtubs, or combing out and cleansing, in a manner that will not bear description, their children's hair. Spanish colour prevailed, and Spanish smells.

Still pursuing her way without hesitation, Mrs. Wilders presently turned up another steep alley bearing the historic name of "Red Hot Shot Ramp," and paused opposite a gateway leading into a dirty courtyard. The place was a kind of livery or bait stable patronised by muleteers and gipsy dealers, who brought in horses from Spain.

Picking her steps carefully, Mrs. Wilders entered the stable-yard.

"Benito Villegas?" she asked in fluent Spanish, of the ostler, who stared with open-mouthed surprise at this apparition of a fine lady in such a dirty locality.

"Benito, the commission agent and guide? Yes, señora, he is with his horses inside," replied the ostler, pointing to the stable-door.

"Call him, then!" cried Mrs. Wilders, imperiously. "Think you that I will cross the threshold of your piggery?" and she waited, stamping her foot impatiently whilst the man did her bidding.

In another minute he came out with Benito Villegas, the man in the brown suit, who had spoken to Mrs. Wilders in the Commercial Square.

"Cypriana," he began at once, in a half-coaxing, half-apologetic tone.

"Silence! Answer my questions, or I will thrash you with your own whip. How dared you intrude yourself upon me to-day?"

"Forgive me! I was so utterly amazed. I thought some bright vision had descended from above, sent, perhaps, by the Holy Virgin"—he crossed himself devoutly—"I could not believe it was you."

"Thanks! I am not an angel from heaven, I know, but let that pass. Answer me! How dared you speak to me to-day?"

"The sight of you awoke old memories; once again I worshipped you— your shadow—the ground on which you trod. I thought of how you once returned my love."

"Miserable cur! I never stooped so low."

"You would have been mine but for that cursed Englishman who came between us, and whom you preferred. What did you gain by listening to him? He lured you from your home—"

"No more! The villain met with his deserts. He is dead—dead these years—and with him all my old life. That is what brings me here. Attend now, Benito Villegas, to what I say!"

"I am listening," he answered, cowering before her, and in a tone of mingled fear and passion. It was evident this strange woman exercised an extraordinary influence over him.

"Never again must you presume to recognise me—to address me, anywhere. If you do, take care! I am a great lady now—the wife of an English general. I have great influence, much power, and can do what I please with such scum as you. I have been with my husband just now to the Convent, the palace of the Governor, and I have but to ask to obtain your immediate expulsion from the Rock. Do not anger or oppose me, man, or beware!"

Benito looked at her with increasing awe.

"Obey my behests, on the other hand, and I will reward you. Ask any favour! Money?"—she quickly took out a little purse and handed him a ten-pound note—"here is an earnest of what I will give you. Interest? Do you want the good-will of the authorities—a snug appointment in the Custom-house, or under the police? They are yours."

"I am your slave; I will do your bidding, and ask nothing in return but your approval."

"Nothing! You grow singularly self-denying, Señor Benito."

"The señora will really help me?" said Benito, now cringing and obsequious. "One small favour, then. I am tired of this wandering life. Here to-day in Cadiz; Ronda, Malaga, to-morrow. At everybody's beck and call—never my own master, not for an hour. I want to settle down."

"To marry?" inquired Mrs. Wilders, contemptuously. "In your own station? That is better."

"I have not forgotten you, señora. But the wound was beginning to heal—"

She held up her hand with a menacing gesture.

"I will not deny that I have cast my eyes upon a maiden that pleases me," Benito confessed. "I have known her from childhood. Her friends approve of my suit, and would accept me; but what lot can I offer a wife?"

"Well, how is it to be mended?"

"For a small sum—five hundred dollars—I could purchase a share in these stables."

"You shall have the money at once as a gift."

"I will promise in return never to trouble you again."

"I make no conditions; only I warn you if you ever offend, if you ever presume—"

"I shall fully merit your displeasure."

"Enough said!" she cut him short. "You know my wishes; see that they are fulfilled. You shall hear from me again. For the present, good-day."

She gathered up the skirts of her dress, turned on her heel, and swept out of the place.

In the gateway she ran up against Serjeant McKay, who had been hovering about the stables from the moment he saw Mrs. Wilders enter the courtyard. He had seen nothing of what passed inside, and as the interview with Benito occupied some time he had grown uneasy. Fearing something had happened to the general's wife, he was on the point of going in to look after her when he met her coming out.

"You have been following me," said Mrs. Wilders, sharply, and jumping with all a woman's quickness at the right conclusion. "Who set you to spy on me?"

"I beg your pardon, madam; I am not a spy," said the young serjeant, formally saluting.

"Don't bandy words with me. Tell me, I insist!"

"The general was afraid something might happen to you. He thought you might need assistance—perhaps lose your way."

She looked at him very keenly as he said these last words, watching whether there was any covert satire in them.

But McKay's face betrayed nothing.

"How long have you been at my heels? How much have you seen?"

"I followed you from the Convent, madam, to this door. I have seen nothing since you went in here."

"I daresay you are wondering what brought me to such a place. A person in whom I take a great interest, an old woman, lives here. I knew her years ago. Psha! why should I condescend to explain? Look here, Mr. Sergeant" — she took out her purse and produced a sovereign—"take this, and drink my health!"

The sergeant flushed crimson, and drew himself up stiffly, as he said, with another formal salute, "Madam, you mistake!"

"Strange!" she exclaimed, scornfully. "I thought all soldiers liked drink. Well, keep the money; spend it as you like."

"I cannot take it, madam; I am paid by the Queen to do my duty."

"And you will not take a bribe to neglect it? Very fine, truly! General Wilders shall know how well you executed his commands. But there!—I have had enough of this; I wish to return to the yacht. Show me the shortest way back to the water side. Lead on; I will follow you."

Sergeant McKay took a short cut down the steep steps, and soon regained the Waterport. There Mrs. Wilders hailed a native boat, and, without condescending to notice the orderly further, she seated herself in the stern-sheets and was rowed off to the *Arcadia*.

CHAPTER VIII
A SOUTHERN PEARL

"Mariquita! Ma—ri—kee—tah!"

A woman's voice, shrill and quavering, with an accent of anger that increased each time the summons was repeated.

"What's come of the young vixen?" went on the speaker, addressing her husband, the Tio Pedro, who sat with her behind the counter of a small tobacconist's shop—an ugly beldame, shrank and shrivelled, with grey elf-locks, sunk cheeks, and parchment complexion, looking ninety, yet little more than half that age. Women ripen early, are soon at their prime, and fade prematurely, under this quickening Southern sun.

The husband was older, yet better preserved, than his wife—a large, stout man, with a fierce face and black, baleful eyes. All cowered before him except La Zandunga, as they called his wife here in Bombardier Lane. He was at her mercy—a Spaniard resident on the Rock by permit granted to his wife—a native of Gibraltar, and liable to be expelled at any time unless she answered for him.

The shop and stock-in-trade were hers, not his, and she ruled him and the whole place.

"Mariquita!" she called again and again, till at length, overflowing with passion, she rushed from behind the counter into the premises at the back of the shop.

She entered a small but well-lighted room, communicating with a few square feet of garden. At the end was a low fence; beyond this the roadway intervening between the garden and the Line wall, or seaward fortifications.

La Zandunga looked hastily round the room. It contained half-a-dozen small low tables, drawn near the window and open door, and at these sat a posse of girls, busy with deft, nimble fingers, making cigarettes and cigars. These workpeople were under the immediate control of Mariquita, the mistress's niece. She was popular with them, evidently, for no one would answer when La Zandunga shrieked out an angry inquiry to each.

No answer was needed. There was Mariquita at the end of the garden, gossiping across the fence with young Sergeant McKay.

It was quite an accident, of course. The serjeant, returning to his quarters from Waterport, had seen Mariquita within, and made her a signal she could not mistake.

"I knew you would come out," he said, pleasantly, when she appeared, shy and shrinking, yet with a glad light in her eyes.

"*Vaya!* what conceit! I was seeking a flower in the garden," she answered demurely; but her low voice and heightened colour plainly showed that she was ready to come to him whenever he called—to follow him, indeed, all over the world.

She spoke in Spanish, with its high-flown epithets and exaggerated metaphor, a language in which Stanislas McKay, from his natural aptitude and this charming tutorship, had made excellent progress.

"My life, my jewel, my pearl!" he cried.

A pearl, indeed, incomparable and above price for all who could appreciate the charms and graces of bright blooming girlhood.

Mariquita Hidalgo was still in her teens—a woman full grown, but with the frank, innocent face of a child. A slender figure, tall, but well-rounded and beautifully poised, having the free, elastic movement of her Spanish ancestors, whose women are the best walkers in the world. She had, too, the olive complexion as clear and transparent as wax, the full crimson lips, the magnificent eyes, dark and lustrous, the indices of an ardent temperament capable of the deepest passion, the strongest love, or fiercest hate.

A very gracious figure indeed was this splendid specimen of a handsome race, as she stood there coyly talking to the man of her choice.

The contrast was strongly marked between them. She, with raven hair, dark skin, and soft brown eyes, was a perfect Southern brunette: quick, impatient, impulsive, easily moved. He, fresh-coloured, blue-eyed, with flaxen moustache, stalwart in frame, self-possessed, reserved, almost cold and impassive in demeanour, was as excellent a type of a native of the North.

"What brings you this way, Señor don Sargento, at this time of day?" said Mariquita. "Was it to see me? It was unwise, indiscreet; my aunt—"

"I have been on duty at Waterport," replied McKay, with a rather ungallant frankness that made Mariquita pout.

"It is plain I am only second in your thoughts. Duty—always duty. Why did not you come last night to the Alameda when the band played?"

"I could not, star of my soul! I was on guard."

"Did I not say so?—duty again! And to-morrow? It is Sunday; you promised to take me to Europa to see the great cave. Is that, too, impossible?"

McKay shook his head laughingly, and said—

"You must not be angry with me, Mariquita; our visit to Europa must be deferred; I am on duty every day. They have made me orderly—"

"I do not believe you," interrupted the girl, pettishly. "Go about your business! Do not trouble to come here again, Don Stanislas. Benito will take me where I want to go."

"I will break Benito's head whenever I catch him in your company," said the young serjeant, with so much energy that Mariquita was obliged to laugh. "Come, dearest, be more reasonable. It is not my fault, you know; I am never happy away from your side. But, remember, I am a soldier, and must obey the orders I receive."

"I was wrong to love a soldier," said Mariquita, growing sad and serious all at once. "Some day you will get orders to march—to India, Constantinople, Russia—where can any one say?—and I shall never see you more."

This trouble of parting near at hand had already arisen, and half-spoilt McKay's delight at the prospect of sailing for the East.

"Do you think I shall ever forget you? If I go, it will be to win promotion, fame—a better, higher, more honourable position for you to share."

It was at this moment that La Zandunga interrupted the lovers with her resonant, unpleasant voice.

"My aunt! my aunt! Run, Stanislas! do not let her see you, in Heaven's name!"

The Serjeant disappeared promptly, but the old virago caught a glimpse of his retreating figure.

"With whom were you gossiping there, good-for-nothing?" cried La Zandunga, fiercely. "I seemed to catch the colour of his coat. If I thought it was that son of Satan, the serjeant, who is ever philandering and following you about—Who was it, I say?"

Mariquita would not answer.

"In with you, shameless, idle daughter of pauper parents, who died in my debt, leaving you on my hands! Is it thus that you repay me my bounty—the home I give you—the bread you eat? Go in, jade, and earn it, or I'll put you into the street."

The girl, bending submissively under this storm of invective and bitter reproach, walked slowly towards the house. Her aunt followed, growling fiercely.

"Cursed red-coat!—common, beggarly soldier! How can you, an Hidalgo of the best blue blood, whose ancestors were settled here before the English robbers stole the fortress—before the English?—before the Moors! You, an Hidalgo, to take up with a base-born hireling cut-throat—"

"No more, aunt!" Mariquita turned on her with flashing eyes. "Call me what you like, you shall not abuse him—my affianced lover—the man to whom I have given my troth!"

"What!" screamed the old crone, now furious with rage. "Do you dare tell me that—to my face? Never, impudent huzzy—never, while I have strength and spirit and power to say you no—shall you wed this hated English mercenary—"

"I will wed no one else."

"That will we see. Is not your hand promised—"

"Not with my consent."

"—Promised, formally, to Benito Villegas—my husband's cousin?"

"I have not consented. Never shall I agree. Benito is a villain. I hate and detest him!"

"Tell him so to his face, evil-tongued slut!—tell him if you dare! He is now in the house. That is why I came to fetch you. I saw him approaching."

"He knows my opinion of him, but if you wish it, aunt, he shall hear it again," said the young girl, undaunted; and she walked on through the workroom, straight into the little shop.

Benito was seated at the counter, talking confidentially, and in a very low voice, with Tio Pedro.

"Are the bales ready, uncle? In two days from now we can run them through like oil in a tube."

"Have you settled the terms?"

"On both sides. Here the inspectors were difficult, but I oiled their palms. On the other side the Custom-house officers are my friends. All is straight and easy. The tobacco must be shipped to-morrow—"

"In the same *falucha*?"

"Yes; for Estepona. Be ready, then, at gunfire—"

He stopped suddenly as Mariquita came in.

"Beautiful as a star!" was his greeting; and in a fulsome, familiar tone he went on—"You are like the sun at noon, my beauty, and burn my heart with your bright eyes."

"Insolent!" retorted Mariquita. "Hold your tongue."

"What! cross-grained and out of humour, sweetest? Come, sit here on my knee and listen, while I whisper some good news."

"Unless you address me more decently, Benito Villegas, I shall not speak to you at all."

"Good news! what then?" put in Tio Pedro, in a coaxing voice.

"My fortune is made. I have found powerful friends here upon the Rock. Within a few days now, through their help, I shall be part owner of la Hermandad Stable; and I can marry when I please."

"Fortunate girl!" said Tio Pedro, turning to Mariquita.

"It does not affect me," replied the girl, with chilling contempt. "Had you the wealth of the Indies, Benito Villegas, and a dukedom to offer, you should never call me yours."

Benito's face grew black as thunder at this unequivocal reply.

"Don't mind her, my son," said the old man. "She has lost her senses: the evil one has bitten her."

"Say, rather, one of those accursed red-coats," interposed his wife, "who has cast a spell over her. I thought I saw him at the garden just now. If I was only certain—"

"Silly girl, beware!" cried Benito, with bitter meaning. "I know him: hateful, despicable hound! He is only trifling with you. He cares nothing for you; you are not to his taste. What! He, a Northern pale-faced boor, choose you, with your dark skin and black hair! Never! I know better. Only to-day I saw him with the woman he prefers—a fair beauty light-complexioned like himself."

He had touched the Southern woman's most sensitive chord. Jealousy flashed from her eyes; a pang of painful doubt shot through her, though she calmly answered—

"It is not true."

"Ask him yourself. I tell you I saw them together: first near our stables, and then down by Waterport—a splendid woman!"

Waterport! McKay had told her he was returning from that part of the Rock. There was something in it, then. Was he playing her false? No. She would trust him still.

"I do not believe you, Benito. Such suspicions are worthy only of a place in your false, black heart!" and with these words Mariquita rushed away.

CHAPTER IX
OFF TO THE WARS

Next morning there was much stir and commotion in the South Barracks, where "lay" the Royal Picts—to use a soldier's phrase. The few words let drop by General Wilders, and overheard by Sergeant McKay, had been verified. "The route had come," and the regiment was under orders to join the expeditionary army in the East.

A splendid body, standing eight hundred strong on parade: strong, stalwart fellows, all of them, bronzed and bearded, admirably appointed, perfectly drilled—one of many such magnificent battalions, the flower of the British army, worthily maintaining the reputation of the finest infantry in the world.

Alas! that long years of peace should have rusted administrative machinery! That so many of these and other brave men should be sacrificed before the year was out for want of food, fuel, and clothing—the commonest supplies.

There seemed little need to improve a military machine so perfect at all its points. But the fastidious eye of Colonel Blythe, who commanded the Royal Picts, saw many blemishes in his regiment, and he was determined to make the most of the time still intervening before embarkation. Parades were perpetual; for the inspection of arms and accoutrements, for developing manual dexterity, and efficiency in drill. Still he was not satisfied.

"We must have a new sergeant-major," said the old martinet to his adjutant in the orderly-room.

The post was vacant for the moment through the promotion of its late holder to be quartermaster.

"Yes, sir; the sooner the better. The difficulty is to choose."

"I have been thinking it over, Smallfield, and have decided to promote Hyde. Send for him."

Colour-sergeant Hyde, erect, self-possessed—a pattern soldier in appearance and propriety—presently marched in and stood respectfully at "attention" before his superior.

"Sergeant Hyde!" said the colonel, abruptly, "I am going to make you a sergeant-major."

"Thank you, sir," said Hyde, saluting; "I had rather not take it."

"Heavens above!" cried the colonel, fiercely. He was of the old school, and used expletives freely. "You must be an idiot!"

"I am sensible, sir, of the honour you would do me, but—"

"Nonsense, man! I insist. I must have you."

"No, sir," said Hyde, firmly, "I must decline the honour."

"Was there ever such an extraordinary fellow? Why, man alive! it will reinstate you—"

"I must beg, sir," said Hyde, hastily interrupting, and looking with intention towards the adjutant.

"Yes, yes! I understand," said the colonel. "Leave us, Mr. Smallfield; I wish to speak to Sergeant Hyde alone."

"You have my secret, Colonel Blythe," said Hyde, when the adjutant had left the room, "but I have your promise."

"I was near forgetting it, I confess; but I was so upset, so put out, at your cursed obstinacy. Why will you persist in keeping in the background? Accept this promotion, and you shall have a commission before the year is out."

"I do not want a commission; I am perfectly happy as I am."

"Was there ever such a pig-headed fellow? Come, Hyde, be persuaded." The colonel got up from his seat and walked round to where the sergeant stood, still erect and motionless. "Come, Rupert, old comrade, old friend," and he put his hand affectionately on the sergeant's shoulder.

The muscles of the sergeant's face worked visibly.

"It's no use, Blythe; I am dead to the world. I have no desire to rise."

"But it's so aggravating; it puts me in such a hole," said the colonel, striding up and down the office. "You're just the man we want—superior in every way. You would hold your own so well with the other non-commissioned officers. I do wish—Where am I to find another?"

"I can tell you, if you will listen to my advice."

"Yes? Speak out."

"Young McKay; he would make an excellent sergeant-major."

"I know him—a smart, sensible, intelligent young fellow. But has he ballast—education?"

"He is better born than you or me, colonel. A lad of excellent parts and first-rate education. Bring him on, and he will do you and the regiment credit yet."

The colonel sat down again at his desk, and seemed lost in thought.

"I must ask Smallfield. Call in the adjutant, will you?" he added, in a voice that implied their conventional relations as superior officer and sergeant were resumed.

Half an hour later McKay was standing in Hyde's place, receiving the same offer, but accepting, although diffidently.

"I am not fit for the post, sir," he protested.

"That's my affair. I have selected you for reasons of my own, and the responsibility is mine."

"I will try my best, sir; that is all I can say."

"It's quite enough. Do your best, and you will satisfy me."

"I can't think why he chose me," confided Stanislas to his friend Hyde, later on, in the sergeants' mess.

"Can't you?" replied his friend, drily. "It's a case of hidden merit receiving its right reward."

"I have never thought that the colonel noticed me, or distinguished me from any of the other sergeants," said Stanislas.

"Probably your good qualities were pointed out to him," replied Hyde, still in the same tone. "Or your fine friends and relations have used their influence."

"It is little likely; and, as I tell you, I don't understand it in the least."

"Leave it so. No doubt you will find out some day. In the meantime do justice to your recommendation, whoever gave it. You have got your foot on the ladder now, but no one can help you to climb; that must depend upon your own exertions."

"Yes, but you can help me, Hyde, with your advice, encouragement, support. I am very young to be put up so high, and over men of standing and experience like yourself."

"You will have no more loyal subordinate than me, Sergeant-major McKay. Come to me whenever you are in trouble or doubt. I will do all I can, you may depend. I like you, boy, and that's enough said."

The old sergeant seized McKay's hand, shook it warmly, and then abruptly quitted the room.

Stanislas was eager to tell this pleasing news of his promotion to Mariquita; but she was the last person to hear it, notwithstanding. McKay entered at once upon his new duties, and they kept him close from morning till night. A good sergeant-major allows himself no leisure. He is the first on parade, the last to leave it. He is perpetually on the move; now inspecting guards and pickets, now superintending drills, while all day long he has his eye upon the conduct of the non-commissioned officers, and the demeanour and dress of the private men.

There was no time to hang about the tobacconist's shop in Bombardier Lane, waiting furtively for a chance of seeing Mariquita alone. They kept their eye upon her, too; and when at last he tore himself away from his new and absorbing duties he paid two or three visits to the place before he could speak to her.

Mariquita received him coldly—distantly.

They were standing, as usual, on each side of the low fence at the end of the garden.

"What's wrong, little star? How have I offended you?"

"I wonder that you trouble to come here at all, Don Stanislas. It's more than a week since I you."

"I have been so busy. My new duties: they have made me, you know—"

"Throw that bone to some other dog," interrupted Mariquita, abruptly. "I am to be no longer deceived by your pretended duties. I know the truth: you prefer some other girl."

"Mariquita!" protested McKay.

"I have heard all. Do not try to deny it. She is tall and fair; one of your compatriots. You were seen together."

"Where, pray? Who has told you this nonsense?"

"At Waterport. Benito saw you."

McKay laughed merrily.

"I see it all. Why, you foolish, jealous Mariquita, that was my general's wife—a great lady. I was attending and following her about like a lackey. I would not dare to lift my eyes to her even if I wished, which is certainly not the case."

Mariquita was beginning to relent. Her big eyes filled with tear, and she said in a broken voice, as though this quarrel with her lover had pained her greatly—

"Oh, oily-tongued! if only I could believe you!"

"Why, of course it's true. Surely you would not let that villain Benito make mischief between us? But, there; time is too precious to waste in silly squabbles. I can't stay long; I can't tell when I shall come again."

"Is your love beginning to cool, Stanislas? If so, we had better part before—"

"Listen, dearest," interrupted McKay; "I have good news for you," and he told her of his unexpected promotion, and of the excellent prospects it held forth.

"I am nearly certain to win a commission before very long. Now that we are going to the war—"

"The war!" Mariquita's face turned ghastly white; she put her hand upon her heart, and was on the point of falling to the ground when McKay vaulted lightly over the fence and saved her by putting his arm round her waist.

"Idiot that I was to blurt it out like that, after thinking all the week how best to break the news! Mariquita! Mariquita! speak to me, I implore you!"

But the poor child was too much overcome to reply, and he led her, dazed and half-fainting, to a little seat near the house, where, with soft caresses and endearing words, he sought to restore her to herself.

"The war!" she said, at length. "It has come, then, the terrible news that I have so dreaded. We are to part, and I shall never, never see you again."

"What nonsense, Mariquita! Be brave! Remember you are to be a soldier's wife. Be brave, I say."

"They will kill you! Oh! if they only dared, I would be revenged!"

"Bravo, my pet! that is the proper spirit. You would fight the Russians, wouldn't you?"

"I would do anything, Stanislas, to help you, to shield you from harm. Why can't I go with you? Who knows! I might save you. I, a weak, helpless girl, would be strong if you were in danger. I am ready, Stanislas, to sacrifice my life for yours."

Greatly touched by the deep devotion displayed by these sweet words, McKay bent his head and kissed her on the lips.

But at this moment the tender scene was abruptly ended by the shrill, strident tones of La Zandunga's voice.

"So I have caught you, shameless girl, philandering again with this rascally red-coat. May he die in a dog-kennel! Here, in my very house! But, I promise you, it is for the last time. *Hola!* Benito! Pedro! help!" and, screaming wildly, the old crone tore Mariquita from McKay's side and dragged her into the house.

The young sergeant, eager to protect his love from ill-usage, would have followed, but he was confronted by Benito, who now stood in the doorway, black and menacing, with a great two-edged Albacete knife in his hand.

"Stand back, miscreant, hated Englishman, or I will stab you to the heart."

Nothing daunted by the threat, McKay advanced boldly on Benito; with one hand he caught his would-be assailant by the throat; with the other the wrist that was lifted to strike. A few seconds more, and Benito had measured his length on the ground, while his murderous weapon had passed into the possession of McKay.

Having thus disposed of one opponent, McKay met a second, in the person of Tio Pedro, who, slower in his movements, had also come out in answer to his wife's appeal.

"Who are you that dares to intrude here?" asked Pedro, roughly. "I will complain to the town major, and have you punished for this."

"Look to yourself, rather!" replied McKay, hotly. "I stand too high to fear your threats. But you, thief and smuggler, I will bring the police upon you and your accomplice, who has just tried to murder me with his knife."

Tio Pedro turned ghastly pale at the sergeant-major's words. He had evidently no wish for a domiciliary visit, and would have been glad to be well rid of McKay.

"Let him be! Let him be!" he said, attempting to pacify Benito, who, smarting from his recent overthrow, seemed ready to renew the struggle.

"Let him be! It is all a mistake. The gentleman has explained his business here, and nothing more need be said."

"Nothing more!" hissed Benito, between his teeth. "Not when he has insulted me—struck me! Nothing more! We shall have to settle accounts together, he and I. Look to yourself Señor Englishman. There is no bond that does not some day run out; no debt that is never paid."

McKay disdained to notice these threats, and, after waiting a little longer in the hope of again seeing Mariquita, he left the house.

It was his misfortune, however, not to get speech with her again before his departure. The few short days intervening before embarkation were full of anxiety for him, and incessant, almost wearisome, activity. He had made himself one moment of leisure, and visited Bombardier Lane, but without result. Mariquita was invisible, and McKay was compelled to abandon all hope of bidding his dear one good-bye.

But he was not denied one last look at the girl of his heart. As the regiment, headed by all the bands of the garrison, marched gaily down to the New Mole, where the transport-ship awaited it, an excited throng of spectators lined the way. Colonel Blythe headed his regiment, of course, and close behind him, according to regulation, marched the young sergeant-major, in brave apparel, holding his head high, proudly conscious of his honourable position. The colonel and the sergeant-major were the first men down the New Mole stairs; and as they passed McKay heard his name uttered with a half-scream.

He looked round hastily, and there saw Mariquita, with white, scared face and streaming eyes.

What could he do? It was his duty to march on unconscious, insensible to emotion. But this was more than mortal man could do. He paused, lingering irresolutely, when the colonel noticed his agitation, and quickly guessed the exact state of the case.

"'The girl I left behind me,' eh, sergeant-major? Well, fall out for a minute or two, if you like"—and, with this kindly and considerate permission, McKay took Mariquita aside to make his last *adieux*.

"*Adios! vida mia*" [good-bye, my life], he was saying, when the poor girl almost fainted in his arms.

He looked round, greatly perplexed, and happily his eye fell upon Sergeant Hyde.

"Here, Hyde," he said, "take charge of this dear girl."

"What! sergeant-major, have you been caught in the toils of one of these bright-eyed damsels? It is well we have got the route. They are dangerous cattle, these women; and, if you let them, will hang like a mill-stone round a soldier's neck."

"Pshaw! man, don't moralise. This girl is my heart's choice. Please Heaven I may return to console her for present sorrow. But I can't wait. Help me: I can trust you. See Mariquita safely back to her home, and then join us on board."

"I shall be taken up as a deserter."

"Nonsense! I will see to that with the adjutant. We do not sail for two hours at least; you will have plenty of time."

Sergeant Hyde, although unwillingly, accepted the trust, and thus met Mariquita for the first time.

CHAPTER X
A GENERAL ACTION

A long low line of coast trending along north and south as far as the eye could reach; nearest at hand a strip of beach, smooth shingle cast up by the surf of westerly gales; next, a swelling upland, dotted with grazing cattle, snug homesteads, and stacks of hay and corn; beyond, a range of low hills, steep-faced and reddish-hued.

The Crimea! The land of promise; the great goal to which the thoughts of every man in two vast hosts had been turned for many months past. On the furze-clad common of Chobham camp, on the long voyage out, at Gallipoli, while eating out their hearts at irritating inaction; on the sweltering, malarious Bulgarian plains, fever-stricken and cholera-cursed; at Varna, waiting impatiently, almost hopelessly, for orders to sail, twenty thousand British soldiers of all ranks had longed to look upon this Crimean shore. It was here, so ran the common rumour, that the chief power of the mighty Czar was concentrated; here stood Sebastopol, the famous fortress, the great stronghold and arsenal of Southern Russia; here, at length, the opposing forces would join issue, and the allies, after months of tedious expectation, would find themselves face to face with their foe.

No wonder, then, that hearts beat high as our men gazed eagerly upon the Crimea. The prospect southward was still more calculated to stir emotion. The whole surface of that Eastern sea was covered with the navies of the Western Powers. The long array stretched north and south for many a mile; it extended westward, far back to the distant horizon, and beyond: a countless forest of masts, a jumble of sails and smoke-stacks, a crowd of fighting-ships and transports, three-deckers, frigates, great troopers, ocean steamers, full-rigged ships—an Armada such as the world had never seen before. A grand display of naval power, a magnificent expedition marshalled with perfect precision, moving by day in well-kept parallel lines; at night, motionless, and studding the sea with a "second heaven of stars."

Day dawned propitious on the morning of the landing: a bright, and soon fierce, sun rose on a cloudless sky. At a given signal the boats were lowered—a nearly countless flotilla; the troops went overboard silently and with admirable despatch, and all again, by signal, started in one long perfect line for the shore. Within an hour the boats were beached, the troops sprang eagerly to land, and the invasion was completed without accident, and unopposed.

The Royal Picts, coming straight from Gibraltar, had joined the expedition at Varna without disembarking. The regiment had thus been long on ship-board, but it had lost none of its smartness, and formed up on the beach with as much precision as on the South Barracks parade. It fell into its place at once, upon the right of General Wilders's brigade, and that gallant officer was not long in welcoming it to his command.

Everyone was in the highest health and spirits, overflowing with excitement and enthusiasm. At the appearance of their general, the men, greatly to his annoyance, set up a wild, irregular cheer.

"Silence, men, silence! It is most unsoldierlike. Keep your shouting till you charge. Here, Colonel Blythe, we will get rid of a little of this superfluous energy. Advance, in skirmishing order, to the plateau, and hold it. There are Cossacks about, and the landing is not yet completed. But do not advance beyond the plateau. You understand?"

The regiment promptly executed the manœuvre indicated, and gained the rising ground. The view thence inland was more extended, and at no great distance a road crossed, along which was seen a long line of native carts, toiling painfully, and escorted by a few of the enemy's horse.

"We must have those carts." The speaker was a staff-officer, the quartermaster-general, an eagle-eyed, decisive-speaking, short, slender man, who was riding a splendid charger, which he sat to perfection. "Colonel Blythe! send forward your right company at the double, and capture them."

"My brigadier ordered me not to advance," replied the old colonel, rather stolidly.

"Do as I tell you; I will take the responsibility. But look sharp!"

Already, no doubt under orders from the escort, the drivers were unharnessing their teams, with the idea of making off with the cattle. The skirmishers of the Royal Picts advanced quickly within range, and opened fire—the first shots these upon Russian soil—and some of them took effect. The carts were abandoned, and speedily changed masters.

"We shall want those carts," said old Hyde, abruptly, to his friend the sergeant-major. They had watched this little episode together.

"Yes, I suppose they will come in useful."

"I should think so. Are you aware that this fine force of ours is quite without transport? At least, I have seen none. Do you know what that means?"

"That we shall have to be our own beasts of burden," said McKay, laughing, as he touched his havresack. It was comfortably lined with biscuit and cold salt pork—three days' rations, and the only food that he or his comrades were likely to get for some time.

"I'm not afraid of roughing it," said the old soldier. "I have done that often enough. We have got our greatcoats and blankets, and I daresay we shan't hurt; but I have seen something of campaigning, and I tell you honestly I don't like the way in which we have started on this job."

"What an inveterate old grumbler you are, Hyde! Besides, what right have you to criticise the general and his plans?"

"We have entered into this business a great deal too lightly, I am quite convinced of that," said Hyde, positively. "There has been no sufficient preparation."

"Nonsense, man! They have been months getting the expedition ready."

"And still it is wanting in the most necessary things. It has to trust to luck for its transport," and the old sergeant pointed with his thumb to the captured carts. "We may, perhaps, get as many more; but, even then, there won't be enough to supply us with food if we go much further inland; we may never see our knapsacks again, or our tents."

"We shan't want them; it won't do us any harm to sleep in the open. Napoleon always said that the bivouac was the finest training for troops."

"You will be glad enough of shelter, sergeant-major, before to-night's out, mark my words! The French are better off than we are; they have got everything to their hands—their shelter-tents, knapsacks, and all. They understand campaigning; I think we have forgotten the art."

"As if we have anything to learn from the French!" said the self-satisfied young Briton, by way of ending the conversation.

But Sergeant Hyde was right, so far as the need for shelter was concerned. As evening closed in, heavy clouds came up from the sea, and it rained in torrents all night.

A miserable night it was! The whole army lay exposed to the fury of the elements on the bleak hillside, drenched to the skin, in pools and watercourses, under saturated blankets, without fuel, or the chance of lighting a bivouac fire. It was the same for all; the generals of division, high staff-officers, colonels, captains, and private men. The first night on Crimean soil was no bad precursor of the dreadful winter still to come.

Next day the prospect brightened a little. The sun came out and dried damp clothes; tents were landed, only to be re-embarked when the army commenced its march. This was on the third day after disembarkation, when, with all the pomp and circumstance of a parade movement, the allied generals advanced southward along the coast. They were in search of an enemy which had shown a strange reluctance to come to blows, and had already missed a splendid opportunity of interfering with the landing.

The place of honour in the order of march was assigned to the English, who were on the left, with that flank unprotected and "in the air"; on their right marched the French; on whose right, again, the Turks; then came the sea. Moving parallel with the land-forces, the allied fleets held undisputed dominion of the waters. A competent critic could detect no brilliant strategy in the operations so far; no astute, carefully calculated plan directed the march. One simple and primitive idea possessed the minds of the allied commanders, and that was to come to close quarters, and fight the Russians wherever they could be found.

There could be only one termination to such a military policy as this when every hour lessened the distance between the opposing forces. At the end of the first day's march, most toilsome and trying to troops still harassed by fell disease, it was plain that the enemy were close at hand. Large bodies of their cavalry hung black and menacing along our front— the advance guards these of a large force in position behind. Any moment might bring on a collision. It was nearly precipitated, and prematurely, by the action of our horse—a small handful of cavalry, led by a fiery impatient soldier, eager, like all under his command, to cross swords with the enemy.

A couple of English cavalry regiments had been pushed forward to reconnoitre the strength of the Russians. The horsemen rode out in gallant style, but were checked by artillery fire; a British battery galloped up and replied. Presently the round-shot bounded like cricket balls, but at murderous pace, across the plain. More cavalry went forward on our side, and two whole infantry divisions, in one of which was the Royal Picts, followed in support.

Surely a battle was close at hand. But nothing came of this demonstration. Why, was not quite clear, till Hugo Wilders, who was a captain in the Royal Lancers, came galloping by, and exchanged a few hasty words with the general, his cousin Bill.

"What's up, Hugo?" The general was riding just in front of the Royal Picts, and his words were heard by many of the regiment.

"Just fancy! we were on the point of having a brush with the Cossacks, when Lord Raglan came up and spoiled the fun."

"Do you know why?"

"Yes; I heard him talking to our general—I am galloping, you know, for Lord Cardigan, who was mad to be at them, I can tell you, but he wasn't allowed."

"They were far too strong for you; I could see that myself."

"That's what Lord Raglan said. As if any one of us was not good enough for twenty Russians! But he was particularly anxious, so I heard him say, not to be drawn into an action to-day."

"No doubt he was right," replied old Wilders. "Only it can't be put off much longer. Unless I am greatly mistaken, to-morrow we shall be at it hammer and tongs."

"I hope I shall be somewhere near!" cried Hugo, gaily. "But where are the Royal Picts? Oh! here! I want to give Anastasius good-day."

He found his younger brother was carrying the regimental colours, and the two young fellows exchanged pleasant greetings. It was quite a little family party, for just behind, in the centre of the line, stood Sergeant-major McKay, the unacknowledged cousin. How many of these four Wilders would be alive next night?

No doubt a battle was imminent. It was more than possible that there would be a night attack, so both armies bivouacked in order of battle, ready to stand up in their places and fight at the first alarm.

But the night passed uneventfully. At daybreak the march was resumed, and the day was still young when the allies came upon what seemed a position of immense strength, occupied in force by the Russian troops.

It was a broad barrier of hills, at right angles with the coast, lying straight athwart our line of march. The hills, highest and steepest near the water's edge, were still difficult in the centre, where the great high road to Sebastopol pierced the position by a deep defile; beyond the road, slopes more gentle ended on the outer flank in the tall buttresslike Kourgané Hill. All along the front ran a rapid river, the Alma, in a deep channel. Villages nestled on its banks—one near the sea, one midway, one on the extreme right; and all about the low ground rich vegetation flourished, in garden, vineyard, and copse.

These were the heights of the Alma—historic ground, hallowed by many memories of grim contest, vain prowess, glorious deeds, fell carnage, and hideous death.

"We are in for it now, my boy," whispered Sergeant Hyde, who was one of the colour-party, and stood in the centre of the column, near McKay.

"What is it?" asked the young sergeant-major eagerly. "A fight?"

"More than that—a general action. In another hour or two we shall be engaged hotly along the whole line. Some of us will lose the number of our mess before the day is done."

The Royal Picts formed part of the second division, under the command of Sir de Lacy Evans, a fine old soldier, who had seen service for half a century. This division was on the right of the English army. On the left of Sir de Lacy Evans was the Light Division, beyond that the Highlanders and Guards. The Third Division was in reserve behind the Second, the Fourth far in the rear, still near the sea-shore.

The march had hitherto been in columns, a disposition that lent itself readily to deployment into line—the traditional formation, peculiar to the British arms, and the inevitable prelude to an attack.

The order now given to form line was, therefore, promptly recognised as the signal for the approaching struggle. It was rendered the more necessary by the galling fire opened upon our troops by the enemy's batteries, which crowned every point of vantage on the hills in front.

Grandly, and with admirable precision, the three leading divisions of the British army formed themselves into the historic "Thin Red Line," renowned in the annals of European warfare, from Blenheim to Waterloo.

This beautiful line, so slender, yet so imposing in its simple, unsupported strength, was more than two miles long, and faced the right half of the Russian position. As the divisions stood, the Guards and Highlanders confronted the Kourgané Hill, with its greater and lesser redoubts, armed with heavy guns and held by dense columns of the enemy. Next them was the Light Division, facing the vineyards and hamlets to the left of the great high road; before them were other earth-works, manned by a no less formidable garrison and artillery. The Second Division lay across the high road, opposite the village of Bourliouk, high above which was an eighteen-gun battery and great masses of Russian troops.

General Wilders's brigade was on the extreme right of the British front; its right regiment was the Royal Picts, the very centre this of the battle-field, midway between the sea and the far left; and here the allied generals had their last meeting before the combat commenced.

A single figure, sitting straight and soldier-like in his saddle, with white hair blanched in the service of his country—a service fraught with the perils and penalties of war, as the empty sleeve bore witness—this single figure rode a little in advance of the British staff. It was Fitzroy Somerset, now Lord Raglan, the close comrade and trusted friend of the Iron Duke, by whose side he had ridden in every action in Spain. His face was passive and serene. Contentment shone in every feature. His martial spirit was stirred by the sights and sounds of battle, once so familiar to him, but now for forty years unheard. But the calm demeanour, the quiet voice, the steady, unflinching gaze, all indicating a noble unconsciousness of danger, were those of the chance rider in Rotten Row, not of a great commander carrying his own life and that of thousands in his hand.

The man who came to meet him was a soldier too, but of a different type, cast in another mould—a Frenchman, emotional, easily excited, quick in gesture, rapid-speaking, with a restless, fiery eye. St. Arnaud, too, had long tried the fortunes of war. His was an intrepid, eager spirit, but he was torn and convulsed with the tortures of a mortal sickness, and at times, even at this triumphant hour, his face was drawn and pale with inward agony.

They were near enough, these supreme chiefs, for their conversation, or parts of it, to be heard around. But they spoke in French, and few but McKay understood the purport of all they said.

"I am ready to advance at any moment," said Lord Raglan. "I am only waiting for the development of your attack."

"Bosquet started an hour ago, but he has a tremendous climb up those cliffs."

It was General Bosquet's business to assault the left of the Russian position, strong in natural obstacles, and almost inaccessible to troops.

At this moment an aide-de-camp ventured to ride forward to his general's side, and said—

"Do you hear that firing, my lord? I think the French on the right are warmly engaged."

"Are they?" replied Lord Raglan, doubtfully; "I can't catch any return fire."

"In any case," observed St. Arnaud, quickly, "it is time to lend him a hand. The Prince Napoleon and Canrobert shall now advance."

"The sooner the better," said Lord Raglan, simply; "I must wait till their attack is developed before I can move."

"You shall not wait long, my friend."

The next instant the French mounted messengers were scouring the plain. St. Arnaud paused a moment, then, gathering up his reins, he put spurs to his horse and galloped away, saluted as he went by a loud and hearty cheer.

The sound must have gladdened the heart of the gallant Frenchman, for he promptly reined in his horse, and, rising in his stirrups, responded with a loud "Hurrah for Old England!" given in ringing tones, and in excellent English. Then, still followed by cheers, he went on his way.

It is but poor fun waiting while others begin a great game—poor fun and dangerous too, as the English line presently realised, while they looked impatiently for the order to advance. The Russian gunners had got their range, and were already plying them with shot and shell. At the first gun, fired evidently at the British staff, Lord Raglan, as cool and self-possessed as ever, turned to General Wilders, and said, briefly—

"Your men had better lie down."

"May I not cast loose cartridges first, my lord?" said the old soldier, anxious to prepare for the serious business of the day.

"With all my heart! But be quick; they must not stand up here to be shot at for nothing." Then Lord Raglan himself, erect and fearless, resumed his observation of the advancing French columns.

"Dear, dear! how slow they are!" cried the eager voice of Airey, the quartermaster-general.

"Look! they are checked!" said another; "they can't stomach the climb."

"They have a tough job before them," said a third. "It will try them hard."

That the French were in difficulties was evident, for now an aide-de-camp came galloping from Bosquet with the grave news that the division was in danger. He was followed by another prominent person on St. Arnaud's staff, bringing an earnest entreaty that the English should not delay their advance. A fierce storm of iron hail, moreover, made inaction more and more intolerable.

The time was come! Lord Raglan turned and spoke five words to General Airey. The next minute staff-officers were galloping to each division with the glad tidings: "The line will advance!"

All along it men rose from the ground with a resolute air, fell into their ranks, and then the "Thin Red Line," having a front of two miles and a depth of two men, marched grandly to the fight.

It is with the doings of the Second Division, or more exactly with Wilders's brigade of that body, that we are now principally concerned.

The task before it was arduous and full of danger, demanding devoted courage and unflinching hearts.

At the moment of the advance the village immediately in front of them burst into flames—a fierce conflagration, lighted by the retreating foe. The dense columns of smoke hid the batteries beyond, and magnified the dangers of attack; the fierce fire narrowed the path of progress and squeezed in the advancing line. On the left, the Light Division, moving forward with equal determination, still further limited the ground for action; and, thus straitened and compressed, the division marched upon a small front swept by a converging fire. So cruelly hampered was the Second Division, so stinted in breathing space, that a portion of General Wilders's command was shut out of the advancing line, and circled round the right of the burning village.

In this way the Royal Picts got divided; part went with the right of the brigade, still under the personal direction of its brigadier; part stuck to the main body, and followed on with the general tide of advance. With the latter went the headquarters of the regiment; its colonel, colours, and sergeant-major.

They were travelling into the very jaws of death, as it seemed. Progress was slow, and hindered by many vexatious obstacles—low walls and brushwood, ruined cottages, and many dangerous pitfalls on the vine-clad slopes—obstacles that forbade all speed, yet gave no cover from the pitiless fire that searched every corner, and mowed men down like grass.

Casualties were terribly numerous; yet still the line, undaunted but with sadly decreasing numbers, kept on its perilous way. Presently, having won through the broken ground, a new barrier interposed. They came upon the rapid river, rushing between steep banks, and deep enough to drown all who risked the fords. But there was no pause or hesitation; the men plunged bravely into the water, and, battling with the torrent, crossed, not without difficulty and serious loss.

Colonel Blythe, with the Royal Picts, was one of the first men over. He rode a snow-white charger, which he put bravely at the steep bank, and clambered up with the coolness of one who rode well to hounds. He gained the top, and served as a rallying-point for the shattered remnant of his regiment, which there quickly re-formed with as much coolness and fastidious nicety as on a barrack-square at home.

They were under shelter here, and, pausing to recover breath, could look round and watch how the fight fared towards the left.

At this moment the Light Division had effected a lodgment in the great redoubt; but, even while they gazed, the Russian reserves were forcing back the too-presumptuous few. Behind, a portion of the brigade of Guards was advancing to reinforce the wavering line and renew the attack. Beyond, further on the left, in an échelon, advanced three lines, one behind the other, the Highlanders and their stout leader, Sir Colin Campbell.

It was only a passing glimpse, however, that our friends obtained. Their leader knew that the fortunes of the day were still in doubt, and that every man must throw his weight into the scale if victory was to be assured.

The line was again ordered to advance. The slope was steeper now; they were scaling, really, the heights themselves. Just above them yawned the mouths of the heavy guns that had been dealing such havoc while they were painfully threading the intricacies of the low ground.

"We must drive them out of that!" shouted old Blythe. "That battery has been playing the mischief with us all along. Now, lads, shoulder to shoulder; reserve your fire till we are at close quarters, then give them the cold steel!"

The Royal Picts set up a ringing cheer in cordial response to their chieftain's call. The cheer passed quickly along the line, and all again pressed forward in hot haste, with set teeth, and bayonets at the charge.

A withering fire of small arms met the Royal Picts as they approached the battery; it was followed by the deafening roar of artillery; and the murderous fire of the guns, great and small, nearly annihilated the gallant band. Small wonder, then, that the survivors halted irresolute, half disposed to turn back. Colonel Blythe was down. They missed his encouraging voice; his noble figure was no more visible, while his fine old white charger, riderless, his flanks streaming with gore, was galloping madly down the hill. Many more officers were laid low by this murderous discharge; amongst others, Anastasius Wilders had fallen, severely wounded, and his blood had spurted out in a great pool upon the colour he carried.

All this happened in less time than it takes to describe. It was one of those moments of dire emergency, of great opportunity—suddenly arising, gone as swiftly beyond recall, unless snatched up and dealt with by a prompt, audacious spirit.

Young McKay saw it with the unerring instinct of a true soldier. He acted instantaneously, and with bold decision.

Stooping over his prostrate cousin, who lay entangled amidst the folds of the now crimson silk, he gently detached the colour, and, raising it aloft, cried—

"Come on, Royal Picts!"

The men knew his voice, and, weakened, though not dispirited, they gallantly responded to the appeal. Once more the line pressed forward. The short space between them and the earthwork was quickly traversed. Before the artillery could deal out a second salvo, the Royal Picts were over the parapet and in the thick of the Russians, bayoneting them as they stood at their guns.

The battery was won.

"Well done, sergeant-major—right well done! I saw it all. It shan't be forgotten if we two come out of this alive!"

The speaker was Colonel Blythe, who, happily, although dismounted by the shot that wounded his horse, had so far escaped unhurt.

"But this is no time for compliments; we must look to ourselves. The enemy is still in great strength. They are bringing up the reserves."

Above the battery a second line of columns loomed large and menacing. Was this gallant handful of Englishmen, which had so courageously gained a footing in the enemy's works, to bear the brunt of a fresh conflict with a new and perfectly fresh foe? The situation was critical. To advance would be madness; retreat was not to be thought of; yet it might cost them their lives to maintain the ground they held.

While they paused in anxious debate, there came sounds of firing from their right, aimed evidently at the Russians in front of them, for the shot and shell ploughed through the ranks of the foe.

"What guns can those be?" asked Colonel Blythe. "They are catching them nicely in flank."

"French, sir, I expect," replied McKay. "That is the side of their attack."

"Those are English guns, I feel sure. I know the crack they make."

He was right; the guns belonged to Turner's battery, brought up at the most opportune juncture by Lord Raglan's express commands. To understand their appearance, and the important part they played in deciding the battle on this portion of the field, we must follow the other wing of the Royal Picts, which, when separated from the rest of the brigade, passed round the right flank of the village.

Hyde was with this detachment, and, as he afterwards told McKay, he saw Lord Raglan and his staff ride forward, alone and unprotected, across the river, straight into the enemy's position. In the river two of his staff were shot down, and the commander-in-chief promptly realised the meaning of this fire.

"Ah!" he cried. "If they can enfilade us here, we can certainly enfilade them on the rising ground above. Bring up some guns!"

It was not easy travelling for artillery, but Turner was a man whom no difficulties dismayed. Within an hour a couple of his guns had been dragged up the steep gradient, were unlimbered, and served by the officers themselves.

It was the fire of this artillery that relieved the Royal Picts of their most serious apprehensions. It tided them over the last critical phase of the hotly-contested action, and completed the discomfiture of the enemy on this side.

Matters had gone no less prosperously on the left. The renewed attack of the Light Division, supported by the Guards, had ended in the capture of the great redoubt; while Sir Colin Campbell, a veteran warrior, at the head of his "bare-legged savages," as they were christened by their affrighted foe, had made himself master of the Kourgané Hill.

CHAPTER XI
AFTER THE BATTLE

The Battle of the Alma was won! Three short hours had sufficed to finish it, and by four o'clock the enemy was in full retreat. It was a flight rather than a retreat—a headlong, ignominious stampede, in which the fugitives cast aside their arms, accoutrements, knapsacks, everything that could hinder them as they ran. Pursuit, if promptly and vigorously carried out, would assuredly have cost them dear. But the allies were short of cavalry; the British, greatly weakened by their losses in this hard-fought field, could spare no fresh troops to follow; the French, although they had scarcely suffered, and had a large force available, would do nothing more; St. Arnaud declared pursuit impossible, and this, the first fatal error in the campaign, allowed the beaten general to draw off his shattered battalions.

But, if the allied leaders rejected the more abiding and substantial fruits of victory, they did not disdain the intoxicating but empty glories of an ovation from their troops. The generals were everywhere received with loud acclaims.

Deafening cheers greeted Lord Raglan as he rode slowly down the line. The cry was taken up by battalion after battalion, and went echoing along—the splendid, hearty applause of men who were glorifying their own achievements as well.

There was joy on the face of every man who had come out of the fight unscathed—the keen satisfaction of success, gloriously but hardly earned. Warm greetings were interchanged by all who met and talked together. Thus Lord Raglan and Sir Colin Campbell, both Peninsular veterans, shook hands in memory of comradeship on earlier fields. Few indeed had thus fought together before; but none were less cordial in their expressions of thankfulness and cordial good-will. They told each other of their adventures in the day—its episodes, perils, narrow, hair-breadth escapes! they inquired eagerly for friends; and then, as they learnt gradually the whole terrible truth, the awful price at which victory had been secured, moments that had been radiant grew overcast, and short-lived gladness fled.

"Next to a battle lost, nothing is so dreadful as a battle won," said Wellington, at the end, too, of his most triumphant day. The slaughter is a sad set-off against the glory; groans of anguish are the converse of exulting cheers. The field of conquest was stained with the life's blood of thousands. The dead lay all around; some on their backs, calmly sleeping as though death had inflicted no pangs; the bodies of others were writhed and twisted with the excruciating agony of their last hour. The wounded in every stage of suffering strewed the ground, mutilated by round shot and shell, shattered by grape, cut and slashed and stabbed by bayonet and sword.

Their cries, the loud shriek of acute pain, the long-drawn moan of the dying, the piercing appeal of those conscious, but unable to move, filled every echo, and one of the first and most pressing duties for all who could be spared was to afford help and succour.

Now the incompleteness of the subsidiary services of the English army became more strikingly apparent. It possessed no carefully organised, well-appointed ambulance trains, no minutely perfect field-hospitals, easily set up and ready to work at a moment's notice; medicines were wanting; there was little or no chloroform; the only surgical instruments were those the surgeons carried, while these indispensable assistants were by no means too numerous, and already worked off their legs.

Parties were organised by every regiment, with stretchers and water-bottles, to go over the field, to carry back the wounded to the coast, and afford what help they could. The Royal Picts, like the rest, hasten to send assistance to their stricken comrades. The bandsmen, who had taken no part in the action, were detailed for the duty, and the sergeant-major, at his own earnest request, was put in charge.

As they were on the point of marching off, General Wilders rode up. He had been separated, it will be remembered, from part of his brigade, and had still but a vague idea of how it had fared in the fight.

"I saw nothing of you, colonel, during the action. Worse luck I went with the wrong lot, on the right of the village."

"It is well some of the regiment escaped what we went through," said Colonel Blythe, sadly. "My left wing was nearly cut to pieces. I was never under such a fire."

"How many have you lost, do you suppose?"

"We are now mustering the regiment: a sorrowful business enough. Seven officers are missing."

"What are their names?"

"Popham, Smart, Drybergh, Arrowsmith—"

"Anastasius—my young cousin—is he safe?" hastily interrupted the general.

Colonel Blythe shook his head.

"I missed him half way up the hill; he was carrying the regimental colour, but when we got into the battery it was in the sergeant-major's hands. I wish to bring his—the sergeant-major's—conduct especially before your notice, general."

"The sergeant-major's? Very good. But if he took the colour he must know what happened to Anastasius. Call him, will you?"

Sergeant-major McKay came up and saluted.

"Mr. Wilders, sir," he told the general, "was wounded as we were breasting the slope."

"You saw him go down? Where was he hit?"

"I hadn't time to wait, sir."

"I should think not," interrupted Colonel Blythe; "but for him, general, we should never have carried the battery. I was dismounted, the men were checked, and just at the right moment the sergeant-major led them on."

"Bravely done, my lad! You shall hear of this again; I will make a special report to the commander of the forces. But there, that will keep. We must see after this poor boy."

"I was just sending off a party for the purpose," said the colonel.

"That's right. You have some idea, I suppose"—this was to McKay—"of the place where Mr. Wilders fell?"

"Certainly, sir. I think I can easily find it."

"Very well; show us the way. And you, Powys"—this was to the aide-de-camp—"ride over to the Royal Lancers and tell Hugo Wilders what has happened."

Then the little band of Good Samaritans set out upon its painful mission. The autumn evening was already closing in; the night air blew chill across the desolate plain; already numbers of men were busy amongst the wounded, assuaging their thirst from water-bottles, covering the prostrate forms with blankets, and lending the surgeons a helping hand.

Half an hour brought the searchers of the Royal Picts to where young Anastasius Wilders lay. McKay was the first to find him, and he raised a shout of recognition as he ran forward to the wounded officer. Unslinging his water-bottle, he put it to his cousin's lips; but young Wilders waved the precious liquid aside, saying, although in a feeble voice—

"Thank you; but I can wait. Give it to that poor chap over there; he is far worse hit than I am."

It was a private of the regiment, whose breast a bullet had pierced, and whose tortures seemed terrible.

But now the rest of the party came up. General Wilders dismounted, flask in hand, and the wounded lad was rewarded for his self-denial.

A surgeon, too, had arrived, and he was anxiously questioned as to the nature of young Wilders's wound.

The right leg had been shattered below the knee by a round shot; the wound had bled profusely, but the poor lad managed to stanch it with his shirt.

"Can you save it?" whispered the general.

"Impossible!" replied the surgeon, in the same tone.

"We must amputate above the knee at once," and he turned up his sleeves and gave instructions to an assistant to get ready the instruments.

The operation, performed without chloroform, and borne with heroic fortitude, was over when Hugo Wilders rode up to the spot. Anastasius recognised his brother, and answered his anxious, sorrowful greeting with a faint smile.

"What is to be done with him now?" asked the general.

"We must get him on board ship—to-night, if possible; but how?"

"We will carry him every inch of the way," said one of the bandsmen of the Royal Picts. Young Wilders was idolised by the men.

"It is three miles to the sea-shore: a long journey."

"They can march in two reliefs, four carrying, four resting," said McKay.

"You must be very careful," said the surgeon.

"Never fear! We will carry him as easy as a baby in its cot," replied one of the soldiers.

"Yes, yes! you can trust us," added McKay.

"Are you going with them?" asked the general.

"I should like to do so, sir."

"And of course I shall go too," added Captain Wilders; and the procession, thus formed, wended its way to the shore.

It was midnight before McKay and the stretcher-party were relieved of their precious charge, and when they had seen the wounded officer embarked in one of the ship's boats, accompanied by his brother, they laid down where they were to rest and await the daylight.

Soon after dawn they were again on the move making once more for the heights above the river, where they had left their regiment. Once more, too, they traversed the battle-field, with its ghastly sights and distressing sounds. It was still covered with the bodies of the dead and dying, their numbers greatly increased, for many of the wounded had succumbed to the tortures of the night. The figures of ministering comrades still moved to and fro, and men of all ranks were busily engaged in the good work.

There were others whose action was more open to question—camp-followers and sutlers, dropped from no one knew where, who lurked in secret hiding-places, and issued forth, when the coast seemed clear, to follow their loathsome trade of robbing the dead.

McKay's little party, as they trudged along, suddenly put up one of these evil birds of prey almost at their feet. The man rose and ran for his life, pursued by the maledictions of the Royal Picts.

"Stop him! Stop him!" they cried, and the fugitive was met and turned at every point. But he doubled like a hare, and had nearly made his escape when he fell almost into the arms of Sergeant Hyde.

"Stick to him!" cried McKay. "We will hand him over to the provost-marshal, who will give him a short shrift."

A fierce struggle ensued between the fugitive and his captor, the result of which seemed uncertain; but the former suddenly broke loose, and again took to his heels. He made towards the French lines, and disappeared amongst the clefts of the steep rocks.

When McKay joined Hyde, he said to him, rather angrily—

"Why did you let the fellow go?"

"I did my best, but he was like an eel. I had far rather have kept him. I have wanted the scoundrel these dozen years."

"You know him, then?"

"Yes," replied Hyde, sternly. "I know him well, but I thought that he was dead. It is better so; we have a long account to settle, and the day of reckoning will certainly come."

Thus ended the first collision between the opposing armies: the first great conflict between European troops since Waterloo. The credit gained by the victors, whose prowess echoed through the civilised world, was greater, perhaps, than the results achieved. The Alma, as we shall see, might have paved the way, under more skilful leadership, to a prompt and glorious termination of the war. But, if it exercised no sufficient influence upon the larger interests of the campaign, the battle greatly affected the prospects of the principal character in this story.

Sergeant-major McKay was presently informed that, in recognition of the signal bravery he had displayed at the storming of the Causeway battery, his name had been submitted to the Queen for an ensign's commission in the Royal Picts.

CHAPTER XII
CATCHING A TARTAR

After their victory at the Alma the allies tarried long on the ground they had gained. There were many excuses, but no sound reasons, for thus wasting precious moments that would never return. It was alleged that more troops had to be landed; that the removal of the sick and wounded to ship-board consumed much time; that further progress must be postponed until the safest method of approaching Sebastopol had been discussed in many and lengthy councils of war.

Yet at this moment the great fortress and arsenal lay at their mercy. They had but to put out their hands to capture it. Menschikoff's beaten army was long in rallying, and when at last it resumed the coherence of a fighting force its leader withdrew it altogether from Sebastopol, thus abandoning the fortress to its fate.

Its chief fortifications now were on the northern side, that nearest the allies, and within a short day's march. Only one redoubt—the so-called Star Fort—was of any formidable strength, and as this was close to the sea-shore it was exposed to the bombardment of the fleets. But the Star Port lay before the French, supposing that the original order of march was preserved; and the French, exaggerating its powers of resistance, could not be persuaded to face the risks of assault. The fact was, St. Arnaud lay dying, and for the moment all vigour was gone from the conduct of the French arms.

Little doubt exists to-day that the northern fortifications could not have resisted a determined attack. That it was not attempted was another grave error; to be followed by yet another, when, after a hazardous detour—the well-known "flank march"—the allies transferred themselves to the southern side of Sebastopol, and again neglected a palpable opportunity. The north side might be fairly well protected; the south was practically defenceless; a few weak earth-works, incomplete, and without artillery, were its only bulwarks; its only garrison were a few militia battalions and some hastily-formed regiments of sailors from the now sunken Russian ships of war.

It must undoubtedly have fallen by a *coup de main*. But generals hesitated and differed, bolder spirits were overruled, undue weight was given to the too-cautious counsels of scientific soldiers, and it was decided to sit down before and slowly besiege the place.

The chance on which the allies turned their backs was quickly seized by the enemy. One of the brightest pages in modern military annals is that which records how the genius and indomitable energy of one man improvised a resolute and protracted defence; and none have done fuller justice to Todleben than the foes he so long and gallantly kept at bay.

The allies now entered, almost with light hearts, upon a siege that was to last for eleven weary months and prove the source of unnumbered woes. In a comfortable leisurely fashion they proceeded to break ground, to open trenches, and approach the enemy's still unfinished works by parallel and sap. The siege-train—the British War Minister's fatal gift, encouraging as it did the policy of delay—was landed, as were vast supplies of ammunition and warlike stores. Tents, too, were brought up to the front, and the allied encampment soon covered the plateau from the Tchernaya to the sea. The troops soon settled down in their new quarters, and the heights before Sebastopol grew gradually a hive of military industry, instinct with warlike sounds, teeming with soldier life.

The Royal Picts found themselves posted on the uplands above the Tchernaya valley, very near the extreme right of the British front, and here they took their share of the duties that now fell upon the army, furnishing fatigue-parties to dig at the trenches, and armed parties to cover them as they worked, and pickets by day and night to watch the movements of the enemy.

Since McKay's official recommendation for a commission, he had been entrusted with duties above his position as sergeant-major. The adjutant had been badly wounded at the Alma, and it was generally understood that when promoted McKay would succeed him. Meanwhile he was entrusted with various special missions appertaining to the rank he soon expected to receive.

One of these was his despatch to Balaclava to make inquiries for the knapsacks of the regiment. They had been left on board ship, and the transport had been expected daily in Balaclava harbour. The men were sadly in want of a change of clothes, and neither these nor the little odds and ends that go to make up a soldier's comfort were available until they got their packs. McKay was directed to take a small party with him to land the much-needed baggage and have it conveyed by hook or crook to the front.

He left the camp late in the afternoon, and, striking the great Woronzoff Road just where it pierced the Fediukine Heights, descended it until he reached the Balaclava plain. A few miles beyond, the little town itself was visible, or, more exactly, the forest of masts that already crowded its little land-locked port.

Here, on the right of the communications between the English army and its base, a long range of redoubts had been thrown up and garrisoned by the Turks. These crowned the summit of a range of low hillocks, and, in marching to his point, McKay paused on the level ground between two hills. The Turks on sentry gave him a "Bono Johnny!" as he passed, by way of greeting; but they were far too lazy and too sleepy to do more.

It was evident they kept a poor look-out, and doubtful strangers were as free to pass as British friends. Just upon the rear of No. 3 Redoubt McKay and his men came upon a fellow crouching low amongst the broken ground. McKay would have passed by without remark, but his first look at the stranger, who wore no uniform and seemed a harmless, unoffending Tartar peasant, was followed by a second and keener gaze. He thought he recognised the man; he certainly had seen his face before. Directing his men to seize him, he made a longer and closer inspection, and found that it was the ruffian whom they had surprised and chased on the heights above the Alma the morning after the battle.

"He is up to no good," said McKay. "We must take him along with us."

But where? The job they were on was a definite one; not the capture of chance prisoners, which would certainly delay them on the road.

Still, remembering the last occasion on which he had seen this man, and the mysterious remarks that Hyde had let fall concerning him, McKay felt sure the fellow was not what he seemed. This Tartar dress must be a disguise: how could Hyde have made the acquaintance years before of a Tartar peasant in the Crimea?

Certainly the man must go with them, and therefore, placing him securely in the midst of his party, McKay marched on. If nothing better offered, he would hand his prisoner over to the Commandant of Balaclava on arrival there.

But as they trudged along, and, leaving the cavalry-encampment on their right, approached the ground occupied by the Highland brigade, they encountered its general—McKay had seen him at the Alma—riding out, accompanied by his staff.

The quick eye of Sir Colin Campbell promptly detected the prisoner. He rode up at once to the party, and said, in a sharp, angry tone—

"What are you doing with that peasant? Don't you know that the orders are positive against molesting the inhabitants? Who is in command of this party?"

McKay stood forth and saluted.

"You? A sergeant-major? Of the Royal Picts, too! You ought to know better. Let the man go!"

"I beg your pardon, Sir Colin," began McKay; "but—"

"Don't argue with me, sir; do as I tell you. I have a great mind to put you in arrest."

McKay still stood in an attitude of mute but firm protest.

"What does the fellow mean? Ask him, Shadwell. I suppose he must have some reason, or he would not defy a general officer like this."

Captain Shadwell, one of Sir Colin's staff, took McKay aside, and, questioning him, learnt all the particulars of the capture. McKay told him, too, what had occurred at the Alma.

"The fellow must be a spy," said Sir Colin, abruptly, when the whole of the facts were repeated to him. "We must cross-question him. I wonder what language he speaks."

The general himself tried him with French; but the prisoner shook his head stupidly. Shadwell followed with German, but with like result.

"I'll go bail he knows both, and English too, probably. He ought to be tried in Russian now: that's the language of the country. He is undoubtedly an impostor if he can't speak that. I wish we could try him in Russian. If he failed, the provost-marshal should hang him on the nearest post."

This conversation passed in the full hearing of McKay, and when Sir Colin stopped the sergeant-major stepped forward, again saluted, and said modestly—

"I can speak Russian, sir."

"You? An English soldier? In the ranks, too? Extraordinary! How on earth—but that will keep. We will put this fellow through his facings at once. Ask him his name, where he comes from, and all about him. Tell him he must answer; that his silence will be taken as a proof he is not what he pretends. No real Tartar peasant could fail to understand Russian."

"Who and what are you?" asked McKay. And this first question was answered by the prisoner with an alacrity that indicated his comprehension of every word that had been said. He evidently wished to save his neck.

"My name is Michaelis Baidarjee. Baidar is my home; but I have been driven out by the Cossacks to-day."

It was a lie, no doubt. Hyde had recognised him as a very different person.

"Ask him what brings him into our lines?" said Sir Colin, when this answer had been duly interpreted.

"I came to give valuable information to the Lords of the Universe," he replied. "The Russians are on the move."

"Ha!" Sir Colin's interest was aroused. "Go on; make him speak out. Say he shall go free if he tells us truly all he knows."

"Where are the Russians moving?" asked McKay.

"This way"—the man pointed back beyond Tchorgorum. "They are collecting over yonder, many, many thousands, and are marching this way."

"Do you mean that they intend to attack us?"

"I think so. Why else do they come? Yesterday there were none. All last night they were marching; to-morrow, at dawn, they will be here."

"Who commands them?"

"Liprandi. I saw him, and they told me his name."

"This is most important," said Sir Colin; "we must know more. Find out, sergeant-major, whether he can go back safely."

"Back within the Russian lines?"

"Exactly. He might go and return with the latest news."

"You would never see the fellow again, Sir Colin. He is only humbugging us—"

"Put the question as I direct you," interrupted the general, abruptly. "What we want is information; it must be got by any means."

"Yes, I will go," the prisoner promised, joining his hands with a gesture as if taking an oath; "and I would return this very night; you shall have the exact numbers; shall know the road they are coming, when to expect them—all."

"Let him loose, then," said the general; "but warn him, if he plays us false, that he had better not fall into our clutches again."

"You may trust him not to do that, sir," said McKay, rather discontented at seeing his prisoner so easily set free.

The general ignored the remark, but he was evidently displeased at its tone, for he now turned sharply on McKay, saying—

"As regards you—how comes it you speak Russian?"

"I was born in Moscow."

"Of Russian parents?"

"My father was a Pole by birth, but by extraction a Scotchman."

"What is your name?"

"McKay—Stanislas Anastasius Wilders McKay."

"Ah! Stanislas; I understand that. But how is it you were christened Wilders? And Anastasius, too—that is a family name, I think. Are you related to Lord Essendine?—a Wilders, in fact?"

"Yes, sir, by my mother's side."

"And yet you have taken the Queen's shilling! Strange! But it is no business of mine. Young scapegrace, I suppose—"

"My character is as good as—" "yours," McKay would have said, but his reverence for the general's rank restrained him. "I enlisted because I could not enter the British army and be a soldier in any other way."

"With your friends'—your relatives'—approval?"

"With my mother's, certainly; and of those nearest me."

"Do you know General Wilders—here in the Crimea, I mean?"

"My regiment is in his brigade."

"Yes, yes! I am aware of that. But have you made yourself known to him, I mean?"

The young sergeant-major knew that his gallantry at the Alma had won him his general's approval, but he was too modest to refer to that episode.

"I have never claimed the relationship, sir," he answered, simply, but with proud reticence; "it would not have beseemed my position."

"Your sentiments do you credit, young man. That will do; you can continue your march. Good-day!"

They parted; McKay and his men went on to Balaclava, the general towards the Second Division camp.

"Curious meeting, that, Shadwell," said Sir Colin. "If I come across Wilders I shall tell him the story. He might like to do his young relative—a smart soldier evidently, or he would not be a sergeant-major so early—a good turn."

CHAPTER XIII
"NOT WAR!"

The spy, whatever his nationality, and however questionable his antecedents, was right in the intelligence he had communicated. A large Russian force was even then on the march from Tchorgorum, pointing straight for the Balaclava plain. The enemy had regained heart; emboldened by the constant influx of reinforcements, and the inactivity of the allies, he had grown audacious, and was ready to try a vigorous offensive. A blow well aimed at our communications and delivered with intention might drive us back on our ships, perhaps into the sea.

McKay had passed the night at Balaclava. The transport with the knapsacks was not yet in port, and he was loth to return to camp empty-handed. But next morning, soon after daylight, news came back to the little seaside town that another battle was imminent, on the plains outside.

The handful of Royal Picts were promptly mustered by their young commander, and marched in the direction of the firing, which was already heard, hot and heavy, towards the east.

As they left Balaclava, they encountered a crowd of Turkish soldiers in full flight, making madly for the haven, and shouting, "Ship! ship!" as they ran. McKay, gathering from this stampede that already some serious conflict had begun, hurried forward to where he found a line of red-coats drawn up behind a narrow ridge which barred the approaches to Balaclava.

This was the famous 93rd, in its now historic formation—another "Thin Red Line," which received undaunted, and only two deep, the onslaught of the Russian horse.

The regiment was under the personal control of its brigadier, stout old Sir Colin, who, with his staff, stood a little withdrawn, but closely observing all that passed. He recognised McKay, and called out abruptly—

"Halloa! where have you dropped from?"

"I heard the firing, sir, met the Turks retreating, and brought up my party to reinforce and act as might be ordered."

"It was well done, man. But, enough; get yourselves up into line there on the left, and take the word from the colonel of the 93rd."

"We have our work cut out for us, sir," said one of his staff to Sir Colin.

"We have, but we'll do it. This gorge must be held to the death. You understand that, Colonel Ainslie—to the death?"

"You can trust us, Sir Colin."

"I think so; but I'll say just one word to the men," and, while the enemy's cavalry were still some distance off, the general rode slowly down the line, speaking his last solemn injunction—

"Remember, men, there is no retreat from here. You must die where you stand."

One and the same answer rose readily to every lip—

"Ay! ay! Sir Colin; we'll do that!" shouted the gallant Scots.[1]

[1] Historical. *cf.* Kinglake's "Crimea," v. 80.

Their veteran leader's head was clear; his temper cool and self-possessed. He held these brave hearts in hand like the rider of a high-couraged horse, and knew well when to restrain, when to let go.

As the Russians approached, a few eager spirits would have rushed forward from their ranks to encounter their foe in the open plain; but Sir Colin's trumpet voice checked them with a fierce—

"Ninety-third! Ninety-third! None of that eagerness!"

And then a minute or two later came the signal for the whole line to advance. The Highlanders, and those with them, swiftly mounted to the crest of the ridge, and met the charging cavalry with a withering volley. A second followed. The enemy had no stomach for more; reining in their horses, they wheeled round and fell back as they had come.

This, however, was only the beginning of the action. Heavy columns of the enemy now appeared in sight, cavalry and infantry, with numerous artillery crowning the eastern hills. A portion occupied the redoubts abandoned by the Turks, and the attitude of the Russians was so menacing that it seemed unlikely we could stay their onward progress.

For the moment no troops could be interposed but the British cavalry— the two brigades, Light and Heavy—which had their encampment in the plain, and had been under arms, commanded by Lord Lucan, since daybreak.

"We must have up the First and Fourth Divisions," Lord Raglan had said, when he arrived on the battle-field soon after eight in the morning; at first he had treated the news of the Russian advance lightly. Many such moves had been reported on previous days, and all had ended in nothing. "Let the Duke of Cambridge and Sir George Cathcart have their orders at once. We must trust to the cavalry till the infantry come up. Tell Scarlett to support the Turks."

But the Turks had given way before General Scarlett could stiffen their courage, and as his brigade, that of heavy cavalry, trotted towards the redoubts, other and more stirring work offered itself. The head of a great column of Russian horse, three thousand sabres, came over the crest of the hill and invited attack.

Scarlett saw his opportunity, and, with true soldierly promptitude, seized it. He wheeled his squadrons into line and charged. Three went against the front, five against the right flank, one against the left.

The intrepid "Heavies," outnumbered fivefold, dashed forward at a hand gallop, and were soon swallowed up in the solid mass. But it could not digest the terrible dose. Just eight minutes more and the Russian column wavered, broke, and turned.

It was a fine feat of arms, richly meriting its meed of praise.

"Well done! well done!" was the message that came direct from Lord Raglan, on the hills above.

"Greys! Gallant Greys!" cried Sir Colin Campbell, galloping up to one of the regiments that had made this charge. "I am sixty-one years old, but if I were young I should be proud to be in your ranks!"

"What luck those Heavies have!" shouted another and a bitterly discontented spectator of their prowess.

It was Lord Cardigan who, at the head of the Light Brigade, sat still in his saddle, looking on.

Yet it was no one's fault but his own that he had not been also engaged. His men were within striking distance; they were bound, moreover, by the clearest canons of the military art to throw their weight upon the exposed flank of the discomfited foe.

But Lord Cardigan had strangely—obstinately, indeed—misunderstood his orders, and, although chafing angrily at inaction, conceived that it was his bounden but distasteful duty to halt where he was.

"Why don't he let us loose at them? Was there ever such a chance?" muttered Hugo Wilders, audibly, and within earshot of his chief. He was again riding as extra aide to Lord Cardigan, who turned fiercely on the speaker.

"How dare you, sir, question my conduct? You shall answer for your insubordination—"

"Let me implore you, my lord, to advance," said another voice, entreating earnestly, that of Captain Morris, a cavalry officer who knew war well, and who was, for the moment, in command of a magnificent regiment of Lancers.

"It is not your business to give me advice," replied the general, haughtily. "Wait till I ask for it."

"But, my lord, see! the Russians are reeling from the charge of the Heavies. Now if ever—"

"Enough, Captain Morris. My orders were to defend this position; and here I shall stay. I was told to attack nothing unless they came within reach. The enemy has not yet done that."

So the chance of annihilating the Russian cavalry was lost, and the Light Brigade thought that its chances of distinction were also gone for the day. Alas! the hour of its trial was very close at hand.

Lord Raglan had waited anxiously for the infantry divisions he had ordered up. The first, under the Duke of Cambridge, was now close at hand, and the fourth, led by Sir George Cathcart, had arrived at a point whence it might easily have reached out a hand to recover the redoubts. But Cathcart's advance was so leisurely that Lord Raglan feared he would be too late to prevent the Russians from carrying off the guns they had captured from the Turks. The enemy, it must be understood, were showing manifest signs of despondency: their shattered cavalry had gone rapidly to the rear, and their infantry had halted irresolute, inclined also to retreat.

"This is the moment to strike them," decided Lord Raglan. "They are evidently losing heart, and we ought to get back the redoubts easily. I will send the cavalry. They are almost on the spot, and at any rate can get quickly over the ground. Ride, sir," to an aide-de-camp, "and tell Lord Lucan to recover the heights. Tell him he will have infantry, two whole divisions, in support."

They watched the aide-de-camp deliver his message; but still Lord Lucan, who was in supreme command of the cavalry, made no move.

"What is he at?" cried Lord Raglan, testily. "He is very long about it."

"There is no time to lose, my lord," interposed the quartermaster-general, who had been intently watching the redoubts with his field-glasses. "I can see them bringing teams of horses into the redoubts. They evidently mean to carry off our guns."

The necessity for action was more than ever urgent and immediate.

"Lord Lucan must be made to move. Here, Airey! send him a peremptory order in writing."

The quartermaster-general produced pencil and paper from his sabretash, and wrote as follows:—

"Lord Raglan wishes the cavalry to advance rapidly to the front, and try to prevent the enemy from carrying away the guns. Immediate."

"That will do," said Lord Raglan. "Let your own aide-de-camp carry the order. He is a cavalry officer, and can explain, if required."

It was Nolan, the enthusiastic, ardent, devoted cavalry soldier, heart and soul, and overflowing now with joy at his mission, and the chances of distinction it offered the cavalry. A fine, fearless horseman, he galloped at a breakneck pace down the steep and rocky sides of the plateau, and quickly reached Lord Lucan's side.

The general read his orders, with lips compressed and lowering brow.

"You come straight from Lord Raglan? But, surely, you are General Airey's aide-de-camp?"

"Lord Raglan himself entrusted me with the message."

"I can't believe it. It is utterly impracticable: for any useful purpose. Quite unequal, quite inadequate, to the risks and frightful loss it must entail."

The impetuous aide-de-camp showed visible signs of impatience. While the general debated and discussed his orders, instead of executing them with instant, unquestioning despatch, a great opportunity was flitting quickly by.

"Lord Raglan's orders are"—Nolan spoke with an irritation that was disrespectful, almost insubordinate—"his lordship's orders are that the cavalry should attack immediately."

"Attack, sir!" replied Lord Lucan, petulantly; "attack what? What guns?"

"There, my lord, is your enemy," replied Nolan, with an excited wave of his arm; "there are your guns!"

The exact meaning of the gesture no man survived to tell, but its direction was unhappily towards a formidable Russian battery which closed the gorge of the north valley, and not to the heights crowned by the captured redoubts.

Lord Lucan, heated by the irritating language of his junior officer, must have lost his power of discrimination, for although his first instructions clearly indicated the guns in the redoubt, and his second, brought by Nolan, obviously referred to the same guns, the cavalry general was misled—by his own rage, or Nolan's sweeping gesture, who shall say?—misled into a terrible error.

He conceived it to be his duty to send a portion of his cavalry against a formidable battery of Russian guns, well posted as they were, and already sweeping the valley with a well-directed, murderous fire.

Of the two cavalry brigades, the Light was still fresh and untouched by the events of the day. The Heavy Brigade, as we have seen, had already done splendid service in routing the Russian cavalry. The turn of the Light Brigade had come, although, unhappily, the task entrusted to it was hopeless, foredoomed to failure from the first.

It stood close by, proudly impatient, its brigadier, Lord Cardigan, at its head.

To him the divisional general imparted Lord Raglan's order.

"You are to advance, Lord Cardigan, along the valley, and attack the Russians at the far end," was the order he gave.

"Certainly, sir," replied Lord Cardigan, without hesitation. "But allow me to point out to you that the Russians have a battery in the valley in our front, and batteries and riflemen on each flank."

"I can't help that," said Lord Lucan; "Lord Raglan will have it so. You have no choice but to obey."

Lord Cardigan saluted with his sword; then, rising in his stirrups, he turned to his men, and cried aloud in a full, firm voice—

"The brigade will advance!"—to certain death, he might have added, for he knew it, although he never quailed. But, settling himself in his saddle, as though starting on a promising run with hounds, and not on a journey from which there was no return, he said, with splendid resignation, as he prepared to lead the charge—

"Here goes for the last of the Brudenells!"[2]

[2] The family name of the Earls of Cardigan was Brudenell.

All this had passed in a few minutes, and then three lines of dauntless horsemen—in the first line, Dragoons and Lancers; in the second, Hussars; in the third, Hussars and more Dragoons—galloped down the north valley on their perilous and mistaken errand.

They were already going at full speed, when a single horseman, with uplifted arm and excited gesture, as though addressing the brigade, crossed their front. It was Nolan, who thus seemed to be braving the anger of Lord Cardigan by interfering with the leadership of his men.

What brought Nolan there? The inference is only fair and reasonable that at the very outset he had recognised the misinterpretation of Lord Raglan's orders, and was seeking to change the direction of the charging horsemen, diverting them from the Russian battery towards the redoubts, their proper goal.

Fate decreed that this last chance of correcting the terrible error should be denied to the Light Brigade. A Russian shell struck Nolan full in the chest, and "tore a way to his heart." By his untimely death the doom of the light cavalry was sealed.

As the devoted band galloped forward to destruction, all who observed them stood horror-stricken at the amazing folly of this mad, mistaken charge.

"Great heavens!" cried Lord Raglan. "Why, they will be destroyed! Go down, Calthorpe, and you, Burghersh, and find out who is responsible for this frightful mistake!"

"Magnificent!" was the verdict of Bosquet, a friendly but experienced French critic. "But it is not war."

Not war—murder, rather, and sudden death.

The ceaseless fire of the guns they faced wrought fearful havoc in the ranks of the horsemen as they galloped on. Still the survivors went forward, unappalled; but it was with sadly diminished numbers that they reached the object of their attack. The few that got to the guns did splendid service with their swords. The gunners were cut down as they stood, and for the moment the battery was ours. But it was impossible to hold it; the Light Brigade had almost ceased to exist. Presently its shattered remnants fell slowly back, covered by the Heavies against the pursuit of the once more audacious Russian cavalry.

Barely half an hour had sufficed for the annihilation of nearly six hundred soldiers, the flower of the British Light Horse. The northern valley was like a shambles, strewn with the dead and dying, while all about galloped riderless horses, and dismounted troopers seeking to regain their lines on foot. Quite half of the whole force had been struck down, among the rest Hugo Wilders, whose forehead a grape-shot had pierced.

The muster of regiments after such a fight was but a mournful ceremony. When at length the now decimated line was re-formed, the horror of the action was plainly seen.

"It was a mad-brained trick," said Lord Cardigan, who had marvellously escaped—"a monstrous blunder, but it was no fault of mine."

"Never mind, my lord!" cried many gallant spirits. "We are ready to charge again!"

"No, no, men," replied Lord Cardigan, hastily; "you have done enough."

It was at this moment that Lord Raglan rode up, and angrily called Lord Cardigan to account.

"What did you mean, sir, by attacking guns in front with cavalry, contrary to the usages of war?"

"You must not blame me, my lord," replied Lord Cardigan. "I only obeyed the orders of my superior officer," and he pointed to Lord Lucan, whom Lord Raglan then addressed with the severe reproof—

"You have sacrificed the Light Brigade, Lord Lucan. You should have used more discretion."

"I never approved of the charge," protested Lord Lucan.

"Then you should not have allowed it to be made."

The battle of Balaclava was practically over, and, although they had suffered no reverse, its results were decidedly disadvantageous to the allies. The massacre of the Light Brigade encouraged the Russian general to advance again; his columns once more crossed the Woronzoff road, and re-occupied the redoubts in force. The immediate result was the narrowing of the communications between the front and the base. The use of a great length of this Woronzoff road was forbidden, and the British were restricted to the insufficient tracks through Kadikoi. A principal cause this of the difficulties of supply during the dread winter now close at hand.

Another lesser result of the Russian advance was that McKay and his men that afternoon were unable to rejoin their regiment by the road they had travelled the day before. He returned to camp by a long and circuitous route, through Kadikoi, instead of by the direct Woronzoff road.

It was late in the day, therefore, when he was once more at his headquarters. He had much to tell of his strange adventures on these two eventful days, and the colonel, who had at once sent for him, kept him in close colloquy, plying him with questions about the battle, for more than an hour. It was not till he had heard everything that Colonel Blythe handed the sergeant-major a bundle of letters and papers, arrived that morning by the English mail.

"There is good news for you, McKay," said he. "I was so interested in your description that I had forgotten to tell you. Let me congratulate you; your name is in the *Gazette*," and the Colonel, taking McKay's hand, shook it warmly.

McKay carried off his precious bundle to his tent, and, first untying the newspaper, hunted out the *Gazette*.

There it was—

"The Royal Picts—Sergeant-Major Stanislas Anastasius Wilders McKay to be Ensign, *vice* Arrowsmith, killed in action."

They had lost no time; the reward had followed quickly upon the gallant deed that deserved it. Barely a month had elapsed since the Alma, yet already he was an officer, bearing the Queen's commission, which he had won with his own right arm.

His letters were from home—from his darling mother, who, in simple, loving language, poured forth her joy and pride.

"My dearest, bravest boy," she said, "how nobly you have justified the choice you made; you were right, and we were wrong in opposing your earnest wish to follow in your poor father's footsteps—would that he had lived to see this day! It was his spirit that moved you when, in spite of us all, of your uncles' protests and my tears, you persisted in your resolve to enlist. They said you had disgraced yourself and us. It was cruel of them; but now they are the first to come round. I have heard from both your uncles; they are, of course, delighted, and beg me to give you their heartiest good wishes. Uncle Ralph said perhaps he would write himself; but he is so overwhelmed with work at the Munitions Office he may not have time. Uncle Barto you will, perhaps, see out in the Crimea; he has got command of the *Burlington Castle*, one of the steamers chartered from his Company, and is going at once to Balaclava.

"Oh, my sweet son be careful of yourself!" went on the fond mother, her deep anxiety welling forth. "You are my only, only joy. I pray God hourly that He may spare your precious life. May He have you in His safe keeping!"

The reading of these pleasant letters occupied Stanislas till nightfall. Then, utterly wearied, but with a thankful, contented heart, he threw himself upon the ground, and slept till morning.

When he issued forth from his tent it was to receive the cordial congratulations of his brother officers. Sergeant Hyde came up, too, a little doubtfully, but McKay seized his hand, saying—

"You do not grudge me my good luck, I hope, old friend?"

"I, sir?"—the address was formal, but the tone was full of heartfelt emotion. "You have no heartier well-wisher than Colour-Sergeant Hyde. Our relative positions have changed—"

"Nothing can change them, or me, Hyde. You have always been my best and staunchest friend. It is to your advice and teachings that I owe all this."

"Go on as you have begun, my boy; the road is open before you. Who knows? That field-marshal's baton may have been in your pack after all!"

While they still talked a message was brought to McKay from General Wilders; the brigadier wished to see him at once.

"How is this, Mr. McKay?" said the general. "So you pretend to be a cousin of mine? Sir Colin Campbell has told me of his meeting with you, and now I find your name in full in the *Gazette*."

"It is no pretence, sir," replied Stanislas, with dignity.

"What! You call yourself a Wilders! By what right?"

"My mother is first cousin to the present Lord Essendine."

"Through whom?"

"Her father, Anastasius Wilders."

"I know—my father's brother. Then you belong to the elder branch. But I never heard that he married."

"He married Priscilla Coxon in 1805."

"Privately?"

"I believe not. But it was much against his father's wish, and his wife was never recognised by the family. His widow—you know my grandfather died early--married a second time, and thus increased the breach between the families."

"It's a strange story. I don't know what to think of it. These statements of yours—can they be substantiated?"

"Most certainly, sir, by the fullest proof. Besides, the present Lord Essendine is quite aware of my existence, and has acknowledged my relationship."

"Never openly: you must admit that."

"No, we were simple people; not grand enough, I suppose, for his lordship. At any rate, we were too proud to be patronised, and preferred to go our own way."

"I acknowledge you, Mr. McKay, without hesitation, and am proud to own so gallant a young man as my relative. You have indeed maintained the soldierly reputation of our family. Shake hands!"

"You are very kind, sir; I hope to continue to deserve your good opinion," and McKay rose to take his leave.

"Stay, Cousin McKay, I have more to say to you. What is this Sir Colin tells me about your speaking Russian?"

Stanislas explained.

"It may prove extremely useful; we have not too many interpreters in the army. I shall write to headquarters and report your qualifications. Do you speak any other languages?"

"French, Spanish, and a little Turkish."

"By Jove! you ought to be on the staff; they want such men as you. Can you sit on a horse?"

"I have ridden bare-backed many a dozen miles across the moors at home."

"Faith! I will take you myself. I want an extra aide-de-camp, and my cousin shall have the preference. I will send to Colonel Blythe at once; be ready to join me. But how about your kit? You will want horses, uniform, and—Forgive me, my young cousin: but how are you off for cash? You must let me be your banker."

McKay shook his head, gratefully.

"Thank you, sir; but I have been supplied from home. One of my uncles— my mother's half-brother—is well-to-do, and he sent me a remittance on hearing of my promotion."

"Well, well, as you please; but mind you come to me if you want anything. I shall expect you to take up your duties to-morrow." They were interrupted by all the bugles in the brigade sounding the assembly. "What is it? The alarm?"

"I can hear file-firing, sir, from the front."

"An attack, evidently. Hurry back to your camp; the regiment will be turned out by the time you get there!"

As McKay left the general's tent he met Captain Powys.

"The outposts have been driven in on Shell Hill and the enemy is advancing in force," said the aide-decamp. "We shall have another battle, I expect. It is our turn to-day."

This was Colonel Fedeoroff's forlorn hope against our extreme right: the sequel to Balaclava, the prelude of Inkerman—a sharp fight while it lasted, but promptly repulsed by our men.

CHAPTER XIV
THE GOLDEN HORN

Since the English and French armies had established themselves in the Crimea and the magnitude of their undertaking grew more and more apparent, they had found their true base of operations at Constantinople. Here were collected vast masses of supplies and stores, waiting to be forwarded to the front; here the reinforcements—horse, foot, and guns—paused ere they joined their respective armies; here hospitals, extensive, but still ill-organised and incomplete, received the sick and wounded sent back from the Crimea; here also lingered, crowding the tortuous streets of Mussulman Stamboul and filling to overflowing the French-like suburb of Pera, a strange medley of people, a motley crew of various faiths and many nationalities, polyglot in tongue and curiously different in attire, drawn together by such various motives as duty, mere curiosity, self-interest, and greed. Jews, infidels, and Turks were met at every corner: the first engaged in every occupation that could help them to make money, from touting at the bazaars to undertaking large contracts and selling bottled beer; the second, representatives going or coming from the forces now devoted to upholding the Crescent; the third, mostly apathetic, self-indulgent, corpulent old Mussulmans riding in state, accompanied by their pipe-bearers, or sitting half-asleep in coffee-houses or at the doors of their shops. Now and again a bevy of Turkish ladies glided by: mere peripatetic bundles of white linen, closely-veiled and yellow-slippered; or a Greek in his white petticoat, fierce in aspect and armed to the teeth; or an Armenian merchant, Arnauts, Bashi-Bazouks, French Spahis, the Bedouins of the desert, but half-disguised as civilised troops, while occasionally there appeared, amidst the heterogeneous throng, the plain suit of grey dittoes worn by the travelling Englishman, or the more or less simple female costumes that hailed from London or Paris.

Misseri's hotel did a roaring trade. It was crowded from roof-tree to cellar. Rooms cost a fabulous price. Mrs. Wilders managed to be very comfortably lodged there notwithstanding.

She still lingered in Constantinople. Her anxiety for her husband forbade her to leave the East, although she told her friends it was misery for her to be separated from her infant boy. She might have had a passage home in a dozen different steamers returning empty, all of them in search of fresh freights of men or material; or there was Lord Lydstone's yacht still lying in the Golden Horn and ready to take her anywhere if only she said the word. But that, of course, was out of the question, as she had laughingly told her husband's cousin more than once when he had placed the *Arcadia* at her disposal.

They met sometimes, but never on board the yacht, for that would have outraged Mrs. Wilders's nice sense of propriety. It was generally at Scutari, where poor young Anastasius Wilders lay hovering between life and death, for Mrs. Wilders, with cousinly kindliness, came frequently to the wounded lad's bedside.

She was bound for the other side of the Bosphorus as she went downstairs one fine morning towards the end of October, dressed, as usual, to perfection.

A man met her as she crossed the threshold, a man dressed like, and with the air of, an Englishman—a pale-faced, sandy-haired man, with white eyebrows, rather prominent cheek-bones, and a retreating chin.

"Good morning, my dear madam." He spoke with just the faintest accent, betraying that English was not his native tongue. "Like a good Sister, going to the hospital again?"

Mrs. Wilders bowed, and, with heightened colour, sought to pass hastily on.

"What! not one word for so old a friend?" He spoke now in French—perfect Parisian French.

"I wish you would not address me in public: you know you promised me that," replied Mrs. Wilders, in a tone of much vexation, tinged with the respect that is born of fear.

"Forgive me, madam, if I have presumed. But I thought you would wish to hear the news."

"News! Of what?"

"Another battle, a fierce, terrible fight, in which, thank Heaven! the English have suffered defeat!" He spoke with an exultation that proved him to be a traitor, or no Englishman.

"A battle? The English defeated?"

"Yes; thank Heaven, beaten, massacred, disastrously defeated! It is only the beginning of the end. We shall hear soon of far worse. The Czar is gathering together all his strength; what can the puny forces of the allies do against him? They will be outnumbered thousands to one—annihilated before they can escape to their ships."

"Pshaw! What do I care! Whether they are driven away from the Crimea, or remain, is much the same to me. But, after all, this is mere talk; you can't terrify me by such vapourings."

"I tell you I know this for a fact. The Russian forces in the Crimea have been continually reinforced for weeks past. I know it; I saw them. I was there, in their midst, not many days ago. Besides, I am behind the scenes, deep in their counsels. Rely upon it, the allies are in imminent danger. You will hear soon of another and far greater fight, after which it will be all over with your friends!"

"Well, well! my friends, as you call them, must look to themselves. Still, this is mere talk of what may be. Tell me what has actually occurred. There has been a battle: are many slain? General Wilders—is he safe?"

"You need have no apprehensions for your dear husband, madam; his command was not engaged. The chief brunt of the fight fell upon the cavalry, who were cut to pieces."

"What of young Wilders? Hugo Wilders, I mean—Lord Lydstone's brother."

"His name is returned amongst the killed. It will be a blow for the noble house of Essendine, and not the only one."

"What do you mean?"

"The other brother, young Anastasius, whom you are going to see, cannot survive, I hear."

"Poor young fellows!" said Mrs. Wilders, with a well-assumed show of feeling.

"You pity them? I honour your sentiments, madam; but, nevertheless, they can be spared, especially by you."

"What do you mean?" she asked, quickly.

"I mean that after they are gone only one obstacle intervenes between you and all the Essendine wealth. If Lord Lydstone were out of the way, the title and its possession would come, perhaps, to your husband, certainly to your son."

"Silence! Do not put thoughts into my head. You must be the very fiend, I think."

"I know you, Cyprienne, and every move of your mind. We are such old friends, you see," he said, with a sneering, cynical smile. "And now, as before, I offer you my help."

"Devil! Do not tempt me!"

He laughed—a cold, cruel, truculent laugh.

"I know you, I repeat, and am ready to serve you as before. Come, or send, if you want me. I am living here in this hotel; Mr. Hobson they call me—Mr. Joseph Hobson, of London. My number is 73. Shall I hear from you?"

"No, no! I will not listen to you. Let me go!" And Mrs. Wilders, breaking away from him, hurried down the street.

It was not a long walk to the waterside. There she took a caique, or local boat, with two rowers in red fezzes, and was conveyed across the Bosphorus to the Asiatic side.

Landing at Scutari, Mrs. Wilders went straight to the great palace, which was now a hospital, and treading its long passages with the facility of one who had travelled the road before, she presently found herself in a spacious, lofty chamber filled with truckle-beds, and converted now into a hospital-ward.

"How is he?" she asked, going up at once to a sergeant who acted as superintendent and head nurse.

"Mr. Wilders, ma'am?" replied the sergeant, with a shake of the head.

"No improvement?"

"Far worse, ma'am, poor young chap! He died this morning, soon after daylight."

"And my lord—was his brother present?"

"Lord Lydstone watched with him through the night, and was here by the bedside when he died."

"Where is he now? Lord Lydstone, I mean."

"He went back on board his yacht, ma'am, I think. He said he should like a little sleep. But he is to be here again this afternoon, for the funeral."

"So soon?"

"Oh, yes! ma'am. It must take place at once, the doctors say."

Mrs. Wilders left the hospital, hesitating greatly what she should do. She would have liked to see and speak with Lydstone, but she had enough good feeling not to intrude by following him on board the yacht.

Then she resolved to attend the funeral too. It would show her sympathy, and Lord Lydstone would be bound to notice her.

He did see her, and came up after the ceremony to shake her hand.

"I am so sorry for you," she began.

"It is too terrible!" he exclaimed. "Both in one day."

He had heard of Balaclava, then.

"But I can't talk about it to-day. I will call on you to-morrow, if I may, in the morning. I am going back to England almost at once."

He came next day, and she received him in her little sitting-room at Misseri's.

"You know how I feel for you," she said, giving him both her hands, her fine eyes full of tears. "They were such splendid young fellows, too. It is so sad—so very sad."

"I am very grateful for your sympathy. But we will not talk about them, please," interrupted Lord Lydstone.

"You have my warmest and most affectionate sympathy. Is there anything I can do to console you, to prove to you how deeply, how sincerely, I feel for you?"

Her voice faltered, and she seemed on the point of breaking down.

"What news have you of the general?" asked Lord Lydstone, rather abruptly, as though to change the conversation.

"Good enough. He is all right," said Mrs. Wilders, dismissing inquiry for her husband in these few brusque words.

"I can't think of him just now," she went on. "It is you and your great sorrow that fill all my heart. Oh, Lydstone! dear Lord Lydstone, the pity of it!"

This tender commiseration was very captivating. But the low, sweet voice seemed to have lost its charm.

"I think I told you yesterday, Mrs. Wilders, that I intended to return to England," said Lord Lydstone, in a cold, hard voice.

"Yes; when do you start?"

"To-morrow, I think. Have you any commands?"

"You do not offer me a passage home?"

"Well, you see, I am travelling post haste," he answered. "I shall only go in the yacht as far as Trieste, and then on overland. I fear that would not suit you?"

"I should be perfectly satisfied"—she was not to be put off—"with any route, provided I go with you."

"You are very kind, Mrs. Wilders," he said, more stiffly, but visibly embarrassed. "I think, however, that as I shall travel day and night I had better—"

"In other words, you decline the pleasure of my company," she said, in a voice of much pique.

It was very plain that she had no longer any influence over him.

"But why are you in such a desperate hurry, Lord Lydstone?" she went on.

"I have had letters, urging me to hurry home. My father and mother are most anxious to see me; and now, after what has happened, it is right that I should be at their side."

"You are a good son, Lord Lydstone," she said, but there was the slightest sneer concealed beneath her simple words.

"I have not been what I ought, but now that I am the only one left I feel that I must defer to my dear parents' wishes in every respect." He said this with marked emphasis.

"They have views for you, I presume?" Mrs. Wilders asked, catching quickly at his meaning.

"My mother has always wanted me to settle down in life, and my father has urged me—"

"To marry. I understand. It is time, they think, for you to have sown your wild oats?"

"Precisely. I have liked my freedom, I confess. Now there are the strongest reasons why I should marry."

"To secure the succession, I suppose."

"We have surely a right to look to that!" said Lord Lydstone, rather haughtily.

"Oh! of course. Everyone is bound to look after his own. And the young lady—has she been found?"

Lord Lydstone coloured at this point-blank question.

"I have been long paying my addresses to Lady Grizel Banquo," he said.

"Oh! she is your choice? I have often seen her and you together."

"We have been friends almost from childhood; and it seems quite natural—"

"That you should tie yourself for life to a red-headed, raw-boned Scotch girl."

"To an English lady of my own rank in life," interrupted Lord Lydstone, sternly, "who will make me an honest, faithful helpmate, as I have every reason to hope and believe."

"You are just cut out for domestic felicity, Lord Lydstone. I can see you a staid, sober English peer, a pattern of respectability, the stay and support of your country, obeyed with reverent devotion by a fond wife, bringing up a large family—"

"As young people should be brought up, I hope—the girls as modest, God-fearing maidens; the boys to behave like gentlemen, and to tell the truth."

"A very admirable system of education, I'm sure. By-and-bye we shall see how nearly you have achieved your aim."

She was disappointed and bitterly angry, feeling that he had rebuffed and flouted her.

"We part as friends, I hope?" said Lord Lydstone, rising to go.

"Oh, certainly! why not?" she answered carelessly.

"I trust you will continue to get good news from Cousin Bill."

"And I that you will have a speedy voyage home. It would be provoking to be delayed when bound on such a mission."

Then they parted, never to meet again.

CHAPTER XV
THE LAST OF LORD LYDSTONE

The mixed population of Constantinople in these busy, stirring times was ripe for any great surprise. It was much moved and excited by a startling bit of news that spread very rapidly next day.

An atrocious murder had been committed on the Stamboul side, near the Bridge of Boats.

Certainly, murders were not unknown in this hive of complex life, harbouring as it did the very scum and refuse of European rascality. But the victims were mostly vile, nameless vagabonds, low Greeks, Maltese suttlers, Italian sailors, or one or other of the hybrid mongrel ruffians following in the track of our armies, any of whom might be sent to their long account without being greatly missed.

It was otherwise now: the murdered man was a prominent personage, an Englishman of high rank, a rich and powerful representative of a great people. No wonder that Constantinople was agitated and disturbed.

On this occasion Lord Lydstone was the murdered man.

He had been found at daybreak by the Turkish patrol, lying in a doorway just where he had fallen dead, stabbed to the heart.

The body was taken to the nearest guard, and inquiries were instituted. A card-case found on the body led to identification, and a report made to the British Embassy set in motion the law and justice of the peace.

Nothing satisfactory or conclusive was brought to light. No one could account for his lordship's presence in that, the lowest quarter of the city; the only clue to his movements was furnished by his steward and body-servant on board the yacht.

The valet came on shore and gave his evidence before the informal court, which was dealing with the case at the British Embassy, presided over by the *attachés*.

"When did you see his lordship last?"

"Last night. My lord dined on board alone. He appeared depressed, and altogether low. He told me he should go to bed early."

"And did he?"

"No. Late in the evening a shore-boat came off—one of those caiques, I think they called them—with a letter, very urgent."

"For Lord Lydstone?"

"For his lordship. He seemed much disturbed on reading it."

"Well?"

"My lord called me and said he would dress to go on shore. I gave him out the suit which he was wearing when the body was found."

"He said nothing about the letter, or its contents?"

"Oh, no! My lord was never given to talking much, although I was his confidential valet since he left college. He never spoke to me of his affairs. My lord always kept his distance, as it was proper he should."

"Could you tell at all what became of this letter?"

"My lord put it in his pocket when he was dressed."

"You are certain of this?"

"Most positive."

"Was any such letter found in the pockets of the deceased?" asked the *attaché* of the Turkish police, through the dragoman of the Embassy.

Nothing of the kind had been found.

"The letter was no doubt removed purposely. This would destroy all trace of its origin. It was evidently a snare, a bait to lure the poor lord on shore," said one *attaché* to another.

"It is curious that he should have been so ready to swallow it."

"There must have been something peculiarly persuasive in the letter."

"But we have heard that he was much distressed, or annoyed, at receiving it."

"Persuasive in a good or bad sense—probably the latter. At any rate, it was sufficient to lure him on shore."

"Of course there is something beneath all this: some intrigue, perhaps."

"The old story, 'who is she?' I suppose."

"But I thought he was devoted to his cousin, the fair Mrs. Wilders."

"Is she still in Constantinople?"

"Yes, I think so. Still at Misseri's, I believe."

"I wonder whether she has yet heard about this horrible affair. Some one ought to break it to her."

But no one was needed for a task from which all shrank, with not unnatural hesitation. While they still talked, a message was brought in to the effect that Mrs. Wilders was in the antechamber, and her first words, when one of the *attachés* joined her, plainly showed that she had heard of Lord Lydstone's death.

"What a horrible, frightful business!" she said, in a voice broken with emotion. "Oh! this wicked, accursed town! How did it happen? Do tell me all you know."

"We are completely in the dark. We know nothing more than that Lord Lydstone was found stabbed at daylight this morning in the streets of Stamboul."

"What could have taken him there?"

The *attaché* shrugged his shoulders.

"There is nothing to show, except that he was inveigled by some mysterious communication—a letter sent on board the yacht."

"Inveigled for some base purpose—robbery, perhaps?"

"Very probably. When the body was found, it had been rifled of everything—watch, money, rings: everything had gone."

Mrs. Wilders sighed deeply. It might have been a sigh of relief, but to the *attaché* it seemed a new symptom of horror.

"But how imprudent—how frightfully imprudent—of the poor dear lord to venture alone, and so late at night, into that vile quarter. What could have tempted him?"

"That's what we are all asking. Some unusually powerful motive must have influenced him, we may be sure, and that I hope we may still ascertain. It will be the first step towards detecting the authors of the crime."

"They will be discovered, you think?"

"No efforts will be spared, you may be sure. The means at our disposal are not very first-rate, perhaps, but we have been promised the fullest help by the Turkish Minister of Police, and we shall leave no stone unturned."

"Oh! I do so hope that the villains will be discovered. Is there anything I can do?"

"Hardly, Mrs. Wilders. But, as you are the only representative of the family, it would be well perhaps for you to go on board the yacht. Poor

Lord Lydstone's papers and effects should be sealed up. One of us will accompany you."

"I shall be delighted to be of any use. When shall we start?"

"The sooner the better," said the *attaché*, Mr. Loftus by name; and, leaving the inquiry, the two took boat, and were presently alongside the *Arcadia*.

They were received by the captain, a fine specimen of a west-country sailor, a hardy seaman, well schooled in his profession, who had long commanded a vessel in the Mediterranean trade, and was thus well qualified to act as sailing-master in the *Arcadia's* present cruise.

But Captain Trejago was soft-hearted, easily led, especially by any daughter of Eve, and he had long since succumbed to the fascinations of Mrs. Wilders's charms. From the day she first trod the deck of the yacht he had become her humblest, perhaps, but most devoted, admirer and slave.

They exchanged a few words of sympathy and condolence.

"You have lost a good friend, Captain Trejago," said the lady.

"He was that, ma'am. My lord was one of the finest, noblest men that ever trod in shoe-leather. And you, ma'am—it must be very terrible for you."

"Losing him in such a way, it is that which embitters my grief. But this gentleman"—she turned to Mr. Loftus—"comes from the Embassy to seal up his lordship's papers."

"Quite right, ma'am. That ought to be done without delay."

"We can go down into the cabin, then?" said Mrs. Wilders.

"Why! surely, ma'am, you ought to know the way. Mr. Hemmings"—this was the valet—"is not on board, as you know: but I will send the second steward if you want any help."

Assisted by the steward, Mr. Loftus proceeded in a business-like manner to place the seals of the Embassy upon the desk, drawers, and other receptacles in Lord Lydstone's cabin. While they were thus employed, Mrs. Wilders sat at the cabin-table under the skylight, her head resting on one hand, and in an attitude that indicated the prostration of great sorrow. The other hand was on the table, fingering idly the various objects that strewed it. There were an inkstand, a pen-tray, a seal, a blotting-book or portfolio, and many other odds and ends.

This blotting-book, with the same listless, aimless action, Mrs. Wilders presently turned to, and turned over the leaves one by one.

Between two of them she came upon a letter, left there by accident, or to be answered perhaps that day.

The feminine instinct of curiosity Mrs. Wilders possessed in no common degree. To look at the letter thus exposed, however unworthy the action, was a temptation such a woman could not resist. She began to read it, almost as a matter of course, but carelessly, and with no set purpose, as though it was little likely to contain matter that would interest her. But after the first few lines its perusal deeply absorbed her. A few lines more, and she closed the book, leaving her hand inside, and looked round the cabin.

Mr. Loftus and his assistants were still busily engaged upon their official task. Neither of them was paying the slightest attention to her.

With the hand still concealed inside the blotter, she folded up this missive which seemed so interesting and important, and, having thus got it into a small compass, easily and quickly transferred it to her pocket.

She looked anxiously round, fearing she might have been observed. But no one had noticed her, and presently, when Mr. Loftus had completed his work, they again left the yacht for the shore.

So soon as Mrs. Wilders regained the privacy of her own room at Misseri's, which was not till late in the day, she took out the letter she had laid hands on in the cabin of the yacht, and read it through slowly and carefully.

It was from Lord Lydstone's father, dated at Essendine Towers, the principal family-seat.

"My dear boy," so it ran, "your mother and I are very grateful to you for your very full and deeply interesting letter, with its ample, but most distressing, account of our dear Anastasius. It is a proud, but melancholy, satisfaction to know that he has maintained the traditions of the family, and bled, like many a Wilders before him, for his country's cause. His condition must, however, be a constant and trying anxiety, and I beseech you, more particularly on your mother's account, to keep us speedily informed of his progress. It is some consolation to think that you are by his side, and it is only right that you should remain at Constantinople so long as your brother is in any danger.

"But do not, my dear boy, linger long in the East. We want you back with us at home. This is your proper place—you who are our eldest born, heir to the title and estates—you should be here at my side. There are other urgent reasons why you should return. You know how anxious we are that you should marry and settle in life. We are doubly so now. Your brothers before this hateful war broke out made the succession, humanly speaking, almost secure. But the chances of a campaign are unhappily most uncertain. Anastasius has been struck down; we may lose him, which Heaven forbid; a Russian bullet may rob us any day of dear Hugo too. In such a dire and grievous calamity, you alone—only one single, precious life—would remain to keep the title in our line. Do not, I beseech you, suffer it to continue thus. Come home; marry, my son; give us another generation of descendants, and assure the succession.

"I have never made any secret of my wishes in this respect; but I have never told you the real reasons for my deep anxiety. It was my father's earnest hope—he inherited it from his father, as I have from mine—that the title might never be suffered to pass to his brother Anastasius's heirs. My uncle had married in direct opposition to his father's orders, in an age when filial disobedience was deemed a very heinous offence, and he was cut off with a shilling. I might say that he deserved no better; but he did not long survive to bear the penalty of his fault. He left a child—a daughter, however—to whom I would willingly have lent a helping hand, but she spurned all my overtures in a way that grieved me greatly, although I never openly complained. That branch of the family has continued estranged from us; and I am certainly indisposed to reopen communications with them.

"Yet the existence of that branch cannot be ignored. It might, at any time, through any series of mishaps of a kind I hardly like to contemplate, but, nevertheless, quite possible in this world of cross-purposes and sudden surprises, become of paramount importance in the family; for in point of seniority it stands next to ourselves. The next heir to the title, after you and your brothers, is the grandson of Anastasius Wilders, a lad of whom I know nothing, except that he is quite unfitted to assume the dignity of an Earl of Essendine, should fate ever will it that he should succeed. This unfitness you will readily appreciate when I tell you that he is at present a private soldier in a marching-regiment in the East. Stranger still, this regiment is the same as that in which poor Anastasius is serving—the Royal Picts. The young man's name is McKay—Stanislas Anastasius Wilders McKay. I have never seen him; but I am satisfied of his existence, and of the absolute validity of his claims. My agents have long had their eye on him, and through them I have full information of his movements and disposition. He appears a decent, good sort of youth. But I feel satisfied that we ought, as far as is possible by human endeavour, to prevent his becoming the head of the family.

"You are now in possession of the whole of the facts, my dear Lydstone, and I need scarcely insist upon the way in which you are affected by them. You will not hesitate, I am sure, after reading this letter, to return to England the moment you can leave your poor brother."

There was more in the letter, but it dealt with purely business matters, which did not interest the person who had become clandestinely possessed of it.

To say that Mrs. Wilders read this letter with surprise would inadequately express its effect upon her. She was altogether taken aback, dismayed, horror-stricken at its contents.

Now, when chance, or something worse, had cleared the way towards the great end, after which she had always eagerly, but almost hopelessly, hankered, a new and entirely unexpected obstacle suddenly supervened.

Another life was thrust in between her and the proximate enjoyment of high rank and great wealth.

Who was this interloper—this McKay—this private soldier serving in the ranks of the Royal Picts? What sort of man? What were his prospects—his age? Was it likely that he would stand permanently in her way?

These were facts which she must speedily ascertain. The regiment to which he belonged was in the Crimea, part of her uncle's brigade. Surely through him she might discover all she wanted to know. But how could this be best accomplished?

The more she thought over it, the more convinced she was that she ought to go in person to the Crimea, to prosecute her inquiries on the spot. While still doubtful as to the best means of reaching the theatre of war, it occurred to her that she could not do better than make use of Lord Lydstone's yacht.

It would have to go home eventually—to be paid off and disposed of by Lord Lydstone's heirs. But there was surely no immediate hurry for this, and Mrs. Wilders thought she had sufficient influence with Captain Trejago to persuade him, not only to postpone his departure, but to take a trip to the Crimea.

In this she was perfectly successful, and the day after Lord Lydstone's funeral the *Arcadia*, with a fine breeze aft, steered northward across the Black Sea.

It reached Balaclava on the morning of the 5th of November, and Mrs. Wilders immediately despatched a messenger on shore to inform the general of her arrival. That day, however, the general and his brigade were very busily employed. It was the day of Inkerman!

CHAPTER XVI
"HARD POUNDING"

Mr. Hobson, as he called himself, had been perfectly right when he gleefully assured Mrs. Wilders that the Russians were gathering up their strength for a supreme effort against the allies. Reinforcements had been steadily pouring into the Crimea for weeks past—two of the Czar's sons had arrived to stir up the enthusiasm of the soldiers. Menschikoff, who still commanded, counted confidently upon inflicting exemplary chastisement upon the invaders. He looked for nothing less, according to an intercepted despatch, than the destruction or capture of the whole allied army.

No doubt the enemy had now an overwhelming superiority in numbers. The total land forces under Prince Menschikoff's command, including the garrison of Sebastopol, were 120,000 strong. Those numbers included a large body of cavalry and a formidable field artillery.

The entire allied army was barely half that strength. It was called upon, moreover, to occupy an immense front—a front which extended from the sea at Kamiesch to the Tchernaya, and from the Tchernaya, by a long and circuitous route, back to the sea at Balaclava. This line, offensive as regards the siege-works, but defensive along the unduly extended and exposed right flank at Balaclava, was close on twenty miles. The great length of front made severe demands upon the allied troops; it could only be manned by dangerously splitting up their whole strength into many weak units, none of which could be very easily or rapidly reinforced by the rest.

Perhaps the weakest part of the whole line was the extreme right, held at this moment by the British Second Division. Here, on an exposed and vitally important flank, the whole available force was barely 3,000 men. For some time past it had been intended to fortify this flank by field-works, armed with heavy artillery. But, although the necessity for protecting it was thus admitted, the urgency was not exactly understood, or at least was subordinated to other operations; as a matter of fact, this flank was "in the air," to use a military phrase, lying quite open and exposed, with only an insufficient, greatly harassed garrison on the spot, and no supports or reserves near at hand.

The utmost assistance on which this small body could count, as was afterwards shown, under stress, too, of most imminent danger, was 14,000 men. Not that all these numbers were fully available at any one time; they were constantly affected and diminished by casualties in the height and heat of the action; so that never were there more than 13,000, French and English, actually engaged.

On the other hand, the Russian attacking force was 70,000 strong, and they had with them 235 guns.

It was in truth another battle of giants, like Waterloo. "Hard pounding," as the great duke said of that other fight; a fierce trial of strength; a protracted, seemingly unequal, struggle between the dead weight of the aggregate many and the individual prowess of the undaunted, indomitable few.

The enemy's plan of action had been minutely and carefully prepared. We know it now. He meant to use his whole strength along his entire front—in part with feigned and deceiving demonstrations to "contain" or hold inactive the troops that faced him, in part with determined onslaught, delivered with countless thousands, in massive columns, against the reputed weakest point of our line.

This plan Menschikoff hastened to put into execution. Time pressed: the enemy had learnt through spies that an assault on Sebastopol was close at hand. Besides, the Grand Dukes had arrived, and the troops, worked up to the highest pitch of loyal fanatic fervour, were mad to fight under the eyes of the sons of their father, the holy Czar.

Dawn broke late on that drear November morning: November the 5th—a day destined to be ever memorable in the annals of British arms: a dawn that was delayed and darkened by dense, driving mists, and rain-clouds, black and lowering.

Nothing, however, had broken the repose of the British camp, or hinted at the near approach of countless foes.

The night had been tranquil; the enemy quiet; only, in the valley beneath our pickets on the Inkerman heights, some sentries had heard the constant rumbling of wheels, but their officers to whom they reported did not interpret the same aright, as the movement of artillery.

An hour or more before daylight the church-bells of Sebastopol rang out a joyous peal. Why not? It was the Sabbath morning. But these chimes, alas! ushered in a Sunday of struggle and bloodshed, not of peaceful devotion and prayer.

The outlying pickets had been relieved, and were marching campwards; the Second Division had had its customary "daylight parade"; the men had stood to their arms for half-an-hour, and, as nothing was stirring, had been dismissed to their tents; the fatigue-parties had been despatched for rations, water, fuel—in a word, the ordinary daily duties of the camp had commenced, when the sharp rattle of musketry rang out angrily, and well sustained in the direction of our foremost picket on Shell Hill.

"That means mischief!" The speaker was General Codrington, who, according to invariable rule, had ridden out before daylight to reconnoitre and watch the enemy. "Halt the off-going pickets; we may want all the men we can lay hands on."

Then this prompt and judicious commander proceeded to line the Victoria ridge, which faced Mount Inkerman, with the troops he had thus impounded, and galloped off to put the rest of his brigade under arms.

The firing reached and roused another energetic general officer, Pennefather, who now commanded the Second Division in place of De Lacy Evans.

"Sound the assembly!" he cried. "Let the division stand to its arms. Every man must turn out: every mother's son of them. We shall be engaged hot and strong in less than half-an-hour."

As pugnacious as any terrier, Pennefather, with unerring instinct, smelt the coming fight.

His division was quickly formed on what was afterwards called the "Home Ridge," and which was its regular parade-ground. But the general had no idea of awaiting attack in this position. It was his plan rather to push forward and fight the enemy wherever he could be found. With this idea he sent a portion of his strength down the slope to "feed the pickets," as he himself called it, whilst another was advanced to the right front under General Wilders, and with this body went the Royal Picts. The Second Division benefited greatly by this advance, for the Russians were now absolute masters of the crest of the Inkerman hill, where they established their batteries, and poured forth volley after volley, all of which passed harmlessly over the heads of our men. Meanwhile the alarm spread. A continuous firing, momentarily increasing in vigour, showed that this was no affair of outposts, but the beginning of a great battle. The bulk of the allied forces were under arms, and notice of the attack had been despatched to Lord Raglan at the English headquarters.

In less than a quarter-of-an-hour, long before 7 a.m., Lord Raglan was in his saddle, ready to ride wherever he might be required most.

But whither should he go? The battle, as it seemed, was waging all around him, on every side of the allied position. A vigorous fire was kept up from Sebastopol; down in the Tchernaya valley the army, supposed to be still under Liprandi, but really commanded by Gortschakoff, had advanced towards the Woronzoff road, and threatened to repeat the tactics of Balaclava by attacking with still greater force the right rear of our position; last of all, around Mount Inkerman, the unceasing sound of musketry and big guns betrayed the development of a serious attack.

Lord Raglan was not long in doubt. He knew the weakest point of the British position, and rightly guessed that the enemy would know it too.

"I shall go to Inkerman," he said. "That is their real point, I feel sure. And we must have up all the reinforcements we can muster. You, Burghersh, tell Sir George Cathcart to move up his division and support Pennefather and Brown. You, Steele, beg General Bosquet to lend me all the men he can spare."

Pennefather had his hands full by the time Lord Raglan arrived. With a paltry 3,000 odd men he was confronting 25,000; but, happily, the morning was so dark and the brushwood so thick that his men were hardly conscious that they were thus outnumbered.

Not that they would have greatly cared; they were manifestly animated with a dogged determination to deny the enemy every inch of the ground, and with unflagging courage they disputed his advance, although they were so few. Once more it was the "Thin Red Line" against the heavy column: hundreds against thousands, a task which for any other troops would have been both hopeless and absurd.

But Pennefather's people stoutly held their own. On his left front, one wing of the 49th Regiment routed a whole Russian column, and drove it back at the point of the bayonet down the hill; to give way in turn, but not till it was threatened by 9,000 men. Next, four companies of the Connaught Rangers stoutly engaged twenty times their number, and only yielded after a stubborn fight. General Buller came up next, with a wing of the 77th, which was faced by a solid mass five times as strong.

"There are the Russians," cried Egerton, who commanded the 77th. "What shall we do, general?"

"Charge them!" was Buller's prompt reply.

The next instant the slender line, with a joyous hurrah, was engulfed in a giant column. The effect was instantaneous. The Russian column reeled before the fiery charge, wavered, then broke and fled.

More to the right, Mauleverer prolonged the line with the 30th, and gave so good an account of the Russians in his front that they, too, fell back in disorder; and Bellairs, with a party of the 49th, was equally triumphant.

Beyond these forces, General Wilders, with whom young McKay now rode as extra aide, led a fraction of his brigade, including the Royal Picts, against the Sandbag Battery, a point deemed important because it commanded the extreme right of the position.

On the far sides of the slopes, beyond the battery were 4,000 Russian troops, and the mere sight of Wilders with his deployed line sufficed to shake the steadiness of the foe. The Russian bugles sounded a retreat, the leading companies faced about, and, communicating the panic to those behind the hill, the whole mass gave way and ran down the slope, followed by a destructive fire from the British line.

Thus ended the first phase of this unequal contest. Pennefather had triumphed to an extent of which neither he nor his heroes were fully aware. Barely 1,200 men had routed 15,000! The few had achieved a decisive victory over the many.

But the struggle had only just begun. Many more and still severer trials awaited our starving, weary, sorely-beset soldiers that day.

The enemy had numberless fresh and still untried troops at hand. Column after column had been moving steadily forward, some from the town, some from the eastern side of the Tchernaya, and already the Russian generals were in a position to renew the fight. A new onslaught was now organised, to be made by 19,000 men under cover of ninety guns.

So far in those early days of the battle the brunt of it had fallen upon the Second Division, supported by a portion of the Light. Stout old General Pennefather had had the supreme control throughout.

"I will not interfere with you," Lord Raglan said, as, standing by his staff, he watched the progress of the fight from the ridge. "You know your ground, as you have occupied it so long with your camp. I'm sure I can trust you."

"Thank you, my lord. I'll do my best, never fear," replied Pennefather.

"Their artillery fire is very troublesome, and must be over-mastered. If I could only get up some of the siege-train guns to help you. Let some one go back to the artillery park, and tell them I want a couple of eighteen pounders."

An aide-de-camp at once galloped off with the order, but two or three eventful hours elapsed before these guns were brought to bear upon the action.

Pennefather's men, although for the moment triumphant, had their hands full. They showed an undaunted front or "knotted line" of fighting-men: the remnants of the pickets, fragments, and odds-and-ends of many regiments, mixed up and intermingled, still in contact with the enemy, and so far still without supports.

Officers came back rather despondingly to ask for help.

"I cannot send you a single man," was the firm reply to one applicant. "You must stand your ground somehow."

"We should be all right, sir, but the men have run out of ammunition."

"It's no use. I can't give you a round. What does it matter? Don't make difficulties. Stick to your bayonets. And remember you've got to hold on where you are, or we shall be driven into the sea."

The want of cartridges was what the troops felt most direly. They growled savagely and grumbled at the mismanagement that kept back these indispensable supplies.

Only here and there the energetic action of a few shrewd officers did something to mend the mischief.

Thus the Royal Picts benefited by the astute promptitude of long-headed Sergeant Hyde. He was acting as quartermaster, and as such had been left behind in camp, although sorely against his will, when the rest of the regiment went out to fight. But he had heard the long, well-sustained roll of musketry-fire, and it satisfied one not new to war that a very close contest had begun.

"They'll soon fire away their cartridges at this rate," he said to himself. "If I could only get the ammunition-reserves up to them! I'll do it." And on his own responsibility he laid hands on all the beasts in camp: spare chargers, officers' ponies, and other animals, and quickly loaded them with the cartridge-boxes. Then, leading the cavalcade, he hurried to the front, asking as he went for the Royal Picts.

He found his regiment in the Sandbag Battery, and they received him, so soon as his errand was known, with a wild cheer.

"Excellently done!" cried Colonel Blythe. "You have a good head on your shoulders, Hyde: ammunition was the one thing we needed."

"Yes," shouted a brawny soldier, "we were just killed for want of cartridges."

"And want of food," grumbled another; "sorra bite nor sup since yesterday."

"Sergeant darling," said a third, "won't you sound the breakfast-bugle? Fighting on an empty stomach is but a poor pastime."

Thus, in the interval between two combats, but always under a galling and destructive fire, they joked and bandied words with a freedom that discipline would not have tolerated at any other time.

"I think, colonel, I could bring up the rations: biscuits and cold pork, anyhow," suggested Hyde.

"And the grog-tub: don't forget that, sergeant" cried a fresh voice.

"By all means, Hyde, get us what you can," replied Blythe; "the men are all fasting, and some sort of a meal would be very good for them, only you must keep a sharp look-out for us. We may not be still here when you return."

This Sandbag Battery, which for the moment the Royal Picts still held, was the object of ceaseless contention that day. Although at best but an empty prize, useful to neither side, because its parapet was too high to be fired over, the battery was lost and won, captured and recaptured, constantly during the battle.

Even now the Russians, regaining heart, had made it the first aim of their fresh attack.

General Dannenberg, who was now in chief command, had a twofold object: he was resolved to press the centre of the English position and at the same time vigorously attack the right, throwing all his weight first upon the Sandbag Battery.

The small force under General Wilders, which included the Royal Picts, soon began to feel the stress of this renewed onslaught.

"They are coming on again and in great numbers, sir," said McKay to his general.

"I see, and menacing both our flanks. We shall be surrounded and swallowed up if we don't take care."

"Some support ought to be near by this time, sir," replied McKay.

"Ride back, and see. I don't want to be outflanked."

McKay retired and presently came upon two battalions of Guards, Grenadiers and Fusiliers, advancing under the command of the Duke of Cambridge.

"General Wilders, sir, is very hard pressed in the Sandbag Battery," said McKay, briefly.

"I'll march at once to his aid," replied the duke, promptly.

"Sir George Cathcart and part of the Fourth Division are coming up, and not far off," added one of the staff; "we won't wait for any one. Ride on ahead, sir," — this was to McKay, — "and let your general know he is about to be supported by her Majesty's Guards."

CHAPTER XVII
A COSTLY VICTORY

Now followed one of the fiercest and bloodiest episodes of the day.

Wilders had made the best show with his little band and clung tenaciously to the battery yet. The Russians came on and on, with stubborn insistence, and all along the line a hand-to-hand fight ensued. Numbers told at length, and the small garrison was slowly forced back, after enduring serious loss.

It was in this retreat that General Wilders received a dangerous wound: a fragment of a shell tore away the left leg below the knee.

"Will some one kindly lift me from my horse?" he said quietly, schooling his face to continue calm, in spite of the agony he endured.

McKay was on the ground in an instant and by his general's side.

"Don't mind me, my boy" said the general. "Leave me with the doctors."

"On no account, sir; I should not think of it." "Yes, yes. They want every man. Attach yourself to Blythe; he will command the brigade now. Do not stay with me: I insist."

McKay yielded to the general's entreaties, but first saw the wounded man bestowed in a litter and carried to the rear.

Then he joined Colonel Blythe.

But now fortune smiled again. Our artillery had stayed the Russian advance; and the Grenadier Guards, followed by the Fusiliers, once more regained the coveted but worthless stronghold.

They could not hold it permanently, however: the tide of battle ebbed and flowed across it, and the victory leant alternately to either side. The Guards fought like giants, outnumbered but never outmatched, wielding their weapons with murderous prowess, and, when iron missiles failed them, hurling rocks—Titan-like—at their foes.

Even when won this Sandbag Battery was a perilous prize: tempting the English leaders to adventure too far to the front and to leave a great gap in the general line of defence unoccupied and undefended.

Lord Raglan saw the error and would have skilfully averted the impending evil.

"That opening leaves the left of the Guards exposed," he said to Airey. "Tell Cathcart to fill it."

"You are to move to the left and support the Guards," was the message conveyed to Cathcart, "but not to descend or leave the plateau. Those are Lord Raglan's orders."

But Sir George chose to interpret them his own way, and already—with Torrens's brigade and a weak body at best—he had gone down the hill to join the Guards. In the sharp but misdirected encounter which followed, the general lost his life, and his force, with the Guards, were for a time cut off from their friends.

A Russian column had wedged in at the gap and for a time forbade retreat, but it was at length sheered off by the first of the French reinforcements; and the intercepted British, in greatly diminished numbers, by degrees won their way home.

This fighting around the Sandbag Battery had cost us very dear: Cathcart was killed, the Guards were decimated, and Wilders's brigade, now commanded by Colonel Blythe, had fallen back, spent and disorganised. So serious indeed were these losses that for the next hour the brigade possessed no coherent shape, and only by dint of the unwearied exertions of its officers was it rallied sufficiently to share in the later phases of the fight.

Meanwhile the centre of our line, where Pennefather stood posted on the Home Ridge, had been furiously assailed. Gathering their forces under shelter of a deep ravine, the Russian general sent up column after column, first against the left and then against the right of the Ridge. Gravely weakened by his early encounter, Pennefather had only a handful of his own men to meet this attack. They were now pressed back indeed, although their general was beginning to wield detachments from other commands. A portion of the Fourth Division had been put under his orders.

General Cathcart, just before his death, had come to him with a battalion of the Rifle Brigade.

"They can do anything," he had said. "Where are they wanted most?"

"Everywhere!" had been old Pennefather's reply.

But now, having at hand this splendid body of infantry, of whom their leader had been so pardonably proud, he hurled them at the flank of a column that was forcing back its own men.

The effect of the charge was instantaneous: the Russians could not withstand it; and, the men of the Second Division again advancing, the foe was pressed as far as the Barrier, where he was held at bay.

But the left of the ridge was still menaced, although the centre was cleared. On this flank Pennefather disposed of some new troops, also of the Fourth Division: the 63rd and part of the 21st.

He rode up to their head and made them a short but stirring address.

"Now, Sixty-third, let's see what metal you are made of! The enemy is close upon you: directly you see them, fire a volley and charge!"

His answer was a vehement cheer. The 63rd fired as it was ordered, and then drove the Russians down the hill.

One more trial awaited Pennefather at this period of the battle. His right, on the Home Ridge, was now assailed; but here again the 20th, with their famous Minden yell—an old historical war-cry, always cherished and secretly practised in the corps—met and overcame the enemy. They were actively supported by the 57th, the gallant "Diehards," a title they had earned at Albuera, one of the bloodiest of the Peninsular fights.

Thus, for the second time, Pennefather stood victorious on the ground he so obstinately held. After two hours of incessant fighting the Russians had made no headway. But although twice repulsed they had inflicted terrible losses on our people. They had still in hand substantial supports untouched; they had brought up more and more guns; they were as yet far from despondent, and their generals might still count upon making an impression by sheer weight of numbers alone.

As for ourselves, the English were almost at the end of their resources. There were no fresh troops to bring up; only the Third Division remained in reserve, and it was fully occupied in guarding the trenches.

The French, it is true, could have thrown the weight of many thousands into the scale; but General Canrobert had not set his more distant divisions in motion, and the only troops that could affect the struggle—Bosquet's—were still far to the rear.

In the contest that was now to be renewed the balance between the offensive forces was more than ever unequal.

Dannenberg gathered together upon the northern slopes of Mount Inkerman some 17,000 men, partly those who had been already defeated, but were by no means disheartened, and partly perfectly fresh troops. On the other hand, Pennefather's force was reduced to a little over 3,000, to which a couple of French regiments might now be added, 1,600 strong. The Russians had a hundred guns in position; the allies barely half that number.

Yet in the struggle that was imminent the battle of Inkerman was practically to be decided.

The Russian general had now resolved to make a concentrated attack in column upon Pennefather's Ridge. He sent up another great mass from the quarry ravine, flanked and covered by crowds of skirmishers. In the centre, the vanguard pressed forward swiftly, drove back the slender garrison of the Barrier, and advanced unchecked towards the Ridge. There were no English troops to oppose their advance; a French battalion only was close at hand, and they seemed to shrink from the task of opposing the foe.

"They do not seem very firm, these Frenchmen," said Lord Raglan, who was closely watching events. "Why, gracious goodness, they are giving way! We must strengthen them by some of our own men. Bring up the 55th—they have re-formed, I see. Stay! what is that?"

As he spoke, an English staff officer was seen to ride up to the wavering French battalion. From his raised hand and impassioned gestures he was evidently addressing them. He was speaking in French, too, it was clear, for his harangue had the effect of restoring confidence in the shaken body. The battalion no longer stood irresolute, but advanced to meet the foe.

"Excellently done!" cried Lord Raglan. "Find out for me at once who that staff-officer is."

An aide-de-camp galloped quickly to the spot, and returned with the answer—

"Mr. McKay, my lord, aide-de-camp to General Wilders."

"Remember that name, Airey, and see after the young fellow. But where is his general?"

"Wounded, and gone to the rear, my lord," was the reply.

The bold demeanour of the French battalion restrained the advancing enemy until some British troops could reach the threatened point. Then together they met the advance. The Russian attack was now fully developed, and his great column was well up the slopes of the ridge. While the French, animated by the warm language of Pennefather, stopped its head, a mad charge delivered by a small portion of the 55th broke into its flank.

The Russians halted, hesitating under this unexpected attack. Pennefather instantly saw the check, and gave voice to a loud "hurrah." The cry was taken up by his men, and the French drums came to the front and sounded the *pas de charge*. With a wild burst of enthusiasm, the allies, intermingled, raced forward, and once again the foe was driven down the hill. At the same time his flanking columns were met and forced back on the left by the 21st and the 63rd.

The Barrier was again re-occupied by our troops, and the third, the chief and most destructive Russian onslaught, had also failed.

The day was still young; it was little past 9 a.m., and the battle as yet was neither lost nor won.

The Russians had been three times discomfited and driven back, but they still held the ground they had first seized upon the crests of the Inkerman hill, and, seemingly, defied the allies to dislodge them.

The English were far too weak to do this. Our whole efforts were concentrated upon keeping the enemy at bay at the Barrier, where Blythe, now in chief command, managed with difficulty, and with a very mixed force, to beat off assailants still pertinacious and tormenting.

The French were now coming up in support, but of their troops already on the ground two battalions had gone astray, wandering off on a fool's errand towards the pernicious Sandbag Battery, where they, too, were destined to meet repulse.

Indeed, the Russians, despite their last discomfiture, were regaining the ascendant.

But now the sagacious forethought of Lord Raglan was to bear astonishing fruit. It has been told in the previous chapter how he was bent upon bringing up some of the siege-train guns, and how he had despatched a messenger for them. His aide-de-camp had found the colonel of the siege-park artillery anticipating the order. Two 18-pounders, which since Balaclava had been kept ready for instant service, were waiting to be moved. There were no teams of horses at hand to drag them up to the front, but the man-harness was brought out, and the willing gunners cheerily entered the shafts, and threw themselves with fierce energy into the collars. Officers willingly lent a hand, and thus the much-needed ordnance was got up a long and toilsome incline.

It was a slow job, however, and two full hours elapsed before they were placed in position on the right flank of the Home Ridge.

"At last!" was Lord Raglan's greeting; "now, my lads, load and fire as fast as you can."

The artillery officers themselves laid their guns, which were served and fired with promptitude and precision.

Now followed a short but sanguinary duel. The Russian guns answered shot for shot, and at first worked terrible havoc in our ranks.

Colonel Gambier of the artillery was struck down: other officers were wounded, and many of the men.

Still Lord Raglan stood his ground, watching the action with keen interest and the most admirable self-possession. He was perfectly unmoved by the heavy fire and the carnage it occasioned.

One or two of his staff besought him to move a little further to the rear, but he met the suggestion with good-natured contempt.

"My lord rather likes being under fire than otherwise," whispered one aide-de-camp to another.

He certainly took it uncommonly cool, and in the thick of it could unbend with kindly condescension when a sergeant who was passing had his forage-cap knocked off by the wind of a passing shot.

"A near thing that, my man," he said, smiling.

The sergeant—it was Hyde, returning from the Barrier, where he had been with more ammunition—coolly dusted his cap on his knee, replaced it on his head, and then, formally saluting the Commander-in-Chief, replied with a self-possession that delighted Lord Raglan—

"A miss is as good as a mile, my lord."

Through all this the 18-pounders kept up a ceaseless and effective fire. They were clearly of a heavier calibre than any the Russians owned, and soon the weight of their metal and our gunners' unerring aim began to tell upon the enemy's ranks.

The Russian guns were frequently shifted from spot to spot, but they could not escape the murderous fire.

At last, in truth, the Russian hold on Inkerman hill was shaken to the core.

Victory at last was in our grasp, and, but for the old and fatal drawback of insufficient numbers, the battle must have ended in a complete disaster for the Russian arms. A vigorous offensive, undertaken by fresh troops, must have ended in the speedy overthrow, possibly annihilation, of the enemy.

But the only troops available for the purpose were the French. Bosquet had now come up with his brigade, and D'Autemarre, released by Gortschakoff's retreat, had followed with a second. There were thus some seven or eight thousand French available. Still Canrobert was disinclined to move.

He was now with Lord Raglan on the Ridge, with his arm in a sling, for he had just been struck by a shrapnel-shell.

He was downcast and dejected, for Bosquet had gone off on a wild-goose chase after two errant battalions, and had shared in their repulse. Just now, indeed, so far from proving the saviours of the hard-pressed English, our French allies were themselves in retreat.

Lord Raglan strove to reassure his colleague.

"All is going well, my general," he said; "we are winning the day."

"I wish I could think so," replied Canrobert.

"Well, but listen to the message my aide-de-camp has brought from General Pennefather. What did he say, Calthorpe?"

"General Pennefather, my lord, says he only wants a few fresh troops to follow the enemy up now, and lick them to the devil. These are his very words, my lord."

Lord Raglan laughed heartily, and translated his stout-hearted lieutenant's language literally for Canrobert.

"Ah! what a brave man!" cried the French general, lighting up. "A splendid general, a most valiant man."

"You see now, general; one more effort and the day is ours. Won't you help?"

"But, my lord, what can I do? The Russians are all round us still, and in great strength. See there, there, and there," he cried, pointing with his unwounded arm.

"Tell General Pennefather to come and speak to me at once," Lord Raglan now said to the aide-de-camp, hoping that the gallant bearing of the victorious veteran would infuse fresh hope in Canrobert.

Now General Pennefather galloped up, as radiantly happy as any schoolboy who has just finished his fifteenth round.

"I should like to press them, my lord. They are retreating already, and we could give a fine account of them."

"What have you left to pursue with?" asked Lord Raglan, still hoping to encourage the French to undertake the offensive.

"Seven or eight hundred now, in the first brigade alone."

"To pursue thousands!" exclaimed Canrobert, when this was interpreted to him; "you must be mad! I will have nothing to do with this; we have done enough for one day."

Now again, as on the Alma, when the heights had been carried by storm, the fruits of victory were lost by our unenterprising, over-cautious allies.

This, indeed, is the true story of Inkerman, as told on incontestable evidence of the great historian of the war. The French did not rescue the English from disaster; they were themselves repulsed. At the close of the action, when they might have actively pursued, their irresolution robbed the victory of its most decisive results.

It was a terrible and far too costly victory, after all. The English army, already terribly weak, suffered such serious losses in the fight that there were those who would have at once re-embarked the remnants and raised the siege. Retreat on the morrow of victory would have been craven indeed, but to stand firm with such shattered forces was a bold and hazardous resolve, for which Lord Raglan deserves the fullest credit, and the coming winter, with its terrible trials, was destined to put his self-reliance to the proof.

It is time to return more particularly to our friends, who took part in this hard-fought, glorious action.

By midday the worse part of the battle was over, and although Colonel Blythe still clung to his Barrier, whence he launched forth small parties to harass the retreating foe, McKay was released of his attendance upon the acting brigadier, and suffered to follow his own general to the rear.

They had carried poor old Wilders in a litter to one of the hospital marquees in the rear of the Second Division camp. The aide-de-camp found him perfectly conscious, with two doctors by his side.

McKay was allowed to enter into conversation with his chief.

"How does it go?" asked the old general, feebly, but with eager interest.

"The enemy are in full retreat, sir; beaten all along the line."

"Thank Heaven!" said the general, as he sank back upon his pillow.

"How are you, sir?"

"Very weak. My fighting days are done."

"You must not say that, sir; the doctors will soon pull you round. Won't you?" said McKay, looking round at the nearest surgeon's face.

"Of course. I have no fear, provided only the general will keep quiet, and—"

"That means that I should go," said the aide-de-camp. "I shall be close at hand, sir, for I mean to be chief nurse," and he left the tent.

Outside the surgeon ended the sentence he had left incomplete.

"The general," he said, "will be in no immediate danger if we could count upon his having proper care. With that, I think we could promise to save his life."

"He shall have the most devoted attention from me," began McKay.

"We know that. But he wants more: the very best hospital treatment, with all its comforts and appliances; and how can we possibly secure these here on this bleak plateau?"

Just then one of the general's orderlies came in sight and approached McKay.

"A letter, sir, for the general, marked 'Immediate.'"

"The general can attend to no correspondence. You know he has been desperately wounded."

"Yes, sir, but the messenger would not take that for an answer."

"Who is he?"

"A seaman from Balaclava, belonging to some yacht that has just arrived."

"Lord Lydstone's perhaps. That would indeed be fortunate," went on McKay, turning to the doctor. "It is the general's cousin, you know; and on board the yacht—if we could get him there?"

"That is not impossible, I think. In fact, it would have to be done."

"Well, on board the yacht he would get the careful nursing you speak of. Is he well enough, do you think, to read this letter?"

"Under the circumstances, yes. Give it me, and I will take it in to the general."

A few minutes later McKay was again called in to the marquee.

"Oh, McKay, I wish you would be so good—" began the wounded man. "This letter, I mean, is from Mrs. Wilders; she has just arrived."

"Here, in the Crimea, sir?"

"Yes, she has come up in Lord Lydstone's yacht, and I want you to be so good as to go to her and break the news." He pointed sadly down the bed towards his shattered limb.

"Of course, sir, as soon as I can order out a fresh horse I will go to Balaclava. Perhaps I had better stay on board for a time, and make arrangements to receive you; if Lord Lydstone will allow me, that is to say."

"Lord Lydstone is not there. Mrs. Wilders tells me she has come up alone, and in the very nick of time. But now be off, McKay, and lose no time. Be gentle with her: it will be a great shock, I am afraid."

The aide-de-camp galloped off on his errand, and finding a boat from the yacht waiting by the wharf in Balaclava harbour he put up his horse and went off to the *Arcadia*. She was still lying outside.

McKay's appearance was not exactly presentable. He had been turned out at daybreak with the rest of the division at the first alarm, and had had no time to attend to his toilette, such as it was in these rough campaigning days. Since then he had been in his saddle for several hours and constantly in the heat and turmoil of the fight. His clothes were torn, mud-encrusted, and bloodstained; his face was black and grimy with gunpowder smoke.

But he had no thought of his looks as he sprang on to the white, trimly-kept deck of the yacht.

Captain Trejago met him.

"Who are you?" asked the sailing-master, rather abruptly.

"I wish to see Mrs. Wilders," replied McKay, still more curtly.

"You had better wash your face first," said Captain Trejago, very jealous of the proper respect due to Mrs. Wilders. "It is uncommonly dirty."

"And so would yours be if you had been doing what I have."

"What might that be?"

"Fighting."

"Perhaps you are ready to begin again? If so, I'm your man. But you will have to wait till we get on shore."

"Pshaw! don't be an idiot. We have been engaged with the Russians ever since daybreak. But there, this is mere waste of breath. I tell you I want to see Mrs. Wilders. I come from the general. I am his aide-de-camp. Show the way, will you?"

"It may be as you say," muttered Trejago, not half satisfied. "But you will have to wait till Mrs. Wilders says she will receive you."

"What's the matter? Who is this person?"

It was the voice of Mrs. Wilders, who now advanced from the stern of the yacht, having seen but not overheard the latter part of the altercation.

McKay stepped forward.

"I have brought you a message from the general."

"Why did he not come himself?"

"It was quite impossible."

"I particularly begged him to come. Who, pray, are you? Stay!" she went on, "I ought to know your face. We have met before: at Gibraltar, was it not?"

"Yes, at Gibraltar. I was the general's orderly sergeant."

"And do you still hold the same distinguished position?"

"No, Mrs. Wilders," said McKay, simply; "I am now a commissioned officer, and have the honour to be the general's aide-de-camp."

"Rapid promotion that: I hope you deserved it. May I ask your name?"

"McKay—Stanislas McKay."

Could it be possible? The very man she was in search of the first to speak to her on arrival here at Balaclava! Surely there must be some mistake! Mastering her emotion at the suddenness of this news, she said—

"You will forgive my curiosity, but have you any other Christian names?"

"My name in full is Stanislas Anastasius Wilders McKay."

"That answer is my best excuse for asking you the question. You are, then, our cousin?"

McKay bowed.

"I have heard of you," said Mrs. Wilders. "Allow me to congratulate you," and she held out her hand.

CHAPTER XVIII
A NOVEMBER GALE

"Will you not come down into the cabin?" said Mrs. Wilders, civilly; "the lunch is still on the table, and I daresay you will be glad of something to eat."

"I have not touched food all day, Mrs. Wilders."

"You must have been very busy, then?"

"Surely you have heard what has happened this morning?"

Mrs. Wilders looked at him amazed.

"A desperate battle has been fought."

"Another!" She thought of what Mr. Hobson had told her. "How has it ended? In whose favour? Are we safe here?"

"There is no cause for alarm. The Russians have been handsomely beaten again; but we have suffered considerable loss," he said, hesitating a little, fearing to be too brusque with his bad news.

"Is that why the general could not come?"

"Exactly. He has had a great deal to do."

"Nothing should have prevented him from coming here."

It never seemed to have occurred to her that he had been in any danger; nor, as McKay noticed, had she asked whether he was safe and well.

"It was quite impossible for him to come. He—he—"

"Pray go on! You are very tantalising."

"The general has been badly wounded," McKay now blurted out abruptly.

"Dear! dear!" she said, rather coolly. "I am very sorry to hear it. When and how did it occur?"

McKay explained.

"Poor dear!" This was the first word of sympathy she had spoken, and even now she made no offer to go to him.

"The doctors think there is no great danger if—"

"Danger!" This seemed to rouse her. "I trust not."

"No danger," went on McKay, "if only he can be properly nursed. They were glad to hear of the arrival of the yacht, and think he ought to be moved on board."

"Oh, of course this will be the best place for him. When can he be brought? I suppose I ought to go to him. Will it be possible to get a conveyance to the front?"

"Nothing but an ambulance, I fear. And you know there is no road."

"Upon my word I hardly know what to say."

"We could manage a saddle-horse for you, I daresay."

"I'm a very poor horsewoman: you see I'm half a foreigner. No; the best plan will be to stay on board and get everything ready for the poor dear man. When may we expect him?"

"The doctors seem to wish the removal might not be delayed. You may see us in the morning."

"So, then, I am to have the pleasure of meeting you again, Mr. McKay?"

"I should be sorry to leave the general while I can be of any use. He has been a kind friend to me."

"And you are a relation. Of course it is very natural you should wish to be at his side. I am sure I shall be delighted to have your assistance in nursing him," said Mrs. Wilders, very graciously; and soon afterwards McKay took his leave.

"So that is the last stumbling-block in my son's way: a sturdy, self-reliant sort of gentleman, likely to be able to take care of himself. I should like to get him into my power: but how, I wonder, how?"

Next day they moved the wounded general to Balaclava, and got him safely on board the *Arcadia*. He was accompanied by a doctor and McKay.

Mrs. Wilders received her husband with the tenderest solicitude.

"How truly fortunate I came here!" she said, with the tears in her eyes.

"Lydstone made no objection, then? Has he remained at Constantinople?" the general asked, feebly.

"Lydstone? Don't you know? He—" But why should she tell him? It would only distress him greatly, and, in his present precarious condition, he should be spared all kind of emotion. With this idea she had begged Captain Trejago to say nothing as yet of the sad end of his noble owner.

"Will it not be best to get the general down to Scutari?" she asked the doctor.

"In a day or two, yes. When he has recovered the shaking of the move on board."

"The captain wanted to know. He has no wish to go inside the harbour, as it is so crowded; but he would not like to remain long off this coast. It might be dangerous, he says."

"A lee-shore, you know," added Captain Trejago, for himself. "Look at those straight cliffs; fancy our grinding on to them, with a southerly, or rather a south-westerly, gale!"

"Is there any immediate prospect of bad weather?" asked McKay. He and the sailing-master were by this time pretty good friends.

"I don't much like the look of the glass. It's rather jumpy; if anything, inclined to go back."

"What should you do if it came on dirty?" the skipper was asked.

"Up stick, and run out to get an offing. It would be our only chance, with this coast to leeward."

Three or four days later the skipper came with a long face to the doctor.

"I like the look of it less and less. The glass has dropped suddenly: such a drop as I've never seen out of the tropics. Is there anything against our putting to sea this afternoon?"

It so happened that General Wilders was not quite so well.

"I'd rather you waited a day or two," replied the surgeon. "It might make all the difference to the patient."

"Well, if it must be," replied the captain, very discontentedly.

"It's his life that's in question."

"Against all of ours. But let it be so. We'll try and weather the storm."

Next morning, about dawn, it burst upon them—the memorable hurricane of the 14th November, which did such appalling damage on shore and at sea. Not a tent remained standing on the plateau. The tornado swept the whole surface clean.

At sea the sight as daylight grew stronger was enough to make the stoutest heart, ignorant landsman's or practised seaman's, quail. A whole fleet—great line-of-battle ships, a crowd of transports under sail and steam—lay at the mercy of the gale, which increased every moment in force and fury. The waves rose with the wind, and the white foam of "stupendous" breakers angrily lashed the rock-bound shore.

"Will you ride it out?" asked McKay of the captain, as the two stood with the doctor crouched under the gunwale of the yacht and holding on to the shrouds.

"Why shouldn't we?" replied Trejago, shortly, as though the question was an insult to himself and his ship.

"That's more than some can say!" cried the doctor, pointing to one great ship, the ill-fated *Prince*, which had evidently dragged her anchors and was drifting perilously towards the cliffs.

"Our tackle is sound and the holding is good," said Trejago, hopefully. "But we ought not to speak so loud. It may alarm Mrs. Wilders."

"Does she not know our danger? Some one ought to tell her. You had better go, McKay."

The aide-de-camp made rather a wry face. He was not fond of Mrs. Wilders, whose manner, sometimes oily, sometimes supercilious, was too changeable to please him, and he felt that the woman was not true.

However, he went down to the cabin, where he found Mrs. Wilders, with a white, scared face, cowering in a corner as she listened to the howling of the storm.

"Is there anything the matter?" she cried, springing up as he appeared. "Is there any danger?"

"I trust not; still, it is well to be prepared."

"For what? Do you mean that we may be lost, drowned—here, in sight of port—all of us—my dear general and myself? It is too dreadful! Why does not the captain run inside the harbour and put us on dry ground?"

"I fear it would be too great a risk to try and make the mouth of the harbour in this gale."

"Then why don't you seek help from some of the other ships—the men-of-war? There are plenty of them all around."

"Every ship outside Balaclava is in the same stress as ourselves. They could spare us no help, even if we asked for it."

"What, then, are we to do?—in Heaven's name!"

"Trust in Providence and hope for the best! But I think—if I might suggest—it would be as well to keep the general in ignorance of our condition, which is not so very desperate after all."

"How do you mean?"

"'Our cables are stout,' Captain Trejago says, and we ought to be able to ride out the storm."

And the *Arcadia* did so gallantly all that day, in the teeth of the hurricane, which blew with unabated fury for many more hours, and in spite of the tempest-torn sea, which now ran mountains high.

All through that anxious day Trejago kept the deck, watching the sky and the storm. It was late in the afternoon when he said, with a sigh of relief—

"The wind is hauling round to the westward; I expect the gale will abate before long."

He was right, although to eyes less keen there was small comfort yet in the signs of the weather.

It was an awful scene—ships everywhere in distress: some on the point of foundering, others being dashed to pieces on the rocks. The great waves, as they raged past in fearful haste, bore upon their foaming crests great masses of wreck, the dread vestiges of terrible disasters. Amongst the floating timbers and spars, encumbered with tangles of cordage, floated great bundles of hay, the lost cargo of heavily-laden transports that had gone down.

Still, as Trejago said, there was hope at last. The gale had spent its chief force and was no longer directly on shore. The more pressing and immediate danger was over.

"It won't do to stop here, though," he went on, "not one second longer than we can help. Now that there is a slant in the wind we can run south under a close-reefed trysail and storm-jib. What say you, doctor?"

"I'll step down and see the general."

"Don't lose any time. I should like to slip my cable this next half-hour. I shan't be happy till we've got sea-room."

McKay went below with the doctor, and, while the latter sat with his patient, the aide-de-camp had a short talk with Mrs. Wilders.

"The captain wants to put to sea."

"Never! not in this storm!"

"It is abating fast. Besides, he says it will be far safer to be running snug under storm-canvas than remaining here on this wild coast."

"I hope he will do no such thing. It will be madness. I must speak to him at once."

She seized a shawl, and, throwing it over her head, ran up on deck.

McKay followed her and was by her side before she had left the companion-ladder.

"Take care, pray. There is a heavy sea on still and the deck is very slippery. I will call Captain Trejago if you will wait here."

"One moment; do not leave me, Mr. McKay. What an exciting, extraordinary scene! But how terrible!"

The yacht rode the waves gallantly: now on their crest, now in the trough between two giant rollers, and always wet with spray. Fragments of wreck still came racing by, borne swiftly by the waters and adding greatly to the horrors of the dread story they told.

"There must have been immense loss among the shipping," said McKay. "It is a mercy and a marvel how we escaped."

"The poor things! To be lost—cast away on this cruel, inhospitable land. How very, very sad!"

"It is safer, you see, to leave this dangerous anchorage. Do you still want the captain? He is busy there forward."

For the moment everyone was forward: they were all intent on the straining cables and the muddle of gear that would have to be cleared or cut away when they got up sail.

So Mrs. Wilders and McKay stood at the cabin companion alone—absolutely alone—with the raging elements, the whistling wind still three parts of a gale, and the cruel, driving sea.

"Shall I fetch the captain?" McKay repeated.

"No, no! Don't disturb him; no doubt he is right. I will go below again. This is no place for me." She took one long, last survey of the really terrifying scene, but then, quite suddenly, there burst from her an exclamation of horror.

"There! there! Mr. McKay, look: on that piece of timber—a figure, surely—some poor shipwrecked soul! Don't you see?"

McKay, shading his eyes, gazed intently.

"No. I can make nothing out," he said at length, shaking his head.

"How strange! I can distinguish the figure quite plainly. But never mind, Mr. McKay; only do something. Give him some help. Try to save him. Throw him a rope."

McKay obediently seized a coil of rope, and, approaching the gunwale, said, quickly—

"Only you must show me where to throw."

"There, towards that mast; it's coming close alongside."

In her eagerness she had followed him, and was close behind as he gathered up the rope in a coil to cast it.

Once, twice, thrice, he whirled it round his head, then threw it with so vigorous an action that his body bent over and his balance was lost.

He might have regained it, but at this supreme moment a distinct and unmistakeable push in the back from his companion completed his discomfiture.

He clutched wildly at the shrouds with one hand—the other still held the rope; but fruitlessly, and in an instant he fell down—far down into the vortex of the seething, swirling sea.

"Ah, traitress!" he cried, as he sank, fully conscious, as it seemed, of the foul part she had played.

Had she really wished to drown him? Her conduct after he had disappeared bore out this conclusion.

One hasty glance around satisfied her that McKay's fall had been unobserved. If she gave the alarm at once he might still be saved.

"Not yet!" she hissed between her teeth. "In five minutes–it will be too late to help him. The waters have closed over him—let him go down, to the very bottom of the sea."

But she was wise in her fiendish wickedness, and knew that as they had been seen last together she must account for McKay's disappearance. At the end of an interval long enough to make rescue impossible she startled the whole yacht with her screams.

"Help! Help! Mr. McKay! He has fallen overboard!"

They came rushing aft to where she stood once more holding on to the top of the companion, and plied her with questions.

"There! there! make haste!" she cried—"for Heaven's sake make haste!"

"A boat could hardly live in this sea," said Captain Trejago, gravely. "Still, we must make the attempt. Who will go with me?" he asked, and volunteers soon sprang to his side.

It was a service of immense danger, but the boat was lowered, and for more than half-an-hour made such diligent search as was possible in the weather and in the sea.

After that time the boat was brought back to the yacht by its brave but disappointed crew.

"No chance for the poor chap," said Captain Trejago, shaking his head despondingly in reply to Mrs. Wilders's mute but eager appeal.

Soon afterwards they got up the anchor, and the yacht sped southward under a few rags of sail.

CHAPTER XIX
UNCLE AND NEPHEW

It will be well to relieve at once the anxiety which the reader must feel—unless I have altogether failed to interest him—in the fate of my hero, Stanislas McKay.

He was not drowned when, through the fiendish intervention of Mrs. Wilders, he fell from the deck of the *Arcadia*, and was, as it seemed, swallowed up in the all-devouring sea.

He went under, it is true, but only for a moment, and, coming once more to the surface, by a few strong strokes swam to a drifting spar. To this he clung desperately, hoping against hope that he might yet be picked up from the yacht. Unhappily for him, the waves ran so high that the boat under Trejago's guidance failed to catch sight of him, and, as we know, returned presently to the *Arcadia*, after a fruitless errand, as was thought.

Very shortly the yacht and the half-submerged man parted company. The former was steered for the open sea; the latter drifted and tossed helplessly to and fro, growing hourly weaker and more and more benumbed, but always hanging on with convulsive tenacity to the friendly timber that buoyed him up, and was his last frail chance of life.

All night long he was in the water, and when day dawned it seemed all over with him, so overpowering was his despair. Consciousness had quite abandoned him, and he was almost at the last gasp when he was seen and picked up by a passing steamship, the *Burlington Castle*.

"Where am I?" he asked, faintly, on coming to himself. He was in a snug cot, in a small but cosy cabin.

"Where you'd never have been but for the smartness of our look-out man," said a steward at his bedside. "Cast away, I suppose, in the gale?"

"No: washed overboard," replied McKay, "last evening."

"Thunder! and in the water all those hours! But what was your craft? Who and what are you?"

"I was on board the yacht *Arcadia*. My name is Stanislas McKay. I am an officer of the Royal Picts—aide-de-camp to General Wilders. Where am I?" he repeated.

"You'll learn that fast enough; with friends, anyhow. Doctor said you weren't to talk. But just drink this, while I tell the captain you've come to. He hasn't had sight of you yet; we hauled you aboard while it was his watch below."

Five minutes more and the captain, a jolly English tar, red in face and round in figure, came down, with a loud voice and cheering manner, to welcome his treasure-trove.

"Well, my hearty, so this is how I find you, eh? Soused in brine. Why, I hear they had to hang you up by the heels to let the water run out of your mouth. Come, Stanny, my boy, this won't do."

"Uncle Barto!"

"The same: master of the steamship *Burlington Castle*, deep in deals— timbers for huts—and other sundries, now lying in Balaclava, waiting to be discharged. But, my dearest lad, you've had a narrow squeak. Tell me, how did it happen, and when?"

"I fell overboard, and I've been all night in the water: that's all."

He did not choose as yet to make public his suspicions as to the real origin of his nearly fatal accident.

"I always said you had nine lives, Stanny, only don't go using them up like this. There's not a tom-cat could stand it."

"Were you out in the gale, uncle?"

"Ay; and weathered it. At dawn, after the first puff, I knew we'd have a twister, so I got up steam and regularly worked against it. Made a good offing that way, and when the storm abated came back here. We were close in when we picked you up on a log."

"It was a providential escape," said Stanislas, thankfully. "I thought it was all over with me."

"We'll set you up in no time, never fear. But tell more about yourself. Jove! you are a fine chap, Stanny. Why, you'll die a general yet, if the Russians'll let you off a little longer, and you're not wanted for the House of Peers."

"What do you mean, uncle?"

"Why, of course, you haven't heard. There's trouble among your fine relations. Lord Essendine has lost all his sons."

"All?"

"Yes; all. Hugo was killed, as you know; Anastasius died at Scutari; and Lord Lydstone, two days later, was found dead in the streets of Stamboul."

"Dead? How? What did he die of, uncle?"

"A stab in the heart. He was murdered."

"And I—"

He understood now the cause of the foul blow struck at him, and the base attempt to get him also out of the way.

"You are now next heir to the peerage, in spite of all they may say. But you'll find my lord civil enough soon. He'll be wanting you to go straight home."

"And leave the army? Not while there's fighting to be done, Uncle Barto. I may not be much good as I am, but I'll do all I can, trust me. I ought to be getting on shore and back to the front."

"My doctor will have a word to say to that. He won't let you be moved till you're well and strong."

But on the second day McKay, thanks to kindly care and plenty of nourishment, was able to leave his cot, and on the third morning he was determined to return to his duty.

"I won't baulk you, Stanny," said his uncle; "good soldiers, like good sailors, never turn their backs on their work. But mind, this ship is your home whenever and wherever you like to come on board; and if you want anything you have only to ask for it, d'ye hear?"

McKay promised readily to draw upon his uncle when needful, and then, his horse being still at Balaclava, he once more got into the saddle and rode up to camp.

The journey prepared him a little for what he found. All the way from Balaclava his horse struggled knee-deep in mud: a very quagmire of black, sticky slush. Yet this was the great highway—the only road between the base of supply and an army engaged eight miles distant in an arduous siege. Along it the whole of the food, ammunition, and material had to be carried on pony-back, or in a few ponderous carts drawn by gaunt, over-worked teams, which too often left their wheels fast-caught in the mire.

At the front—it had been raining in torrents for hours—the mud was thicker, blacker, and more tenacious. Tents stood in pools of water; their occupants, harassed by trench duty, lay shivering within, half-starved and wet.

McKay made his way at once to the colonel and reported his return.

"Oh! so you've thought fit to come back," said Colonel Blythe, rather grumpily. Since war and sickness had decimated his battalion he looked upon every absentee, from whatever cause, right or wrong, as a recreant deserter.

"I was with my general, sir," expostulated Stanislas.

"The general has no need of an aide-de-camp now. We want every man that can stand upright in his boots. I have given up the command of the brigade myself so as to look the better after my men."

McKay accepted the reproof without a murmur, and only said—

"Well, sir, I am here now, and ready to do whatever I may be called upon. I feel my first duty is to my own colonel and my own corps."

"Do you mean that, young fellow?" said the colonel, thawing a little.

"Certainly, sir."

"Because they want to inveigle you away—on the staff. Lord Raglan has sent to inquire for you."

"I have no desire to go, sir," said McKay, simply; although his face flushed red at the compliment implied by the Commander-in-Chief's message.

"It seems he was pleased with the way you rallied those Frenchmen, and he has heard you are a good linguist, and he wants to put you on the staff."

"I had much rather stay with the regiment, sir," said McKay.

"Are you quite sure? You must not stand in your own light. This is a fine chance for you to get on in the service." The colonel's voice had become very friendly.

"I know where my true duty lies, sir; I owe everything to you and to the regiment. I should not hesitate to refuse an appointment on the general staff if it were offered me now." McKay did not add that his future prospects were now materially changed, and that it was no longer of supreme importance to him to rise in his profession.

"Give me your hand, my boy," said Colonel Blythe, visibly touched at McKay's disinterestedness. "You are proving your gratitude in a way I shall never forget. But let us talk business. You know I want you as adjutant."

"I shall be only too proud to act, sir."

"I must have a good staff about me. We are in great straits; the regiment will go from bad to worse. There are barely 200 'duty' men now, and it will soon be a mere skeleton, unless we can take good care of the rest."

"Yes, sir," said McKay, feeling constrained to say something.

"They are suffering—we all are, but the men most of all—from exposure, cold, want of proper clothing, and, above all, from want of proper food. This is what I wish to remedy. They are dying of dysentery, fever, cholera—I don't know what."

"The doctor, sir?"

"Can do nothing. He has few drugs; but, as he says, that would hardly matter if the men could have warmth and nourishment."

"Something might be done, sir, with system; the quartermaster—"

"You are right. Let us consult him. Hyde is still acting, and he has already proved himself a shrewd, hard-headed old soldier."

Quartermaster-sergeant Hyde—for he had accepted the grade, although unwillingly—came and stood "at attention" before his superiors.

"As to food, sir," he said, "the men might be provided with hot coffee, and, I think, hot soup, on coming off duty. I am only doubtful as to the sufficiency of fuel."

"There is any quantity of drift-wood just now—wreckage—floating in Balaclava Harbour," suggested McKay.

"We must have it sir, somehow," said Hyde, eagerly. "But can we get it up to the front?"

"We'll lay an embargo on all the baggage-animals in camp. Take the whole lot down to Balaclava, and lay hands on every scrap of timber."

"As to clothing, sir, an uncle of mine has come up with a heavily-laden ship—hutting-timbers mostly, but he may have some spare blankets, sailors' pea-jackets, jerseys, and so forth."

"And boots, long boots or short—all kinds will be acceptable. Get anything and everything that is warm. I'll pay out of my own pocket sooner than not have them. When can you start, Hyde?"

"Now, sir, if that will suit Mr. McKay, and I can have the horses."

The matter was speedily arranged, and in the early afternoon our hero and Hyde were jogging back to Balaclava, at the head of a string of animals led and ridden by a small selected fatigue-party of regimental batmen and grooms.

It was the first occasion on which the two friends had conversed freely together for months.

McKay had most to tell. He spoke first of the offer to go on the headquarter-staff which he had refused. Then of the strange accidents by which he had become heir presumptive to the earldom of Essendine. Last of all, of the narrow escape he had of his life.

Hyde pressed him on this point.

"You fell overboard—lost your balance, eh? Entirely your own doing? Mrs. Wilders did not help you at all?"

"How on earth, Hyde, did you guess that? I never hinted at such a thing."

"I know her—do not look surprised—I know her, and have done so intimately for years. There is nothing she would stick at if she saw her advantage therefrom. You were in her way; she sought to remove you, as, no doubt, she, or some one acting for her, had removed Lord Lydstone, and—and—for all I know, ever so many more."

"Can she be such a fiendish wretch?"

"She is a demon, Stanislas McKay. Beware how you cross her path. But let her also take heed how she tries to injure you again. She will have to do with me then."

"Why, Hyde! what extraordinary language is this? What do you know of Mrs. Wilders? What can you mean?"

"Some day you shall hear everything, but not now. It is too long a story. Besides, here we are at Balaclava. Do you know where your uncle's ship lies?"

—

CHAPTER XX
RED TAPE

"What! back again so soon, Stanny," was Captain Faulks's greeting as McKay stepped on board the *Burlington Castle*. "I am right glad to see you. Is that a friend of yours?" pointing to Hyde. "He is welcome too. What brings you to Balaclava?"

McKay explained in a few words the errand on which they had come.

"Drift-wood—is that what you're after? All right, my hearties, I can help you to what you want. My crew is standing idle, and I will send the second officer out with them in the boats. They can land it for you, and load up your horses."

Before the afternoon Hyde started for the camp with a plentiful supply of fuel, intending to return next morning to take up any other supplies that could be secured. McKay tackled his uncle on this subject that same evening.

"Blankets? Yes, my boy, you shall have all we can spare, and I daresay we can fit you out with a few dozen jerseys, and perhaps some seamen's boots."

"We want all the warm clothing we can get," said McKay. "The men are being frozen to death."

"I tell you what: there were five cases of sheepskin-jackets I brought up—*greggos*, I think they call them—what those Tartar chaps wear in Bulgaria.'"

"The very thing! Let's have them, uncle."

"I wish you could, lad; but they are landed and gone into the store."

"The commissariat store? I'll go after them in the morning."

"It'll trouble you to get them. He is a hard nut, that commissariat officer, as you'll see."

Mr. Dawber, the gentleman in question, was a middle-aged officer of long standing, who had been brought up in the strictest notions of professional routine. He had regulations on the brain. He was a slave to red tape, and was prepared to die rather than diverge from the narrow grooves in which he had been trained.

The store over which he presided was in a state of indescribable chaos. It could not be arranged as he had seen stores all his life, so he did nothing to it at all.

When McKay arrived early next day, Mr. Dawber was being interviewed by a doctor from a hospital-ship. The discussion had already grown rather serious.

"I tell you my patients are dying of cold," said the doctor. "I must have the stoves."

"It is quite impossible," replied Mr. Dawber, "without a requisition properly signed."

"By whom?"

"It's not my place, sir, to teach you the regulations, you will find that no demands can be complied with unless they have been through the commanding officer of the troops, the senior surgeon, the principal medical officer, the senior commissariat officer, the brigadier, and the general of division. Bring me a requisition duly completed, and you shall have the stoves."

"But it is monstrous: preposterous! There is not time. It would take a week to get these signatures, and I tell you my men are dying."

"I can't help that; you must proceed according to rule."

"It's little short of murder!" said the doctor, now furious.

"And what can I do for you?" said Mr. Dawber, ignoring this remark, and turning to another applicant, a quartermaster of the Guards.

"I have come for six bags of coffee."

"Where is your requisition?"

The quartermaster produced a large sheet of foolscap, covered with printing and ruled lines, a mass of figures, and intricate calculations.

Mr. Dawber seized it, and proceeded to verify the totals, which took him half-an-hour.

"This column is incorrectly cast; in fact, the form is very carelessly filled in. But you shall have the coffee—if we can find it."

Further long delay followed, during which Mr. Dawber and his assistant rummaged the heterogeneous contents of his overcrowded store, and at last he produced five bags, saying—

"You will have to do with this."

"But it is green coffee," said the quartermaster, protesting. "How are we to roast it?"

"That's not my business. The coffee is always issued in the green berry. You will find that it preserves its aroma better when roasted just before use."

"We should have to burn our tent-poles or musket-stocks to cook it," said the quartermaster. "That stuff's no use to me," and he went away grumbling, leaving the bags behind him.

McKay followed him out of the store.

"You won't take the coffee, then?"

"Certainly not. I wish I had the people here that sent out such stuff."

"May I have it?"

"If you like. It's all one to me."

"Give me the requisition, then."

Armed with this important document, he returned, and accosted Mr. Dawber.

"He has changed his mind about the coffee. You can give it to me; I will see that he gets it. Here is the requisition."

The commissariat officer was only too pleased to get rid of the bags according to form.

McKay next attacked him about the *greggos*. Despairing, after all he had heard, of getting them by fair means, he resolved to try a stratagem.

"You received yesterday, I believe, a consignment from the *Burlington Castle?*"

"Quite so. There are the chests, still unpacked. I have not the least idea what's inside."

"You have the bill of lading, I suppose?"

"Certainly."

"May I look at it? I come from the *Burlington Castle,* and the captain thinks he was wrong to have sent you the cases without passing the bill of lading through the commissariat officer at headquarters."

"I believe he is right. Here is the bill; it has not Mr. Fielder's signature. This is most irregular. What shall I do?"

"You had better give me back the bill of lading and the cases until the proper formalities have been observed."

"You are perfectly right, my dear sir, and I am extremely obliged to you for your suggestion."

A few minutes later McKay had possession of the cases. With the help of some of his uncle's crew he moved them back to the seaside, where he waited until Hyde's arrival from the front. Then they loaded up the *greggos* on the baggage-animals, and returned to camp in triumph.

From that day the men of the Royal Picts were fairly well off. Their condition was not exactly comfortable, but they suffered far less than the bulk of their comrades in the Crimea.

Their sheepskin-jackets were not very military in appearance, but they were warm, and their heavy seamen's boots kept out the wet. They had a sufficiency of food, too, served hot, and prepared with rough-and-ready skill, under the superintendence of Hyde.

He had struck up a great friendship with a Frenchman, one of the Voltigeurs, in a neighbouring camp, who, in return for occasional nips of sound brandy, brought straight from the *Burlington Castle*, freely imparted the whole of his culinary knowledge to the quartermaster of the Royal Picts.

"He is a first-class cook," said Hyde to his friend McKay, "and was trained, he tells me, in one of the best kitchens in Paris. He could make soup, I believe, out of an old shoe."

"I can't think how you get the materials for the men's meals. That stew yesterday was never made out of the ration-biscuit and salt pork. There was fresh meat in it. Where did you get it?"

Old Hyde winked gravely.

"If I were to tell you it would get about, and the men would not touch it."

"You can trust me. Out with it."

"There's lots of fresh meat to be got in the camp by those who know where to look for it. Anatole"—this was his French friend—"put me up to it."

"I don't understand, Hyde. What do you mean?"

"I mean that her Majesty's Royal Picts have been feeding upon horseflesh. And very excellent meat, too, full of nourishment when it is not too thin. That is my chief difficulty with what I get."

"It's only prejudice, I suppose," said McKay, laughing; "but it will be as well, I think, to keep your secret."

But horseflesh was better than no meat, and the men of the Royal Picts throve well and kept their strength upon Hyde's soups and savoury stews. Thanks to the care bestowed upon them, the regiment kept up its numbers in a marvellous way—it even returned more men for duty than corps which had just arrived, and the difference between it and others in the camp-grounds close by was so marked that Lord Raglan came over and complimented Blythe upon the condition of his command.

"I can't tell how you manage, Blythe," said his lordship; "I wish we had a few more regiments like the Picts."

"It is all system, my lord, and I have reason, I think, to be proud of ours—that and an excellent regimental staff. I have a capital quartermaster and a first-rate adjutant."

"I should like to see them," said Lord Raglan.

McKay and Hyde were brought forward and presented to the Commander-in-Chief.

"Mr. McKay, I know your name. You behaved admirably at Inkerman. I have just had a letter, too, about you from England."

"About me, my lord?" said Stanislas, astonished.

"Yes, from Lord Essendine, your cousin. And, to oblige him, no less than on your own account, I must renew my offer of an appointment on the headquarter staff."

McKay looked at the colonel and shook his head.

"You are very good, my lord, but I prefer to stay with my regiment."

"Colonel Blythe, you really must spare him to me," said Lord Raglan. "We want him, and more of his stamp."

"Your wishes are law, my lord. I should prefer to keep Mr. McKay, but I will not stand in his way if he desires to go. I shall not miss him so much now that everything is in good working order."

McKay was disposed still to protest, but Lord Raglan cut him short by saying—

"Come over to headquarters to-morrow, and report yourself to General Airey. As for you, my fine fellow," Lord Raglan went on, turning to Hyde, "you are still a non-commissioned officer, I see."

"Yes, my lord, I am only acting-quartermaster."

"Well, I shall recommend you for a commission at once."

"I do not want promotion, my lord," replied Hyde.

"He has refused it several times," added Blythe.

"That's all nonsense! He must take it; it's for the good of the service. I shall send forward your name," and, so saying, Lord Raglan rode off.

Stanislas took up his duties at headquarters next day. He was attached to the quartermaster-general's department, and was at once closely examined as to his capabilities and qualifications by his new chief, General Airey, a man of extraordinarily quick perception, and a shrewd judge of character.

"You speak French? Fluently? Let's see," and the general changed the conversation to that language. "That's all right. What else? Italian? German? Russian?—"

"Yes, sir, Russian."

"You ought to be very useful to us. But you will have to work hard, Mr. McKay, very hard. There are no drones here."

McKay soon found that out. From daybreak to midnight everyone at headquarters slaved incessantly. Horses stood ready saddled in the stables, and officers came and went at all hours. Men needed to possess iron constitution and indomitable energy to meet the demands upon their strength.

"Lord Raglan wants somebody to go at once to Kamiesch," said General Airey, coming out one morning to the room in which his staff-assistants worked and waited for special instructions. There was no one there but McKay, and he had that instant returned from Balaclava. "Have you been out this morning, Mr. McKay? Yes? Well, it can't be helped; you must go again."

"I am only too ready, sir."

"That's right. Lord Raglan does not spare himself, neither must you."

"I know, sir. How disgraceful it is that he should be attacked by the London newspapers and accused of doing nothing at all!"

"Yes, indeed! Why, he was writing by candle-light at six o'clock this morning, and after breakfast he saw us all, the heads of departments and three divisional generals. Since then he has been writing without intermission. By-and-by he will ride through the camp, seeing into everything with his own eyes."

"His lordship is indefatigable: it is the least we can do to follow his example," said McKay, as he hurried away.

This was one of many such conversations between our hero and his new chief. By degrees the quartermaster-general came to value the common-sense opinion of this practical young soldier, and to discuss with him unreservedly the more pressing needs of the hour.

There was as yet no improvement in the state of the Crimean army; on the contrary, as winter advanced, it deteriorated, pursued still by perverse ill-luck. The weather was terribly inclement, alternating between extremes. Heavy snowstorms and hard frosts were followed by thaws and drenching rains. The difficulties of transport continued supreme. Roads, mere spongy sloughs of despond, were nearly impassable, and the waste of baggage-animals was so great that soon few would remain.

To replace them with fresh supplies became of paramount importance.

"We must draw upon neighbouring countries," said General Airey, talking it over one day with McKay. "It ought to have been done sooner. But better now than not at all. I will send to the Levant, to Constantinople, Italy—"

"Spain," suggested McKay.

"To be sure! What do you suppose we could get from Spain?"

"Thousands of mules and plenty of horses."

"It is worth thinking of, although the distance is great," replied the quartermaster-general. "I will speak to Lord Raglan at once on the subject. By-the-way, I think you know Spanish?"

"Yes," said McKay, "fairly well."

"Then you had better get ready to start. If any one goes, I will send you."

This was tantamount to an order. General Airey's advice was certain to be taken by Lord Raglan.

Next morning McKay started for Gibraltar, specially accredited to the Governor of the fortress, and with full powers to buy and forward baggage-animals as expeditiously as possible.

CHAPTER XXI
AGAIN ON THE ROCK

McKay travelled as far as Constantinople in one of the man-of-war despatch-boats used for the postal service. There he changed into a transport homeward bound, and proceeded on his voyage without delay.

But half-an-hour at Constantinople was enough to gain tidings of the *Arcadia* and her passengers.

The yacht, he learnt, had left only a week or two before. It had lingered a couple of months at the Golden Horn, during which time General Wilders lay between life and death.

Mortification at last set in, and then all hope was gone. The general died, and was buried at Scutari, after which Mrs. Wilders, still utilising the *Arcadia*, started for England.

The yacht, a fast sailer, made good progress, and was already at anchor in Gibraltar Bay on the morning that McKay arrived.

"Shall I go on board and tax her with her misdeeds?" McKay asked himself. "No; she can wait. I have more pressing and more pleasant business on hand."

His first visit was to the Convent. "You shall have every assistance from us," said the Governor, Sir Thomas Drummond. "But what do you propose to do, and how can I help?"

"My object, sir, is to collect all the animals I can in the shortest possible time. I propose, first, to set the purchase going here—under your auspices, if you agree—then visit Alicante, Valencia, Barcelona, and ship off all I can secure."

"An excellent plan. Well, you shall have my hearty co-operation. If there is anything else—"

An aide-de-camp came in at this moment and whispered a few words in his general's ear.

"What! on shore? Here in the Convent, too? Poor soul! of course we will see her. Let some one tell Lady Drummond. Forgive me, Mr. McKay:

a lady has just called whom I am bound by every principle of courtesy, consideration, and compassion to see at once. Perhaps you will return later?"

McKay bowed and passed out into the antechamber. On the threshold he met Mrs. Wilders face to face.

"You—!" she gasped out, but instantly checked the exclamation of chagrin and dismay that rose to her lips.

"You hardly expected to see me, perhaps; but I was miraculously saved."

McKay spoke slowly, and the delay gave Mrs. Wilders time to collect herself.

"I am most thankful. It has lifted a load off my mind. I feared you were lost."

"Yes; the sea seldom gives up its prey. But enough about myself. You are going in to see the general, I think; do not let me detain you."

"I shall be very pleased to see you on board the yacht."

"Thank you, Mrs. Wilders; I am sure you will. But to me such a visit would be very painful. My last recollections of the *Arcadia* are not too agreeable."

"Of course not. You were so devoted to my poor dear husband."

Mrs. Wilders would not acknowledge his meaning.

"But I shall see you again before I leave, I trust."

"My stay here is very short. I am only on a special mission, and I must return to the Crimea without delay. But we shall certainly meet again some day, Mrs. Wilders; you may rely on that."

There was meaning, menace even, in this last speech, and it gave Mrs. Wilders food for serious thought.

McKay did not pause to say more. He was too eager to go elsewhere.

His first visit, as in duty bound, had been to report his arrival and set on foot the business that had brought him. His second was to see sweet Mariquita, the girl of his choice.

They had exchanged several letters. His had been brief, hurried accounts of his doings, assuring her of his safety after every action and of his unalterable affection; hers were the artless outpourings of a warm, passionate nature tortured by ever-present heartrending anxiety for the man she loved best in the world. There had been no time to warn her of his visit to Gibraltar, and his appearance was entirely unexpected there.

Things were much the same at the cigar-shop. McKay walked boldly in and found La Zandunga, as usual, behind the counter, but alone. She got up, and, not recognising him, bowed obsequiously. Officers were rare visitors in Bombardier Lane and McKay's staff-uniform inspired respect.

"You are welcome, sir. In what can we serve you? Our tobacco is greatly esteemed. We import our cigars—the finest—direct from La Havanna; our cigarettes are made in the house."

"You do not seem to remember me," said McKay, quietly. "I hope Mariquita is well?"

"Heaven protect me! It is the Sergeant—"

"Lieutenant, you mean."

"An officer! already! You have been fortunate, sir." La Zandunga spoke without cordiality and was evidently hesitating how to receive him. "What brings you here?"

"I want to see Mariquita." The old crone stared at him with stony disapproval. "I have but just arrived from the Crimea to buy horses and mules for the army."

"Many?" Her manner instantly changed. This was business for her husband, who dealt much in horseflesh.

"Thousands."

"Won't you be seated, sir? Let me take your hat. Mariqui—ta!" she cried, with remarkable volubility. The guest was clearly entitled to be treated with honour.

Mariquita entered hastily, expecting to be chidden, then paused shyly, seeing who was there.

"Shamefaced, come; don't you know this gentleman?" said her aunt, encouragingly. "Entertain him, little one, while I fetch your uncle."

"What does it mean?" asked Mariquita, in amazement, as soon as she could release herself from her lover's embrace. "You here, Stanislas: my aunt approving! Am I mad or asleep?"

"Neither, dearest. She sees a chance of profit out of me—that's all. I will not baulk her. She deserves it for leaving us alone," and he would have taken her again into his arms.

"No, no! Enough, Stanislas!" said the sweet girl, blushing a rosy red. "Sit there and be quiet. Tell me of yourself: why you are here. The war, then, is over? The Holy Saints be praised! How I hated that war!"

"Do not say that, love! It has been the making of me."

"Nothing would compensate me for all that I have suffered these last few months."

"But I have gained my promotion and much more. I can offer you now a far higher position. You will be a lady, a great lady, some day!"

"It matters little, my Stanislas, so long as I am with you. I would have been content to share your lot, however humble, anywhere."

This was her simple, unquestioning faith. Her love filled all her being. She belonged, heart and soul, to this man.

"You will not leave me again, Stanislas?" she went on, with tender insistence.

"My sweet, I must go back. My duty is there, in the Crimea, with my comrades—with the army of my Queen."

"But if anything should happen to you—they may hurt you, kill you!"

"Darling, there is no fear. Be brave."

"Oh, Stanislas! Suppose I should lose you—life would be an utter blank after that; I have no one in the world but you."

McKay was greatly touched by this proof of her deep-seated affection.

"It is only for a little while longer, my sweetest girl! Be patient and hopeful to the end. By-and-by we shall come together, never to part again."

"I am weak, foolish—too loving, perhaps. But, Stanislas, I cannot bear to part with you. Let me go too!"

"Dearest, that is quite impossible."

"If I was only near you—"

"What! you—a tender woman—in that wild land, amidst all its dangers and trials!"

"I should fear nothing if it was for you, Stanislas. I would give you my life; I would lay it down freely for you."

He could find no words to thank her for such un-selfish devotion, but he pressed her to his heart again and again.

He still held Mariquita's hand, and was soothing her with many endearing expressions, when La Zandunga, accompanied by Tio Pedro, returned.

The lovers flew apart, abashed at being surprised.

McKay expected nothing less than coarse abuse, but no honey could be sweeter than the old people's accents and words.

"Do not mind us," said La Zandunga, coaxingly.

"A pair of turtle-doves," said Tio Pedro: "bashful and timid as birds."

"Sit down, good sir," went on the old woman: "you can see Mariquita again. Let us talk first of this business."

"You want horses, I believe?" said Tio Pedro. "I can get you any number. What price will you pay?"

"What they are worth."

"And a little more, which we will divide between ourselves," added the old man, with a knowing wink.

"That's not the way with British officers," said McKay, sternly.

"It's the way with ours in Spain."

"That may be. However, I will take five hundred from you, at twenty pounds apiece, if they are delivered within three days."

Tio Pedro got up and walked towards the door.

"I go to fetch them. I am the key of Southern Spain. When I will, every stable-door shall be unlocked. You shall have the horses, and more, if you choose, in the stated time."

"One moment, Señor Pedro; I want something else from you, and you, señora."

They looked at him with well-disguised astonishment.

"I have long loved your niece; will you give her to me in marriage?"

"Oh! sir, it is too great an honour for our house. We—she—are all unworthy. But if you insist, and are prepared to take her as she is, dowerless, uncultured, with only her natural gifts, she is yours."

"I want only herself. I have sufficient means for both. They may still be modest, but I have good prospects—the very best. Some day I shall inherit a great fortune."

"Oh! sir, you overwhelm us. We can make you no sufficient return for your great condescension. Only command us, and we will faithfully execute your wishes."

"My only desire is that you should treat Mariquita well. Take every care of her until I can return. It will not be long, I trust, before this war is ended, and then I will make her my wife."

McKay's last words were overheard by a man who at this moment entered the shop.

It was Benito, who advanced with flaming face and fierce, angry eyes towards the group at the counter.

"What is this—and your promise to me? The girl is mine; you gave her to me months ago."

"Our promise was conditional on Mariquita's consent," said La Zandunga, with clever evasion. "That you have never been able to obtain."

"I should have secured it in time but for this scoundrel who has come between me and my affianced bride. He'll have to settle with me, whoever he is," and so saying, Benito came closer to McKay, whom hitherto he had not recognised. "The Englishman!" he cried, starting back.

"Very much at your service," replied McKay, shortly. "I am not afraid of your threats. I think I can hold my own with you as I have done before."

"We shall see," and with a muttered execration, full of hatred and malice, he rushed from the place.

When, an hour or two later, Mrs. Wilders hunted him up at the Redhot Shell Ramp, she found him in a mood fit for any desperate deed. But, with native cunning, he pretended to show reluctance when she asked him for his help.

"Who is it you hate? An Englishman? Any one on the Rock?" he said. "And what do you want done? I have no wish to bring myself within reach of the English law."

"It is an English officer. He is here just now, but will presently return to the Crimea."

"What is his name?" asked Benito, eagerly, his black heart inflamed with a wild hope of revenge.

"McKay—Stanislas McKay, of the Royal Picts."

It was his name! A fierce, baleful light gleamed in Benito's dark eyes; he clenched his fists and set his teeth fast.

"You know him?" said Mrs. Wilders, readily interpreting these signs of hate.

"I should like to kill him!" hissed Benito.

"Do so, and claim your own reward."

"But how? When? Where?"

"That is for you to settle. Watch him, stick to him, dog his footsteps, follow him wherever he goes. Some day he must give you a chance."

"Leave it to me. The moment will come when I shall sheathe my knife in his heart."

"I think I can trust you. Only do it well, and never let me see him again."

CHAPTER XXII
MR. HOBSON CALLS

The *Arcadia* went direct from Gibraltar to Southampton, where Mrs. Wilders left it and returned to London.

It was necessary for her to review her position and look things in the face. Her circumstances were undoubtedly straitened since her husband's death. She had her pension as the widow of a general officer—but this was a mere pittance at best—and the interest of the small private fortune settled, at the time of the marriage, on her and her children, should she have any. Her income from both these sources amounted to barely £300 a year—far too meagre an amount according to her present ideas, burdened as she was, moreover, with the care and education of a child.

But how was she to increase it? The reversion of the great Wilders estates still eluded her grasp; they might never come her way, whatever lengths she might go to secure them.

"Lord Essendine ought to do something for me," she told herself, as soon as she was settled in town. "It was not fair to keep the existence of this hateful young man secret; my boy suffers by it, poor little orphan! Surely I can make a good case of this to his lordship; and, after all, the child comes next."

She wrote accordingly to the family lawyers, Messrs. Burt and Benham, asking for an interview, and within a day or two saw the senior partner, Mr. Burt.

He was blandly sympathetic, but distant.

"Allow me to offer my deep condolence, madam; but as this is, I presume, a business visit, may I ask—"

"I am left in great distress. I wish to appeal to Lord Essendine."

"On what grounds?"

"My infant son is the next heir."

"Nay; surely you know—there is another before him?"

"Before my boy! Who? What can you mean? Impossible! I have never heard a syllable of this. I shall contest it."

It suited her to deny all knowledge, thinking it strengthened her position.

"That would be quite useless. The claims of the next heir are perfectly sound."

"It is sheer robbery! It is scandalous, outrageous! I will go and see Lord Essendine myself."

"Pardon me, madam; I fear that is out of the question. He is in Scotland, living in retirement. Lady Essendine's health has failed greatly under recent afflictions."

"He must and shall know how I am situated."

"You may trust me to tell him, madam, at once; and, although I have no right to pledge his lordship, I think I can safely say that he will meet you in a liberal spirit."

So it proved. Lord Essendine, after a short interval, wrote himself to Mrs. Wilders a civil, courtly letter, in which he promised her a handsome allowance, with a substantial sum in cash down to furnish a house and make herself a home.

Although still bitterly dissatisfied with her lot, she was now not only fortified against indigence, but could count on a life of comfort and ease. She established herself in a snug villa down Brompton way—a small house with a pretty garden, of the kind now fast disappearing from what was then a near suburb of the town. It was well mounted; she kept several servants, a neat brougham, and an excellent cook.

There she prepared to wait events, trusting that Russian bullet or Benito's Spanish knife might yet rid her of the one obstacle that still stood between her son and the inheritance of great wealth.

It was with a distinct annoyance, then, while leading this tranquil but luxurious life, that her man-servant brought in a card one afternoon, bearing the name of Hobson, and said, "The gentleman hopes you will be able to see him at once."

"How did you find me out?" she asked, angrily, when her visitor—the same Mr. Hobson we saw at Constantinople—was introduced.

"Ah! How do I find everything and everybody out? That's my affair—my business, I may say."

"And what do you want?" went on Mrs. Wilders, in the same key.

"First of all, to condole with you on the loss of so many near relatives. I missed you at Constantinople after Lord Lydstone's sad and dreadful death."

Mrs. Wilders shuddered in spite of herself.

"You suffer remorse?" he said, mockingly.

She made a gesture of protest.

"Sorrow, I should say. Yet you benefited greatly."

"On the contrary, not at all. Another life still intervenes."

"Another! and you knew nothing of it! Impossible!"

"It is too true. I am as far as ever from the accomplishment of my hopes."

"Who is this unknown interloper?"

"An English officer, at present serving in the Crimea. His name is McKay: Stanislas McKay."

"The name is familiar; the Christian name is suggestive. Do you know whether he is of Polish origin?"

"Yes, I have heard so. His father was once in the Russian army."

"It is the same, then. There can be no doubt of it. And you would like to see him out of the way? I might help you, perhaps."

"How? I have my own agents at work."

"He is in the Crimea, you say?"

"Yes, or will be within a few weeks."

"If we could inveigle him into the Russian lines he would be shot or hanged as a traitor. He is a Russian subject in arms against his Czar."

"It would be difficult, I fear, to get him into Russian hands."

"Some stratagem might accomplish it. You have agents at work, you say, in the Crimea?"

"They can go there."

"Put me in communication with them, and leave it all to me."

"You will place me under another onerous obligation, Hippolyte."

"No, thanks. I am about to ask a favour in return. You can help me, I think."

"Yes? Command me."

"You have many acquaintances in London; your late husband's friends were military men. I want a little information at times."

Mrs. Wilders looked at him curiously.

"Why don't you call things by their right names? You would like to employ me as a spy—is that what you mean?"

"Well, if you like to put it so, yes. I suppose I can count upon you?"

"I am sorry not to be able to oblige you, but I am afraid I must say no."

"You are growing squeamish, Cyprienne, in your old age. To think of your having scruples!"

"I despise your sneers. It does not suit me to do what you wish, that's all; it would be unsafe."

"What have you to lose?"

"All this." She waved her hand round the prettily-furnished room. "Lord Essendine has been very kind to me, and if there were any suspicions—if any rumour got about that I was employed by or for you—he would certainly withdraw the income he gives me."

Mr. Hobson laughed quietly.

"You have given yourself away, as they say in America; you have put yourself in my hands, Cyprienne. I insist now upon your doing what I wish."

"You shall not browbeat me!" She rose from her seat, with indignation in her face. "Leave me, or I will call the servants."

"I shall go straight to Lord Essendine, then, and tell him all I know. How would you like that? How about your allowance, and the protection of that great family? Don't you know, foolish woman, that you are absolutely and completely in my power?"

Mrs. Wilders made no reply. Her face was a study; many emotions struggled for mastery—fear, sullen obstinacy, and impotent rage.

"Come, be more reasonable," went on Mr. Hobson, "Our partnership is of long standing; it cannot easily be dissolved; certainly not now. After all, what is it I ask you? A few questions put adroitly to the right person, an occasional visit to some official friend; to keep your eyes and ears open, and be always on the watch. Surely, there is no great trouble, no danger, in that?"

"If you will have it so, I suppose I must agree. But where and how am I to begin?"

"I leave it all to you, my dear madam; you are much more at home in this great town than I am. I can only indicate the lines on which you should proceed."

"How shall I communicate with you?"

"Only by word of mouth. When you have anything to say, write to me— there is my address"—he pointed to his card—"Duke Street, St. James's. Write just three lines, asking me to lunch, nothing more; I shall understand."

"And about this hated McKay?"

"Let me know when he returns to the Crimea. We shall be able to hit upon a plan then. But it will require some thought, and a reckless, unscrupulous tool."

"I know the very man. He is devoted to my interests, and a bitter enemy of McKay's."

"We shall succeed then, never fear," and with these words Mr. Hobson took his leave.

CHAPTER XXIII
WAR TO THE KNIFE

Since we left him at Gibraltar McKay had led a busy life. The "Horse Purchase" was in full swing upon the north front, where, in a short space of time, many hundreds of animals were picketed ready for shipment to the East. Having set this part of his enterprise on foot, he had proceeded to the Spanish ports on the Eastern coast and repeated the process.

Alicante was the great centre of his operations on this side, and there, by means of dealers and contractors, he speedily collected a large supply of mules. They were kept in the bull-ring and the grounds adjoining, a little way out of the town. A number of native muleteers were engaged to look after them, and McKay succeeded in giving the whole body of men and mules some sort of military organisation.

They were a rough lot, these local muleteers, the scum and riff-raff of Valencia—black-muzzled, dark-skinned mongrels, half Moors, half Spaniards, lawless, turbulent, and quarrelsome.

Fights were frequent amongst them—sanguinary struggles, in which the murderous native knife played a prominent part, and both antagonists were often stabbed and slashed to death.

The local authorities looked askance at this gathering of rascaldom, and gave them a wide berth. But McKay went fearlessly amongst his reprobate followers, administering a rough-and-ready sort of discipline, and keeping them as far as possible within bounds.

It was his custom to pay a nightly visit to his charge. He went through the lines, saw that the night-patrols were on the alert, and the rest of the men quiet.

Repeatedly the overseers next him in authority cautioned him against venturing out of the town so late.

"There are evil people about," said his head man, a worthy "scorpion," whom he had brought with him from Gibraltar. "Your worship would do better to stay at home at night."

"What have I to fear?" replied McKay, stoutly. "I have my revolver; I can take care of myself."

They evidently did not think so, for it became the rule for a couple of them to escort him back to town without his knowledge.

They followed at a little distance behind him, carrying lanterns, and keeping him always in sight.

One night McKay discovered their kind intentions, and civilly, but firmly, put an end to the practice.

Next night he was attacked on his way back to the hotel. A man rushed out on him from a dark corner, and made a blow at his breast with a knife. It missed him, although his coat was cut through.

A short encounter followed. McKay was stronger than his assailant, whom he speedily disarmed; but he was not so active. The fellow managed to slip through his fingers and run; all that McKay could do was to send three shots after him, fired quickly from his revolver, and without good aim.

"Scoundrel! he has got clear away," said McKay, as he put up his weapon. "Who was it, I wonder? Not one of my own men; and yet I seemed to know him. If I did not think he was still at Gibraltar, I should say it was that miscreant Benito. I shall have to get him hanged, or he will do for me one of these days."

The pistol-shots attracted no particular attention in this deserted, dead-alive Spanish town, and McKay got back to his hotel without challenge or inquiry.

A day or two later, as the organisation of his mule-train was now complete, and transports were already arriving to embark their four-footed freight, he returned to Gibraltar, meaning to go on to the Crimea without delay.

Of course he went to Bombardier Lane, where he was received by the old people like a favourite son.

Mariquita, blushing and diffident, was scarcely able to realise that her Stanislas was now at liberty to make love to her, openly and without question.

The time, however, for their tender intercourse was all too short. McKay expected hourly the steamer that was to take him eastward, and his heart ached at the prospect of parting. As for Mariquita, she had alternated between blithe joyousness and plaintive, despairing sorrow.

"I shall never see you again, Stanislas," she went on repeating, when the last mood was on her.

"Nonsense! I have come out harmless so far; I shall do so to the end. The Russians can't hurt me."

"But you have other enemies, dearest—pitiless, vindictive, and implacable."

"Whom do you mean? Benito?"

"You know without my telling you. He has shown his enmity, then? How? Oh, Stanislas! be on your guard against that black-hearted man."

Should he tell her of his suspicions that it was Benito who had attacked him at Alicante? No; it would only aggravate her fears. But he tried, nevertheless, to verify these suspicions without letting Mariquita know the secret.

"Is Benito at Gibraltar?" he asked, quietly,

"We have not seen him for weeks. Since—since—you know, my life!—since you came to our house he has kept away. But I heard my uncle say that he had left the Rock to buy mules. He was going, I believe, to Alicante. Did you see him there?"

"I saw many ruffians of his stamp, but I did not distinguish our friend."

"You must never let him come near you, Stanislas. Remember what I say. He is treacherous, truculent—a very fiend."

"If he comes across my path I will put my heel upon him like a toad. But let us talk of something more pleasant—of you—of our future life. Shall you like to live in England, and never see the sun?"

"You will be my sun, Stanislas."

"Then you will have to learn English."

"It will be easy enough if you teach me."

"Some day you will be a great lady—one of the greatest in London, perhaps. You'll have a grand house, carriages, magnificent dresses, diamonds—"

"I only want you," she said, as she nestled closer to his side.

It was sad that stern duty should put an end to these pretty love passages, but the moment of separation arrived inexorably, and, after a sad, passionate leave-taking, McKay tore himself away.

Mariquita for days was inconsolable. She brooded constantly in a corner, weeping silent tears, utterly absorbed in her grief. They considerately left her alone. Since she had become the affianced wife of a man of McKay's rank and position, both the termagant aunt and cross-grained uncle had treated her with unbounded respect. They would not allow her to be vexed or worried by any one, least of all by Benito, who, as soon as the English officer was out of the way, again began to haunt the house.

It was about her that they were having high words a day or two after McKay's departure.

Mariquita overheard them.

"You shall not see her, I tell you!" said La Zandunga, with shrill determination. "The sweet child is sad and sick at heart."

"She has broken mine, as you have your word to me. I shall never be happy more."

He spoke as though he was in great distress, and his grief, if false, was certainly well feigned.

"Bah!" said old Pedro. "No man ever died of unrequited love. There are as good fish in the sea."

"I wanted this one," said Benito, in deep dejection. "No matter; I am going away. There is a fine chance yonder, and I may perhaps forget her."

"Where, then?" asked the old woman.

"In the Crimea. I start to-morrow."

"Go, in Heaven's keeping," said Tio Pedro.

"And never let us see you again," added La Zandunga, whose sentiments towards Benito had undergone an entire change in the last few months.

"May I not see her to say good-bye?"

"No, you would only agitate her."

"Do not be so cruel. I implore you to let me speak to her."

"Be off!" said the old woman, angrily. "You are importunate and ill-bred."

"I will not go; I will see her first."

"Put him out, Pedro; by force, if he will not go quietly."

Tio Pedro rose rather reluctantly and advanced towards Benito.

"Hands off!" cried the young man, savagely striking at Pedro.

"What! You dare!" said the other furiously. "I am not too old to deal with such a stripling. Begone, I say, quicker than that!" and Tio Pedro pushed Benito towards the door.

There was a struggle, but it was of short duration. Within a few seconds Benito was ejected into the street.

By-and-by, when the coast was clear, and Mariquita felt safe from the intrusion of the man she loathed, she came out into the shop.

By this time the place was quiet. Tio Pedro had gone off to a neighbouring wine-shop to exaggerate his recent prowess, and La Zandunga sat alone behind the counter.

"Where is Benito? Has he gone?" asked Mariquita, nervously.

"Yes. Did he frighten my sweet bird?" said her aunt, soothing her. "He is an indecent, ill-mannered rogue, and we shall be well rid of him."

"Well rid of him? He really leaves us, then? For the Crimea?"

"You have guessed it. Yes. He thinks there is a chance of finding fortune there."

Was that his only reason? Mariquita put her hand upon her heart, which had almost ceased beating. She was sick with apprehension. Did not Benito's departure forebode evil for her lover?

Just then her eye fell upon a piece of crumpled paper lying on the floor — part of a letter, it seemed. Almost mechanically — with no special intention at least — she stooped to pick it up.

"What have you got there?" asked her aunt.

"A letter."

"It must be Benito's; he probably dropped it in the scuffle. Do you know that he dared to raise his hand against my worthy husband?"

"If it is Benito's I have no desire to touch it," said Mariquita, disdainfully.

"Throw it into the yard, then," said her aunt.

Mariquita accordingly went to the back door and out into the garden, round which she walked listlessly, once or twice, forgetting what she held in her hand.

Then she looked at it in an aimless, absent way, and began to read some of the words.

The letter was in Spanish, written in a female hand. It said —

"Wait till he goes back to the Crimea, then follow him instantly. On arrival at Balaclava go at once to the Maltese baker whose shop is at the head of the bay near Kadikoi; he will give you employment. This will explain and cover your presence in the camp. You will visit all parts of it, selling bread. You must hang about the English headquarters; he is most often there; and remember that he is the sole object of your errand. You must know at all times where he is and what he is doing.

"Further instructions will reach you through the baker in the Crimea. Obey them to the letter, and you will receive a double reward. Money to any amount shall be yours, and you will have had your revenge upon the man who has robbed you of your love."

After reading this carefully there was no doubt in Mariquita's mind that Benito's mission was directed against McKay. Her first thought was the urgency of the danger that threatened her lover; the second, an eager desire to put him on his guard. But how was she to do this? By letter? There was no time. By a trusty messenger? But whom could she send? There was no one from whom she could seek advice or assistance save the old people; and in her heart, notwithstanding their present extreme civility, she mistrusted both.

She was sorely puzzled what to do, but yet resolved to save her lover somehow, even at the risk of her own life.

CHAPTER XXIV
AT MOTHER CHARCOAL'S

With the return of spring brighter days dawned for the British troops in the East. The worst troubles were ended; supplies of all kinds were now flowing in in great profusion; the means of transport to the front were enormously increased and improved, not only by the opportune arrival of great drafts of baggage-animals, through the exertions of men like McKay, but by the construction of a railway for goods traffic.

The chief difficulty, however, still remained unsolved: the siege still slowly dragged itself along. Sebastopol refused to fall, and, with its gallant garrison under the indomitable Todleben, still obstinately kept the Allies at bay.

The besiegers' lines were, however, slowly but surely tightening round the place. Many miles of trenches were now open and innumerable batteries had been built and armed. The struggle daily became closer and more strenuously maintained. The opposing forces—besiegers and besieged— were in constant collision. Sharpshooters interchanged shots all day long, and guns answered guns. The Russians made frequent sorties by night; and every day there were hand-to-hand conflicts for the possession of rifle-pits and the more advanced posts.

It was a dreary, disappointing season. This siege seemed interminable. No one saw the end of it. All alike—from generals to common men—were despondent and dispirited with the weariness of hope long deferred.

Why did we not attack the place? This was the burden of every song. The attack—always imminent, always postponed—was the one topic of conversation wherever soldiers met and talked together.

It was debated and discussed seriously, and from every point of view, in the council-chamber, where Lord Raglan met his colleagues and the great officers of the staff. It was the gossip round the camp-fire, where men beguiled the weary hours of trench-duty. It was tossed from mouth to mouth by thoughtless subalterns as they galloped on their Tartar ponies for a day's outing to Kamiesch, when released from sterner toil.

The attack! To-morrow—next day—some day—never! So it went on, with a wearisome, monotonous sameness that was perfectly exasperating.

"I give you Good-day, my friend. Well, you see the summer is now close at hand, and still we are on the wrong side of the wall."

The speaker was M. Anatole Belhomme, Hyde's French friend. They had met outside a drinking-booth in the hut-town of Kadikoi. Hyde was riding a pony; the other was on foot.

"Ah! my gallant Gaul, is it you?" replied Hyde. "Let's go in and jingle glasses together, hey?"

"A little tear of cognac would not be amiss," replied the Frenchman, whose excessive fondness for the fermented liquor of his country was the chief cause of his finding himself a sergeant in the Voltigeurs instead of chief cook to a Parisian restaurant or an English duke.

Hyde hitched up his pony at the door, and they entered the booth, seating themselves at one of the tables, if the two inverted wine-boxes used for the purpose deserved the name. There were other soldiers about, mostly British: a couple of sergeants of the Guards, an assistant of the provost-marshal, some of the new Land Transport Corps, and one or two Sardinians, in their picturesque green tunics and cocked hats with great plumes of black feathers.

The demand for drink was incessant and kept the attendants busy. There were only two of them: the proprietress, a dark-skinned lady, familiarly termed Mother Charcoal, and a mite of a boy whom the English customers called the "imp" and the French *polisson* (rogue).

Mother Charcoal was a stout but comely negress, hailing originally from Jamaica, who had come to Constantinople as stewardess in one of the transport-ships. Being of an enterprising nature, she had hastened to the seat of war and sunk all her ready-money in opening a canteen. She was soon very popular with the allied troops of every nationality and did a roaring trade.

"Some brandy—your best, my black Venus!" shouted Hyde.

"Who you call names? Me no Venus."

"Well, Mrs. Charcoal, then; that name suits your colour."

"What colour? You call me coloured? I no common nigger, let me tell you, sah; I a Georgetown lady. Me wash for officers' wives and give dignity-balls in my own home. Black Venus! Charcoal! You call me my right name. Sophimisby Cleopatra Plantagenet Sprotts: that my right name."

"Well, Mrs. S.C.P.S., I can't get my tongue round them all; fetch the brandy or send it. We will talk about your pedigree and Christian names some other time."

This chaffing colloquy had raised a general laugh and put Hyde on good terms with the company.

"What news from the front, sergeant?" asked one of the Land Transport Corps, a new comer.

"Nothing much on our side, except that they say there will be a new bombardment in a few days. But the French, were pretty busy last night, to judge from the firing."

"What was it?"

"Perhaps our friend here can tell you" and he turned to Anatole, asking the question in French.

"A glorious affair, truly!" replied the Frenchman, delighted to have an opportunity of launching out.

"I was there—I, who speak to you."

"Tell us about it," said Hyde; "I will interpret it to these gentlemen."

"The Russians, you must understand, have been forming ambuscades in front of our bastion Du Mât, which have given us infinite trouble. Last night we attacked them in three columns, 10,000 strong, and drove them out."

"Well done!"

"It was splendidly done!" went on Anatole, bombastically. "Three times the enemy tried to retake their ambuscades; three times we beat them back at the point of the bayonet, so!"

And the excitable Frenchman jumped from his seat and went through the pantomime of charging with the bayonet.

"You lost many men?"

"Thousands. What matter? we have many more to come. The Imperial Guard has landed, and the reserve, are at Constantinople."

"Yes, and there are the 'Sardines,'" said another pointing to the new uniform.

"Plenty of new arrivals. M. Soyer, the great cook, landed yesterday."

"What on earth brings him?"

"He is going to teach the troops to make omelettes and biscuit-soup."

"We were ahead of him in that, I think," said Hyde, winking at Anatole.

"He is with Miss Nightingale, you know, who has come out as head nurse."

"Heaven bless her!"

"Well, for all the new arrivals, we don't get on very fast with the siege."

"Why don't they go into the place, without all this shilly-shallying?" cried an impetuous Briton. "We'd take the place—we, the rank and file—if the generals only would let us do the work alone."

"They are a poor lot, the generals, I say."

"Halt, there! not a word against Lord Raglan," cried Hyde.

"He is so slow."

"Yes, but he is uncommon sure. Have you ever seen him in action? I have. He knows how to command: so quiet and self-possessed. Such a different man from the French generals, who always shout and swear and make such a confounded row. What do you think of your generals, Anatole?"

"Canrobert is an imbecile; he never knows his own mind."

"Well, we shan't be troubled with him much longer," said a fresh arrival. "Canrobert has just resigned the chief command."

"Impossible!" said Anatole, when the news was interpreted to him.

"It is perfectly true, I assure you," replied the last speaker. "I have just come from the English headquarters, and saw the new French commander-in-chief there. Palliser, I think they call him."

"Pélissier," said the French sergeant, correcting him. "That is good news. A rare old dog of war that. We shan't wait long to attack if he has the ordering."

"They say the Russian generals have changed lately. Gortschakoff has succeeded Mentschikoff."

"Confound those koffs! They are worse than a cold in the head."

"And just as difficult to get rid of. I'd like to wring their necks, and every Russian's at Sebastopol."

"Mentschikoff could not have been a bad fellow, anyway."

"How do you know that?"

"Why, one of our officers who was taken prisoner at Inkerman has just come back to camp. I heard him say that while he was in Sebastopol he got a letter from his young woman at home. She said she hoped he would take Mentschikoff prisoner, and send her home a button off his coat."

"Well?"

"The letter was read by the Russian authorities before they gave it him, and some one told the general what the English girl had said."

"He got mad, I suppose?"

"Not at all. He sent on the letter to its destination, with a note of his own, presenting his compliments, and regrets that he could not allow himself to be taken prisoner, but saying that he had much pleasure in inclosing the button, for transmission to England."

"A regular old brick, and no mistake! We'll drink his health."

It was drunk with full honours, after which Hyde, finding the party inclined to be rather too noisy, got up to go.

"Here!" he cried out, "some of you. What have I got to pay? Hurry up, my dusky duchess; I want to be off. Come, don't keep me waiting all day," and he struck the table impatiently with his riding-whip.

Mother Charcoal's assistant, "the imp," ran up.

"How much?"

"One dollar: four shilling," said the lad, in broken English.

"There's your money!" cried Hyde, throwing it down, "and a 'bob' for yourself. Stop!" he added. "Who and what are you? I have seen you before."

The lad, a mere boy, frail-looking and slightly built, but with a handsome, rather effeminate-looking face, tried to slink away.

"What's your name?" went on Hyde. ~

"Pongo," replied the boy.

"That's no real name. Smacks of the West Coast of Africa. Who gave it you?"

"Mother Charcoal."

"What's your country? What language do you talk?"

"English."

"Monstrous little of that, my boy. What's your native lingo, I mean? Greek, Turkish, Italian, Coptic—what?"

"Spanish," the boy confessed, in a low voice.

Hyde looked at him very intently for a few seconds; then, without further remark, walked out with his French friend.

But he did not do more than say good-bye outside the shanty; and, leaving his horse still hitched up near the door, he presently re-entered the canteen.

The place had emptied considerably, and he was able to take his seat again in a corner without attracting much attention. For half-an-half or more he watched this boy, who seemed to interest him so much.

"There's not a doubt of it. I must know what it means," and he beckoned the "imp" towards him.

"How did you get to the Crimea?" he asked, abruptly, speaking in excellent Spanish, when the lad, shyly and most reluctantly, came up to him. "What brings you here? I must and will know. It is very wrong. This is no place for you."

"I came to save him; he is in pressing danger," said the boy, whose large eyes were now filled with tears.

"Does he know you are in the Crimea?"

"I have been unable to find him. I lost all my money; it was stolen from me directly I landed, and, if I had not found this place with the black woman, I should have starved."

"Poor child! Alone and unprotected in this terrible place. It was sheer madness your coming."

"But I could tell him in no other way."

"Tell him what?"

"He has two bitter and implacable enemies, who are sworn to take his life."

Hyde shook his head gravely.

"It is true, as Heaven is my witness—perfectly true. But read this if you doubt me," and the boy, who was no other than Mariquita in disguise, produced the scrap of paper she had picked up in the shop in Bombardier Lane.

"I did not doubt your words. I was thinking of those enemies—one of them, at least—and wondering why she is permitted to live."

He took the letter, and read it slowly.

"Her handwriting! I was sure of it. To whom was this addressed?"

"Benito Villegas. Perhaps you know him—he is a native of the Rock."

"I remember him years ago. And has he carried out these instructions? Is he here?"

"I cannot make out. I have looked for him, but have been unable to find him."

"Not at the address stated here? You have been to it?"

"Several times, but have never seen him."

"He is probably in some disguise; that would suit his purpose best. We will hunt him up, never fear. But Stanislas must first be warned."

"You will go to him—at once?"

"This very day. And you—won't you come too?"

"No, no! I cannot." Mariquita blushed crimson. "He would chide me. It is wrong, I know; I have no right to be here, but he was in such danger. I risked everything: his displeasure, my life, my good name."

"Yes," said Hyde, thoughtfully; "this is no place for you; it is a pity you came to it. Still, we should not have known but for you; as it is, you had better stay here."

"With Mother Charcoal?"

"Just so. She is a worthy old soul, and can be trusted. It will be best, I think, to tell her the exact state of the case. Leave that to me."

"You will not delay in warning Stanislas?" said Mariquita, placing her hand on his arm.

"No; I will go directly after I have spoken to our black friend. Be easy in your mind, little woman, or Señor Pongo, or whatever you like to be called, and expect to see me again, and perhaps some one else you know, within a day or two from now."

Fate, however, decreed that Hyde should be unavoidably delayed in his errand of warning.

On leaving Mother Charcoal's shanty the second time, he found that his horse had disappeared. It had been hitched up to a hook near the doorway, in company with several others, and all were now gone.

"Some mistake? Scarcely that. One of those rascally sailor thieves, rather; not a four-footed beast is safe from them. What a nuisance it is! I suppose I must walk back to camp."

What chafed Hyde most was the delay in getting to headquarters. He had already made up his mind to find McKay as soon as he could, and tell him exactly what had occurred.

"He will, of course, think first of Mariquita; but that matter can be easily settled. We will send her on board one of the hospital-ships, where she will be with nurses of her own sex. What is really urgent is that McKay should look to himself. We must manage, through his interest and authority, to make a thorough search for this villain Benito, and get him expelled from the Crimea. That would make McKay safe, if only for a time, although I suppose Cyprienne would soon devise some new and more diabolical scheme. If I could only get on a little faster! It is most annoying about the horse. I will go straight to headquarters on foot, taking the camp of the Naval Brigade on my way."

There was wisdom in this last resolution. The sailors' camp was the Crimean pound. All animals lost or strayed, or, more exactly, stolen, if the truth is to be told, found their way to it. Jack did a large business in horseflesh. Often enough a man, having traced his missing property, was obliged to buy it back for a few shillings, or a glass or two of grog.

It was a general joke in the Crimea that the infantry were better mounted than the cavalry, and that the sailors had the pick of the infantry horses.

"I suppose I must go to the sailors' camp, but it's rather out of my road," said Hyde, as he trudged along under the hot sun.

Many more fortunate comrades, all mounted, overtook and passed him on the way. Each time he heard the sound of hoofs his rage increased against the dishonest rogue who had robbed him of his pony.

"Like a lift, guv'ner?" said a voice behind him. "You shall have this tit chape. Half a sov., money down."

Hyde turned, and saw a blue-jacket astride of the missing pony.

"Buy it, you rascal! why it belongs to me! Where did you get it?"

"I found it, yer honour."

"Stole it, you mean. Get off this instant, or I'll give you up to the provost!" And, so saying, Hyde put out his hand to seize the reins.

"Avast heaving there, commodore," said Jack, digging his heels into the horse, and lifting it cleverly just out of Hyde's reach. "Who finds keeps. Pay up, or you shan't have him. Why, I deserve a pound for looking after the dumb baste."

Hyde looked around for help, but no one was in sight. He was not to be baulked, however, and made a fresh attempt to get alongside the pony. But each time the sailor forged a little ahead, and this tantalising game continued for half-an-hour.

At last, disgusted and despairing, Hyde thought it better to make terms. He was losing valuable time.

"I give in, you rogue! Pull up, and you shall have your money."

"Honour bright, guv'ner?"

"Here it is," said Hyde, taking out the money.

"It's a fair swap. Hand over the money."

"No; you give up the pony first."

"I shan't. That's not my way of doing business."

"You shall!" cried Hyde, who had been edging up towards the sailor, and now suddenly made a grab at his leg.

He caught it, and held it with an iron grip. But Jack was not disposed to yield quietly. With a loud oath, he struck viciously at the pony's side with his disengaged foot.

It was a lively little beast, and went off at once, Hyde still clinging tenaciously to his prey.

But Jack was determined not to be beaten. With one hand he tried to beat off Hyde, and with the other incited the pony to increase its pace.

In the end Hyde was thrown to the ground, and received two nasty kicks—one in the forehead, the other in the breast—from the heels of the excited horse.

The sailor got clear away, and our friend Hyde was picked up senseless half-an-hour later by a passing ambulance-cart, and carried back to camp.

VOLUME II

CHAPTER I
SECRET SERVICE

McKay, on returning to the Crimea, had resumed his duties at headquarters. He was complimented by Lord Raglan and General Airey on the manner in which he had performed his mission.

"Matters have improved considerably in the month or two you were absent," said the latter to him one day. "Thanks to the animals you got us, we have been able to bring up sufficient shot and shell."

"When is the new bombardment to take place, sir?"

"At once."

"And the attack?"

"I cannot tell you. Some of the French generals are altogether against assaulting the fortress. They would prefer operations in the open field."

"What do they want, sir?"

"They would like to divide the whole allied forces into three distinct armies: one to remain and guard the trenches, another to go round by sea, so as to cut the Russian communications; and the third, when this is completed, to attack the Mackenzie heights, and get in at the back of the fortress."

"It seems rather a wild plan, sir."

"I agree with you—wild and impossible."

"Does the French commander-in-chief approve of it, sir?"

"General Canrobert does; but I think we have nearly seen the last of him. I expect any day to hear that he has given up the command."

"Who will succeed him, sir?"

"Pélissier, I believe—a very different sort of man, as we shall see."

A few days later the change which has already been referred to took place, and Marshal Pélissier came over to the English headquarters to take part in a council of war. All the principal general officers of both armies were present, and so was McKay, whose perfect acquaintance with French made him useful in interpreting and facilitating the free interchange of ideas.

The new French commander-in-chief was a prominent figure at the council—a short, stout, hard-featured man, brusque in movements and abrupt in speech; a man of much decision of character, one who made up his mind quickly, was intolerant of all opposition, and doggedly determined to force his will upon others.

When it came to the turn of the French generals to speak, one of them began a long protest against the attack as too hazardous. Several others brought forward pet schemes of their own for reducing the place.

"Enough!" said Pélissier, peremptorily. "You are not brought here to discuss whether or how we should attack. That point is already settled by my lord and myself."

He looked at Lord Raglan, who bowed assent.

"We have decided to attack the outworks on the 7th of the month."

"But I dissent," began General Bosquet.

"Did you not hear me? I tell you we have decided to attack. You are only called together to arrange how it can best be carried out."

"I have a paper here in which I have argued out the principles on which an attack should be conducted," said another, General Niel, an engineer.

"Ah!" said Pélissier, "you gentlemen are very clever—I admit your scientific knowledge—but when I want your advice I will ask for it."

While this conversation was in progress, the English officers present were whispering amongst themselves with undisguised satisfaction at finding that the new commander-in-chief of the French, unlike his predecessor, was well able to keep his subordinates in order; and, all useless discussion having been cut short, the plan of attack was soon arranged.

"Well," said Lord Raglan, "it is all clear. We shall begin by a heavy cannonade."

"To last four-and-twenty-hours," said Pélissier, "and then the assault."

"At what hour?" asked Lord Raglan.

"Daylight, of course!" cried two or three French generals in a breath.

"One moment," interposed General Airey. "Day-break is the time of all others that the enemy would expect an attack; they would therefore be best prepared for it then."

A sharp argument followed, and lasted several minutes, each side clinging tenaciously to its own opinion.

"Do not waste your energies, gentlemen," said Marshal Pélissier, again interfering decidedly. "Lord Raglan and I have settled that matter for ourselves. The attack will take place at five o'clock in the afternoon. That will allow time for us to get established in the enemy's works in the night after we have carried them."

"Of course, gentlemen," said Lord Raglan, in breaking up the council, "you will all understand the importance of secrecy. Not a word of what has passed here must be repeated outside. It would be fatal to success if the enemy got any inkling of our intentions."

"It's quite extraordinary," said General Airey to McKay and a few more, as they passed out from the council-chamber, "how the enemy gets his information."

"Those newspaper correspondents, I suspect, are responsible," said another general. "They let out everything, and the news, directly it is printed, is telegraphed to Russia."

"That does not entirely explain it. They must be always several weeks behind. I am referring more particularly to what happens at the moment. Everything appears to be immediately known."

"Why, only the other day a Russian spy walked coolly through our second parallel," said a French officer, "and counted the number of the guns. He passed himself off as an English traveller."

"Great impudence, but great pluck. I wish we had men who would do the same. That's what I complain of. We want a better organised secret service, and men like Wellington's famous Captain Grant in the Peninsular War, bold, adroit, and quick-witted, ready to run any risks, but bound to get information in the long run. I wish I could lay my hands on a few Captain Grants."

McKay smarted under the sting of these reproaches, feeling they applied, although scarcely so intended, to him. But there was no man, after all, on the headquarter staff better fitted to remove them. With his enterprising spirit and intimate acquaintance with many tongues, he ought to be able to secure information that would be useful to his chiefs.

Full of this idea, he rode down that afternoon to Balaclava, the centre of all the rascaldom that had gathered around the base of the Crimean army. He was in search of agents whom he could employ as emissaries into the enemy's lines.

Putting up his horse, he mixed amongst the motley crowd that thronged the "sutlers' town," as it was called, which had sprung up half-a-mile outside Balaclava, to accommodate the swarms of strangers who, under the strict rule of Colonel Harding, had been expelled from the port itself.

The place was like a fair—a jumble of huts and shanties and ragged canvas tents, with narrow, irregular lanes between them, in which the polyglot traders bought and sold. Here were grave Armenians, scampish Greeks from the Levant, wild-eyed Bedouins, Tartars from Asia Minor, evil-visaged Italians, scowling Spaniards, hoarse-voiced, slouching Whitechapel ruffians, with a well-developed talent for dealing in stolen goods.

As McKay stood watching the curious scene, and replying rather curtly to the eager salesmen, who pestered him perpetually to buy anything and everything—food, saddlery, pocket-knives, horse-shoes, fire-arms, and swords—he became conscious of a stir and flutter among the crowd. It presently became strangely silent, and parted obsequiously, to give passage to some great personage who approached.

This was Major Shervinton, the provost-marshal, supreme master and autocrat of all camp-followers, whom he ruled with an iron hand. Close behind him came two sturdy assistants—men who had once been drummers, and were specially selected in an army where flogging was the chief punishment for their prowess with the cat-o'-nine-tales.

Woe to the sutler, whatever his rank or nation, who fell foul of the terrible provost! Summary arrest, the briefest trial, and a sharp sentence peremptorily executed, in the shape of four dozen, was the certain treatment of all who offended against martial law.

"Hullo, McKay!" cried Shervinton, a big, burly, pleasant-faced man, whose cheery manner was in curious contrast with his formidable functions. "What brings a swell from headquarters into this den of iniquity? Lost your servant, or looking out for one? Don't engage any one without asking me. They are an abominable lot, and deserve to be hanged, all of them."

"You are the very fellow to help me, Shervinton," and McKay, taking the provost-marshal aside, told him his errand.

"I firmly believe every second man here is a spy, or would be if he had the pluck."

"Are any of them, do you think, in communication with the Russians?"

"Lots. They come and go through the lines, I believe, as they please."

"I wish I could find a few fellows of this sort."

"Perhaps I can put you in the way; only I doubt whether you can trust to a single word that they will tell you."

"But where shall we come upon them?"

"The best plan will be to consult Valetta Joe, the Maltese baker at the end of the lines. I have always suspected him of being a Russian spy; but I dare say we could buy him over if you want him. If he tries to play us false we will hang him the same day."

Valetta Joe was in his bread-store—a small shed communicating with the dark, dirty, semi-subterranean cellar behind, in which the dough was kneaded and baked. The shed was encumbered with barrels of inferior flour, and all around upon shelves lay the small short rolls, dark-looking and sour-tasting, which were sold in the camp for a shilling a piece.

"Well, Joe, what's the news from Sebastopol to-day?" asked Shervinton.

"Why you ask me, sare? I a poor Maltee baker—sell bread, make money. Have nothing to do with fight."

"You rascal! You know you're in league with the Russians. I have had my eye on you this long time. Some of these days we'll be down upon you like a cart-load of bricks."

"You a very hard man, Major Shervinton, sare—very unkind to poor Joe. I offer you bread every day for nothing; you say No. Why not take Joe's bread?"

"Because Joe's a scoundrel to offer it. Do you suppose I am to be bribed in that way? But here: I tell you what we are after. This gentleman," pointing to McKay, "wants news from the other side."

"Why you come to me? I nothing to do with other side."

"You can help him, you know that, and you must; or we will bundle you out of this and send you back to Constantinople."

The provost-marshal's manner was not to be mistaken.

"What can I do, sare?"

"Find out some one who can pass through the lines and bring or send him to my friend."

"Who is this gentleman?"

"He is one of Lord Raglan's staff; his name is Mr. McKay."

A close observer would have seen that the baker started slightly at the name and that he bent an eager, inquisitive look upon McKay.

"Will the gentleman give promise to do no harm to me or my people?"

"So long as you behave properly,—yes."

"I think I know some one, then."

"Produce him at once."

"He not here to-day; out selling bread. Where he find you, sare, to-morrow, or any time he have anything to tell?"

"Let him come to the headquarters and ask for my tent," said McKay. "There is my name on a piece of paper; if he shows that to the sentry they will let him through."

"Very good, sare; you wait and see."

"No humbug, mind, Joe; or I'll be down on you!" added the provost-marshal. "Is that all you want, McKay?"

Our hero expressed himself quite satisfied, and, with many thanks to the provost-marshal, he remounted and rode away.

CHAPTER II
AMONG THE COSSACKS

McKay was in His tent next morning finishing dressing when his servant brought him a piece of crumpled paper and said there was a messenger waiting to see him. The paper was the pass given the day before to Valetta Joe; its bearer was a nondescript-looking ruffian, in a long shaggy cloak of camel's hair, whose open throat and bare legs hinted at a great scantiness of wardrobe beneath. He wore an old red fez, stained purple, on the back of his bullet-head; he had a red, freckled face, red eyebrows, red eyes, red hair, and a pointed red beard, both of which were very ragged and unkempt.

"Have you got anything to tell me?" asked McKay, sharply, in English; and when the other shook his head he tried him in French, Spanish, and last of all in Italian.

"News," replied the visitor, at length, laconically; "ten dollars."

McKay put the money in his hand and was told briefly—

"To-morrow—sortie—Woronzoff Road."

And this was all the fellow would say.

McKay passed on this information to his chief, but rather doubtfully, declining to vouch for it, or say whence it had come.

It was felt, however, that no harm could be done in accepting the news as true and preparing for a Russian attack. The event proved the wisdom of this course. The sortie was made next night. A Russian column of considerable strength advanced some distance along the Woronzoff Road, but finding the English on the alert immediately retired.

The next piece of information that reached McKay from the same source, but by a different messenger, was more readily credited. He learnt this time that the Russians intended to establish a new kind of battery in front of the Karabel suburb.

"What kind?" asked McKay.

The messenger, a hungry-looking Tartar who spoke broken English, but when encouraged explained himself freely in Russian, said—

"Big guns; they sink one end deep into the ground, the other point very high."

"I understand. They want to give great elevation, so as to increase the range."

"Yes, you see. They will reach right into your camp."

Again the information proved correct. Within a couple of days the camps of the Third and Fourth Divisions, hitherto deemed safe from the fire of the fortress, were disturbed by the whistling of round-shot in their midst. The fact was reported in due course to headquarters.

"You see, sir, it is just what I was told," said McKay to General Airey.

"Upon my word, you deserve great credit. You seem to have organised an intelligence department of your own, and, what is more to the purpose, your fellow seems always right."

McKay was greatly gratified at this encouragement, and eager to be still more useful. He visited the Maltese baker again, and urged him to continue supplying him with news.

"Trust to Joe. Wait one little bit; you know plenty more."

Several days passed, however, without any fresh news. Then a new messenger came, another Tartar, a very old man with a flowing grey beard, wearing a long caftan like a dressing-gown to his heels, and an enormous sheepskin cap that came far down over his eyes, and almost hid his face. He seemed very decrepit, and was excessively stupid, probably from old age. He looked terribly frightened when brought to McKay's tent, stooping his shoulders and hanging his head in the cowering, deprecating attitude of one who expects, but would not dare to ward off, a blow.

He was tongue-tied, for he made no attempt to speak, but merely thrust forward one hand, making a deep obeisance with the other. There was a scrap of paper in the extended hand, which McKay took and opened curiously. A few lines in Italian were scrawled on it.

"The Russians are collecting large forces beyond the Tchernaya," ran the message. "Expect a new attack on that side."

"Who gave you this?" asked McKay, in Russian.

The old fellow bowed low, but made no answer.

He repeated the question in Italian and every other language of which he was master, but obtained no reply. The man remained stupidly, idiotically dumb, only grovelling lower and more abjectly each time.

"What an old jackass he is! I shall get nothing out of him, I'm afraid. But it won't do to despise the message, wherever it comes from. Take him outside," he said to his orderly, "while I go and see the general." "You have no idea where this news comes from?" was General Airey's first inquiry.

"The same source, I don't doubt; but of course I can't vouch for its accuracy."

"It might be very important," the general was musing. "I am not sure whether you know what we contemplate in these next few days?"

"In the direction of the Tchernaya, sir?"

"Precisely. Now that the Sardinian troops have all arrived, Lord Raglan thinks we are strong enough to extend our position as far as the river."

"I had heard nothing of it, sir?"

"If this news be true, the Russians appear to be better informed than you are, McKay."

"And are preparing to oppose our movement?"

"That's just what I should like to know, and what gives so much importance to these tidings. I only wish we could verify them. Where is your messenger? Who is he?"

"A half-witted old Tartar; you will get nothing out of him, sir. I have been trying hard this half-hour."

"But you know where the news comes from. Could you not follow it up to its source?"

"I will do so at once, sir;" and within half-an-hour McKay was in his saddle, riding down to Balaclava.

Valetta Joe was in his shop, distributing a batch of newly-baked bread to a number of itinerant vendors, each bound to retail the loaves in the various camps.

McKay waited until the place was clear, then accosted the baker sharply.

"What was the good of your sending that old numbskull to me?"

"He give you letter. You not understand?"

"Yes, yes, I understand; but I want to be certain it is true."

"When Joe tell lies? You believe him before; if you like, believe him again."

"But can't you tell me more about it? How many troops have the Russians collected? Since when? What do they mean to do?"

"You ask Russian general, not me; I only know what I hear."

"But it would be possible to tell, from the position of the enemy, something of their intentions. I could directly if I saw them."

"Then why you not go and look for yourself?" asked Joe, carelessly; but there was a glitter in his eyes which gave a deep meaning to the simple question.

"Why not?" said McKay, whom the look had escaped. "It is well worth the risk."

"I'll help you, if you like," went on Joe, with the same outwardly unconcerned manner.

"Can you? How?"

"Very easy to pass lines. You put on Tartar clothes same as that old man go to you to-day. He live near Tchorgaun; he take you right into middle of Russian camp."

"When can he start?" asked McKay eagerly, accepting without hesitation all the risks of this perilous undertaking.

"To-night, if you choose. Come down here by-and-by; I have everything ready."

McKay agreed, and returned to headquarters in all haste, where he sought out his chief and confided to him his intentions.

"You are really prepared to penetrate the enemy's lines? It will be a daring, dangerous job, McKay. I should be wrong to encourage you."

"It is of vital importance, you say, that we should really know what the enemy is doing beyond the Tchernaya. I am quite ready to go, sir."

"Lord Raglan—all of us—indeed, will be greatly indebted to you if you can find out. But I do not like this idea of the disguise, McKay. You ought not to go under false colours."

"I should probably learn more."

"Yes; but do you know what your fate would be if you were discovered?"

"I suppose I should be hanged, sir," said McKay, simply.

"Hanged or shot. Spies—everyone out of uniform is a spy—get a very short shrift at an enemy's hand. No; you must stick to your legitimate dress. I am sure Lord Raglan would allow you to go under no other conditions."

"As you wish, sir. Only I fear I should not be so useful as if I were disguised."

"It is my order," said the general, briefly; and after that there was nothing more to be said.

McKay spent the rest of the afternoon at his usual duties, and towards evening, having carefully reloaded his revolver, and filled his pockets with Russian rouble notes, which he obtained on purpose from the military chest, he mounted a tough little Tartar pony, used generally by his servant, and trotted down to the hut-town.

Valetta Joe heard with marked disapprobation McKay's intention of carrying out his enterprise without assuming disguise.

"You better stay at home: not go very far like that."

"Lend me a *greggo* to throw over my coat, and a sheepskin cap, and I shall easily pass the Cossack sentries. Where is my guide?"

"Seelim—Jee!" shouted Joe, and the old gentleman who had visited McKay that morning came ambling up from the cellar below.

"Is that old idiot to go with me? Why, he speaks no known tongue!" cried McKay.

"Only Tartar. You know no Tartar? Well, he understand the stick. Show it him—so," and Joe made a motion of striking the old man, who bent submissively to receive the blow.

"Does he know where he is to take me? What we are going to do?"

"All right. You trust him: he take you past Cossacks." Joe muttered a few unintelligible instructions to the guide, who received them with deep respect, making a low bow, first to Joe and then to McKay.

"I give him *greggo* and cap: you put them on when you like."

McKay knew that he could only pass the British sentries openly, showing his uniform as a staff officer, so he made the guide carry the clothes, and the two pressed forward together through Kadikoi, towards the formidable line of works that now covered Balaclava.

He skirted the flank of one of the redoubts, and, passing beyond the intrenchments, came at length to our most advanced posts, a line of cavalry vedettes, stationed at a considerable distance apart.

"I am one of the headquarter staff," he said, briefly, to the sergeant commanding the picket, "and have to make a short reconnaissance towards Kamara. You understand?"

"Are we to support you, sir?"

"No; but look out for my coming back. It may not be till daybreak, but it will be as well, perhaps, to tell your men who I am, and to expect me. I don't want to be shot on re-entering our own lines."

"Never fear, sir, so long as we know. I will tell the officer, and make it all right."

McKay now rode slowly on, his guide at his horse's head. They kept in the valleys, already, as night was now advancing, deep in shade, and their figures, which could have been clearly made out against the sky if on the upper slopes, were nearly invisible on the lower ground.

It was a splendid summer's evening, perfectly still and peaceful, with no sounds abroad but the ceaseless chirp of innumerable grasshoppers, and the faint hum of buzzing insects ever on the wing. Only at intervals were strange sounds wafted on the breeze, and told their own story; the distant blare of trumpets, and the occasional "thud" of heavy cannon, gun answering gun between besiegers and besieged. As they fared along, McKay once or twice inquired, more by gesture than by voice, how far they had to go.

Each time the guide replied by a single word—"Cossack"—spoken almost in a whisper, and following by his placing finger on lip.

Half-a-mile further, the guide motioned to McKay to dismount and leave his horse, repeating the caution "Cossack!" in the same low tone of voice.

McKay, who had now put on the *greggo* and sheepskin cap, did as he was asked, and the two crept forward together, having left the horse tethered to a bush, the guide explaining by signs that they would presently come back to it.

A little farther and he placed his hand upon McKay's arms, with a motion to halt.

"H—sh!" said the old man, using a sound which has the same meaning in all tongues, and held up a finger.

McKay listened attentively, and heard voices approaching them. Instinctively he drew his revolver and waited events. The voices grew plainer and plainer, then gradually faded away.

"Cossack!" repeated the guide, and McKay gathered that these were a couple of Cossack sentries, from whose clutches he had narrowly escaped.

Again our hero was urged forward, and this time with all speed. The guide ran, followed by McKay, for a couple of hundred yards, then halted suddenly. What next? He had thrown himself on the ground, and seemed closely examining it; in this attitude he crept forward cautiously.

The movement was presently explained. A slight splash told of water encountered. He had been in search of the river, and had found it. This was the Tchernaya—a slow sluggish stream, hidden amidst long marshy grass, and everywhere fordable, as McKay had heard, at this season of the year.

The guide now stood up and pointed to the river, motioning McKay to enter it and cross.

Our hero stepped in boldly, and in all good faith, expecting his guide to follow. But he was half-way towards the other bank, and still the old man had made no move.

Why this hesitation?

McKay beckoned to him to come on. The guide advanced a step or two, then halted irresolute.

McKay grew impatient, and repeated his motion more peremptorily. The guide advanced another step and again halted. He seemed to suffer from an invincible dislike to cold water.

"Is he a cur or a traitor?" McKay asked himself, and drew his revolver to quicken the old man's movements, whichever he was.

The sight of the weapon seemed to throw the guide into a paroxysm of fear. He fell flat on the ground, and obstinately refused to move.

All this time McKay was in the river, up to his knees, a position not particularly comfortable. Besides, valuable time was being wasted—the night was not too long for what he had to do. Hastily regaining the bank, he rejoined the guide where he lay, and kicked him till he stood erect.

"You old scoundrel!" cried McKay, putting his revolver to his head. "Come on! do you understand? Come on, or you are a dead man!"

The gesture was threatening, not that McKay had any thought of firing. He knew a pistol-shot would raise a general alarm. Still the old man, although trembling in every limb, would not move.

"Come on!" repeated McKay, and with the idea of dragging him forward he seized him fiercely by the beard.

To his intense surprise, it came off in his hand.

"Cursed Englishman!" cried a voice with which he was perfectly familiar, and in Spanish. "You are at my mercy now. You dare not fire; your life is forfeited. The enemy is all around you. I have betrayed you into their hands."

"Benito! Can it be possible?" But McKay did not suffer his astonishment to interfere with his just revenge.

"On your knees, dog! Say your prayers. I will shoot you first, whatever happens to me."

"You are too late!" cried Benito, wrenching himself from his grasp, and whistling shrilly as he ran away.

McKay fired three shots at him in succession, one of which must have told, for the scoundrel gave a great yell of pain.

The next instant McKay was surrounded by a mob of Cossacks and quickly made prisoner.

They had evidently been waiting for him, and the whole enterprise was a piece of premeditated treachery, as boldly executed as it had been craftily planned.

McKay's captors having searched his pockets with the nimbleness of London thieves, and deprived him of money, watch, and all his possessions, proceeded to handle him very roughly. He had fought and struggled desperately, but was easily overpowered. They were twenty to one, and their wild blood was aroused by his resistance. He was beaten, badly mauled, and thrown to the ground, where a number of them held him hand and foot, whilst others produced ropes to bind him fast. The brutal indignities to which he was subjected made McKay wild with rage. He addressed them in their own language, protesting vainly against such shameful ill-usage.

"Hounds! Miscreants! Sons of burnt mothers! Do you dare to treat an English officer thus? Take me before your superior. Is there no one here in authority? I claim his protection."

"Which you don't deserve, scurvy rogue," said a quiet voice. "You are no officer—only a vile, disreputable spy."

"I can prove to you—"

"Bah! how well you speak Russian. We know all about you; we expected you. But enough: we must be going on."

"I don't know who you may be," began McKay, hotly, "but I shall complain of you to your superior officer."

"Silence!" replied the other, haughtily. "Have I not told you to hold your tongue? Fill his mouth with clay, some of you, and bring him along."

This fresh outrage nearly maddened McKay.

"You shall carry me, then," he spluttered out, from where he still lay upon the ground.

"Ah! we'll see. Get up, will you! Prick him with the point of your lance, Ivanovich. Come, move yourself," added the officer, as McKay slowly yielded to this painful persuasion, "move yourself, or you shall feel this," and the officer cracked the long lash of his riding-whip.

"You shall answer for this barbarity," said McKay "I demand to be taken before the General at once."

"You shall see him, never fear, sooner than you might wish, perhaps."

"Take me at once before him; I am not afraid."

"You will wait till it suits us, dog; meanwhile, lie there."

They had reached a rough shelter built of mud and long reeds. It was the picket-house, the headquarters of the troop of Cossacks, and a number of them were lying and hanging about, their horses tethered close by.

The officer pointed to a corner of the hut, and, giving peremptory instructions to a couple of sentries to watch the prisoner, for whom they would have to answer with their lives, he disappeared.

Greatly dejected and cast down at the failure of his enterprise, and in acute physical pain from his recent ill-usage and the tightness of his bonds, McKay passed the rest of the night very miserably.

Dawn came at length, but with it no relief. On the contrary, daylight aggravated his sufferings. He could see now the cruel scowling visages of his captors, and the indescribable filth and squalor of the den in which he lay.

"Get up!" cried a voice; but McKay was too much dazed and distracted by all he had endured to understand that the command was addressed to him.

It was repeated more arrogantly, and accompanied by a brutal kick.

He rose slowly and reluctantly, and asked in a sullen voice—

"Where are you taking me?"

"Before his Excellency. Step out, or must we prick you along?"

A march of half-an-hour under a strong escort brought them to a large camp. They passed through many lines of tents, and halted presently before a smart marquee.

The Cossack officer in charge entered it, and presently returned with the order—

"March him in!"

McKay found himself in the presence of a broadly-built, middle-aged man, in the long grey great-coat worn by all ranks of the Russian army, from highest to lowest, and the flat, circular-topped cap carried also by all.

There was nothing to indicate the rank of this personage but a small silver ornament on each shoulder-strap, and another in the centre of the cap. At a button-hole on his breast, however, was a small parti-coloured rosette, the simple record of orders and insignia too precious to carry in the field.

There was unbounded arrogance and contempt in his voice and manner as he addressed the prisoner, who might have been the vilest of created things.

"So"—he spoke in French, like most well-educated Russians of that day, to show their aristocratic superiority—"you have dared, wretch, to thrust yourself into the bear's mouth! You shall be hanged in half-an-hour."

"I claim to be treated as a prisoner of war," said McKay, boldly.

"You! impudent rogue! A low camp-follower! A sneaking, skulking spy—taken in the very act! You!"

"I am a British officer!" went on McKay, stoutly. He was not to be browbeaten or abashed.

"Where is your uniform?"

"Here!" replied McKay, throwing open the *greggo*, which he still wore, and showing the red waistcoat beneath, and the black breeches with their broad red stripe.

"You said he was a civilian in Tartar disguise," said the general,—for such was the officer's rank,—turning to one of his staff and seeming rather staggered at McKay's announcement. He spoke in Russian.

"Take care, Excellency; the prisoner speaks Russian."

"Is that so?" said the general to McKay. "An unusual accomplishment that, in English officers, I expect."

"Yes, I am acquainted with Russian," said McKay. Why should he deny it? They had heard him use that language at the time of his capture.

"How and when did you learn it?"

"I do not choose to say. What can that matter?"

Again the staff-officer interposed and whispered something in the general's ear.

"Of course; I had forgotten." Then, turning to McKay, he went on: "What is your name?"

"McKay."

"Your Christian names in full?"

"Stanislas Anastasius Wilders McKay."

"Exactly. Stanislas Alexandrovich McKay. I knew your father when he was a captain in the Polish Lancers; was he not?"

"I cannot deny it."

"He was a Russian, in the service of our holy Czar, and you, his son, are a Russian too."

"It is false! I am an Englishman. I have never yielded allegiance to the Czar."

"You will find it hard to evade your responsibility. It is not to be put on or off like a coat. You were born a Russian subject, and a Russian subject you remain!"

"I bear a commission in the army of the British Queen. I dare you to treat me as a Russian now!"

"We will treat you as we find you, Mr. McKay: as an interloper disguised for an improper purpose within our lines."

"What shall you do with me?" asked McKay, in a firm voice, but with a sinking heart.

"Hang you like a dog to the nearest tree. Or, stay! out of respect for your father, whom I knew, and if you prefer it, you shall be shot."

"I am in your power. But I warn you that, if you execute me, the merciless act will be remembered throughout Europe as an eternal disgrace to the Russian arms."

This bold speech was not without its effect. The general consulted with his staff, and a rather animated discussion followed, at the end of which he said —

"I am not to be deterred by any such threats: still, it will be better to refer your case to my superiors. I shall send you into Sebastopol, to be dealt with as Prince Gortschakoff may think fit, only do not expect more at his hands than at mine. Rope or rifle—one of them will be your fate. See he is sent off, Colonel Golopine, will you? And now take him away."

McKay was marched out of the marquee, still under the escort of Cossacks. But outside he was presently handed over to a fresh party; they brought up a shaggy pony—it might have been the fellow of the one he had left behind the previous night—and curtly bade him mount. When, with hands still tied, he scrambled with difficulty into his saddle, they tied his legs together by a long rope under the pony's belly, and, placing him in the centre of the escort, they started off at a jog-trot in the direction of the town.

CHAPTER III
A PURVEYOR OF NEWS

Mr. Hobson gave his address at Duke Street, St. James's, a lodging-house frequented by gentlemen from the neighbouring clubs. But he was never there except asleep. There was nothing strange in this as none of the occupants of the house were much there, except at night-time—they lived at their clubs.

So, for all the landlady knew, did Mr. Hobson. But we know better. He had no club, and his daily absence from breakfast—simply a cup of coffee and a roll, which he took in the French fashion, early—till late at night was to be accounted for by his constant presence at his office or place of business, although it was both and neither. This was in a little street off Bloomsbury, the first floor over a newspaper shop.

Mr. Hobson passed here as an agent for a country paper. It was supposed to be his business to collect and transmit news to his principals at a large seaport town on the East Coast. These were days before the present development of newspaper enterprise, when leading provincial journals have their own London offices and a private wire. Mr. Hobson's principles were very liberal according to the idea of that time; they seemed to grudge no expense with regard to the transmission of news.

Telegrams were costly things in those days, but Mr. Hobson sometimes sent off half-a-dozen in the course of a morning. He was served too, and exceedingly well, by special agents of his own, who came to him at all hours—in cabs driven recklessly, or on foot, in a stealthy, apologetic way, as though doubtful whether the news they brought would be acceptable.

The office upstairs bore out the notion of the news-agency. Its chief furniture consisted of two long, sloping tables, on which lay files of daily papers. There was one big book-case handy near the fireplace, and over the desk at which Mr. Hobson sat. On the shelves of this were ranged a couple of dozen volumes, each bearing a label on which were various letters and numerals.

On the desk itself were the usual writing appliances, a large pair of scissors, and a wide-mouthed bottle of gum.

Let us look in at Mr. Hobson on his first arrival at his office, soon after eight o'clock.

His first business was to ring his bell, which communicated with the shop below.

"My papers! It is past eight."

"Here they are, sir, the whole lot—*Times*, *'Tizer*, *Morning Chronicle*, and *Morning Post*."

"Why do you oblige me to ask for them? Can't you bring them as I have told you? It makes me so late with my work." And, having delivered himself of these testy remarks, he threw himself into an arm-chair and proceeded to devour the morning's news.

"Nothing fresh from the East?" As he now talked to himself, this smooth-shaven, typical Englishman spoke, strange to say, in French. "Have Messieurs the correspondents no news? No letter in the *Post*? None in the *Morning Chronicle*? How disappointing! Ha! what's this? Two columns in the *Times*. How admirably that excellent paper is served! Let's see what it says."

He hastily ran his eye down the columns, muttering to himself: "Ha! mostly strong language—finding fault. How kind of you to be dissatisfied with the administration, and to tell us why. The siege practically suspended, eh? Fuses won't fit the shells—so much the better, then the mortars can't fire.

"But that's no news: my friends and good masters will have found that out for themselves. Anything else? 'Our new battery, which is only seven hundred yards from the enemy's guns, is nearly completed.' Which battery does he mean? Has he referred to it before?"

And Mr. Hobson, as we shall still call him, got up from his seat and took a volume down from the shelf. It was labelled "T. 14, M. 55." These expressions expanded meant that it contained extracts from the *Times*, the 14th volume, for May, 1855.

After referring to an alphabetical index, he quickly turned over the leaves of the book till he found a certain page.

"Ah! here it is," he said. "'We have commenced another battery just in front of the quarries, the nearest to the enemy's works. It will be armed with the heaviest ordnance,' &c. &c. And now it is nearly ready. That must be passed on without delay."

Mr. Hobson turned to his desk and indited a telegram. It was addressed to Arrowsmith, Hull, and said—

"New shop, as already indicated, will be opened at once. Let our Gothenburg correspondent know."

"I will take it over myself. But let me first see whether there is anything to add."

He resumed his reading, and presently came to the following passage:—

"'Lord Lyons had just returned from a cruise in the Black Sea. This confirms my impression that some new movement is contemplated. Regiments have been placed under orders, and there is great stir among the fleet. A secret expedition is on the point of being despatched somewhere, but the real destination no one as yet knows. Camp-gossip is, of course, busy; but I will not repeat the idle and misleading rumours that are on every lip.'

"Another expedition planned! I must know more of this. Where can it be going? Is it meant for the Sea of Azof and Kertch, like the last, which alarmed us so, and never got so far?

"What a business that was! We heard of it long beforehand; preparations for transport, and the embarkation of the troops. The fleet left Kamiesch, steering northward, past Sebastopol, and we thought the latter would be attacked. But lo! next morning the enemy were not in sight; the fleet had returned to Kamiesch Bay. What did it mean? It was weeks before I learnt the right story, and then it came from Paris. General Canrobert had changed his mind. The Emperor had told him not to send away any troops, but to keep all concentrated before Sebastopol. So the expedition to Kertch—for it was directed against Kertch, and the northward move was only intended to deceive us—all ended in smoke. Can they be going again to Kertch? It is hardly likely. They have some deeper designs, I feel sure. This would tally with my latest advice. Let me read once more what the Prince says."

He took a key from his pocket, opened his desk, and unlocked an inner receptacle, from which he took a letter in cypher.

"'We have learnt,' he read, fluently, without using any key, 'that the enemy contemplate a great change in their plan of operations. It is reported that they propose to raise the siege, or at least reduce it to a mere blockade. The great bulk of the allied army would then be transferred to sea to another point where it would take the field against our line of communications. It is essential that we should know at the earliest date whether there is any foundation in this report. Use every endeavour to this end.'

"Yes; there can be no doubt that this surmise is corroborated by the latest news. But I must have more precise and correct information without delay. How is it to be obtained? Which of my agents can help me best? Lavitsky? He works in Woolwich Arsenal—he might know if more wheeled transport had been ordered. Or Bauer, at Portsmouth—he would know of any movements in the fleet. Or—

"Of course!" and he slapped his forehead, despising his own stupidity. "Cyprienne—she can, and must, manage this."

He proceeded to put back the papers into the secret drawer; he replaced the volume on the shelf, and, taking the telegram he had written in his hand, left the office, carefully locking the door behind him.

Hailing a cab, he was driven first to a telegraph-station, where he sent off his despatch, only adding the words:—

"Other important transactions in the shipping interest will shortly be undertaken; more precise details will speedily follow."

Then he directed the cabman to drive to Thistle Grove, Brompton.

"Is Mrs. Wilders visible yet?" he asked the servant, on reaching her house.

"Madame does not receive so early," replied the man, a foreigner, speaking broken English, who was new to the establishment, and had never seen Mr. Hobson before.

"Take in my name!" said Mr. Hobson, peremptorily. "It is urgent, say. I must see her at once."

"I will tell madame's maid."

"Do so, and look sharp about it. Don't trouble about me—be off and tell the maid. I know my way;" and Mr. Hobson marched himself into the morning-room.

This room, in the forenoon, was on the shady side of the house—it looked on to a pretty garden, a small, level lawn of intensely green grass, jewelled with flowers. The windows, reaching to the ground, were wide open, and near one was drawn a small round table, on which was set a dainty breakfast-service of pink-and-white china, glistening plate, and crimson roses, standing out in pleasant relief upon the snowy damask.

"Beyond question, madame has a knack of making herself comfortable. I have seldom seen a cosier retreat on a broiling summer's day, and in this dusty, dirty town. She has not breakfasted yet, nor, except for my cup of coffee, have I. I will do myself the pleasure of joining her. A cutlet and a glass of cool claret will suit me admirably just now, and we can talk as we eat."

While he stood there, admiring cynically, Mrs. Wilders came in.

She was in a loose morning wrapper of pale pink, and had seemingly taken little trouble with her day's toilette as yet. Her *negligé* dress hinted at hurry in leaving her room, and she addressed her visitor in a hasty, impatient way.

"What is this so urgent that you come intruding at such an unseemly hour?"

"You grow indolent, my dear madame. Why, it is half-past eleven."

"I have not yet breakfasted."

"So I see. I am delighted. No more have I."

"Was it to ask yourself to breakfast that you came here this morning?"

"Not entirely; another little matter brought me; but we can deal with the two at the same time. Pray order them to serve: I am excessively hungry."

Mrs. Wilders, without answering, pettishly pulled the bell.

"Lay another cover," she told the man, "and bring wine with the breakfast. You will want it, I suppose," she said to her guest; "I never touch it in the morning."

"How charmingly you manage! You have a special gift as a housewife. What a delightful meal! I have seen nothing more refined in Paris."

There was a delicious lobster-salad, a dish of cold cutlets and jelly, and a great heap of strawberries with cream.

"Now get to business," said Mrs. Wilders, in a snarling, ill-tempered way; "let's have it out."

"It's a pity you are out of humour this morning," observed Mr. Hobson, with a provoking forbearance. "I have come to find fault."

Mrs. Wilders shrugged her shoulders, implying that she did not care.

"It may seem ungracious, but I must take you to task seriously. How is it you give me no news?"

"I tell you all I hear; what more do you want?"

"A great deal. Look here, Cyprienne, I am not to be put off with stale, second-hand gossip—the echoes of the Clubs; vague, empty rumours that are on everybody's tongue long before they come to me. I must have fresh, brand-new intelligence, straight from the fountain-head. You must get it for me, or—"

The old frightened look which we have seen on Mrs. Wilders's face before when brought into antagonism with this man returned to it, and her voice was less firm, her manner less defiant, as she said—

"Spare me your threats. You know I am most anxious to oblige you—to help you."

"You have put me off too long with these vague promises. I must have something more tangible at once."

"It is so difficult to find out anything."

"Not if you go the right way to work. A woman of your attractions, your cleverness, ought to be able to twist any man round her finger. You have done it often enough already, goodness knows. Now, there's old Faulks; when did you see him last?"

"Not a week ago."

"And you got nothing out of him? I thought he was devoted to you."

"He is most attentive, most obliging, but still exceedingly wary. He will talk about anything rather than business. I have tried him repeatedly. I have introduced the subject of his nephew, of whom he is now so proud."

"Your enemy, you mean—that young McKay."

"Exactly. I thought that by bringing the conversation to the Crimea I might squeeze out something important. But no! he is always as close as an oyster."

"He will be ready enough to talk about his dear nephew before long. You may look out for some startling news about McKay."

"Really?" said Mrs. Wilders, growing suddenly excited. "Your plan has succeeded, then?"

"Any day you may hear that he has been removed effectually, and for ever, from your path. But for the moment that will keep. What presses is that you should squeeze old Faulks. There is something that I must know to-day, or to-morrow at latest. You must go and see him at once."

"At his office?"

"Why not?"

"But on what pretence? I have never been there as yet. He has always come here to lunch or dine. He is fond of a good dinner."

"Ask him again."

"But I could do that by letter. He may suspect me if I go to him without some plausible excuse."

"Trump up some story about his nephew. Only get to him; he will soon give you an opening you can turn to account. I trust to your cleverness for that; only lose no time."

"Must I go to-day?"

"This very afternoon; directly you leave the house."

CHAPTER IV
IN WHITEHALL

The Military Munitions' department was one of a dozen or more seated at that period in and about Whitehall. Its ostensible functions, as its title implied, were to supply warlike and other stores to the British army when actively engaged. But as wars had been rare for nearly half-a-century it had done more during that time towards providing a number of worthy gentlemen with comfortable incomes than in ministering to the wants of troops in the field.

It was an office of good traditions: highly respectable, very old-fashioned, slow moving, not to say dilatory, but tenacious of its dignity as regards other departments, and obstinately wedded to its own way of conducting the business of the country.

The most prominent personage in the department for some little time before the outbreak of hostilities with Russia, and during the war, was Mr. Rufus Faulks, brother to the Captain Faulks we met on board the *Burlington Castle*, and also uncle to Stanislas McKay.

Mr. Faulks had entered the office as a lad, and, after long years of patient service, had worked his way up through all the grades to the very top of the permanent staff. He had no one over him now but the statesman who, for the time being, was responsible for the department in Parliament—a mere politician, perfectly raw in official routine, who had the good taste and better sense to surrender himself blindly to the guidance of Mr. Faulks. What could a bird of passage know of the deep mysteries of procedure it took a life-time to learn?

He was the true type and pattern of a Government official. A prim, plethoric, middle-aged little man; always dressed very carefully; walking on the tips of his toes; speaking precisely, with a priggish, self-satisfied smirk, and giving his opinion, even on the weather, with the air of a man who was secretly better informed than the rest of the world.

He was very punctual in his attendance at the office, passing the threshold of the private house in a side-street near Whitehall, where the department was lodged all by itself, every morning at eleven, and doing the same thing every day at the same time with the most praiseworthy, methodical precision. His first step was to deposit his umbrella in one corner, his second to hang his hat in another, his third to take an old office-coat out of a bottom drawer in his desk, substituting it for the shiny black frock-coat he invariably wore; then he looked through his letters, selected all of a private and confidential nature, and placing the morning's *Times* across his knees deposited himself in an arm-chair near the fire. He was supposed to be digesting the morning's correspondence, and no one during this the first half-hour of his attendance would have ventured to intrude upon him unsummoned.

It was with a very black face, therefore, that when thus occupied upon the morning that Mr. Hobson visited Mrs. Wilders he saw his own private messenger enter the room.

"What is it, Lightowlar? I have forbidden you to disturb me till twelve."

"Beg pardon, sir; very sorry, sir!" replied the messenger, who had been confidential valet to a Cabinet Minister, and prided himself on the extreme polish of his language and demeanour. "I am aware that you have intimidated your disapprobation of unseasonable interruption, but—"

"Well, well! out with it, or take yourself off."

"Sir 'Umphry, sir; he have just come to the office quite unforseen."

Sir Humphrey Fothergill was the Parliamentary head of the office at this time.

"Sir Humphrey here! What an extraordinary thing!"

The proper time for the appearance of this great functionary was at 4 p.m., on his way to the House and Mr. Faulks felt quite annoyed at the departure from the ordinary rule.

"Sir 'Umphry 'ave took us all aback, sir. His own messenger, Mr. Sprott, was not in the way for the moment, and Sir 'Umphry expressed himself in rather strong terms."

"Serve Sprott right. But what has all that to do with me?"

"Sir 'Umphry, sir, 'ave sent, sir"—the man could hardly bring himself to convey the message; "he 'ave sent, sir, to say he wishes to see you at once."

"Me? At this hour? Impossible!"

This pestilent Sir Humphrey was upsetting every tradition of the office.

Mr. Faulks again settled himself in his arm-chair, with the air of a man who refused to move—out of his proper groove.

"Mr. Faulks! Mr. Faulks!" Another unseemly intrusion. This time it was Sprott, the chief messenger, flurried and frightened, no doubt, by recent reproof. "Sir Humphrey's going on awful, sir; he's rung his bell three times, and asked how long it took you to go upstairs."

Sullenly, and sorely against his will, Mr. Faulks rose and joined his chief.

"I have asked for you several times," said Sir Humphrey Fothergill, a much younger man than Mr. Faulks, new to official life, but a promising party politician, with a great belief in himself and his importance as a member of the House of Commons; "you must have come late."

"Pardon me, I was here at my usual time; but in the thirty-five years that I have had the honour to serve in the Military Munition Department I never remember a Parliamentary chief who came so early as you."

"I shall come when I choose—in the middle of the night, if it suits me or is necessary, as is more than probable in these busy times."

Mr. Faulks waved his hands and bowed stiffly, as much as to say that Sir Humphrey was master of his actions, but that he need not expect to see him.

"You all want stirring up here," said Sir Humphrey abruptly. "It is high time to give you a fillip."

"I am not aware—" Mr. Faulks began, in indignant protest, but his chief cut him short.

"Did you read what happened in the House last night?"

"I have only just glanced at the *Times*," replied Mr. Faulks, in a melancholy voice, thinking how rudely his regular perusal of the great journal had been interrupted that morning.

"It's not pleasant reading. There was a set attack upon this department, and they handled us very roughly, let me tell you. It made my ears tingle."

"We have been abused cruelly—unfairly abused for the last twelve months," said Mr. Faulks with a most injured air.

"You richly deserved it. Amongst you the troops in the Crimea have been dying from starvation, perishing from cold."

"I can assure you that is distinctly unjust. I can assure you great quantities of warm clothing were dispatched in due course."

"Ay, but when?"

"I can't give you the exact dates, but we have been advised of their arrival these last few weeks."

"Warm clothing in May? A very seasonable provision! But it's all of a piece. How about those fuzes?"

"To what do you refer, may I ask?" said Mr. Faulks very blandly; but his blood was boiling at the indignity of being lectured thus by a young man altogether new to the office.

"It is all in this morning's *Times*. The siege is at a standstill; the fuzes won't fit the shells. There are plenty of 10-inch fuzes, but only 13-inch shells. Who is to blame for that?"

"Our ordnance branch, I fear. But it shall be seen to: I will address a communication to the head, calling his attention to the error."

"And when will he get the letter?"

"In the course of the next two or three days."

"And his reply will take about the same time to reach you, I suppose?"

"Probably: more or less."

"Where is the office of the ordnance branch? In this house?"

"Oh, no!" replied Mr. Faulks, in a voice full of profound pity for the lamentable ignorance of his chief. "It is at No. 14."

"Just round the corner—in fact, half-a-dozen yards off?"

"Yes, about that."

"Well, look here, Mr. Faulks: you just put on your hat and go round the corner and see the head of the ordnance branch, and settle all this with him in the next five minutes, d'ye hear?"

"What, I? personally? That would be altogether against precedent and contrary to the rules of the office. I really must decline to introduce such a radical change."

"You will obey my order, this very instant! It is utterly preposterous to waste six days sending letters backwards and forwards about a paltry matter that can be settled by word of mouth in as many minutes. No wonder the troops have died like rotten sheep!"

"I have been five-and-thirty years in this office—" began Mr. Faulks.

"Oh! don't bother me with your historical reminiscences," said Sir Humphrey, cutting him short.

"And never, during all that period—" went on Mr. Faulks, manfully.

"—Have you done anything to-day that could be put off till to-morrow? But now go and see about this at once—do you understand?—and then come back to me; I have other matters to arrange. We have news that a fresh expedition will shortly start for Kertch, and we are requested to send out with all dispatch considerable supplies of salt rations."

"It will be necessary to refer to the Admiralty: they will require proper notice."

"You will get the rations within twenty-four hours, notice or no notice. But we will discuss that by-and-by. Meanwhile, hurry off to the ordnance branch."

Mr. Faulks went to the door, protesting and muttering to himself.

"Stay! one word more! It is wrong of me, perhaps, to hint that your zeal requires any stimulus, Mr. Faulks."

"Hardly, I hope. I have endeavoured for the last five-and-thirty years—"

"Yes, yes, we know all about that. But I have been told that you looked for some special recognition of your services—a decoration, the Order of the Bath—from the last Administration. Now, unless you bestir yourself, don't expect anything of the kind from us."

"I do not pretend to say that I have earned the favour of my Sovereign; but in any case it would depend upon her most gracious Majesty whether—"

"Don't make any mistake about it. You can only get the Bath through the recommendation of your immediate superiors. There's stimulus, if you want it. But don't let me detain you any more."

Mr. Faulks went slowly downstairs, and still more slowly resumed his out-of-door frock-coat; he took up his hat and stick in the same deliberate fashion, and started at a snail's pace for round the corner.

He drawled and dawdled through the business, which five minutes' sharp talk could have ended, and it was nearly lunch-time before he returned to his chief.

"Well, you might have been to the Crimea and back!" said Sir Humphrey, impatiently.

"Matters of such moment are not to be disposed of out of hand. Haste is certain to produce dangerous confusion, and it has been my unvaried experience during five-and-thirty years—"

"Which it has taken you to find the shortest way next door. But there! let us get on with our work. Now, about this expedition to Kertch?"

And Sir Humphrey proceeded to discuss and dispose of great questions of supply in a prompt, off-hand way that both silenced and terrified Mr. Faulks.

CHAPTER V
MR. FAULKS TALKS

Mr. Faulks was rather fond of good living, and, as a rule, he never allowed official cares to interfere with his lunch, a meal brought in on a tray from an eating-house in the Strand. To make a proper selection from the bill of fare sent in every morning was a weighty matter, taking precedence over any other work, however pressing.

But to-day he scarcely enjoyed the haricot of lamb with new potatoes and young peas that he found waiting, and slightly cold, when he went downstairs to his own room.

"For two pins I'd take my retirement; I can claim it; where would they be then?"

This estimable personage shared with thousands the strange superstition that the world cannot do without them.

"This cook is falling off most terribly. The lamb is uneatable, the potatoes are waxy, and the peas like pills. Ugh! I never made a worse lunch!"

A large cigar and the perusal of the long-neglected *Times* did not pacify him much, and he was still fretting and fuming when his messenger brought in a three-cornered note and asked if there was any reply.

"The lady, sir—a real lady, I should think—'ave brought it in her own bruffam, and was most particular, sir, as you should 'ave it at once."

Mr. Faulks took the letter and examined it carefully.

"From that charming woman, Mrs. Wilders, my cousin, or rather Stanny's cousin; but his relations are mine. I am his uncle; some day, if he lives, I shall be uncle to an earl. They will treat me better perhaps when I have all the Essendine interest at my back. Whippersnappers like this Fothergill will scarcely dare to snub me then. A good lad Stanislas; I always liked him. I wish he was back amongst us, and not at that horrid war."

"The lady, sir, is most anxious, sir, to have a answer," put in the messenger, recalling Mr. Faulks's attention to the letter.

"Ah! to be sure. One moment," and he read the note:—

"Cannot I see you?" it said. "I am oppressed with fears for our dear Stanislas. Do please spare me a few minutes of your valuable time.

"Cyprienne W."

"I will go down to her at once, say." And, seizing his hat, Mr. Faulks followed the messenger into the street, where he found Mrs. Wilders in her tiny brougham, at the door of the office.

"Oh, how good of you!" she said, putting out a little hand in a perfectly-fitting grey glove. "I would not disturb you for worlds, but I was so anxious."

"What has happened? Nothing serious, I trust?"

"I do not know. I cannot say. I am terribly upset."

"Do tell me all about it."

"Of course; that is why I came. But it will take some time. Will you get into the carriage? Are you going anywhere? I can take you, and tell you upon the road."

"I am afraid I cannot leave just at present." He had misgivings as to his arbitrary young chief. "But if I might suggest, and if you will honour me so far, will you not come upstairs to my room?"

"Oh! willingly, if you will allow me."

This was all that she wished. Very soon, escorted by her obsequious friend, she found herself in his arm-chair, pouring forth a long and intricate, not to say incomprehensible, story about Stanislas McKay. She had heard, she said—it was not necessary to say how--that they meant to send him on some secret expedition, full of danger, she understood, and she thought it such a pity—so wrong, so unfair!

"He ought really to return to England and take up his proper position," she went on. "Lord Essendine wishes it, and so, I am sure, must you."

"No one will be more pleased to welcome him back than myself," said Mr. Faulks. "I should be glad indeed of his countenance and support just now. They do not treat me too well here."

"Can it be possible!" she exclaimed, in a voice of tenderest interest. "You whom I have always thought one of the most useful, estimable men in the public service."

"Things are not what they were, my dear lady; they do not appreciate me here. They deny me the smallest, the most trifling recognition. Would you believe it that, after five-and-thirty years of uninterrupted service, they still hesitate to give me a decoration? I ought to have had the Companionship of the Bath at the last change of Ministry."

"Of course you ought; I have often heard Lord Essendine say so."

"Has he now, really?" asked Mr. Faulks, much flattered.

"Frequently," went on Mrs. Wilders, fluently, availing herself readily of the opening he had given her. "I am sure he has only to know that you are disappointed in this matter and he will give you the warmest support. You know he belongs to the party now in power, and a word from him—"

"If he will deign to interest himself on my behalf the matter is, of course, settled."

"And he shall, rely on me for that."

"How can I ever thank you sufficiently, dear lady, for your most gracious, most generous encouragement? If I can serve you in any way, command me."

"Well, you can oblige me in a little matter I have much at heart."

"Only name it," he cried, earnestly.

"Come and dine with me to-night in Thistle Grove."

"Is that all? I accept with enthusiasm."

"Only a small party: four at the most. You know I am still in deepest mourning. My poor dear general—" she dropped her voice and her eyes.

"Ah!" said Mr. Faulks, sympathetically; "you have known great sorrows. But you must not brood, dear lady: we should struggle with grief." He took her hand, and looked at her in a kindly, pitying way.

The moment was ill-timed for interruption, but the blame was Sir Humphrey's, who now sent the messenger with a fresh and more imperious summons for the attendance of Mr. Faulks.

He got up hurriedly, nervously, saying—

"I must leave you, dear lady; there are matters of great urgency to be dealt with to-day."

"No apologies: it's my fault for trespassing here. I will run away. To-night—do not forget me, at eight," and Mrs. Wilders took her departure.

The little house in Thistle Grove wore its most smiling aspect at evening, with its soft-shaded lamps, pretty hangings, and quantities of variegated, sweet-smelling flowers; it was radiant with light, full of perfume, bright in colour.

Mrs. Wilders's guests were three—Mrs. Jones, a staid, hard-featured, middle-aged lady in deep black, an officer's widow like herself, as she explained, who lived a few doors down, and was an acquaintance of the last month or two, Mr. Hobson, and Mr. Faulks.

The dinner was almost studied in simplicity, but absolutely perfect of its kind. Clear soup, salmon cutlets, a little joint, salad, and quail in vine-leaves. The only wine was a sound medium claret, except at dessert, when, after the French fashion, Mrs. Wilders gave champagne.

Through dinner the talk had been light and trivial, but with dessert and coffee it gradually grew more serious, and touched upon the topics of the day.

"These must be trying times for you Government officials," said Mr. Hobson, carelessly.

"Yes, indeed," replied Mr. Faulks, with a deep sigh. "I often feel that life is hardly worth having."

"The public service is no bed of roses," remarked Mrs. Jones. "It killed my poor dear husband."

"It is so disheartening to slave day after day as you do," went on Mrs. Wilders to Mr. Faulks, "and get no thanks."

"Very much the other thing!" cried Mr. Hobson; "you are about the best abused people in the world, I should say, just now."

"It is hard on us, for I assure you we do our best. We are constantly, uninterruptedly at work. I never know a moment that I may not be wanted — that some special messenger may not be after me. I have to leave my address so that they can find me wherever I am, and at any time."

"Is it so now?" asked Mrs. Wilders. "Cannot you even give me the pleasure of your society for an hour or two without its being known?"

"I do it in this way, dear lady. I leave a sealed envelope on my hall table, which is only opened in case of urgency."

"You don't expect to be summoned to-night, I hope?" inquired the fair hostess.

"I cannot say; it is quite probable."

"There are, perhaps, important movements intended in the Crimea?" asked Mr. Hobson, as he picked his strawberries and prepared himself a sauce of sugar and cream.

"You have heard so?" replied Mr. Faulks.

"There was something in the *Times* this morning from their special correspondent. Some new expedition was talked of."

"They ought to be all shot, these correspondents," said Mr. Faulks, decisively. "They permit themselves to canvass the conduct and character of persons of our position with a freedom that is intolerable."

"Pardon me," said Mr. Hobson, "but as one of the British public, a taxpayer and bearer of the public burden, I feel grateful to these newspaper gentlemen for seeing that our money is properly spent."

"I am sorry to hear you commend them," said Mr. Faulks, in a way that implied much resentment.

"Well, but without them we should hear of nothing that is going on. This new expedition, for instance, which I have a shrewd suspicion covers some deep design."

"You think so, do you? On what ground, pray?" said Mr. Faulks, with the slight sneer of superior knowledge.

"The *Times* man hints as much. There has long been a rumour of some change in the plan of operations, and he seems to be right in his conjecture."

"He knows nothing at all about it—how can he?" said Mr. Faulks, contemptuously.

"You must forgive my differing with you. It is not my business to say how he obtains his information, but I have generally found that he is right. Now, this great expedition—"

"Is all moonshine!" cried Mr. Faulks, losing his temper, and thrown off his guard. "It's quite a small affair—a trip round the Sea of Azof, and the reduction of Kertch."

"The old affair revived, in fact."

"Neither more nor less. There is no intention at the present moment of drawing any large detachment from the siege. On the contrary, every effort is being strained to bring it to an end."

"Quite right too; it ought to be vigorously prosecuted—attack should follow attack."

"We shall hear of one or more before long," went on Mr. Faulks, growing more and more garrulous. "Our advanced trenches are creeping very near, and I expect any day to hear that the French have stormed the Mamelon, and our people the Quarries."

"Indeed? That is very interesting. And we shall take them—do you think?"

"We must. The attacking columns will be of great strength, and the attack will be preceded by a tremendous cannonade."

"So we may expect great news in the next few days?" said Mrs. Wilders, eagerly.

"More bloodshed!" added Mrs. Jones, with a deep sigh. "This terrible war!"

"You can't make omelettes without breaking eggs," said Mr. Hobson, sententiously. "The more terrible a war is, the sooner it is ended."

"We are getting very ghastly in our talk," said Mrs. Wilders. "Suppose we go into the drawing-room and have some tea."

As they passed out of the dining-room, Mr. Hobson managed to whisper a few words.

"I have squeezed him dry: that was all I wanted to know. I need not stay any longer, I think."

"Who knows? His special messenger may come down with the very latest. If so, you ought to be able to extract that from him too."

Mrs. Wilders spoke these words carelessly; but, as often happens, they correctly foretold what presently occurred.

When they were all seated cosily around the tea-table, Mrs. Wilders's man brought in a great dispatch upon a salver.

"For Mr. Faulks," he said, and with an air of the greatest importance the hard-worked, indispensable official tore open the cover.

It contained a few hurried lines from Sir Humphrey Fothergill to the following effect:—

"A telegram has just been received from Lord Raglan. It contains painful news for you; but I thought it best to let you have it at once."

He opened the telegram with trembling hands and read—

"Yesterday, Mr. McKay, of the quartermaster-general's staff, ventured through the enemy's lines in the direction of the Tchernaya to make a special reconnaissance. He unfortunately was captured. I sent a flag of truce into Sebastopol, asking that he might be exchanged, but have been peremptorily refused. Gortschakoff asserts that he is a Russian subject and was taken red-handed as a spy. He is to be executed immediately. Will renew request with strong protest, but fear there is no hope."

Mr. Faulks groaned heavily and let the telegram fall on the ground.

"What has happened?" asked Mrs. Wilders, eagerly.

"You were right—too right. That poor boy—"

"Stanislas?"

"Yes; my poor nephew has fallen into the hands of these bloodthirsty Russians, who are resolved to execute him as a traitor and a spy."

CHAPTER VI
MARIQUITA'S QUEST

Hyde's unfortunate affair with the sailor had ended in a broken rib and a dislocated arm. He was taken back senseless to the camp of the Royal Picts, and for some days required the closest care. It was nearly a week before he so far recovered himself as to be able to give any account of what had occurred, and longer before he remembered accurately what was taking him to headquarters at the time of the accident.

It flashed across him quite suddenly, and with something of a shock, that while he lay there helpless his friend McKay was still in danger.

"When shall I be able to get about again?" he asked the doctor, anxiously.

"You won't be fit for duty, if that's what you're driving at, for many a long day to come."

"I can go about with my arm in a sling. I am beginning to feel perfectly well otherwise."

"What's the good of a soldier with his arm in a sling? No: as soon as you are fit to move I shall have you sent down to Scutari."

"But I don't want to go: I had much rather stay here with the old corps."

He was thinking of the business he had still in hand.

"You will have to obey orders, anyhow, so make up your mind to go."

The regimental surgeon of the Royal Picts was a morose old Scotchman, very obstinate and intolerant of opposition. What he said he stuck to, and Hyde knew that he must prepare to leave the Crimea in a short time, probably before he was strong enough to go in person to headquarters and find out McKay.

It would be necessary, therefore, to find some other messenger, and, after considering what was best to be done, he resolved to beg Colonel Blythe to come and see him, intending to make him his confidant.

"Well, Rupert," said the Colonel—they were alone together—"this is a bad business. Macinlay tells me you won't be fit for duty for months. He is going to send you at once before a medical board."

"It is very aggravating, Colonel, as I particularly wished to be here for the next few weeks.

"To be in at the death, I suppose? We are bound to take the place at the next attack."

"I hope you may. But it is not that. Our friend McKay is in imminent danger."

"What is the nature of the danger?"

"He is pursued by the relentless hate of an infamous woman: one who has never yet spared any who dared to thwart or oppose her."

"What on earth do you mean, Hyde?" The colonel thought the old sergeant was wandering in his mind. "There are no women out here except Mother Charcoal, and a few French *vivandières*. How can any of them threaten McKay?"

"It is as I say, colonel. By-and-by I will tell you everything. But let me implore you to find out McKay at once and bring him to me. I cannot, you see, go to him."

"Is this very urgent?"

"A matter of life and death, I assure you."

"I will order a horse at once. It is all very mysterious and extraordinary; but then you have been a mystery, Rupert Hyde, a riddle and a puzzle, ever since I have known you."

"It will all be unravelled some day, colonel, never fear; but lose no time, let me beg;" and, thus adjured, the colonel presently mounted his horse and galloped over to headquarters.

He arrived there the day after McKay's excursion into the Russian lines. The young staff-officer was still absent, and fears were already entertained as to his safety, although it was not positively known as yet that he had come to harm.

Let us leave Colonel Blythe and other friends exchanging anxious conjectures as to McKay's fate and return to Mariquita, whose misgivings had steadily increased from the day she had last seen Hyde.

He had promised she should see him again, and, perhaps, Stanislas, without delay. Yet this was more than a week since. What had become of the old soldier? Had he fulfilled his mission of warning, or had he been involved in the dire intrigues that threatened her lover?

Her lover, too; her Stanislas—to save whom she had come so far, braving so many dangers, and at the peril of her maidenly self-respect—had anything happened to him?

The terrible uncertainty was crushing her. She must know something, even the worst, or her apprehensions, ever present and hourly increasing, would kill her.

To whom could she turn in this time of cruel suspense? Hyde had deserted her, seemingly; in spite of her heartfelt anxiety she could not bring herself to approach McKay.

One other man there was; that villain, Benito Villegas—the source, in truth, of all her trouble—might give her news. Bad news, possibly, but still news, if only she could lay hands on him. Where and how was he hiding? Every effort to find him had been fruitless hitherto.

At Valetta Joe's they knew no such name, so they told her when she inquired cautiously for Benito from some of the loafers hanging about the shop.

Yet that was the place to which he was to proceed on arrival. The letter she had picked up in Bombardier Lane said so. He must be hiding, or in disguise; and now, when her anxiety for her beloved Stanislas was at its highest pitch, she was more than ever resolved to find out somehow what Benito was doing.

One afternoon, when business was rather slack at Mother Charcoal's, she seized a chance of visiting the hut-town.

"Any work?" she asked, in Spanish, of Valetta Joe himself, whom she met at the door of his shanty.

"What can you do? Where do you come from? Spain?" replied the baker in the same tongue.

"Yes, from Malaga. I can do anything—try me."

"Can you sell bread through the camp? I am a man short, and could take you on, perhaps, until he is better. Come down below, and I will give you a basketful to hawk about."

"I shall have to tell them at the canteen—Mother Charcoal's—that I am going to leave."

"That won't do. You must come at once if you come at all. Which will you do?"

While she still hesitated, a voice from the subterranean regions at the end of the shop fell upon her ear. Her heart gave a great jump at the sound — it was Benito's. "Joe! Joe!" he was crying, in feeble accents.

"It's take it or leave it. There are plenty of your sort about. Well, what do you say?"

"I accept," said Mariquita, eagerly. "When shall I begin work?"

"Now, this minute. Come down and help me to get a batch of bread out of the oven."

They passed down into the cellar by a short ladder, and Mariquita found herself in a dimly-lighted cavernous den, hot and stifling, at one end of which glowed the grate below the oven.

"Joe! Joe!" repeated Benito's voice, and Mariquita, with difficulty, made out his figure lying on a heap of rags in a corner of the cellar.

"Well?" answered Joe, roughly, as soon as he had pointed out the bread-trays and desired her to get them in order. "What's wrong with you now? You are always groaning and calling out."

"Water!" asked Benito, piteously. "This place is like a furnace. I am suffering torments from raging thirst and this cruel wound. Accursed Englishman! may I live to repay him!"

"You will have to hurry and get well, or the Russians will save you the trouble," remarked Joe.

"That is my only consolation. It was I who gave him to them."

Although bending busily over her task, Mariquita felt her heart beat faster and faster. These words, which she now overheard through such a strange chance, clearly referred to her lover.

"Will they hang him, do you think?" asked Benito.

"As sure as the sun breeds flies. We have done our business too well to give him a chance of escape."

"Would that I might hold the rope, that I might see his agony, his last convulsions! That I might myself revenge the tortures he has made me bear!"

And Benito sank back upon his miserable bed, groaning with pain.

"Don't whine like that, you miserable cur!" said Joe, brutally. "It's bad enough to have you here at all, without your disturbing the whole place. Why did you come here?"

"Where else could I go? I never expected to get so far. I was faint from loss of blood, and in frightful pain. I thought I should die as I crawled along."

"Better you had than bring me into trouble, as you will if the provost-marshal finds you here."

"It is cowardly of you to ill-treat and upbraid me. Take care! I am helpless now, but by-and-by, when I am well and strong, you shall suffer for your cruelty."

"What! you threaten me? But there, it is idle to waste words on such a wretched rogue; I have other work to do. Now, young imp!" cried Joe, turning to Mariquita, "stir yourself, and let us get out this batch of bread."

The conversation which she had overheard, conveying as it did the confirmation of her worst fears, had agitated Mariquita exceedingly, but she knew that she must control her emotion, and arouse no suspicions in the minds of these villains. Benito, wounded, and in desperate case, was in no position to recognise her, and Joe was, of course, completely in the dark as to whom he had admitted within his shop.

The work in the cellar was not completed and the bread carried upstairs for an hour or more, during which time Mariquita was able to think over and decide what she would do. She had matured her plan when they got upstairs.

"Pay me!" she said, saucily, to Valetta Joe. "I shan't stop here."

"Pay you, vile imp? Why, I only took you on trial!"

"Pay me!" she repeated. "You shan't cheat me."

"I owe you nothing. Be off out of this or you shall feel the weight of my hand."

"Pay me, you swindling old rogue!" shouted Mariquita, in a shrill voice. "I won't go till I get my rights."

"You won't!" cried Joe, as he seized her roughly by the collar and dragged her towards the door.

"Villain! Thief! Murder! Help, help! He is killing me!" cried Mariquita, now at the top of her voice, and this frenzied appeal had the exact effect she hoped. A crowd of camp-followers quickly gathered around the door of the shanty, and with it came a couple of stalwart assistants of the provost-marshal.

"What's all this?" asked one of them, in a peremptory tone. "Leave that lad alone, you old rascal!"

"What's he doing to you?" asked the other.

"He won't pay me my wages," said Mariquita, in a whining, piteous voice. "He owes me three shillings."

"I don't, you lying little ragamuffin! I only took you on trial."

"He does; and he was beating me, ill-using me," went on Mariquita.

"We can't have no disturbance here," said one of the provost-marshal's men. "You must come before the provost, both of you; he'll settle your case in a brace of shakes. Bill, you bring the old man; I'll take charge of the youngster."

And the two guardians of order marched their prisoners through the hut-town to a wooden building at the end, where Major Shervinton dealt out a simple, rough-and-ready justice to the turbulent characters he ruled.

This was precisely what Mariquita had hoped for. What she sought at all hazards was to gain speech of the provost-marshal.

They had to wait for him half-an-hour, and when he appeared there were other cases to be dealt with first.

When it came to Valetta Joe's turn, he stoutly denied the charge of defrauding and ill-using the lad.

"I don't know about the wages, sir," said one of the assistants, "but we caught him in the act of cuffing the boy."

"What does he owe you, my lad?" asked Major Shervinton.

"Nothing," replied Mariquita, trembling and in very imperfect English. "I only wanted to get him here to denounce him as a friend of the Russians and a spy."

"There's not a word of truth in what he says!" cried Joe, looking at her with open-mouthed astonishment.

"We have long had our eye upon you, my friend, you know that; and I shall inquire into this more closely."

"At this moment there is a man—his name is Benito Villegas—in the bakehouse below the shop," said Mariquita. "He is wounded; you will find him there. Go and seize him; make him tell you what he has done with the English officer, Mr. McKay."

"Mr. McKay!" said the provost-marshal, deeply interested at once. "He is absent—missing! Have you heard anything of him or his fate?"

"Make Benito tell you. He has betrayed him into the Russians' hands."

"This is very important intelligence. What you say shall be verified at once. See to the prisoners, one of you, and let some one come with me to Joe's shop."

Major Shervinton made short work of Benito.

"Look here, my fine fellow, you had better make a clean breast of it all. What have you done with Mr. McKay?"

Benito shook his head, groaned, and pointed to his wounded arm.

"I see you have been hit; but that won't prevent your talking. Tell me exactly what happened — it's your only chance; if you don't, we will wait till your arm is healed, and then hang you here in the middle of the hut-town. Come, speak out."

"You will spare my life if I tell you?"

"Perhaps: if it is the truth. We shall have means of finding out. But look sharp!"

In feeble, faltering accents Benito told his story, laying stress on the villainy of others and making light of the part he had himself played.

While the provost-marshal was examining the trembling wretch his assistants had been making a thorough search of the shop. They came presently to their chief, laden with a number of papers: letters, passes signed by Gortschakoff, and other documents of a compromising character, plainly proving that this place had long been the centre of a cunningly-devised secret correspondence with the enemy.

"There's enough to hang you both, and perhaps others too, at home. As for you," he turned to Benito, "I will have you removed to the Balaclava hospital. You will be better looked after there, and we shall have you under our hands when required. Your accomplice, the commander-in-chief will deal with, I trust, very summarily; we have overwhelming proofs of his guilt."

Major Shervinton returned to his office, where the prisoners anxiously awaited his verdict.

"Take Joe away, and put a double sentry over him. I shall ride over to headquarters to report the whole case."

"Oh, good, kind, beneficent sir," began Joe, wringing his hands, "spare me! There no word of truth in all this. I done nothing, I swear. I unjustly accused. I—"

"March him out," said Shervinton. "Such vermin as you must be ruthlessly destroyed.

"And the lad, sir?" asked an assistant.

"To be sure; I had forgotten. Well, boy, you have behaved uncommonly well. What shall we do for you?"

"Nothing," she faltered out, "only save him—save Mr. McKay."

"Mr. McKay! Do you know him? What—when—?" asked Major Shervinton, greatly surprised at the agonised accents in which Mariquita spoke, yet more, seeing that her eyes were filled with tears. "Who are you? Where do you come from?" he went on, examining the little creature attentively.

He noticed now for the first time the delicate skin, the clear-cut, regular features, the lustrous, eyes; he remarked the fragile form, the shy, shrinking manner of the lad, who stood diffidently, deprecatingly, before him, and he said to himself, "What an exceedingly handsome boy! Boy!" he repeated, and now suddenly a doubt crossed his mind as to the proper sex of the young person who evinced such a tender interest in Stanislas McKay.

"Some secret romance, probably," he went on, smiling at the thought, but quickly changing his mood as he remembered how tragic its end was likely to be.

"I will do all I can to save him, rest assured," he went on aloud, "and if we recover him from the clutches of the enemy he shall certainly know how much he owes to you."

The vivid blush that overspread her cheeks at these words betrayed her completely.

"But, my poor child," went on the provost-marshal, in a kindly, sympathetic voice, "what are we to do with you? It was madness, surely, for you to venture here. Have you any friends? Let me see you safe back to them. Where do you live?"

Mariquita in a low voice explained that she was employed at Mother Charcoal's.

"Does she know about you?"

"Yes," acknowledged Mariquita, in a still lower, almost inaudible voice.

"She is a good old soul, and may be trusted to take care of you. Still, her canteen is no place for such as you. You shall stay with her, but only till we can send you on to one of the troopships with female nurses on board."

Having thus decided, Shervinton himself escorted Mariquita to Mother Charcoal's, and then rode on to headquarters.

He arrived there half-an-hour after Colonel Blythe, and the news he brought threw fresh light upon the disappearance of poor McKay.

"There is a woman at the bottom of it, of course," said Sir Richard Airey. "These papers prove it," putting his finger upon the bundle Shervinton had seized at the Maltese baker's.

"Two women, unless I'm much mistaken," replied the provost-marshal, and he went on to tell of Mariquita's devotion.

"Devotion, indeed," said the general, "but to no purpose, I fear. We have little hope of saving McKay. Lord Raglan is in despair. Prince Gortschakoff refuses distinctly to surrender the poor fellow, or spare his life."

"One woman's devotion outmatched by another's reckless greed. But, should McKay be sacrificed, she—his murderess—must not escape," said Blythe, hotly.

"Ah! but how shall we lay hands on her? Who knows her?" asked Sir Richard.

"One of my officers—Hyde. We shall get her through him," and Blythe repeated what the old quartermaster had said that morning.

"Yes, he evidently knows. He would be the best man to pursue her—to bring her to judgment for her villanies. There is enough in these papers to convict her. But he could hardly leave the Crimea just now."

"He happens at this moment to be going down to Scutari, on sick leave: he could easily go on."

"Is he strong enough?"

"He is gaining strength daily; it is only a wounded arm."

"That will be best. I will arrange with Lord Raglan to give him leave, provided he will accept the mission."

Without further delay Blythe went back to his camp and told Hyde all that had occurred.

"Go! Of course I will go. This very day, if the doctor will let me. I will unmask her; I will spoil her game. If I cannot save Stanislas, at least she shall not benefit by her crime."

"You are sure you can find her?"

"Trust me! People in her position are easily found. The first Court Guide will give you her address. She holds her head high, and must pay the penalty of greatness."

The prospect of starting soon for England on such an errand seemed to restore Hyde to energy and strength.

"Not fit to travel!" he said to the doctor, who still expressed some doubts on that head. "Why, I am fit for anything."

"Nonsense, man! You won't be able to use your arm for weeks."

"I shan't want it. My head's sound and clear; that's the chief thing. The moment I get my leave and my orders, I'm off."

They gave Hyde a passage home in the *Himalaya*, a man-of-war transport, and at that time one of the swiftest steamers afloat. At the most, the journey would not occupy more than twelve days or a fortnight. He might not be able or in time to do much for Stanislas in his present peril, but he at least hoped that retribution might follow fast on the betrayal of his friend.

CHAPTER VII
INSIDE THE FORTRESS

It is time to return to Stanislas McKay, whose life, forfeited under the ruthless laws of a semi-barbarous power, still hung by a thread.

He had been taken into Sebastopol by his escort at a rapid pace. It was a ride of half-a-dozen miles, no more, and the greater part of it, when once they regained the Tchernaya, followed the low ground that margins both sides of the river.

McKay could see plainly the English cavalry vedettes in the plain; but, fast bound as he was, it was impossible for him to make any signal to his friends. It was as well that he could not try, for he would certainly have paid the penalty with his life.

They watched him very closely, these wild, unkempt, half-savage horsemen; watched him as though he were a captive animal—a beast of prey which might at any time break loose and rend them.

But the rough uncivilised Cossacks of the Don were not bad fellows after all.

Although they at first looked askance at him when he spoke to them, these simple boors were presently won over by the distress and sufferings of their prisoner.

McKay was in great pain; his bonds cut into his flesh, he was exhausted by the night's work, dejected at the ruin of his enterprise, uneasy as to his fate.

No food had crossed his lips for many hours, his throat was parched and dry under the fierce heat of the sun.

He begged piteously for water, speaking in Russian, and using the most familiar style of address. The men who rode on each side of him soon thawed as he called them "his little fathers," and implored them to give him a drink.

"Presently, at the first halt," they said.

And so he had to battle with his thirst while they still hurried on.

Suddenly the officer in command called a halt—they had now reached the picket-house at Tractir Bridge—and rode out to the flank of the party. He seemed perturbed, anxious in his mind, and raised his hand to shroud his eyes as he peered eagerly across the plain.

"Here!" he shouted, rising in his stirrups and turning round. "Bring up the prisoner."

McKay was led to his side.

"What is the meaning of that?" asked the officer haughtily, speaking in French, as he pointed to a cloud of dust in the distant plain.

"How can I tell you?" replied McKay, shortly: but in his own mind he was certain that this was the contemplated extension of the French and Sardinian lines towards the Tchernaya. For a moment his heart beat high with the hope that this movement might help him to escape.

"You know, you rogue! Tell me, or it will be the worse for you."

"I don't know," replied McKay stoutly; "and if I did I should not tell you."

"Dirty spy! You would have sold us for a price, do the same now by the others. You owe them no allegiance; besides, you are in our power. Tell me, and I will let you go."

"Your bribe is wasted on me. I am a British officer—"

"Pshaw! Officer?" and the fellow raised his whip to strike McKay, but happily held his hand.

"Here! take him back," he said angrily, and McKay was again placed in the midst of the party.

He renewed his entreaties for a drink, and a Cossack, taking pity on him, offered him a canteen.

It was full of *vodkhi*, an ardent spirit beloved by the Russian peasant, half-a-dozen drops of which McKay managed to gulp down, but they nearly burned his throat.

"Water! water!" he asked again.

And the Cossack, evidently surprised at his want of taste, substituted the simpler fluid; but the charitable act drew down upon him the displeasure of his chief.

"How dare you! without my permission?" cried the officer, as he dashed the water from McKay's lips, and punished the offending Cossack by a few sharp strokes with his whip.

"Come, fall in!" the officer next said. "It won't do to linger here." And the party resumed their ride, still in the valley, but as far as possible from the stream.

Every yard McKay's hopes sank lower and lower; every yard took him further from his friends, who were advancing, he felt certain, towards the river. Large bodies of troops, columns of infantry on the march, covered by cavalry and accompanied by guns, were now perfectly visible in the distant plain.

"Look to your front!" cried the Russian officer peremptorily to Stanislas, as he stole a furtive, lingering glance back. "Faster! Spur your horses, or we may be picked up or shot."

All hope was gone now. This was the end of the Tchernaya valley. Up there opposite were the Inkerman heights, the sloping hills that a few months before McKay had helped to hold. This paved, much-worn causeway was the "Sappers' Road," leading round the top of the harbour into the town.

No one stopped the Cossacks.

They passed a picket in a half-ruined guard-house, the roof of which, its door, walls, and windows, were torn and shattered in the fierce and frequent bombardments. Even at that moment a round shot crashed over their heads, took the ground further off, and bounded away. The sentry asked no questions. Some one looked out and waved his hand in greeting to the Cossack officer, who replied, pointing ahead, as the party rode rapidly on.

Time pressed; it promised to be a warm morning. The besiegers' fire, intended no doubt to distract attention from the movements in the Tchernaya, was constantly increasing.

"What dog's errand is this they sent me on?" growled the Cossack officer, as a shell burst close to him and killed one of the escort.

"Faster! faster!"

And still, harassed by shot and shell, they pushed on.

All this time the road led by the water's edge; but presently they left it, and, crossing the head of a creek, mounted a steep hill, which brought them to the Karabel suburb, as it was called, a detached part of the main town, now utterly wrecked and ruined by the besiegers' fire.

The Cossack officer made his way to a large barrack occupying a central elevated position, and dismounted at the principal doorway.

"Is it thou, Stoschberg?" cried a friend who came out to meet him. "Here, in Sebastopol?"

"To my sorrow. Where is the general? I have news for him. The enemy are moving in force upon the Tchernaya."

"Ha! is it so? And that has brought you here?"

"That, and the escort of yonder villain—a rascally spy, whom we caught last night in our lines."

"Bring him along too; the general may wish to question him."

McKay was unbound, ordered to dismount, and then, still under escort, was marched into the building. It was roofless, but an inner chamber had been constructed—a cellar, so to speak—under the ground-floor, with a roof of its own of rammed earth many feet thick, supported by heavy beams. This was one of the famous casemates invented by Todleben, impervious to shot and shell, and affording a safe shelter to the troops.

McKay was halted at the door or aperture, across which hung a common yellow rug. The officers passed in, and their voices, with others, were heard in animated discussion, which lasted some minutes; then the one called Stoschberg came out and fetched McKay.

He found himself in an underground apartment plainly but comfortably furnished. In the centre, under a hanging lamp, was a large table covered with maps and plans, and at the table sat a tall, handsome man, still in the prime of life. He was dressed in the usual long plain great-coat of coarse drab cloth, but he had shoulder-straps of broad gold lace, and his flat muffin cap lying in front of him was similarly ornamented. This personage, an officer of rank evidently, looked up sharply, and addressed McKay in French.

"What is the meaning of this movement in the Tchernaya?" he asked. "You understand French of course? People of your trade speak all tongues."

"I speak French," replied McKay, "but English is my native tongue. I am a British officer—"

"I have told you of his pretensions, Excellency," interposed the Cossack officer.

"Yes, yes! this is mere waste of time. What is the meaning of this movement in the Tchernaya, I repeat? Tell me, and I may save your life."

"You have no right to ask me that question, and I decline to answer it, whatever the risk."

"An obstinate fellow, truly!" said the general, half to himself. "What do you call yourself?"

Then followed a conversation very similar to that which had taken place at Tchorgoun.

"I, too, knew your father," said the general, shaking his head. "It is a bad case; I fear you must expect the worst."

"I shall meet it as a soldier should," replied McKay, stoutly. "But I shall always protest, even with my dying breath, that I have been foully and shamefully used. I appeal to you, a Russian officer of high rank, of whose name I am ignorant—"

"My name is Todleben, of the Imperial Engineers."

McKay started, and, notwithstanding the imminent peril of his position, looked with interest upon the man who was known, even in the British lines, as the heart and soul of the defence.

"I appeal to you, sir," he pleaded, "as a general officer, a man of high honour and known integrity, to protect me from outrage."

"I can do nothing," replied Todleben, gravely, shrugging his shoulders. "The Prince himself will decide. Take him away. I cannot waste time with him if he is not disposed to speak. Let him be kept a close prisoner until the Prince is ready to see him."

The general then bent his head over his plans, and took no further notice of McKay.

Our hero was again marched into the yard, made to remount, re-bound, and led off towards the principal part of the town. They now skirted the ridge of the Karabel suburb, and began to descend. Half way down they came upon a series of excavations in the side of the hill. These were old caves that had been enlarged and strengthened with timbers and earth. Each had its own doorway, a massive piece of palisading. They were used as barracks, casemated, and practically safe during the siege. Into one of these McKay was taken; it was empty; the men who occupied it were on duty just then at the Creek Battery below. In one corner lay a heap of straw and old blankets, filthy, and infested with the liveliest vermin.

One of the escort pointed to this uninviting bed, and told the prisoner he might rest himself there. McKay, weary and disconsolate, gladly threw himself upon this loathsome couch. They might shoot him next morning, but for the time at least he could forget all his cares in sleep.

CHAPTER VIII
FROM THE DEAD

We have seen how the news of Stanislas McKay's capture by the Russians was communicated to his uncle, Mr. Faulks.

Next day the brief telegram announcing it was published in the morning papers, with many strong comments. Although some blamed the young officer for his rashness, and others held Lord Raglan directly responsible for his loss, all agreed in execrating the vindictive cruelty of the uncompromising foe.

General sympathy was expressed for Mr. McKay; the most august person in the land sent a message of condolence to his mother through Lord Essendine, who added a few kindly words on his own account.

"What curse lies heavy on our line? It seems fatal to come within reach of heirship to the family-honours. Ere long there will be no Wilders left, and the title of Essendine will become extinct," wrote the old peer to Mrs. McKay. "Your boy, a fine, fearless young fellow, whom I neglected too long and who deserved a nobler fate, is the latest victim. Pray Heaven he may yet escape! I will strive hard to help him in his present dire peril."

Lord Essendine was as good as his word. He had great influence, political and diplomatic: great friends in high place at every court in Europe. Among others, the Russian ambassador at Vienna was under personal obligations to him of long standing, and did not hesitate when called upon to acknowledge the debt.

Telegrams came and went from London to Vienna, from Vienna to St. Petersburg, backwards and forwards day after day, yet nothing was effected by Lord Essendine's anxious, energetic advocacy. The Czar himself was appealed to, but the Autocrat of All the Russias would not deign to intervene. He was inexorable. The law military must take its course. Stanislas McKay was a traitor and the son of a traitor; he had been actually taken red-handed in a new and still deeper treachery, and he must suffer for his crime.

At the end of the first fortnight McKay's relations and friends in England had almost abandoned hope. This was what Mr. Faulks told Mrs. Wilders, who called every day two or three times, always in the deepest distress.

"Poor boy! poor boy!" she said, wringing her hands. "To be cut off like this! It is too terrible! And nothing—you are sure nothing can be done to save him?"

"Lord Essendine is making the most strenuous efforts; so are we. Even Sir Humphrey Fothergill has been most kind; and the War Minister has repeatedly telegraphed to Lord Raglan to leave no stone unturned."

"And all without effect? It is most sad!" She would have feigned the same excessive grief with the Essendine lawyers, to whom she also paid several visits, but the senior partner's cold eye and cynical smile checked her heroics.

"You will not be the loser by poor McKay's removal," he said, with brutal frankness, one day when she had rather overdone her part.

"As if I thought of that!" she replied, with supreme indignation.

"It is impossible for you not to think of it, my dear madam. It would not be human nature. Why shouldn't you? Mr. McKay was no relation."

"He was my dear dead husband's devoted friend. Nursed him after his wound—"

"I remember to have heard that, and indeed everything that is good, of Mr. McKay. I feel sure he would have made an excellent Earl of Essendine; more's the pity."

"I trust my son, if he inherits, will worthily maintain the credit of the house."

"So do I, my dear madam," said old Mr. Burt, with a bow that made the speech a less doubtful compliment.

"When will it be settled? Why do they hesitate? Why delay?" she said to herself passionately, as she went homewards to Thistle Grove. Her friend Mr. Hobson was there, waiting for her; and she repeated the question with a fierce anxiety that proved how closely it concerned her.

"How impatient you grow! Like every woman. Everything must be done at once."

"I am not safe yet. I begin to doubt."

"Can't you trust me? I have assured you it will end as you wish. When have I disappointed you, Lady Lydstone?"

She started at the sound of this name, once familiar, but surrounded now by memories at once painful and terrible.

"It is the rule in your English peerage that when a son becomes a great peer, and the mother is only a commoner, to give her one of the titles. Your Queen does it by prerogative."

"I might have been Lady Lydstone by right, if I had waited," she said slowly.

"And you repent it? Bah! it is too late. Be satisfied. You will be rich, a great lady, respected—"

She made a gesture of dissent.

"Yes; respected. Great ladies always are. You can marry again—whom you please; me, for instance—"

Again the gesture: dissent mixed with unmistakable disgust.

"You are not too flattering, Cyprienne. Do not presume on my good-nature, and remember—"

"What, pray?"

"What you owe me. I am entitled to claim my reward. You must repay me some day."

"By marrying you?"

Her voice, as usual, began to tremble when she found herself in antagonism with this man.

"If that be the price I ask. Why not? We ought to be happy together. We have so much in common, so many secrets—"

"Enough of this!" she said shortly, but not bravely.

"And to be Lady Lydstone's husband would give me a certain status—a sufficient income. I could help you to educate the boy, whom, by-the-way, I have never seen. Yes; the notion pleases me. I will be your second—I beg your pardon, your third husband, probably your last."

"I must beg of you, Hippolyte, to be careful; I hear some one coming."

It was the Swiss butler, who entered rather timidly to say a gentleman had called on important business.

"What business? Surely you have not admitted him? If so, you shall leave my service. You know it is contrary to my express orders."

"He said you would see him, madam; that he came on the part of a friend, a very ancient friend, whose name I had but to tell you—"

"What name? Go on, François."

"The name—it is difficult. Ru—" he spoke very slowly, struggling with the strangeness of the sounds. "Ru—pert—Gas—"

"Who can this be?" Mrs. Wilders had turned very white and now beckoned Hobson to step out into the garden. "Is it a message from beyond the grave?"

"Coward!" cried her companion contemptuously. "The Seine seldom surrenders its prey. Rupert Gascoigne is dead—drowned, as you know, fourteen years ago."

"But this visitor knew him—he knows of my connection with him. Else why come in his name? Oh, Hippolyte, I tremble! Help me. Support me in my interview with this strange man."

"No; it would not be safe. If he knew Rupert Gascoigne, he may, too, have known Ledantec. I will not meet him."

"Who is the coward now?"

"I do not choose to run unnecessary risks. But I will help you—to this extent. See the man, if you must see him, in the double drawing-room. I will be within call."

"And earshot? I understand."

"Well, what can I overhear—about you, at least—that I do not know already? In any case I could help you."

It was so arranged. Mrs. Wilders bade her servant introduce the stranger, and presently joined him in the adjoining room.

"Mr. Hyde," she began, composedly and very stiffly, "may I inquire the meaning of this intrusion? You are a perfect stranger—"

"Look well at me, Cyprienne Vergette. Have years so changed me—?"

"Rupert? Impossible!" she half-shrieked. "Rupert is dead. He died—was drowned—when—"

"You deserted him, and left him, you and your vile partner, falsely accused of a foul crime."

"I cannot—will not believe it. You are an impostor; you have assumed a dead man's name."

"My identity is easily proved, Cyprienne Vergette, and the relation in which I stand to you."

"What brings you here to vex me, after all these years? I always hated you. I left you—Why cannot you leave me in peace?"

"God knows I had no wish to see or speak to you again. The world was wide enough for us both. We should have remained for ever apart, but for your latest and foulest crime."

"What false, lying charge is this you would trump up against me?"

"The murder of my dearest friend and comrade. Murder twice attempted. The first failed; the second, I fear, will prove fatal. If so, look to yourself, madam."

"What can you do?" she said, impudently, having regained much of her old effrontery.

"Prevent you from reaping the fruits of your iniquity. You know you were never General Wilders's wife; you were always mine. Worse luck!"

"You cannot prove it. You are dead. You dare not reappear."

"Wait and see," he replied, very coolly.

"You have no proofs, I say, of the marriage."

"They are safe at the Mairie, in Paris. French archives are carefully kept. I have only to ask for a certificate; it's easy enough."

"For any one who could go there. But how will you dare to show yourself in Paris? You are proscribed; a price is set on your head. Your life would be forfeited."

"I will risk all that, and more, to ruin your wicked game."

"Do so at your peril."

"You threaten me, vile wretch? Be careful. The measure of your iniquity is nearly full. Punishment must soon overtake you; your misdeeds are well known; your complicity with—"

Why should he tell her? Why warn her of the net that was closing round her, and thus help her to escape from the toils?

But she had caught at his words.

"Complicity?" she repeated, anxiously. "With whom?"

"No matter. Only look to yourself. It is war, war to the knife, unquenchable war between us, remember that."

And with these words he left the house.

Although she had shown a bold front, Mrs. Wilders, as we shall still call her, was greatly agitated by this stormy scene, and it was with a blanched cheek and faltering step that she sought her confederate in the next room.

Mr. Hobson was gone.

"Coward! he has easily taken alarm. To desert me at the moment that I most need advice and help!"

But she did her friend injustice, as a letter that came from him in the course of a few hours fully proved.

"I heard enough," wrote Mr. Hobson, "to satisfy me that the devil is unchained and means mischief. I never thought to see R. G. again. We must watch him now closely, and know all his movements. If he goes to Paris, as I heard him threaten, he will give himself into our hands. I shall follow, in spite of the risks I run. One word of warning to the Prefecture will put the police on his track. Arrest, removal to Mazas, Cayenne, or by the guillotine—what matter which?—will be his inevitable fate. The French law is implacable. His *dossier* (criminal biography) is in the hands of the authorities, and will be easily produced. There must be numbers of people still living in Paris who could identify him at once, in spite of his beard and bronzed face. I can, if need be, although I would rather not make myself too prominent just now. Be tranquil; he will not be able to injure us. It is his own doom that he is preparing."

CHAPTER IX
IN PARIS

Years had passed since Hyde—he was Rupert Gascoigne then—had last been in Paris. The memory of that last sojourn and the horrors of it still clung to him—his arrest, unjust trial, escape. His bold leap into the swift Seine, his rescue by a passing river steamer, on which, thanks to a plausible tale, in which he explained away the slight flesh-wound he had received from the gendarme's pistol, he found employment as a stoker, and so got to Rouen, thence to Havre and the sea.

Willingly he would never have returned to the place where he had so nearly fallen a victim. But he was impelled by a stern sense of duty; he came now as an avenging spirit to unmask and punish those who had plotted against him and his friend—unscrupulous miscreants who were a curse to the world.

He took up his quarters in a large new hotel upon the Boulevards.

Paris had changed greatly in these years. The Second Empire, with its swarm of hastily-enriched adventurers, had already done much to beautify and improve the city. Life was more than ever gay in this the chief home of pleasure-seekers. Luxury of the showiest kind everywhere in the ascendant; smart equipages and gaily-dressed crowds, the shop-fronts glittering with artistic treasures, everyone outwardly happy, and leading a careless, joyous existence.

Englishmen, officers especially, were just now welcome guests in Paris. Mr. Hyde, of the Royal Picts, as he entered himself upon the hotel register, with his soldierly air, his Crimean beard, and his arm in a sling, attracted general attention. He was treated with extraordinary politeness everywhere by the most polite people in the world. When he asked a question a dozen answers were ready for him—a dozen officious friends were prepared to escort him anywhere.

But Rupert Hyde wanted no one to teach him his way about Paris. Within an hour of his arrival, after he had hastily changed the garments he had worn on the night journey, had sallied forth, and, entering the long Rue Lafayette, made straight to the headquarters of the 21st *arrondissement*.

Urgent business of a public nature had brought him to Paris, but this was a private matter which he desired to dispose of before he attended to anything else.

The place he sought was easily found. It was a plain gateway of yellowish-white stone, over which hung a brand-new tricolour from a flag-staff fixed at an angle, and on either side a striped sentry-box containing a *Garde de Paris*.

The gateway led into a courtyard, in which were half-a-dozen loungers, clustered chiefly around the entrance to a handsome flight of stone steps within the building.

Just within this second entrance was a functionary, half beadle, half hall-porter, wearing a low-crowned cocked hat and a suit of bright blue cloth plentifully adorned with buttons, to whom Hyde addressed himself.

"The office of M. the Mayor, if you please."

"Upstairs; take the first turn to the right, and then —"

"But surely I know that voice!" said some one behind Hyde, who had turned round quickly.

"What, you!" went on the speaker; "my excellent English comrade — here in Paris! Oh, joyful surprise!"

"Is it you? M. Anatole Belhomme, of the Voltigeurs? You have left the Crimea? Is Sebastopol taken? the Russians all massacred, then?"

"It is I who was massacred — almost. I received a ball, here in my leg, and was invalided last month. But you also have suffered, comrade." And Anatole pointed to Hyde's arm in a sling.

"Nothing much. Only the kick of a horse; it does not prevent me moving about, as you see."

"But what brings you to Paris, my good friend?"

"I am seeking some family documents — to substantiate an inheritance. They are here in the archives of the Mairie."

"How? You were seeking the office of M. the Mayor? You?" And M. Anatole proceeded to scrutinise Hyde slowly and minutely from head to foot. "You, a veteran with your arm in a sling, and that brown beard — brown mixed with grey. It is strange — most strange."

"Well, comrade," replied Hyde, laughing a little uneasily, "you ought to know me again."

"Lose no time, friend, in getting what you want from the Mairie. Come: I will go with you. Come: you may be prevented if you delay."

These words aroused Hyde's suspicions. Had Cyprienne warned the French police to be on the look-out for him?

"But, Anatole, explain. Why do you lay such stress on this?" he asked.

"Do as I tell you—first, the papers. I will explain by-and-by."

There was no mistaking Anatole, and Hyde accordingly hastened upstairs. Anatole indicated the door of an antechamber, which Hyde entered alone. It was a large, bare room, with a long counter—inside were a couple of desks, and at them sat several clerks—small people wielding a very brief authority—who looked contemptuously at him over their ledgers, and allowed him to stand there waiting without the slightest acknowledgment of his existence for nearly a quarter of an hour.

"I have come for a certificated extract from the registers of a civil marriage contracted here on the 27th April, 184—" he said, at length, in a loud, indignant voice.

The inquiry had the effect of an electrical shock. Two clerks at once jumped from their stools; one went into an inner room, the other came to the counter where Hyde stood.

"Your name?" he asked, abruptly. "Your papers, domicile, place of birth, age. The names of the parties to the contract of marriage."

Hyde replied without hesitation, producing his passport, a new one made out in the name of Hyde, describing his appearance, and setting forth his condition as an officer in Her Britannic Majesty's Regiment of Royal Picts.

While he was thus engaged, an elderly, portly personage, wearing a tricolour sash which was just visible under his waistcoat, came out from the inner room, and, taking up the passport, looked at it, and then at Hyde.

"Is that your name? Yes? It is different," he went on, audibly, but to himself, "although the description tallies. You are an English officer, domiciled at the Hôtel Impérial, Boulevard de la Madeleine. I do not quite understand."

"Surely it is only a simple matter!" pleaded Hyde. "Monsieur, I seek a marriage certificate."

"For what purpose?"

"As a claim for an inheritance."

"Nothing more, eh!" said the Mayor, suspiciously. "Have you any one, any friend, who will answer for you, here?"

"No one nearer than the British Embassy, except—to be sure—" he suddenly thought of Anatole, who still waited outside, and who came in at the summons of his friend.

"Oh, you are with Monsieur?" The official's face brightened the moment he saw Anatole. "It is all right, then. Give the gentleman the certificate. This friend"—he laid the slightest stress on the word—"will be answerable for him, of course."

"Now, Anatole, tell me what all this means," said Hyde, as he left the Mairie with the document he deemed of so much importance in his pocket.

"Not here," said the Frenchman, looking over his shoulder, nervously. "Let us go somewhere out of sight."

"The nearest wine-shop—I have not breakfasted yet, have you? A bottle of red seal would suit you, I dare say," said Hyde, remembering Anatole's little weakness.

"It is not to be refused. I am with you, comrade. At the sign of the 'Pinched Nose' we shall find the best of everything," replied Anatole, heartily, and the pair passed into the street.

It was barely a dozen yards to the wine-shop, and they walked there arm-in-arm in boisterous good-fellowship, elbowing their way through the crowd in a manner that was not exactly popular.

"Take care, imbecile!" cried one hulking fellow whom Anatole had shouldered off the path.

"Make room, then," replied our friend, rudely.

"Would you dare—" began the other, in a menacing voice, adding some words in a lower tone.

"Excuse. I was in the wrong," said Anatole, suddenly humbled.

"You are right to avoid a quarrel," remarked Hyde, when they were seated at table. He had been quietly amused at his companion's easy surrender.

"I could have eaten him raw. But why should I? He is, perhaps, a father of a family—the support of a widowed mother: if I had destroyed him they might have come to want. No; let him go."

"All the same, he does not seem inclined to go. There he is, still lurking about the front of the shop."

"Truly? Where?" asked Anatole, in evident perturbation. "Bah! we will tire him of that. By the time we have finished a second bottle—"

"Or a third, if you will!" cried Hyde, cheerfully.

They had their breakfast—the most savoury dishes; ham and sour crout, tripe after the mode of Caen, rich ripe Roquefort cheese, and had disposed of three bottles of a rather rough but potent red wine, before Anatole would speak on any but the most common-place topics. The Crimea, the dreadful winter, the punishment administered to their common enemy, occupied him exclusively.

But with the fourth bottle he became more communicative.

"You owe a long candle to your saint for your luck to-day in meeting me," he said, with a slight hiccup.

"Ah! how so?"

"Had not I been there to give you protection you would now be under lock and key in the depôt of the Prefecture."

Hyde, in spite of himself, shuddered as he thought of his last detention in that unsavoury prison.

"What, then, have you done, my English friend?" went on Anatole, with drunken solemnity. "Why should the police seek your arrest?"

"But do they? I cannot believe it."

"It is as I tell you. I myself am in the 'cuisine' (the Prefecture). Since my return from the war my illustrious services have been rewarded by an appointment of great trust."

"In other words, you are now a police-agent, and you were set to watch for some one like me."

"Why not you?" asked Anatole, trying, but in vain, to fix him with his watery eyes. "In any case," he went on, "I wish to serve a comrade—at risk to myself, perhaps."

"You shall not suffer for it, never fear, in the long run. Count always upon me."

"They may say that I have betrayed my trust; that I put friendship before duty. That has always been my error; I have too soft a heart."

Anatole now began to cry with emotion at his own chivalrous self-sacrifice, which changed quickly into bravado as he cried, striking the table noisily—

"Who cares? I would save you from the Prefect himself."

At this moment the big man who had been watching at the window returned, accompanied by two others. He walked straight towards the door of the wine-shop.

"*Sacré bleu! le patron* (chief). You are lost! Quick! take me by the throat."

Hyde jumped to his feet and promptly obeyed the curious command.

"Now struggle; throw me to the ground, bolt through the back door," whispered Anatole, hastily.

All which Hyde executed promptly and punctiliously. Anatole suffered him to do as he pleased, and Hyde escaped through the back entrance just as the other policemen rushed in at the front.

"After him! Run! Fifty francs to whoever stops him!"

But Hyde had the heels of them. He ran out and through a little courtyard at the back communicating with the street. There he found a *fiacre*, into which he jumped, shouting to the cabman—

"Drive on straight ahead! A napoleon for yourself."

In this way he distanced his pursuers, and half-an-hour later regained his hotel by a long detour.

Rather agitated and exhausted by the events of the morning, Hyde went upstairs to his own room to rest and review his situation.

"It is quite evident," he said to himself, "that Cyprienne has tried to turn the tables on me. I was too open with her. It was incautious of me to show my hand so soon. Of course the police have been set upon me—the accused and still unjudged perpetrator of the crime in Tinplate Street—by her. But has she acted alone in this?

"I doubt it. I doubt whether she would have come to Paris with that express purpose, or whether the police would have listened to her if she had.

"But who assisted her? Some one from whom she has no secrets. Were it not that such a woman is likely to have set up the closest relations with other miscreants in these past years, I should say that her agent and accomplice was Ledantec. Ledantec is still alive; I know that, for I saw him myself on the field of the Alma, rifling the dead.

"Ledantec! We have an old score to settle, he and I. What if he should be mixed up in this business that brings me to Paris? It is quite likely. That would explain his presence in the Crimea, which hitherto has seemed so strange. I never could believe that so daring and unscrupulous a villain had degenerated into a camp-follower, hungry for plunder gained in the basest way. It could not have been merely to prey upon the dead that he followed in the wake of our army. Far more likely that he was a secret agent of the enemy. If so then, so still, most probably. What luck if these damaging clues that I hold should lead me also to him!

"But it is evident that I shall do very little if I continue to go about as Rupert Hyde. The police are on the alert: my movements would soon be interfered with, and, although I have no fear now of being unable to prove my innocence, arrest and detention of any kind might altogether spoil my game.

"I must assume some disguise, and to protect myself and my case I will do so with the full knowledge of the Embassy. It will do if I go there within an hour. By this evening at latest the police will certainly be here after Rupert Hyde."

It must be mentioned here that the police of Paris are supposed to be acquainted with the names of all visitors residing in the city. The rule may be occasionally relaxed, as now, but under the despotism of Napoleon III. it was enforced with a rigorous exactitude.

Hyde had been barely half-a-dozen hours in Paris, but already his name was inscribed upon the hotel-register awaiting the inspection of the police, who would undoubtedly call that same day to note all new arrivals.

Before starting for the Embassy, Hyde sat down and wrote a couple of rather lengthy letters, both for England, which he addressed, and himself posted at the corner of the Rue Royale.

Thence he went on, down the Faubourg St. Honoré, not many hundred yards, and soon passed under the gateway ornamented with the arms of Great Britain, and stood upon what, by international agreement, was deemed a strip of British soil.

He saw an *attaché*, to whom he quickly explained himself.

"You wish to pursue the investigation yourself, I gather? Is it worth while running such a risk? Why not hand over the whole business to the

Prefecture? I believe they have already put a watch upon the persons suspected."

"I have no confidence in their doing it as surely as I would myself."

Hyde, it will be understood, had his own reasons for not wishing to present himself at the Prefecture.

"You propose to assume a disguise? As you please; but how can we help you?"

"By giving me papers in exchange for my passport, which you can hold, and by sending after me if I do not reappear within two or three days."

"You anticipate trouble, then; danger, perhaps."

"Not necessarily, but it is as well to take precautions."

"Is there anything else?"

"Yes; I should like to bring my disguise and put it on here. In the porter's lodge, a back office—anywhere."

The *attaché* promised to get the ambassador's permission, which was accorded in due course, and that same afternoon Hyde entered the Embassy a well-dressed English gentleman, and came out an evil-looking ruffian, wearing the blue blouse and high silk cap of the working classes. One sleeve of the blouse hung loose across his chest, as though he had lost his arm, but his injured limb was safe underneath the garment. His beard was trimmed close, and on either side of his forehead were two great curls, plastered flat on the temple, after the fashion so popular with French roughs.

In this attire he plunged into the lowest depths of the city.

Amongst the papers seized at the Maltese baker's in Kadikoi were several that gave an address in Paris. This place was referred to constantly as the headquarters of the organisation which supplied the Russian enemy with intelligence, and at which a certain mysterious person—the leading spirit evidently of the whole nefarious company—was to be found.

"I'll find out all about him and his confederates before I'm many hours older," said Hyde, confidently, as he presented himself at the porter's lodge of a tall, six-storied house, of mean and forbidding aspect, close to the Faubourg St. Martin. It was let out in small lodgings to tenants as decayed and disreputable as their domicile.

"M. Sabatier?" asked Hyde, boldly, of the porter.

"On the fifth floor, the third door to the right," was the reply.

Hyde mounted the stairs and knocked at the door indicated.

"Well?" asked an old woman who opened it.

"The patron—is he here? I must speak to him."

"Who are you? What brings you?" The old woman still held the door ajar, and denied him admission.

"I have news from the Crimea—important news—from the Maltese."

"Joe?" asked the old woman, still suspicious.

Hyde nodded, and said sharply—

"Be quick! The patron must know at once. You will have to answer for this delay."

"He is absent—come again to-morrow," replied the old woman, sulkily.

"It will be worse for him—for all of us—if he does not see me at once."

"I tell you he is absent. You must come again;" and with that the woman shut the door in his face.

What was Hyde to do now? Watch outside? That would hardly be safe. The police, he knew, were on the look-out already, and they would be suspicious of any one engaged in the same game.

There was nothing for it but to take the old woman's reply for truth and wait till the following day. Hyde knew his Paris well enough to find a third-class hotel or lodging-house suitable for such a man as he now seemed, and here, after wandering through the streets for hours, dining at a low restaurant and visiting the gallery of a theatre, he sought and easily obtained a bed.

Next day he returned to the Faubourg St. Martin and was met with the same answer. The patron was still absent.

Hyde was beginning to despair; but he resolved to wait one more day, intending, if still unsuccessful, to surrender the business to other hands.

But on the third day he was admitted.

"The patron will see you," said the old woman, as she led him into a small but well-lighted room communicating with another, into which she passed, locking the door behind her.

They kept him waiting ten minutes or more, during which he had an uncomfortable feeling he was being watched, although he could not tell exactly how or from where.

There was really a small eye-hole in the wall opposite, of the kind called in French a "Judas," and such as is used in prisons to observe the inmates of the cells. Through this, Hyde had been subjected to a long and patient examination.

It was apparently satisfactory; for presently the inner door was unlocked, and the old woman returned, followed by a man whom we have seen before.

It was Mr. Hobson in person; Ledantec really, as Hyde immediately saw, in spite of the smug, smooth exterior, the British-cut whiskers, and the unmistakable British garb.

"Here is the patron," said the old woman; "tell him what you have to say."

Hyde, addressing himself to Mr. Hobson, began his story in the most perfect French he could command. He spoke the language well, and had no reason to fear that his accent would betray him.

"The patron speaks no French," put in the old woman. "You ought to know that. Tell me, and I will interpret."

Mr. Hobson played his part closely, that was clear. A Frenchman by birth, he could hardly be ignorant of or have forgotten his own tongue.

Hyde, following these instructions, told his story in the briefest words. How Valetta Joe had been seized, his shop ransacked, and many compromising papers brought to light.

"Ask him how he knows this," said Mr. Hobson quietly.

"My brother has written to me from the Crimea. He was in the camp when the baker was seized."

"What is his brother's name?"

"Eugène Chabot, of the 39th Algerian battalion."

This was a name given in the papers seized.

"Was it he who gave this address? How did the fellow come here? Ask him that."

"Yes," Hyde said; he had learned the patron's address from his brother, who had urged him to come and tell what had happened without a moment's delay.

Mr. Hobson, *alias* Ledantec, had listened attentively to this friendly message as it was interpreted to him bit by bit, but without betraying the slightest concern. Suddenly he changed his demeanour.

"*Ecoutez-moi!*" he cried in excellent French, looking up and darting a fierce look at the man in front of him. "Listen! You have played a bold game and lost it. You did not hold a sufficiently strong hand."

Hyde stood sullenly silent and unconcerned, but he felt he was discovered.

"In your charming and for the most part veracious story there is only one slight mistake, my good friend."

"I do not understand."

"I will tell you. Eugène Chabot, your brother?—yes; your brother. Well, he could not have written to you as you tell me—"

"But I assure you—"

"For the simple reason, that, just one week before the seizure of Valetta Joe, Chabot was killed—in a sortie from the enemy's lines."

"Impossible! I—"

"Have been lying throughout and must take the consequences. You have thrust your head into the lion's jaw. Hold!"

Seeing that Hyde had thrust his one hand beneath his blouse, seeking, no doubt, for some concealed weapon, Hobson suddenly struck a bell on the table before him.

Four men rushed in.

"Seize him before he can use his arm! Seize him, and unmask him!"

The ruffians, laying violent hands on Hyde, tore off his blouse and dragged the wig with its elaborate curls from his head. In the struggle he gave a sharp cry of pain. They had touched too roughly the still helpless arm which hung in its sling beneath the blouse.

"Ah! I knew I could not be mistaken. It is you, then, Rupert Gascoigne! I thought I recognised you from the first, although it is years and years since we met."

"Not quite, villain! Cowardly traitor, murderer, despoiler of the dead!"

"What do you mean by that?"

"That I saw you at your craven work just after the Alma; you ought to have been shot then. The world would have been well rid of a miscreant."

"Pretty language, truly, Mr. Gascoigne! I must strive to deserve it."

"What are you going to do with me?"

"I am not sure. Only do not hope for mercy. You know too much. I might make away with you at once—"

"But why spill blood?" he went on, musing aloud. "The guillotine will do your business in due course if I hand you over to the law. That will be best, safest; the most complete riddance, perhaps."

There was a pause.

"You see you are altogether in my power," said Ledantec, "either way. But I am not unreasonable. I am prepared to spare you—for the present," he said, with an evil smile—"only for the present, and according as you may behave."

"On what conditions will you spare me—for the present?" asked Hyde, elated at the unexpected chance thus given him.

"Tell me how you came to know of this address. Who sent you here?"

"Valetta Joe, the Maltese baker at Kadikoi."

"Describe him to me," asked Ledantec, to try Hyde.

Hyde had seen Joe more than once in his rides through the hut-town, and his answer was perfectly satisfactory.

"Did he send any message?"

"Just what I have told you. I was to let you know of his arrest and of the danger you would run."

Ledantec was deceived by the straightforward and unhesitating way in which Hyde told his story.

"It may be so. At any rate, the warning must not be despised. Whether or not you are to be trusted remains to be seen. But I will keep you safe for a day or two longer and see what turns up. In any case you cannot do much mischief to Cyprienne while shut fast here."

"Cyprienne?" said Hyde, quite innocently.

"I am quite aware of one reason that brought you to Paris, but, as I have said, you cannot well execute your threats so long as we hold you tight."

Hyde shook his head as though these remarks were completely unintelligible. But he laughed within himself at the thought that he had already outwitted both Cyprienne and her accomplice, and that, wherever he was, a prisoner or at large, events would work out her discomfiture without him.

He had no fears for himself. They had promised him at the British Embassy that he should be sought out if he did not reappear within three days. Besides, the French police had their eyes on the house. The tables would presently be turned upon his captors in a way that they little expected.

When, therefore, he was led by Ledantec's orders into a little back room dimly lighted by a window looking on to a blank wall, he went like a lamb. But physically he was not particularly comfortable; there were pleasanter ways of spending the day than tied hand and foot to the legs of a bedstead, and Ledantec's farewell speech was calculated to disturb his equanimity.

"Don't make a sound or a move, mind. If you do—" and he produced a glittering knife, with a look that could not be misunderstood.

CHAPTER X
SUSPENSE

McKay must have slept for many hours. Daylight was fading, and the den he occupied was nearly dark, when he was aroused by the voices of his Russian fellow-lodgers coming off duty for the night.

They were rough, simple fellows most of them: boorish peasants torn from their village homes, and forced to fight in their Czar's quarrel, which he was pleased to call a holy war. Coarse, uncultivated, but not unkindly, and they gathered around McKay, staring curiously at him, and plying him with questions.

His command of their language soon established amicable relations, and presently, when supper was ready, a nauseous mess of *kasha*, or thick oatmeal porridge, boiled with salt pork, they hospitably invited him to partake. He was a prisoner, but an honoured guest, and they freely pressed their flasks of *vodkhi* upon him when with great difficulty he had swallowed a few spoonfulls of the black porridge.

They talked, too, incessantly, notwithstanding their fatigue, always on the same subject, this interminable siege.

"It's weary work," said one. "I long for home."

"They will never take the place; Father Todleben will see to that. Why do they not go, and leave us in peace?"

"It is killing work: in the batteries day and night; always in danger under this hellish fire. This is the best place. You are better off, comrade, than we" (this was to McKay); "for you are safe under cover here, and in the open a man may be killed at any time."

"He has dangers of his own to face," said the under-officer in charge of the barrack, grimly. "Do not envy him till after to-morrow."

McKay heard these words without emotion. He was too wretched, too much dulled by misfortune and the misery of his present condition, to feel fresh pain.

Yet he slept again, and was in a dazed, half-stupid state when they fetched him out next morning and marched him down to the water's edge, where he was put into a man-of-war's boat and rowed across to the north side of the harbour.

Prince Gortschakoff, the Russian commander-in-chief, had sent for him, and about noon he was taken before the great man, who had his headquarters in the Star Fort, well out of reach of the besiegers' fire.

The Prince, a portly, imposing figure, of haughty demeanour, and speaking imperiously, accosted McKay very curtly.

"I know all about you. Whether you are spy or traitor matters little: your life is forfeited. But I will spare it on one condition. Tell me unreservedly what is going on in the enemy's lines."

"I should indeed deserve your unjust epithets if I replied," was all McKay's answer.

"What reinforcements have reached the allies lately?" went on the Prince, utterly ignoring McKay's refusal, and looking at him fiercely. "Speak out at once."

Our hero bore the gaze unflinchingly, and said nothing.

"We know that the French Imperial Guard have arrived, and that many new regiments have joined the English. Is an immediate attack contemplated?"

McKay was still silent.

"Ill-conditioned, obstinate fool!" cried the Prince, angrily. "It is your only chance. Speak, or prepare to die!"

"You have no right to press me thus. I refuse distinctly to betray my own side."

"Your own side! You are a Russian—it is your duty to tell us. But I will not bandy words with you. Let him be taken back to a place of safety and await my orders."

Once more McKay gave himself up for lost. When he regained the wretched casemate that was his prison he hardly hoped to leave it, except when summoned for execution.

But that day passed without incident, a second also, and a third. Still our hero found himself alive.

Had they forgotten him? Or were they too busily engaged to attend to so small a matter as sending him out of the world.

The latter seemed most probable. Another bombardment, the most incessant and terrible of any that preceded it, as McKay thought. Although hidden away, so to speak, in the bowels of the earth, he plainly heard the continuous cannonade, the roar of the round-shot, the murderous music of the shells as they sang through the air, and presently exploded with tremendous noise.

He was to have a still livelier experience of the terrible mischief caused by the ceaseless fire of his friends.

Late in the afternoon of the fourth day he was called forth, always in imminent peril of his life, and taken round the head of a harbour which was filled with men-of-war, past the Creek Battery, and up into the main town. They halted him at the door of a handsome building, greatly dilapidated by round-shot and shell. This was the naval library, the highest spot in Sebastopol, a centre and focus of danger, but just now occupied by the chiefs of the Russian garrison.

McKay waited, wondering what would happen to him, and in a few minutes narrowly escaped death more than once. First a shell burst in the street close to him, and two bystanders were struck down by the fragments; then another shell struck a house opposite, and covered the neighbouring space with splinters large and small; next a round-shot tore down the thoroughfare, carrying everything before it.

It was no safer inside than out. Yet McKay was glad when they marched him in before the generals, who were seated at the open window of the topmost look-out, scanning the besiegers' operations with their telescopes.

"What is the meaning of this fire? Have you any idea?" It was Todleben who asked the question. "Does it prelude a general attack?"

"I cannot tell you," replied McKay.

"Was there no talk in the enemy's lines of an expected assault?" asked another.

"I do not know."

"You must know. You are on the headquarter-staff of the British army."

"Who told you so? You have always denied my claim to be treated as an English officer."

"Because you are a traitor to your own country. But it is as I say. We know as a fact that you belong to Lord Raglan's staff; how we know it you need not ask."

The fact was, of course, made patent by the English commander-in-chief, in his repeated attempts to secure McKay's release and exchange. But the prisoner had been told nothing of these efforts, or of the peremptory refusal that had met Lord Raglan's demands.

"I told you it would be no use," interrupted a third. "He is as obstinate as a mule."

"Stay! what is that?" cried Todleben, suddenly. "Over there, in the direction of the Green Mamelon."

Three rockets were seen to shoot up into the evening sky.

"It is some signal," said another. "Yes; heavy columns are beginning to climb the slopes away there to our left."

"And the British troops are collecting in front of the Quarries."

At this moment the besiegers' fire, which had slackened perceptibly, was re-opened with redoubled strength.

"Let everyone return to his station without delay," said Todleben, briefly. "A serious crisis is at hand. The attack points to the Malakoff, which, as you all know, is the key of our position."

"Hush!" said one of the other generals, pointing to McKay.

"What matter?" replied Todleben. "He can hardly hope to pass on the intelligence."

But the words were not lost upon our hero, although he had but little time then to consider their deep meaning.

"What shall we do with the prisoner?" asked his escort.

"Take him back to his place of confinement."

McKay's heart was lighter that evening than it had been at any time since his capture. He remembered now that this was the 7th of June, the day settled for the night attack upon the Mamelon and Quarries, and he hoped that if these succeeded, as they must, they would probably be followed by a further assault upon the principal inner defences of the town.

He spent the evening and the greater part of the night in the deepest agitation, hoping hourly, momentarily, for deliverance.

None came, no news even; but that the struggle was being fought out strenuously he knew from the absence of the men that occupied his casemate, all of whom were doubtless engaged. But towards daylight one or two dropped in who had been wounded and forced to retire from the batteries. From them he learnt something of what had occurred.

The French had stormed the works on the left of the Russian front, and had carried them once, twice, three times. The Russians had returned again and again to recover their lost redoubts, but had been obliged to surrender them in the end.

In the same way the English had attacked the ambuscades—what we call the Quarries—and between night and dawn the Russians had made four separate attempts to recover what had been lost at the first onslaught.

"And now it is over?"

"No one can say. We have suffered fearfully; we are almost broken down. If the enemy presses we shall have to give up the town."

"Pray God they may come on!" cried McKay, counting the moments till relief came.

But bitter disappointment was again his portion. The day grew on, and, instead of renewed firing, perfect quiet supervened. There was a truce, he was told, on both sides, to bury the dead.

Now followed several dreary days, when hope had sunk again to its lowest ebb, and all his worst apprehensions revived. It was like a living death; he was a close prisoner, and never a word reached him that any of his friends were concerning themselves with his miserable fate.

Again there came a glimpse of hope. Surely there was good cause: in the renewal of the bombardment, which, after an interval of a few days, revived with yet fiercer intention and unwavering persistence.

Surely this meant another—possibly the final—and supreme attack?

The firing continued without intermission for four days. It was increased and intensified by an attack of the allied fleet upon the seaward batteries. This new bombardment made itself evident from the direction of the sounds, and the merciless execution of the fiery rockets that fell raging into the town.

At length, in the dead of night, McKay was aroused from fitful sleep by the beating of drums and trumpets sounding the assembly.

It was a general alarm. Troops were heard hurrying to their stations from all directions, and in the midst of it all was heard—for a moment there had been a lull in the cannonade—a sharp, long-sustained sound of musketry fire.

Evidently an attack, but on what points it was made, and how it fared, McKay at first could have no idea. But, as he listened anxiously to the sounds of conflict, it was clear that the tide of battle was raging nearer to him now than on any previous occasion.

He waited anxiously, his heart beating faster and faster, as each minute the firing grew nearer and nearer. He was in ignorance of the exact nature of the attack until, as on the last occasion, the Russian soldiers came back by twos and threes and re-entered the casemate.

"What is going on in the front?" McKay asked.

"The enemy are advancing up the ravine. We have been driven out of the cemetery, and I doubt whether we shall hold our ground."

"They are coming on in thousands!" cried a new arrival. "This place is not safe. Let us fall back to the Karabel barrack."

"You had better come too," said one soldier thoughtfully to McKay, as he gathered up the long skirts of his grey great-coat to allow of more expeditious retreat.

"All right," said McKay, "I will follow."

And taking advantage of the confusion, during which the sentries on the casemate had withdrawn, he left his prison-chamber and got out into the main road.

The fusilade was now close at hand; bullets whistled continually around and pinged with a dull thud as they flattened against the rocky ground.

The assailants were making good progress. McKay, as he crouched below a wall on the side of the road, could hear the glad shouts of his comrades as, with short determined rushes, they charged forward from point to point.

His situation was one of imminent peril truly, for he was between two fires. But what did he care? Only a few minutes more, if he could but lie close, and he would be once more surrounded by his own men.

While he waited the dawn broke, and he could watch for himself the progress the assailants made. They were now climbing along the slopes of the ravine on both sides of the harbour, occupying house after house, and maintaining a hot fire on the retreating foe. It was exciting, maddening; in his eagerness McKay was tempted to emerge from his shelter and wave encouragement to his comrades.

Unhappily for him, the gesture was misunderstood. The crack of half-a-dozen rifles responded promptly, and a couple of them took fatal effect. Poor Stanislas fell, badly wounded, with one bullet in his arm and another in his leg.

CHAPTER XI
AMONG FRIENDS AGAIN

McKay lay where he fell, and it was perhaps well for him that he was prostrate. The attacking parties soon desisted from firing, and charged forward at racing-pace, driving all who stood before them at the point of the bayonet. They swept over and past McKay, trampling him under foot in their hot haste to demolish the foe.

But the wave of the advance left McKay behind it, and well within the shelter of his own people.

Although badly wounded, he was not disabled, and he took advantage of the first pause in the fight to appeal for help to some men of the 38th who occupied the wall behind which he fell.

"You speak English gallows well for a Rooskie," said one of the men, brusquely, but not without sympathy. "What do you want? Water? Are you badly hit?"

"A bullet in my leg and a flesh-wound in my arm."

"Hold hard! Sawbones will be up soon. Meanwhile, let's try and staunch the blood. We'll tear up your shirt for a bandage."

And with rough but real kindness he tore open McKay's old *greggo* so as to get at his underlinen. This action betrayed the red cloth waistcoat he still wore.

"Why, that's an English staff waistcoat. Quick! How did you come by it, you murdering rogue?"

"I am a staff officer."

"You! What do you call yourself?"

"Mr. McKay, of the Royal Picts: deputy-assistant-quartermaster-general at headquarters."

"Save us alive! This bangs Bannagher. Wait, honey — wait till I call an officer."

Presently, when the wounds had been rudely but effectively bound up, a captain of the 38th came up, and to him McKay made himself known.

"This is no time or place to ask how you came here. Taken prisoner, I suppose?"

"Who are you? What force?"

"Eyre's Brigade: of the Third Division. Told off to attack the Creek Battery. We have carried the cemetery, but what else we've done I have not the least idea."

"Haven't you? Well, I'll tell you. You've taken Sebastopol."

"Not quite, I'm afraid."

"You're well inside the fortress anyway. I can tell you that for certain. Just above is the place in which I was kept a prisoner."

"Is that a fact? By Jove! what tremendous luck!"

"But can you hold your ground?"

"Eyre will. He'll hold on by his eyelids till reinforcements come up, never fear. And the French have promised us support."

"Is yours the only attack?"

"Dear no! The French have gone in at the Malakoff, and our people at the Redan."

"How has it gone—have you any idea?" asked McKay, anxiously.

"No one knows, except the general, perhaps. Here he comes; and he don't look over pleased."

General Eyre, a tall, fierce-looking soldier, strode up with a long step, talking excitedly to a staff-officer, whom McKay recognised as one of Lord Raglan's aides-de-camps.

"Hold our ground!" the general was saying. "Of course we will, to the last. But if the French could only come up in force we might still retrieve the day. You see we are well inside, though I cannot say exactly where."

At this moment the officer who had been speaking to McKay touched his hat and said to the general—

"There is some one here who can tell you, I think, sir."

"Who is that? A prisoner?"

"One of our own people. McKay, of the headquarter staff. A man whom the Russians took, and whom we have just recovered."

"McKay!" cried the aide-de-camp, joyfully. "Where is he?"

Our hero was speedily surrounded by a group of sympathetic friends, to whom he gave a short account of himself. Then he briefly explained to the general the position in which they were.

"It is as I thought," said the general. "We have pierced the Russian works above the man-of-war harbour, and, if reinforced promptly, can take the whole of the line in reverse. Will you let Lord Raglan know? and the attack might then be renewed on this side."

"I fear there is no hope of that," said the aide-de-camp, gloomily.

"Have we failed, then?" asked McKay.

His friend shook his head.

"Completely. I cannot tell why exactly, but I know that part of the French started prematurely. There was some mistake about the signal-rocket. This gave the alarm to the whole garrison."

"Yes; I heard them turning out in the middle of the night."

"And the consequence was they were ready for us at all points. Our attacking parties at the Redan were met with a tremendous fire, and literally mowed down. Our losses have been frightful. All the generals—Sir John Campbell, Lacy, yea, and Shadford—are killed, and ever so many more. It's quite heartbreaking."

"And will nothing more be tried to-day?"

"I fear not, although Lord Raglan is quite ready; but the French are very dispirited. Goodness knows how it will end! The only slice of luck is Eyre's getting in here; but I doubt if he can remain."

"Why not?"

"The enemy's fire is too galling, and it appears to be on the increase."

"I fancy they are bringing the ships' broadsides to bear."

"Yes, and we are bound to suffer severely. But you, McKay; I see you are wounded. We must try and get you to the rear."

"Never mind me," said McKay, pluckily; "I will take my chance and wait my turn."

The chance did not come for many hours. Eyre's brigade continued to be terribly harassed; they were not strong enough to advance, yet they stoutly refused to retire. The enemy's fire continued to deal havoc amongst them; many officers and men were struck down; General Eyre himself was wounded severely in the head.

All this time they waited anxiously for support, but none appeared. At length, as night fell, Colonel Adams, who had succeeded Eyre in the command, reluctantly decided to fall back.

The retreat was carried out slowly and in perfect order, without molestation from the enemy. Now at last the wounded were removed on stretchers as carefully and tenderly as was possible.

McKay's hurts had been seen to early in the day. He was placed as far as possible out of fire, and his strength maintained by such stimulants as were available.

While the excitement lasted his pluck and endurance held out. But there was a gradual falling-off of fire as the night advanced, and the pains of his wounds increased. He suffered terribly from the motion as he was borne back to camp, and when at last they reached the shelter of a hospital-tent in the Third Division camp he was in a very bad way: fits of wild delirium alternated with death-like insensibility.

But he was once more amongst his friends. Next morning Lord Raglan, notwithstanding his heavy cares and preoccupation, sent over to inquire after him.

Many of the headquarter-staff came too, and Colonel Blythe was constantly at his bedside.

On the second day the bullet was removed from the leg, and from that moment the symptoms became more favourable. Fever abated, and the wounds looked as though they would heal "at the first intention."

"He will do well enough now," said the doctor in charge of the case; "but he will want careful nursing—better, I fear, than he can get in camp."

"Why not send him on board a hospital ship? Could he bear the journey to Balaclava?"

"Undoubtedly. I was going to suggest it."

"There is the *Burlington Castle*, his own uncle's ship: she is now fitted up as a hospital, with nurses and every appliance. He will soon get well on board her."

There were other and still more potent aids to convalescence on board the *Burlington Castle*. A band of devoted female nurses tended the sick; and amongst them, demurely clad in a black dress, her now sad white face half hidden under an immense coif, was one who answered to the name of Miss Hidalgo.

It was Mariquita, placed there by the kindness of the military authorities, anxious to make all the return possible by helping in the good work. The relationship of the captain to Stanislas was remembered by Colonel Blythe, and the *Burlington Castle* seemed the fittest place to receive the poor girl.

Good Captain Faulks had been taken into the secret.

"Poor child!" he had said. "I will watch over her for dear Stanny's sake. I was fond of that lad, and she shall be like a daughter to me."

At first she seemed quite dazed and stupefied by her grief. She gave up her lover as utterly lost, and would not listen to the consolation and encouragement offered.

"He'll turn up, my dear," said Captain Faulks; "you'll see. He was not saved from drowning to die by a Russian rope. Wait; he'll weather the storm."

Mariquita would shake her head hopelessly and go about her appointed task with an unflagging but despairing diligence that was touching to see.

Uncle Barto, as he always wished her to call him, was the first to tell her the good news.

"He's found, my dear. What did I tell you? They couldn't keep him; I knew that."

"The Holy Virgin be praised!" cried Mariquita. "But is he well—uninjured? When shall we see him?"

"Soon, my dear, soon. He will be brought—I mean he will-come on board in a few days now."

A simple pressure of the hand, a half-whispered exclamation of joy in her own fluent Spanish, was the only greeting that Mariquita gave her wounded lover when they lifted him on to the deck of the hospital-ship. But the vivid blush that mantled in her cheek, and the glad light that came into her splendid eyes, showed how much she had suffered, and how great was her emotion at this moment of trial.

As for Stanislas, he was nearly speechless with surprise.

"You here, Mariquita! What strange adventure is this? Tell me at once—"

"No, no," interposed the doctor; "it is a long story. You are tired now, and will have plenty of time to hear from Miss Hidalgo all about herself."

It was the telling of this story as she sat by the side of his couch, hand locked in hand, and he learnt by degrees the full measure of her self-sacrificing devotion, that did McKay so much good. It braced and strengthened him, giving him a new and stronger desire to live and enjoy the unspeakable blessing of this true woman's love.

They would have been altogether happy, these long days of convalescence, but for his enforced absence from his duties, and the distressing news that came from the front.

Lord Raglan had never recovered from the disappointment of the 18th of June. The failure of the attack, and the loss of many personal friends, preyed upon his spirits, and he suddenly became seriously ill. He never rallied, sank rapidly, and died in a couple of days, to the great grief of the whole army.

No one felt it more than McKay, to whom the sad news was broken by his old chief.

"It is very painful to think," said Sir Richard Airey, "that he passed away at the moment of failure; that he was not spared to see the fortress fall—for it must fall."

"Of course it must, sir," said McKay. "This last attack ought to have succeeded. The Russians were in sore straits."

"It was the French who spoiled everything by their premature advance. I knew we could do nothing until they had taken the Malakoff. That is the key of the position."

"You are right, sir. I myself heard Todleben say those very words."

"Did you? That is important intelligence. It must not be forgotten when the time comes to organise a fresh attack."

"I shall be well then, I hope, sir, and able to go in with the first column. I think I could show the way."

"At any rate you can say more than most of us, for you have been actually inside the place."

"And shall be again, if you will only wait another month!" cried McKay.

But the doctors laughed at him when he talked like this.

"You will not be able to put your foot to the ground for three months or more, and then you must make up your mind to crutches for another six."

"I shall not see the next attack, then?"

"No; but you will see England before many weeks are gone. We are going to send you home at once."

"But I had much rather not go—" began McKay.

"It's no use talking; everything is settled."

And so it came to pass. The good ship *Burlington Castle*, Bartholomew Faulks, master, having filled up its complement of invalids and wounded men, including Captain Stanislas McKay, steamed westward about the middle of July.

CHAPTER XII
IN LINCOLN'S INN

Ledantec, *alias* Hobson, had at once reported progress to Mrs. Wilders. The day after his arrival in Paris she had heard from him. He wrote—

"Have no fears. The police are on his track. They have his exact description, and are watching at the Mairie. Directly he shows himself he will be arrested as Rupert Gascoigne, tried, condemned. They do these things well in France. You will never hear of him again."

There was much to quiet and console her in these words. After the dreadful surprise of Rupert's reappearance she had been a prey to the keenest anxiety. The whole edifice, built up with such patient, unscrupulous effort, had threatened to crumble away. Bitter disappointment seemed inevitable just when her highest hopes were nearest fulfilment.

But now, thanks to her unscrupulous confederate, the staunch friend who had stood by her so often before, the last and worst difficulty was removed, and everything would be well.

Another day passed without further intelligence from Paris, but Ledantec's silence aroused no fresh apprehensions. Doubtless there was nothing special to tell; matters were progressing favourably, of course; until her husband was actually arrested, she could expect to hear nothing more.

On the evening of the third day, however—that, in fact, following Gascoigne's visit to the Mairie—she had a short letter from Lincoln's Inn. Lord Essendine's lawyers wrote her, begging she would call on them early next day, as they had an important communication to make to her. His lordship himself would be present, and their noble client had suggested, if that would suit her, an appointment for twelve noon.

"At last! They mean to do the right thing at last," she said, exultingly. "The proud old man is humbled; he fears the extinction of his ancient line, and must make overtures now to me. My boy is the heir; they cannot resist his rights; his claim is undeniable. He shall be amply provided for; I shall insist on the most liberal terms."

Fully satisfied of the cause of her summons to Lincoln's Inn, Mrs. Wilders presented herself punctually at twelve. Although she still schooled her face to sorrowful commiseration with the old peer whom fate had so sorely stricken, the elation she felt was manifest in her proud, arrogant carriage, and the triumphant glitter of her bold brown eyes.

Lord Essendine was with the senior partner, Mr. Burt, when she was shown in; and although he arose stiffly, but courteously, from his seat, did not take her outstretched hand, while his greeting was cold and formal in the extreme.

There was a long pause, and, as neither of the gentlemen spoke, Mrs. Wilders began.

"You sent for me, my lord—"

His lordship waved his hand toward Mr. Burt, as though she must address herself to the old lawyer.

"Mrs. Wilders," said Mr. Burt, gravely and with great deliberation— "Mrs. Wilders, if that indeed be your correct appellation—"

And the doubt thus implied, reviving her worst fears, sent a cold shock to her heart.

But she was outwardly brave.

"How dare you!" she cried with indignant defiance in her tone. "Have you only brought me here to insult me? I appeal to your lordship. Is this the treatment I am to expect? I, your cousin's widow—"

"One moment, madam," interposed the lawyer. "To be a widow it is first necessary to have been a wife."

"Do you presume to say I was not General Wilders's wife?" she asked hotly.

"Not his lawful wife. Stay, madam," he said, seeing Mrs. Wilders half rise from her chair. "You must hear me out. We have evidence, the clearest seemingly; disprove it if you can."

"What evidence?"

"The certificate of your other marriage. It is here."

"How came you by it?" she inquired eagerly.

"No matter, it is all in proper form; you could not contest it, understand."

"Well? I never pretended when I gave my hand to Colonel Wilders that I had not been married before. He was well aware of it."

"But not that your first husband was alive at the time."

"It is false! He was dead—drowned; he drowned himself in the Seine."

"Your first husband is alive still, and you know it. You have seen him yourself within these last few days. He is ready to come forward at any time. It is he in fact who has furnished us with these proofs."

"I shall protest, dispute, contest this to the uttermost. It is a base, discreditable plot against a weak, helpless, defenceless woman," said Mrs. Wilders with effrontery; but despair was in her heart.

How Ledantec has deceived her!

"Is that all you have to say to me?" she went on at length after another pause. "You, Lord Essendine—my husband's relative and friend, one of the richest and proudest men in this purse-proud land—how chivalrous, how brave of you, to bring me here to load me with vile aspersions, to rob me of my character; my child, my little friendless orphan boy, of the inheritance which is his by right of birth!"

"Do not let us get into recriminations, madam," said Lord Essendine, speaking for the first time. "It is to speak of your boy, mainly, that I wished for this interview."

"Poor child!"

"Whatever blot may stain his birth, I cannot forget that he has Wilders's blood in his veins. He is Cousin Bill's son still."

"You admit so much? Many thanks," she sneered. "And since these heavy blows have struck us, blow after blow, he is the sole survivor of the house. I am willing—nay, anxious—to recognise him."

"Indeed! How truly generous of you!" There was no telling whether the speech was genuine, or another sneer.

"He cannot bear the title, but I can make him my heir. He may succeed to the position in due course—I hardly care how soon."

"Are you mocking me, Lord Essendine?"

"I am in sober earnest. I will do what I say, but only on one condition."

"And that is?"

"That you give up the child, absolutely, and forever."

"What! part with the only thing left me to love and cherish—"

"One moment, madam," interposed the lawyers "before your emotion overpowers you. We happen to be able to judge of the extent of your affection for your only son."

"How so?"

"We know you care so little for him that for month, you never see the child. It was left in England when you went to the Crimea—"

"With my husband. Besides, I could not have made a nursery of Lord Lydstone's yacht."

"And since you settled in London you have sent it to a nurse in the country."

"It was better for the child."

"No doubt you know best. However, this discussion is unnecessary. Will you comply with his lordship's conditions, and part with the child?"

"Never!"

"Remember, the offer will not be renewed."

"And what, pray, would become of me? You deprive me of everything—present joy in my offspring, his affection in coming years. I shall be alone, friendless—a beggar, perhaps."

"As to that, you must trust to his lordship's generosity."

"Little as you deserve it," added Lord Essendine, meaningfully.

She turned on him at once.

"Of what do you accuse me?"

"Of much that I forbear to repeat now. But I will spare you—I will leave you to your own conscience and—"

"What else, pray?"

"The law. It may seize you yet, madam, and it has a tight grip."

"I shall not remain here to be so grossly insulted. If you have anything more to say to me, my lord, you must write."

"And you refuse to give up the child?"

"You had better put your proposals on paper, Lord Essendine. I may consider them in my child's interests, although the separation would be almost too bitter to bear. I may add, however, that I will consent to nothing that does not include some settlement on myself—"

"As to that," said the lawyer, "his lordship declines to bind himself—is it not so, my lord?"

"Quite; I will make no promises. But she will not find me ungenerous if she will accept my terms."

And so the interview ended. There was no further reference made to the unpleasant facts now brought to light by the letter and documents sent over by Hyde. Mrs. Wilders, as we shall still call her, knew that she could not dispute them; that any protest in the shape of law proceedings would only make more public her own shame and discomfiture. But if she was beaten she would not confess it yet; and at least she was resolved that the enemy who had so ruthlessly betrayed her should not enjoy his triumph.

CHAPTER XIII
HUSBAND AND WIFE

Mrs. Wilders's first and only idea after she left Lincoln's Inn was to get to Paris as soon as she could. She no longer counted on much assistance from Ledantec, nor, indeed, had she much belief in him now; but she yet hoped he might help her to obtain revenge. Whatever it cost her, Rupert Gascoigne must pay the penalty of thwarting her when she seemed on the very threshold of success.

Having desired her maid to pack a few things, she hastily realised all the money she had at command and started by the night-mail for Paris.

Paris! Like the husband she had wronged and deserted, she had not visited the gay city for years. Not since she had thrown in her lot with an unspeakable villain, joining and abetting him in a vile plot against the man to whom she was bound by the strongest ties in life—by loyalty, affection, honour, truth.

"I hate going back there," she told herself, as the Calais express whirled her through Abbeville, Amiens, Creil. "Hate it, dread it, more than I can say."

And this repugnance might be interpreted into some glimmering remnant of good feeling were it not due to vague fears of impending evil rather than to shame and remorse.

She was landed at an early hour at the hotel she resolved to patronise: a quiet, old-fashioned house in the best part of the Rue de Rivoli, overlooking the gardens of the Tuileries.

She was shown to a room, and proceeded at once to correct the ravages of the night journey. A handsome woman still, but vain, like all her sex, and anxious to look her best on every occasion.

Hastily swallowing a cup of coffee, as soon as her toilette was completed she issued forth and took the first cab she could find.

"To the Porte St. Martin," she said; "lose no time."

Arrived there, she alighted, dismissed the cab, and proceeded on foot to the Faubourg St. Martin, to the house we have visited already, and in which our friend Hyde was still a prisoner.

Simply mentioning her name, she passed by the porter with the air of one who knew her road, although it was probably the first time she had come there. On the sixth floor she knocked as Hyde had done, and was admitted much as he had been.

There was no disguise about her, however, and she sent in her name as "Mrs. Wilders, just arrived from England, and most anxious to see Mr. Hobson."

"You, Cyprienne!" said the man we know, who answered to the names of both Hobson and Ledantec. "In Paris! This was quite unnecessary. I am arranging everything. You had my letter?"

"Pshaw! Hippolyte, you can't befool me."

"Why this tone? I tell you I have done everything."

"You may think so, but in the meantime Rupert has stolen a march on me. He has got the papers—"

"Impossible!"

"It is so. Got them, and placed them, with a full statement, in Lord Essendine's hands."

"How do you know this?"

"From Lord Essendine's own lips?"

"How can he have done this? He—a prisoner."

"Are you sure of that?"

"He is fast by the leg. Come and see him. He is in the next room."

"Here? In our power?"

"Yes: let us go and see him at once."

There was a fierce gleam in her eyes, as though she wished to stab him, wherever she found him, to the heart.

Hyde was where we had left him, still bound hand and foot to the bedstead. He had spent a miserable night, he was stiff and sore from his strange position, and they had given him little or no food. But his manner was defiant, and his air exulting, as he saw Ledantec and Cyprienne approach.

"Have you come to release me? It's about time. You will gain nothing by keeping me here."

"Dog! I hate you!" cried Mrs. Wilders, as she struck him a cruel, cowardly blow on the face.

"A pleasant greeting from the woman I made my wife."

"Would that fate had never thrown us together; that I had never heard your name!"

"No one can wish it more sincerely than myself," replied Gascoigne. "It was you who wrecked and ruined my life."

"And what have you done to me, Rupert Gascoigne? Could you not leave me in peace? Why follow me to persecute me, to rob me and my son—"

"Of the proceeds of your infamy?" interrupted Gascoigne, or Hyde, as I prefer to call him; "I will tell you. Because you dared to plot against a man I esteem. Whatever has happened to Stanislas McKay, he owes it, I feel confident, to you. I may never see him again—"

"You never will, and for a double reason. Do not hope, Rupert Gascoigne, to leave this place again."

And she looked capable of taking his life then and there.

"Come, come! Cyprienne; you are going too far. Mr. Gascoigne has not behaved very well, perhaps, but it is not for us to call him to account. We will leave him to the myrmidons of the law. He is wanted, we know, by the police."

"Am I?" said Hyde, mockingly; "so are others, as you will find. At this moment the house is surrounded. The authorities have long had their eye on Hippolyte Ledantec, *alias* Hobson, the Russian spy."

The confederates looked at each other uneasily, and Ledantec said—

"It can hardly be so. But it will be well to ascertain and take precautions. Come! there is a way out of this house known only to me."

And, so saying, he went towards the door, followed by Mrs. Wilders. Suddenly he paused, surprised by a loud knocking outside.

They heard the old woman's voice angrily asking who was there; they heard the reply, spoken loudly and authoritatively.

"The police! Open, in the name of the law. Open! or we shall break the door down."

Next minute the apartment was invaded by a *posse* of police, all of whom were drawn to where Hyde was by his loud cries of "Here! Here!"

"Let no one move," said the chief of the police, briefly. "What is the meaning of this? Who are you?" This was to Ledantec.

"My name is Mr. Hobson, a British subject, and member of the press. I shall require you to explain this intrusion."

"His real name is Ledantec!" cried Hyde, interposing. "Ex-gambler, and now spy in the pay of the Russians. This woman is his accomplice."

"And who may you be?" said the police-officer, turning to Hyde.

"I know this gentleman," put in the *attaché* whom Hyde had seen at the Embassy. "He is a British officer—Mr. Hyde."

"I know better!" cried Ledantec, with a scornful laugh. "I denounce him as Rupert Gascoigne, the perpetrator of the murder in Tinplate Street, fifteen years ago. The case cannot yet be forgotten at the Prefecture."

"Is it possible?" said the chief of the police, looking curiously at Hyde. "Surely I should recognise you. I was one of those from whom you escaped by jumping into the Seine."

"I do not deny that I am the man," replied Hyde, calmly. "But I am innocent, and only ask a fair trial."

"We must arrest you, anyway. Keep what you have to say for the judge. Come! bring them along; it's altogether a fine morning's work."

And within an hour Hyde found himself in his old quarters—a separate cell of the depôt of the Prefecture. The other prisoners were lodged there also, but apart from him and each other.

CHAPTER XIV
THE SCALES REMOVED

The capture made by the police in the Faubourg St. Martin was kept secret. Under the Second Empire nothing was published except with the permission of the authorities, and they had their reasons for not talking too openly of Hyde's arrest. He was a British subject, a military officer moreover, and these were claims to the consideration of French justice that would not have been so readily recognised fifteen years before.

It was, of course, inevitable that the affair of Tinplate Street should be re-opened. But a new complexion was given to it by the recent arrests. Hyde had been interrogated at once by the magistrate who had examined him before; the same man, but so different; no longer insolently positive and threatening unjustly, but bland, considerate, obliging. The fact was he had had a hint from his superiors to treat the Englishman gently.

"The truth must come out now," Hyde had said, when asked if he remembered the circumstances of his former arrest. "You have the real culprit in custody."

"This Ledantec, I suppose?" asked the judge.

"It was he who struck the blow; I saw him with my own eyes, as I told you years ago. Then he escaped by the window into a back-street; I followed him, but he was too quick for me. A cab waited for him, picked him up, and he was driven away."

While Hyde was speaking the judge had turned over the pages of a voluminous document in front of him,—a detailed report of the previous interrogation.

"Your story does not vary. You have either an excellent memory, or—" and the stern magistrate smiled quite archly—"or you are really telling me the truth."

"The truth! I can swear to it."

"What is more, your story is in the main corroborated. Shortly after your escape we laid hands on the very cabman who had helped Ledantec away. He described the scene as you have, and through him we got upon the trace of his fare—Ledantec, as you call him."

"But you never arrested him?"

"Until now he carefully kept away from Paris."

"But you have him now on a double charge."

"Him and his accomplice. Justice will be satisfied, never fear."

"How long will you keep me here?"

"I regret that for the present it will be impossible to release you. We are compelled first to verify the facts before us. But in a few days at the latest I hope your trouble will be at an end. You have powerful friends, Monsieur."

"The British Embassy, I suppose?" said Hyde, complacently.

"Yes; and his Imperial Majesty has deigned to go personally into your case."

"Then I can wait events calmly and without fear."

Presently, when Hyde had been removed, Ledantec was introduced, and was received with the brutal harshness which was the judge's habitual manner towards prisoners.

"Your name, profession, address?" he asked abruptly.

"Silas Hobson, an English journalist, residing in Duke Street, St. James's, London."

"It is false! You have no right to the name of Hobson. You are not an Englishman. You may reside in London, but it is only temporarily."

"Who am I then?" asked Ledantec with a sneer.

"In Paris, at your last visit, you passed as Hippolyte Ledantec, but your real name is Serge Michaelovitch Vasilenikoff. You are a Russian by birth, by profession a gambler, a blackleg, a cheat."

Ledantec, as I shall still call him, merely shrugged his shoulders in sarcastic helplessness at this abuse.

"You are worse. You are a spy in the service of the enemies of the State; an unconvicted murderer—"

He bent his eyes upon the prisoner with a piercing gaze, to watch the effect of this accusation.

Ledantec never blenched, and the judge presently continued—

"You are the real author of the crime in Tinplate Street."

"M. Rupert Gascoigne is your informant, I presume," said Ledantec sneering; "it is easy to rebut a charge by throwing it on another. But you are too clever, M. le Juge, to be imposed upon."

"You at least cannot hoodwink me. We have the fullest evidence, let me tell you, of the crime—all the crimes—laid to your charge. Your accomplice has confessed."

This was said to try the prisoner, and it succeeded, for he started slightly at the word "crimes."

"Accomplice! Of whom do you speak?"

"There is a woman in custody who has been associated with you for years. It was she who instigated you to the robbery and murder of the Baron d'Enot. She joined you when you fled from the gambling-den in Tinplate Street, and shared your flight from Paris. She was with you in St. Petersburg till you separated after a violent quarrel—"

"The blame was hers," interrupted Ledantec.

"Possibly, but you were equally to blame. In any case she left you to shift for herself. She entered a great English family by a false marriage, and, when next you met her, conspired with her to bring the wealth of that family within her grasp. You again became her guilty partner, and plotted to take the life of the heir to a noble English title and great estates."

He was referring now to McKay, but Ledantec, misled by a guilty conscience, was thinking of Lord Lydstone, and his mysteriously sudden death.

"That was her doing!" he cried remorsefully. "In removing Lord Lydstone—"

The judge caught quickly at the new name.

"You removed, or, more plainly, you murdered Lord Lydstone at the instigation of your accomplice—is that so?"

Ledantec would not confess to this, but the judge felt certain that he had come upon the track of another dreadful crime.

"There is enough against you," he went on slowly, "to convict you a dozen times over, enough to send you to the guillotine. Your only hope will be to make a clean breast of everything. By helping us to convict your accomplice you may save your forfeited life."

"But I shall be sent to the galleys; to Toulon or Brest. Life as a French galley-slave is worse than death."

"You will not think so when the alternative is put before you," said the judge, dryly; "and my advice to you is to make a full confession."

Ledantec shook his head, but it was with far less assurance than he had shown at the beginning of his examination. It was clear that he saw himself fast in the toils; that the law held him tight in its clutch; that unqualified submission was the only course to pursue.

He had spoken fully and unreservedly, confessing freely to every guilty deed in his long career of wickedness, possessing the judge with every detail of his own and his accomplice's crimes, when that accomplice was brought up for interrogation in her turn.

She was ghastly pale: the rough ordeal of imprisonment had robbed her dress and demeanour of all its coquetry; but she faced the magistrate with self-possessed, insolent effrontery, and met his stern look with cold, unflinching eyes.

"Why am I brought here?" she began, fiercely. "How dare you detain me? You and your masters shall answer for this ill-usage. I am an English lady, belonging to one of the proudest families in the country. The British Embassy, the British nation, will call you to the strictest account."

"Ta! ta! ta!" said the judge, with a gesture of the hand essentially French; "I think you are slightly mistaken; you are no more English than I am. I know you, and all about you, Cyprienne Vergette—otherwise Gascoigne, otherwise Wilders.

"Shall I tell you a little of your early history? How you eloped from Gibraltar, where your father was Vice-Consul; how you came to Paris with your lover; your marriage, your life, your desertion of your husband, your association with Ledantec, your second marriage, your plots against Milord Essendine and his family, your murder—"

"It is a lie!" she interrupted him, hastily. "I never committed murder."

"You compassed Lord Lydstone's death, although you did not strike the blow. You would have caused the death of another English officer, but, happily, he has escaped your murderous intrigues."

Only that morning the French journals had copied from the English an account of McKay's almost providential escape on the 18th of June.

"But your last attempt has failed utterly. Mr.—" he referred to his papers for the name—"McKay is safe within the British lines. The agent you employed to inveigle him into danger is dead, but with his last breath he confessed that he had had his orders from you. Now, Cyprienne Vergette, what have you to say?"

"I deny everything. I protest against your jurisdiction."

"The Assize Court will hear, but scarcely admit, your plea. That tribunal and its president will deal you as you deserve."

CHAPTER XV
L'ENVOI

The *Burlington Castle* made a short halt at Constantinople, and another, somewhat longer, at Malta; a third was to be made at Gibraltar, where two of our most important characters proposed to leave the ship.

The delay at Malta was to allow Miss Hidalgo to make her appearance in the Supreme Court as principal witness against the baker, Giuseppe Pisani, commonly called Valetta Joe.

The British military authorities in the Crimea had hesitated to deal summarily with the spy's offence. He might have been hanged out of hand under the Mutiny Act; but such swift retribution, however richly merited, was obnoxious to our general's sense of justice.

He preferred to leave the criminal to the ordinary tribunals of his native island. It could adjudge and carry out any punishment short of death, if so inclined. In the Crimea the capital sentence only would have been possible.

The trial was short and summary. Mariquita, dressed still in the sober, quaker-like garb of a hospital-nurse, said what she had to say in a few simple words. Her sweet face and artless manner were the admiration of the whole court, and there was a little round of applause as it came out that she had ventured so far and braved so much out of love for the gallant soldier who was leaning on his crutches close by her side.

Valetta Joe was found guilty and sentenced to imprisonment for four years, and with his conviction the reader's interest in him will probably cease. It disposed of the last of McKay's active enemies; Benito, as we have seen, had died in Balaclava hospital, and Cyprienne Vergette and her accomplice were in the grip of the French law.

The enemies had disappeared; friends only remained. When he landed at Gibraltar numbers came to greet him, from the Governor himself to the Tio Pedro and the old crone his wife. Letters had already assured them of Mariquita's safety, and they wept crocodile tears of joy as they clasped her once more in their arms.

They were her only relatives, and as such McKay was compelled to surrender his love to them for a time. But only for the very briefest time.

He measured their affections at its true value, and had no compunction in asserting his claim over theirs to protect and cherish her.

He easily persuaded them and Mariquita, but with some tender insistence, to hurry on the marriage, and it took place within a few short weeks of their return to the Rock. Why should he wait? He was his own master; the only relative whose consent and approval he coveted—his mother—had already promised gladly to accept the girl of his choice.

His great relatives, the Essendines, might question the propriety of the match, anxious that he should look higher, and find his future bride amongst the aristocracy to which he now rightly belonged.

That was a point on which he meant to please himself, and did.

When, after a short honeymoon at Granada, the young married couple returned to Gibraltar and travelled leisurely homewards, Lord Essendine was one of the first to welcome him on arrival, and to congratulate him on the beauty of his bride.

By-and-by, when the days of mourning were ended, Lady Essendine came out of her strict retirement to present Mrs. McKay at Court; and the handsome Spanish girl with the strange romantic history was one of the greatest successes of the next London season. Ere long the future succession of the Essendine title was assured beyond doubt. McKay was blessed with a numerous family—many sons came to satisfy the head of the house that the title of Essendine and the family name were in no danger of extinction. But Lord Essendine lived for many years after the termination of the Crimean war, and McKay was a general officer and a Knight of the Bath before he became the fifteenth Earl of Essendine.

Having thus disposed of the hero whose early career was so chequered and eventful, I must add a word as to the fate of the other actors in this veracious narrative.

First as to Hyde, who continued to be known by that name to his death, preferring it greatly to the other, with its painful memories. He remained a prisoner in the depôt of the Prefecture only a few days. The confession made by Ledantec and the evidence of other witnesses so amply attested the innocence of the M. Gascoigne accused of the Tinplate Street murder that his release followed as a matter of course. Hyde waited in Paris to hear the issue of the trial of the real offenders, and, painful as it was to be present at the sentence of the woman who had once borne his name, he yet listened without flinching to the whole story. After all, there was a certain relief in knowing that he was well rid of her. It was little likely that the Central prison to which she was consigned in perpetual "reclusion" would ever surrender its prey.

He heard, too, with lively satisfaction, the sentence of his old foe, Ledantec, to hard labour at the galleys for twenty years.

With these trials, and the penalties that followed them, he turned down for ever the dark page of his life, and presently returned to England, where he spent the remainder of his leave with his old friend and comrade, McKay.

After that had expired he returned to the Crimea, and was present at the closing scenes of the war. He continued to serve with the Royal Picts for many years more—the regiment had become his home—and, as he was in due course promoted to the post of paymaster, his position and income were materially changed.

He lived to a green old age, retiring from the service full of rank and honour. Colonel Hyde was long a notable figure at his club in Pall Mall, which gained a new and very popular *chef* when Anatole Belhomme wrote him that he had been summarily dismissed from the French police. Hyde spent a great portion of every year at Essendine Castle, after his friend had succeeded to the estates, and there was no more honoured guest than he at the coming of age of Rupert, Viscount Lydstone, his godson.

The boy whom Mrs. Wilders had hesitated to surrender to old Lord Essendine, from greed rather than maternal instinct, was not neglected by the old peer. After the mother had passed out of sight, the son was brought up decently, given a good education, and eventually started in life. He adopted the military profession, and was not denied the support and encouragement of Stanislas McKay.

Our hero was able to help his uncle, too, the much-aggrieved functionary of the Military Munition Department, and secured for him the decoration he had so long coveted in vain.

Uncle Barto, the worthy captain of the *Burlington Castle*, made a snug fortune by his commercial ventures during the war, and paid regular visits to his nephew, Stanny. Mrs. McKay, or Countess of Essendine as she became, could never forget what she owed for his generous hospitality on board the *Burlington*.

BLUE BLOOD

CHAPTER I

"The idea is simply preposterous. I decline to entertain it. I cannot listen to it—not for one moment. Never!"

The speaker was Mrs. Purling, "heiress of the Purlings"; imperious, emphatic, self-opinionated, as women become who have had their own way all their lives through.

"But, mother," went on Harold, her only son—like herself, large and broadly built; but, unlike her, quiet and rather submissive in manner, as one who had been habitually kept under—"I am really in earnest. I am absolutely sick of doing nothing."

"Because you won't do what you might. There is plenty for you to do. Has not the Duchess asked you to Scotland? You refuse—and such a splendid invitation! I have offered you a yacht. I say you may share a river in Norway with dear Lord Faro. I implore you to drive a coach, to keep racehorses, to take your place in the best society, as the representative of the Purling—"

"Pills?" put in Harold, with a queer smile.

His mother's face grew black instantly.

"Harold, do not dare to speak in that way. My father's memory should be respected by my only son."

Old Purling had made all his money by a certain chemical compound which had been adopted by the world at large as a panacea for every ill. But the heiress of the Purlings hated any reference to the Primeval Pills, although she owed to them her wealth.

"I want a profession," Harold said, returning to his point. "I want regular employment."

"Well, I say go into the Guards."

"I am too old. Besides, peace-soldiering, and in London, would never suit me, I know."

"Read law; it is a gentlemanly occupation."

"But most uninteresting. Now medicine—"

"Do not let me hear the word; the mere idea is intolerable. My son, the heir of the Purlings must not condescend so low."

"Considering my own father was a doctor," cried Harold, rather hotly.

"Not a mere doctor. A man of science, of world-wide repute, is not like a general practitioner, with a red lamp and an apothecary's shop, where he makes up—"

"Pills?" said Harold, again. He was throwing down the gauntlet indeed. Mrs. Purling had never known him like this before.

"Leave the room, Harold. I decline to speak to you further, or again, unless you appear in a more obedient and decorous frame of mind."

That Mrs. Purling was what she was, the chances of her life and her father were principally to blame. He had begun life as an errand-boy, and ended it as a millionnaire; but long before he ended he had forgotten the beginning. He had a sort of notion that he belonged to one of the old families in the county wherein he had bought wide estates, and he himself styled his only daughter "the heiress of the Purlings," as if there had been Purlings back for generations, and he was the last, not the first, of his race. It was he who had indoctrinated her with ideas of her own importance; and these same views had taken so strong a hold of him that he found it quite impossible to mate his daughter according to his mind. He was ambitious, as was natural to a *nouveau riche*; wide awake, or he would not have made so much money. Not one of the crowds of suitors who came forward was exactly to his taste. He would have preferred a man of title, but the peers who were not penniless were too proud; and the best baronet was an aged bankrupt, who had been twice through the courts, and enjoyed an indifferent name. It was strange that Isabel did not cut the Gordian knot, and choose for herself; but she was a dutiful daughter, and little less cautious than her father. In the midst of it all he was called away on some particular business of his own— to another world—and Isabel was left alone, past thirty, and unmarried still.

The *rôle* of single blessedness may be charming to a man of means, but it is often extremely irksome to an heiress in her own right. Miss Purling was like a pigeon that escapes from the inclosure at a match—an aim for every gun around. Great ladies took her up, as a kindness to their younger sons; briefless barristers, with visions of the Woolsack, besought her to help them to the first step—a seat in the House; clergymen with great views prayed her to join them in some stupendous charitable work, that must win for them the lawn-sleeves; more than one impecunious soldier pleaded with her for their tailors, whose bills without her help they were quite unable to pay. She seemed a common prey, fair game for every hand. This developed in her an undue amount of suspicion and a certain hardness of heart. She began to doubt whether there was one disinterested man in the whole world.

But before many years had passed she realised that unless she married there could be no prospect of peace. Already she had quarrelled with a dozen companions of her own sex; she wished now to try one of the other. But men seemed tired of proposing to her. She had the character of being as hard and cold as iron; and no one cared to run his head against a wall. If she wanted a husband now the proposal must come from her. Miss Purling in her heart rather liked the notion; it gave her a chance of posing like a queen in search of a consort, and years of independence had made her very queenlike and despotic indeed. So much so, that the only man to suit her must be a mere cipher without a will of his own; and he was difficult to find. Men of the kind are not plentiful unless they plainly perceive substantial advantage from assuming the part. But few guessed what kind of man would exactly suit Isabel Purling, so there were few pretenders.

Among those who flocked to her *soirées*—she was fond of entertaining in spite of her disabilities as a single woman—was a meek little professor, who lodged in Camden Town, and who came afoot in roomy goloshes, which now and again, in a fit of abstraction, he carried upstairs and laid upon the tea-table or at his hostess's feet, as though the carpet was damp and he feared she might run the risk of catarrh. He was reputed to be extremely erudite, a ripe scholar, and of some fame in scientific research. But of all his discoveries—and he had made many under the microscope and in space— the most surprising was the discovery that a lady who owned a deer-park and many thousands a-year desired him to make her his wife. But he was an obliging little man, always ready to do a kind thing for anybody; and he obliged Miss Purling in the way she wished—after all, at some cost to himself. The marriage meant little less than self-effacement for him; he was to take his wife's name instead of giving her his; he was to forego his favourite pursuits, and from an independent man of science pass into a mere appendage to the Purling property—part and parcel of his wife's goods and chattels as much as the park-palings, or her last-purchased dinner-service of rare old "blue."

It was odd that Miss Purling's choice should have fallen where it did; for her tendencies were decidedly upward, and she would have dearly loved to be styled "my lady," and to have moved freely in the society of the "blue-blooded of the land." It was her distrustfulness which had stood in the way. She feared that in an aristocratic alliance she could not have made her own terms. And with the results of this marriage with Dr. Purling—as he was henceforth styled—she had every reason to be pleased. He proved a most exemplary husband—the chief of her subjects, nothing more; a loyal, unpretending vassal, who did not ask to share the purple, but was content to sit upon the steps of the throne. He continued a shy, reserved, unobtrusive little man to the end of the chapter; and the chapter was closed without unnecessary delay as soon as the birth of a son secured the succession of the Purling estates. Dr. Purling felt there was nothing more required of him, so he quietly died.

His widow raised a tremendous tablet to his memory, eulogising his scientific attainments and domestic worth; but, although she appeared inconsolable, she was secretly pleased to have the uncontrolled education of her infant son. An elderly lady with a baby-boy is like a girl with a doll— just as the little mother dresses and undresses its counterfeit presentment of a child in wax and rags, crooning over its tiny cradle, talking to it in baby-language, pretending to watch with anxious solicitude its every mood, so Mrs. Purling found in Harold a plaything of which she never tired. She coddled and cosseted him to her heart's content. If he had cried for the moon some effort would have been made to obtain for him the loan of that pale planet, or the best substitute for it that could be got for cash. If his finger ached, or he had a pain in his big toe, he was physicked with half the Pharmacopœia; he underwent divers systems of regimen, was kept out of draughts, cautioned against chills, cased in red flannel; he might, to crown all, have been laid by in cotton-wool. His mother's over-much care ought to have killed him; but he had inherited from her a fine physique, and the lad was large-limbed, healthy, and well grown.

And this vigilant supervision was prolonged far beyond the time when youths are emancipated usually from their mother's control. Long after he had left college, and was launched out upon the world, she kept her hands upon the reins, ruling him with a sharp bit, and driving him the road she decided it was best for him to go. Mrs. Purling had grown more and more imperious with advancing years, impatient of contradiction, self-satisfied, very positive that everything she did was right. She could not brook opposition to her wishes. Those who dared to thwart her must do it at their peril; no nature but one entirely subservient would be likely to continue permanently in accord with hers; and it was easy to predict troubles in the future between mother and son unless he yielded always a complete and docile submission to her will.

For a long time Harold wore his chains without a murmur. Obedient deference had been a habit with him from childhood, and, however irksome and galling the slavery, it was not until he had made practical acquaintance with the actual value of the life she wished him to lead that there arose in him a disposition to rebel. Mrs. Purling had all along been chafed with the notion that she did not enjoy that social distinction to which as a wealthy woman she considered herself entitled. In her own estimation she ranked very high; but the best families of the neighbourhood did not accept her valuation. Some went so far as to call her a vulgar old snob; and "snobbish," as we understand the word, she certainly was. She worshipped rank; and it was a very sore point with her that she was not freely admitted into the best society of the county in which she lived. She looked to Harold to redress her wrongs. Where she failed, a handsome young fellow, of engaging presence and heir to a fine estate, must assuredly succeed. He might, if he chose, be acceptable anywhere. There was no limit to her dreams. He might mate with a duke's daughter; and after such an alliance—who would presume to question the social rights of the Purlings?

It was therefore her chief and greatest desire to make a man of fashion of her son. Her purse was long—he might dip into it as deep as he pleased. Let him but take his proper position, on an equality with the noblest and best, and all charges would be gladly defrayed by her. She wanted him to be a dandy, *répandu* in society, a member of the Coaching Club, well known at Prince's, at Hurlingham, at Lord's; sought after by dowagers; intimate with royalties; she would not have seriously resented a reputation for a little wickedness, provided he erred in the right direction—with people of the blue blood, that is to say—and the scandal did not go too far.

Unhappily, Harold's tastes and inclinations lay all in the opposite direction. In external appearance he favoured his mother, in disposition he was his father's son. Like him reserved—he would have been shy but for his training at school and college, which had rubbed the sensitive skin off his self-consciousness; like him studious too, thoughtful, quiet, with scientific tastes and proclivities. His friends in familiar talk called him "Old Steady"; he had never got into debt or serious trouble. Even in the midst of the whirling maze of London life he continued steadfastly sober and sedate.

Here at once was to be found the germ of discord between mother and son, the first gap or chink in their friendly relations, which might widen some day into a yawning breach. But yet Mrs. Purling could find no fault with her son. She might resent the staid sober-mindedness of his conduct; but she was perforce compelled to confess that he was a dear good son, affectionate, devoted, considerate; and there was much solid comfort in the thought that the good name of the Purlings, as well as their substantial wealth, could be safely intrusted to his hands. This she readily allowed; and, had he continued obedient and tractable until he was grey-haired, Mrs. Purling might have gone down into her grave without a shadow of excuse for quarreling with her son.

It was when he was past five-and-twenty that there arose between them misunderstanding, at first only a small cloud no bigger than a man's hand. Harold suddenly declared that he was sick of gallivanting about the fashionable world; sick of idleness—sick of the silly purposeless existence he led; and thereupon announced his intention of studying medicine seriously and as a profession. Mrs. Purling was at first aghast, then argumentative, finally indignant. But Harold remained inflexible, and she grew more and more wrathful. It led at length to something like a rupture between them. She received the news of his success in the schools with grim contempt, condescending only to ask once whether he wished her to buy him a practice, or whether he meant to put up a red lamp at the family-mansion in Berkeley Square.

Her persistent implacability gave Harold much pain, but he did not despair of bringing her round in the end; only, to avoid further dissensions, he wisely resolved to keep out of her way: and as soon as he had gained his diploma he started for Germany, intending to prosecute his studies abroad.

CHAPTER II

It was not until he had been absent more than a year that Mrs. Purling appeared to relent. She began to yearn after her son; she missed him and was disposed to be reconciled, provided he would but meet her half-way. At first she sent olive-branches in the shape of munificent letters of credit over and above his liberal allowance; then came more distinct overtures in lengthy epistles, which grew daily warmer in tone and plainly showed that her resentment was passing rapidly away. These letters of hers were her chief pleasure in life; she prided herself on her ability to wield the pen. When, instead of a few curt sentences in brief acknowledgment of his letters, his mother resumed her old custom of filling several sheets of post with advice, gossip, odds and ends of news, mixed with stray scraps of wisdom culled from Martin Tupper, Harold began to hope that the worst was over and that he would soon be forgiven in set form.

And he was right. Pardon was soon extended to him, not quite unconditional, but weighted merely with terms which—Mrs. Purling thought—no sensible man could hesitate to accept.

She only asked him to settle in life. He must marry some day—why not soon? Not to anybody, of course,—he must be on his guard against foreign intriguing sirens, who would entangle him if they could,—but to some lady of rank and fashion, fitted by birth and breeding to be the mother of generations of Purlings yet to be. This was the condition she annexed to forgiveness of the past; this the text upon which she preached in her letters week after week. The doctrine of judicious marriage appeared in all she wrote with the unfailing regularity of the red thread that runs through all the strands of Admiralty rope.

Harold smiled at the reiteration of these sentiments; smiled, but he had misgivings. Herein might be another source of disagreement between his mother and himself. Would their respective opinions agree as to the style of girl most likely to suit him? Then he began to consider what style of girl his mother would choose; and while he was thus musing there came a missive which plainly showed Mrs. Purling's hand.

"I have been at Compton Revel for a week—"

"I wonder," thought Harold, when he had read thus far, "why they asked her there? My dear old mother must have been in the seventh heaven of delight. She always longed to be on more intimate terms with Lady Calverly."

"I have been at Compton Revel for a week," his mother said, "and met there a Miss Fanshawe, one of Lord Fanshawe's daughters, who seemed to me quite the nicest girl I have ever known. I took to her directly; and without conceit I may be permitted to say that I think she took quite as readily to me. We became immense friends. She was at such pains to be agreeable to an uninteresting old woman like myself that I feel convinced she has a good heart. I confess I was charmed with her. It is not only that she is strikingly handsome, but her whole bearing and her style are so distinguished that she might be descended from a long line of kings—as I make no doubt she is.

"Of course she has moved only in the best circles; her mother being dead, she has been introduced by the Countess of Gayfeather, and goes with her ladyship everywhere. Just imagine, she has been to State-balls at the Palace; the Prince has danced with her, and she has been spoken to by the Princess! You know how I enjoy hearing all the news of the great world, and Miss Fanshawe has been so obliging as to amuse me for hours with descriptions of all she has seen and heard—not a little, I assure you; she is not one of those flighty girls who have no ears but for flattery, no eyes but for young men; she is observant, critical perhaps, but strikingly just in her strictures on what goes on around. I find she has thought out several of the complex problems of our modern high-pressure life; and really she gave me very valuable ideas upon my favourite theory of 'lady-helps,' to which I am devoting now so much of my spare time.

"Miss Fanshawe has promised to pay me a long visit at Purlington some day soon—a real act of kindness which I fully appreciate. It will indeed be a treat to a lonely old woman to find so entertaining a guest and companion.

"When do you think of returning? Gollop tells me there are plenty of pheasants this year. Surely, you have had enough of those dry German *savants* and that dull university-town?"

The hook was rather coarsely baited; it would hardly have deceived the most guileless and unsuspecting. Harold Purling at a glance could read between the lines; he could trace effect to cause, and readily understood why his mother was so anxious for his return.

"One of Lady Gayfeather's girls, is she? I never thought much of that lot. However—but why on earth should Lady Calverly take my dear mother up in this way, at the eleventh hour?"

He would have wondered yet more if he had seen how cordially Mrs. Purling had been welcomed to Compton Revel.

"It is so good of you to come to us," Lady Calverly said, with effusion. "We are so glad to have you here, and have looked forward to it for so long."

For about seventeen years, in fact, during which time Lord and Lady Calverly had completely ignored the existence of their near neighbour, Mrs. Purling. Compton Revel might have been a paradise, and the heiress an exiled peri waiting at the gates.

The party assembled was after Mrs. Purling's own heart. They were all great people, at least in name; and the heiress of the Purlings was heard to murmur that she did like to be in such good society—she felt so perfectly at home. And they all made much of her. One night she was handed in to dinner by a Duke, another by an ex-Cabinet Minister. The latter made her feel proud, for the first time in her life, of her son, and the line he had adopted so sorely against her will.

"Mr. Purling's paper on toxicology," he said, "is quite the cleverest thing that has appeared on the subject. My friend, Sir William—," he mentioned a physician of world-wide repute, "considers that Mr. Purling will go far."

Lady Calverly followed suit by declaring that Mr. Purling was a pattern young man, everyone gave him so good a character. They *did* hope to see him at Compton Revel directly he got back to England.

Then Miss Fanshawe metaphorically prostrated herself before Mrs. Purling, and by judicious phrases and ready sympathy completely won her good-will.

"You certainly made an impression upon her, Phillipa," said Lady Calverly afterwards.

"She is a vain and rather silly old woman," Miss Fanshawe replied. Language that might have opened Mrs. Purling's eyes.

"But I am very glad you became such good friends. Purlington is a very desirable place."

Here, then, was a faint clue to the mystery of Mrs. Purling's tardy reception at Compton Revel. Intrigue—not necessarily base, but covered by the harmless phrase, "It would be so very nice"—was at work to bring about a match between Miss Fanshawe and Harold Purling. She was one of a large family of girls and her father was an impoverished peer. Besides, her career so far had not been an unmixed success. Lady

Gayfeather's young ladies had the reputation of being the "quickest" in the town.

"I have met the son," went on Lady Calverly.

"Yes?" Phillipa's tone was one of absolute indifference.

"He is a gentleman."

"I have always heard of him as a solemn prig—'Old Steady' he was named at college. I confess I have no special leaning to these very proper and decorous youths."

"Do not say that you are harping still on that old affair. I assure you Gilly Jillingham is unworthy of you. You are not thinking still of each other, I sincerely hope?"

"I may be of him," said Phillipa bitterly. "He is not likely to think of any one—but himself."

"I shall never forgive myself for surrendering you to Lady Gayfeather. Nothing but misery seems to hang about her and her house. This last affair—"

There had been a terrible scandal, not many months old, and hardly forgotten yet, which had roused Lady Calverly to remove her cousin, Phillipa Fanshawe, from the evil influences of Lady Gayfeather's set. Whether or not the rescue had come in time it would be difficult to say. Miss Fanshawe could hardly escape scot-free from her associations, nor was it to her advantage that rumour had bracketed her name with that of a successful but not popular man of fashion. There had been a talk of marriage, but he had next to nothing; no more had she.

"We must have an end to all that," said Lady Calverly decisively. "You must promise me to forget Mr. Jillingham for good and all."

"Of course," replied Phillipa; but the pale face and that sad look in her weary eyes belied her words.

It seemed as if she had shot her bolt at the target of life's happiness, and that the arrow had fallen very wide of the gold.

CHAPTER III

When old Purling bought the —shire estates there was an ancient manor-house on the property, a picturesque but inconvenient residence, which did not at all come up to his ideas of a country gentleman's place. It was therefore incontinently pulled down, and one of the most fashionable architects of the day, having *carte blanche* to build, erected a Palladian pile of wide frontage and imposing dimensions on the most prominent site he could find. It ought to have haunted its author like a crime; but he was spared, and the punishment fell upon the innocent who dwelt around. There was no escape from Purlington, so long as you were within a dozen miles of it. Wherever you went and wherever you looked, down from points of vantage or up from quiet dells, this great white caravanserai, with its glittering plate-glass panes and staring stucco, forced itself upon you with the unblushing effrontery of a brazen beauty, with painted face and bedizened in flaunting attire. But the heiress thought it was a very splendid place, with its pineries, conservatories, its acres of glass, and its army of retainers in liveries of rainbow hues. Mrs. Purling was a little afraid of her servants, albeit strong-minded in other respects; but it was natural she should submit to a coachman who had once worn the royal livery, or quail before a butler who had lived with a duke.

The butler met Harold on his return, extending to him a gracious patronising welcome, as if he were doing the honours of his own house.

"Misterarold," he cried, making one word of the name and title, "this is a pleasant surprise. You wus not expected, sir; not in the least."

"My mother is at home?"

"No, sir; out. In the kerridge. She drove Homersham way."

"See after my things. Here are my keys." And Harold passed on to the little morning-room which Mrs. Purling called her own. Having the choice of half-a-dozen chambers, each as big as Exeter Hall, she preferred to occupy habitually the smallest den in the house. To his surprise he found the room not untenanted. A young lady was at the book-case, and she turned seemingly in trepidation on hearing the door open.

"Miss Fanshawe," thought Harold, as he advanced with eyes that were unmistakably critical.

"I must introduce myself," he said. "I am Harold."

"The last of the Saxon kings?"

"No; the first of the Purling princes. I know you quite well. Has my mother never mentioned me?"

"I only arrived yesterday," the young lady replied, rather evading the question.

"My mother must be delighted. She told me she was looking forward eagerly to your promised visit."

"She really spoke of me?"

"In her letters; again and again."

"I hardly thought—"

"That you had taken her by storm? You have; and I was surprised, for she is not easily won."

Not a civil speech, which this girl only resented by placing a pair of old-fashioned double glasses across her small nose, and looking at him with a gravity that was quite comical.

"But now that I have met you I can readily understand."

The same look through the glasses; sphinx-like, she seemed impervious both to depreciation and compliment.

"And she has left you alone all the morning? I am afraid you must have been bored."

"Thank you. I had my work."

It was an exquisite piece of art needlework. Water-lilies and yellow irises on a purple ground. She confessed it was her own design.

"And books?"

He took up Schlegel's *Philosophy of History* in the original.

"You read German?"

"O yes."

"And Italian? and French? and Sanscrit—without doubt?"

"Not quite; but I have looked into Max Müller, and know something of Monier Williams."

And this was one of Lady Gayfeather's girls! Was this a new process, the last dodge in the perpetual warfare between maidens and mankind?

Harold looked at the prodigy.

In appearance she was quite unlike the conventional type of a London young lady of fashion. Her fresh dimpled cheeks wore roses and a pearly bloom that spoke of healthy hours and a tranquil life; her dress was quiet almost to plainness; there was nothing modern in the style of her coiffure; Lobb would not have been proud of her boots. Her fair white hands were innocent of rings; she wore no jewelry; there was no gold or silver about her, except for the gold-rimmed glasses that made so curious a contrast to her young face, with its merry eyes and frame of mutinous curls.

"You will not be angry," said Harold earnestly, "if I tell you that you are not in the least what I expected to find you, Miss Fanshawe—"

"Miss Fanshawe!" Her gay laugh was infectious. "I'm afraid—"

But just now the butler came in to say that the carriage was coming up the drive. Harold went out to meet his mother, without noticing that the young lady also got up and hurriedly left the room.

"It's just like you, you stupid boy!" said the heiress. "Why did you give me no notice?"

"I meant to have written from Paris. But it's all for the best. You were quite right. She is perfectly charming."

"Who?"

"Miss Fanshawe. I have made her acquaintance."

"In town?"

"No, here; in your own morning-room."

"What!" The ejaculation contained volumes. "Was there ever anything so annoying! But it is all your fault for coming so unexpectedly."

"What harm? We introduced ourselves, Miss Fanshawe—"

"Miss Fiddlesticks! That's Dolly Driver, your father's cousin!"

"Indeed! Then I wish I had made the acquaintance of my father's cousins a little earlier in life. Why have I been kept in ignorance of my relatives? Where do they live?"

Mrs. Purling, instead of answering him, took him by the arm abruptly, as if to ask him some searching question; then suddenly checking herself, she said—

"Have you had lunch? It must be ready. Come into the dining-room."

"Will not Miss Driver join us?"

"She will go to the housekeeper's room, where she ought to have been sitting, and not in my boudoir."

"Mother!"

"It's as well to be plain-spoken. Dolly Driver is not of our rank in life. Her parents are miserably poor. Nevertheless,"—as if the crime hardly deserved such liberal pardon,—"I am not indisposed to help them. She is going to a situation."

"Poor girl! Companion or governess? or both?"

"Neither; she will be either housemaid or undernurse."

Harold almost jumped off his chair.

"A girl like that! as a domestic servant! Mother, it's a disgraceful shame!"

"The disgrace is in the language you permit yourself to use to me. Your travels have made you rather boisterous and *gauche*. What disgrace can there be in honest work? Household work is honourable, and was once occupation for the daughters of kings. Happily the world grows more sensible. I look to the day as not far distant when the wide-spread employment of lady-helps will solve that terrible problem—the redundancy of girls."

"My cousin will not continue redundant, I feel sure."

"She is not your cousin."

"Whether or no, she should be spared the degradation you propose. She is a girl of culture, highly educated. You cannot condemn her to the kitchen."

"The lady-helps have their own apartment; but I decline to justify myself."

And Mrs. Purling lapsed into silence. There was friction between them already.

"Where are you going?" she asked, when lunch was over.

"To the housekeeper's room."

"Harold, I forbid you. It's highly improper—it's absolutely indelicate."

"She is my cousin; besides there is a *chaperone*, Mrs. Haigh, or I'll call in the cook."

"Do you mean to set me at defiance?"

"I mean to do what I consider right, even although my views may not coincide with yours, mother."

For the rest of the day, indeed, Harold never left his newly-found cousin's side. The heiress fumed and fretted, and scolded, but all in vain.

There was a new kind of masterfulness about her son which for the moment she was powerless to resist.

"Of course she will dine with us," Harold said. And of course she did, although Mrs. Purling looked as if she wished every mouthful would choke her. Of course Harold called her Dolly to her face; was she not his cousin? Quite as naturally he would have given her a cousinly kiss when he said good-night, but something in her pure eyes and modest face restrained him.

Certainly she was the nicest girl he had ever met in his life.

"Where's Doll?" he asked next morning at breakfast. "Not down?"

"Miss Driver is half-way to London, I hope," replied Mrs. Purling, curtly. She was not a bad general, and had taken prompt measures already to recover from her temporary reverse.

"I shall go after her."

"If you do, you need not trouble to return."

Nothing more was said, but anger filled the hearts of both mother and son.

CHAPTER IV

"I expect my dear friend, Miss Fanshawe, in a few days, Harold. I trust you will treat her becomingly."

"One would think I was a bear just escaped from the Zoo. Why should you fear discourtesy from me to any lady?"

"Because she is a friend of mine. Of late you seemed disposed to run counter to me in every respect."

"I have no such desire, I assure you," said Harold, gravely; and there the matter ended.

The preparation for Miss Fanshawe's reception could not have been more ambitious if she had been a royal princess. With much reluctance Mrs. Purling eschewed triumphal arches and a brass band, but she redecorated the best bedroom, and sent two carriages to the station, although her guest could hardly be expected to travel in both.

"*This* is Miss Fanshawe," said the heiress, with much emphasis—"the Honourable Miss Fanshawe."

"The Honourable Miss Fanshawe is only a very humble personage, not at all deserving high-sounding titles," said the young lady for herself. "My name is Phillipa—to my friends, and as such I count you, dear Mrs. Purling; perhaps some day I may be allowed to say the same of your son."

She spoke rapidly, with the fluent ease natural to a well-bred woman. In the subdued light of the cosy room Harold made out a tall, slight figure, well set off by the tight-fitting ulster; she carried her head proudly, and seemed aristocratic to her finger-tips.

"I should have known you anywhere, Mr. Purling," she went on, without a pause. "You are so like your dear mother. You have the same eyes."

It was a wonder she did not use the adjective "sweet"; for her tone clearly implied that she admired them.

"I hear you are desperately and astoundingly clever," she continued, like the brook flowing on for ever. "They tell me your pamphlet on vivisection was quite masterly. How proud you must be, Mrs. Purling, to hear such civil things said of his books!"

"Do you take sugar?" Harold asked, as he put a cup of tea into a hand exquisitely gloved.

She looked up at him sharply, but failed to detect any satire behind his words.

Harold thought that there was too much sugar and butter about her altogether. Even thus early he felt antipathetic; yet, when they were seated at dinner, and had an opportunity of observing her at leisure, he could not deny that she was handsome, in a striking, queenly sort of way; but he thought her complexion was too pale, and, at times, when off her guard, a worn-out, harassed look came over her face, and a tinge of melancholy clouded her dark eyes. But it was not easy to find her off her guard. The unceasing strife of several seasons had taught her to keep all the world at sword-point; she was armed *cap-à-pie*, and ready always to fight with a clever woman's keenest weapons—her eyes and tongue. Upon Harold she used both with consummate skill; it was clear that she wished to please him, addressing herself principally to him, asking his opinion on scientific questions, coached up on purpose, and listening attentively when he replied.

"How wise you have been to keep away from town these years! One gets so sick of the perpetual round."

"I should have thought it truly delightful," said Mrs. Purling, who, of course, took the unknown for the magnificent.

"Any honest labour would be preferable."

"Turn lady-help; that's my mother's common advice."

"Harold, how dare you suggest such a thing to Miss Fanshawe? Do you know she is a peer's daughter?"

"I thought you said housework would do for the daughters of kings; and you have proposed it to our cousin, Dolly Dri—"

"Were you at Ryde this year, Phillipa?" asked Mrs. Purling, promptly.

"No—at Cowes. We were yachting. Dreary business, don't you think, Mr. Purling?"

"I rather like it."

"Yes, if you have a pleasant party and an object. But mere cruising"— Miss Fanshawe was quick at shifting her ground.

"And you are going to Scotland?"

"Probably; and then for a round of visits. Dear, dear, how I loathe it all! I had far rather stay with you."

The heiress smiled gratefully. It was, indeed, the dearest wish of her heart that Phillipa should stay with her for good and all, and she was at no pains to conceal the fact. To Phillipa she spoke with diffidence, doubting whether this great personage could condescend to favour her son. But there was no lack of frankness in the old lady's speech.

"If you and he would only make a match of it!"

Miss Fanshawe squeezed Mrs. Purling's hand affectionately.

"I like him, I confess. More's the pity. I'm sure he detests me."

"As if it were possible!"

"Trust a girl to find out whether she's appreciated. Mr. Purling, for my sins, positively dislikes me; or else he has seen some one already to whom he has given his heart."

Mrs. Purling shook her head sadly, remembering artful Dolly Driver.

"You do not know all your son's secrets; no mother does."

"I do know this one, I fear."

And then Mrs. Purling described the absurd mistake in identity.

"You are not angry?" she went on. "For my part, I was furious. But nothing shall come of it, I solemnly declare. Harold will hardly risk my serious displeasure; but he shall know that, sooner than accept this creature as my daughter, I would banish him for ever from my sight."

"It will not come to that, I trust," said Phillipa, earnestly, and with every appearance of good faith.

"Not if you will help me, as I know you will."

Mrs. Purling was resolved now to issue positive orders for Harold to marry Miss Fanshawe—out of hand. But next day Phillipa suddenly announced her intention of returning to town.

"You promised to stay at least a month." The heiress was in tears.

"I am heartily sorry; but Cæcilia—Lady Gayfeather—is ill and alone. I must go to her at once."

"You have a feeling heart, Phillipa. This is a sacred duty; I cannot object. But I shall see you again?"

"As soon as I can return, dear Mrs. Purling—if you will have me, that is to say."

The story of Lady Gayfeather's illness was a mere fabrication. What summoned Phillipa to London was this note:

"I *must* see you. Can you be at Cæcilia's on Saturday?—G."

Phillipa sat alone in Lady Gayfeather's drawing-room, when Mr. Jillingham was announced.

"What does this mean?" she asked.

"I'm broke, simply."

"You don't look much like it."

To say the truth, he did not; he never did. He had had his ups and downs; but if he was down he hid away in outer darkness; if you saw him at all, he was floating like a jaunty cork on the very top of the wave. He was a marvel to everyone; it was a mystery how he lasted so long. Money went away from him as rain runs off the oiled surface of a shiny mackintosh coat. And yet he had always plenty of it; eclipses he might know, but they were partial; collapse might threaten, but it was always delayed. He had still the best dinners, the best cigars, the best brougham; was *bien vu* in the best society: had the best boot-varnish in London, and wore the most curly-brimmed hats, the envy of every hatter but his own. To all outward seeming there was no more fortunate prosperous man about town; the hard shifts to which he had been put at times were known only to himself—and to one other man, who had caught him tripping once, and found his account in the fact. The pressure this man excited drove Gilly Jillingham nearly to despair. He was really on the brink of ruin at this moment, although he stood before Phillipa as reckless and defiant as when he had first won her girlish affections, and thrown them carelessly on one side.

"How can I help you?" asked Phillipa, when he had repeated his news.

"I never imagined you could; but you take such an interest in me, I thought you might like to know."

"And you have dragged me up to London simply to tell me this?"

"Certainly. You always took a delight in coming when I called."

It was evident that he had a strong hold over her. She trembled violently.

"Are these lies I hear?" he went on, speaking with mocking emphasis. "Can it be possible you mean to marry that cub?"

"Who has been telling you this?"

"Answer my question."

"What right have you to ask?"

"The best. You know it. Have you not been promised to me since— since—"

"Well, do you wish me to redeem my promise? I am ready to marry you now—to-day, if you please. Ruined as you are, reckless, unprincipled, gambler—I know not what—"

"That's as well. But I am obliged to you; I will not trespass on your good-nature. I shall have enough to do to keep myself."

"We might go to a colony."

"I can fancy you in the bush!"

"Anything would be preferable to the false, hollow life I lead. I want rest. I could pray for it. I long to lay my head peacefully where—"

"Wherever you please. Try Mr. Purling's shoulder. You have my full permission."

Phillipa's eyes flashed fire at this heartless *persiflage*.

"There is no such luck."

"Can he dare to be indifferent? How you must hate him!"

"As I did you."

"And do still? Thank you. But I wish you joy. When is it to be?"

"I tell you there is absolutely nothing between us. Mr. Purling is, to the best of my belief, engaged already."

"Not with his mother's consent, surely? Why, then, has she made so much of you?"

"No; not with her consent; indeed, it is quite against her wish. Mrs. Purling as much as told me that if her son married this cousin he would be disinherited. They do not agree very well together now."

"It's all hers—the old woman's—in her own right?"

"So far as I know."

Gilly Jillingham lay back in his chair and mused for a while.

"It's not a bad game if the cards play true."

His evil genius, had he been present, might have hinted that sometimes the cards played for Mr. Jillingham a little too true.

"Not a bad game. Phillipa, how do you stand with this old beldame?"

"She pretends the most ardent affection for me."

"There are no other relatives, no one she would take up if this son gave unpardonable offence?"

"Not that I know of. Besides, she calls me her dear daughter already."

"And would adopt you, doubtless, if the cub were got out of the way. Yes, it can be done, I believe, and you can do it, Phillipa, if you please. Only persuade the old lady to make you the heiress of the Purlings, and there will be an end to your troubles—and mine."

Soon after this conversation Miss Fanshawe returned to Purlington. The heiress smothered her with caresses.

"I shall not let you go away again. We have missed you more than I can say."

"And you also, Mr. Harold? Are you glad to see me again?"

Harold bowed courteously.

"Of course; I have been counting the hours to Miss Fanshawe's return."

"Fibs! I can't believe it."

By-and-by she came to him.

"Why cannot we be friends, Mr. Purling? It pains me to be hated as you hate me."

"You are really quite mistaken," Harold began.

"I am ready to prove my friendship. I know all about Miss Driver—there!"

"Do you know where she is at this present moment?" Harold asked, eagerly.

"You really wish to know? Your mother will tell me, I daresay. How hard hit you must be! But there is my hand on it. You shall have all the help that I can give."

Next day she told him.

"Miss Driver is at Harbridge."

"In service?"

"No; at home. They live there. Her father is a Custom-house officer."

That evening Harold informed his mother that important business called him away. She remonstrated. How could he leave the house while Miss Fanshawe was still there? What was the business? At least he might tell his mother; or it might wait. She could not allow him to leave.

Mere waste of words; Harold was off next morning to Harbridge, and Phillipa reported progress to her co-conspirator.

"It promises well," said Gilly. "I may be able to muzzle that scoundrel after all."

CHAPTER V

A quaint old red-sandstone town; the river-harbour crowded with small craft, but now and again, like a Triton among the minnows, a timber-brig or a trading-barque driven in by stress of weather. When the tide went out—as it did seemingly with no intention of coming back, it went so far—the long level sands were spotted with groups of fisherfolk, who dug with pitchforks for sand-eels; while in among the rocks an army of children gleaned great harvests of a kind of seaweed, which served for food when times were hard.

These rocks were the seaward barrier and break-water of the little port, and did their duty well when, as now, they were tried by the full force of a westerly gale. It is blowing great guns; the hardy sheep that usually browse upon the upland slopes must starve perforce to-day—they cannot stand upon the steep incline; the cocks and hens of the cottagers take refuge to leeward of their homes; every gust is laden with atoms of sand or stone, which strike like hail or small shot upon the face. See how the waves dash in at the outlying rocks, hurrying onward like blood-hounds in full cry, scuffling, struggling, madly jostling one another in eagerness to be first in the fray; joining issue with tremendous crash, only to be spent, broken, dissipated into thin air. Overhead the sky changes almost with the speed of the blast; sometimes the sun winks from a corner of the leaden clouds and tinges with glorious light the foam-bladders as they burst and scatter around their clouds of spray; in between the headlands the sea is churned into creaming froth, as though the housewives of the sea-gods with unwearying arms were whipping "trifle" for some tremendous bridal-feast.

The houses at Harbridge mostly faced the shore, but all had stone porches, and the doors stood not in front, but at one side. The modest cottage which Mr. Driver called his own was like the rest; but as he enters, for all his care, a keen knife-edged gust of the pushing wind precedes him and announces his return. Next instant the little lobby is filled: a bevy of daughters, the good house-mother, one or two youngsters dragging at his legs, everyone eager to welcome the breadwinner home. They divest him of his wraps, soothing him the while with that tender loving solicitude a man finds only at his own happy hearth.

He unfolds his budget of news: a lugger driven by stress of weather upon the Castle Rock; suspicions of smuggling among the rough beyond Langness Cove; Dr. Holden's new partner arrived last night.

"I have asked him to come up this evening. A decent sort of chap."

Forthwith they fired a volley of questions. Was he old or young, married or single? had he blue eyes or brown? and how was he called?

To all papa makes shift to reply. The name he had forgotten, also the colour of his hair; but the fellow had eyes and two arms and two legs; he did not squint; had a pleasant address and all the appearance of an unmarried man.

"How could you see that, wise father?" asked Doll.

"He looked so sheepish when I mentioned my daughters. Doubtless he had heard of you, Miss Doll, and of your dangerous wiles."

She pinched his ear. They were excellent friends, were father and eldest daughter. Mr. Driver, a scholar and a man of letters, who had been thankful to exchange an uncertain footing upon the lower rungs of the ladder of literature for a small post under Government, had for years devoted his talents to the education of the children. In Dolly, as his most apt pupil, he took a peculiar pride.

"Come in, doctor!" cried Mr. Driver that night. "We are all dying, but only to make your acquaintance."

The new visitor was checked at the very threshold by Dolly's cry—

"Mr. Purling!"

And Harold stood confessed to his cousins without a chance of further disguise.

"Cousin Harold, you mean," he said, as he offered Dolly his hand.

She tried hard to hide her blushes; and then and there Mrs. Driver, after the manner of mothers, built up a great castle in the air, which her husband shook instantly to its foundations by asking unceremoniously and not without a shade of angry suspicion in his tone—

"Why did you not claim relationship this morning?"

He disliked the notion of a man stealing into his house under false colours.

"I waited for you to speak. You heard my name."

"I did not catch it clearly. Besides, I had never heard of you. None of us have. Your mother did not choose to recognise the relationship."

"She called you a tide-waiter," said his wife indignantly.

"At least I'm not a white-tied waiter," cried Mr. Driver, with a laugh, in which all joined. Then in low voice Dolly said—

"I met Mr. Purling at Purlington."

At which her father turned upon her with newly-raised suspicion. Why had she not mentioned the fact before? But something in Mrs. Driver's face deterred him. A woman in these matters sees how the land lies, while the cleverest man is still unable to distinguish it from the clouds upon the horizon-line.

"We are pleased to know you, Harold," said Mrs. Driver, a gentle, soft-voiced motherly person.

"You have really come to practise here?" went on the father, still rather on his guard.

"I wanted sea-air. The change will do me good," replied Harold, rather evasively. "I like the place, too."

Not a doubt of it. Harbridge was after his own heart, and so were some people who lived in it. He found it so much to his taste that he declared within a week or two that he thought of remaining there altogether. He would go into partnership with the local doctor; perhaps he had another partnership also in his eye.

"Can't you see what's going on under your nose, father?" asked Mrs. Driver.

"What do I care? I shall not interfere."

"Mrs. Purling will never give her consent. Poor Doll!"

"*That* for Mrs. Purling and her consent!" said Mr. Driver, snapping his fingers. "Doll is ever so much too good for them—well, not for him; he is an honest, straightforward fellow: but as for that selfish, silly, purse-proud old woman, she may thank Heaven if she gains a daughter like Doll."

That this was not Mrs. Purling's view of the question was plainly evident from a letter which awoke Harold rather rudely from his rosy dreams.

"So at length I have found you out, Harold. I never dreamt you could be so deceitful and double-faced. To talk of clinical lectures in town, and all the time at Harbridge, philandering with that forward, intriguing girl! Only with the greatest difficulty have I succeeded in learning the truth. Phillipa— who, it seems, has known your secret all along, and to whom, I find, you have constantly written—could not continue indifferent to my distress of mind. Although she has shielded you so far with a magnanimity that is truly heroic, she has interposed at length only to save my life.

"I desire you will come to me at once. Do not disobey me, Harold. I am very seriously displeased, and will only consent to forgive the past when I find you ready to bend your stubborn heart to obey my will."

Harold started at once for home. He hoped rather against hope that he might talk his mother over; but her aspect was not encouraging when he met her face to face.

No tragedy-queen could have assumed more scorn. Mrs. Purling, having thrown herself into several attitudes, fell at length into a chair.

"I never thought it," she said; "not from my own and only child. The serpent's tooth hath not such fangs, such power to sting, as the base ingratitude of one undutiful boy. But this fills the cup. I have done with you—for ever, unless you give me your sacred word of honour now, at this minute, never to speak to Dolly Driver again."

"Such a promise would be quite impossible under any circumstances, but I distinctly refuse to give it—upon compulsion."

"Then you have fair warning. Not one penny of my money shall you ever possess. I will never see you again."

"I sincerely trust the last is only an empty threat, my dearest mother."

She made a gesture as though she were not to be beguiled by soft words.

"As for the money, it matters little. Thank God, I have my profession."

"At which you will starve."

"By which I shall earn my bread as my father did. Besides, I can fall back upon the reputation of the Family Pills."

"I see you wish to goad me beyond endurance, Harold. Go!"

"For good and all?"

"Yes; except on the one alternative. Will you give up this idiotic passion? You refuse. It is on your own head, then. Go—go till I send for you, which will be never!"

Harold went without another word—to Harbridge, overcame Dolly's scruples, secured the practice, and within a month was married and settled.

Mrs. Purling, in Phillipa's presence, made a great parade of burning her will.

"He has brought it all on himself, unnatural boy! But you, darling Phillipa, will never treat me thus. *Noblesse oblige.* The bright blue blood that fills your veins would curdle at a *mésalliance*, I know."

Mrs. Purling was quite calm and self-possessed, while Miss Fanshawe, strange to say, seemed agitated enough for both. Her hands trembled, she looked away; only with positive repugnance she submitted to her new mother's affectionate embrace. A woman who is capable of the most cold-blooded calculating intrigue may yet have an access of remorse. Phillipa's heart was heavy now at the moment of her triumph. It cost her more than a passing pang to remember that she had robbed Harold Purling of his birthright, and had turned to her own base purpose the foolish cravings of the silly mother's heart.

But she had put aside self-upbraiding when she met her lover in town.

"Faith, you are a trump, Phillipa; but it's not much too soon. When will you take your reward?"

"Meaning Mr. Jillingham? Is the reward worth taking, I wonder?" For a moment she held him at bay. "Suppose I were to refuse you now at the eleventh hour? It is for you to sue. I am not what I was. Mrs. Purling calls me the heiress of the Purlings, and we may not consider Mr. Gilbert Jillingham a very eligible *parti*."

"You dare not refuse me, Phillipa," said Gilly very seriously. "I should expose your schemes, and we should go to the wall together. No, there is no escape for you now; our interests are identical."

"How am I to introduce you upon the scene?"

"Quite naturally; I shall go and stay at Compton Revel. They will have me, for your sake, if not for my own. I shall begin *de novo*—at the very beginning: be smitten, pay you court, win over the heiress, and propose."

So it fell out, and they also were married before the end of the year.

CHAPTER VI

Mean as had been their conduct towards Mrs. Purling and her son, Phillipa and her husband were not to be classed with common adventurers of the ordinary type. Born in a lower station, Gilly Jillingham might have taken honours as a "prig"; in his own with less luck he might have been an Ishmaelite generally shunned. Phillipa also might have degenerated into a mere soured cackling hanger-on; but they were not pariahs by caste, but Brahmins, and entitled to all due honour so long as they floated on top of the wave. Perhaps if near drowning no finger would have been outstretched to save; but there were plenty to pat them on the back as they disported themselves on the sound dry land. Fair-weather friends and needy relatives rallied round their prosperity, of course; but they were also accepted as successful social facts by the whole of that great world which judges for the most part by appearances, being too idle or too much engrossed by folly to apply more accurate or searching tests. In good society those who cared to talk twice of the matter blamed Harold; he was absent; besides, he had gone to the wall, therefore he must be in the wrong. On the other hand, the Jillinghams deserved the triumph that is never denied success. To Gilly prosperous were forgiven the sins of Gilly in social and moral rags. If scandal like an evil gas had been let loose to crystallise upon Phillipa's good name, the black stains could not adhere long to so charming a person, who made the Purling mansion in Berkeley Square one of the best-frequented and most fashionable in town.

There were many reasons why the Jillinghams should find their account in perpetual junketings. Social excitement was as the breath in Gilly's nostrils; notorious for profuse expenditure even when he was penniless, he was now absolutely reckless with money that was plentiful and moreover not his own. Nor was the constant whirl of gaieties without its charm for Phillipa; it deadened conscience, and consoled in some measure for the neglect and indifference she soon encountered at her husband's hands. But the most potent reason was that it fooled Mrs. Purling to the top of her bent. Self-satisfaction beamed upon her ample face as she found herself at length in constant intercourse and on a social equality—as she thought— with the potentates and powers and great ones of the earth. Gilly Jillingham in the days of his apogee had been the spoiled favourite of more than one titled dame; his success must have been great, to measure it by the envy and hatred he evoked among his fellowmen—even when in the cold shade there were duchesses who fought for him still; and now, when once more in full blossom, all his fair friends were ready to pet him as of old. The form in which their kindness pleased him best—because it was most to his advantage—was in making much of Mrs. Purling. Great people have the knack of putting those whom they patronise on the very best terms with themselves; and Mrs. Purling was so convinced of her success as a leader of fashion that she would have asked for a peerage in her own right, taking for arms three pills proper upon a silver field, if she could have been certain that these honours would not descend to her recreant son.

Whether or not, as time passed, she was absolutely happy, she did not pause to inquire. The devotion of her newly-adopted children was so unstinting, and they kept her so continually busy, that she had not time for self-reproach. It was a disappointment to her that the Jillinghams had no prospect of a family, and her chagrin would have been increased had she known that already a boy and girl had been born to the rightful heirs at Harbridge. But such news was carefully kept from her; she was rigorously cut off from all communication with her son. There was no safety otherwise against mischance; the strange processes of the old creature's mind were inscrutable; she might in one spasm of an awakened conscience undo all. For the Jillinghams were still absolutely dependent upon her; she could turn them out of house and home whenever she pleased. A small settlement was all the real property Phillipa had secured. Although with right royal generosity Mrs. Purling gave her favourites a liberal allowance, and promised them everything when she was gone, yet was she like a crustacean in the tenacity of her grip upon her own. This close-fistedness was exceedingly distasteful to Mr. Jillingham. He had an appetite for gold not easily appeased, and four or five thousand a year was to him but a mouthful to be swallowed at one gulp.

Openly of course he continued on his best behaviour, but behind the scenes he permitted himself to grumble loudly at the old lady's meanness and miserly ways.

"I cannot understand you, Gilbert. I cannot see what you do with all the money you get," said Phillipa reproachfully one day when they were alone, and Gilly was enlarging upon his favourite theme. "You live at free quarters, you have no expenses and ought to have no debts."

"Have you no debts, pray?"

"None that you are ignorant of."

"Look here, Phillipa; listen to me. I spend what I please, how I please. I shall give no account of it to you, nor to any one else in the world."

"It is not necessary. I had rather not be told. I do not care to know," said Phillipa, womanlike, forgetting that she had begun by wishing to be informed. She had her own suspicions, but forbore to question further, lest she might be brought face to face with the outrages she feared he put upon her.

"She will take to counting the potatoes next. It's most contemptible. A mean old brute—"

"I shall not listen to you, Gilbert. You owe her everything."

"Do I? I wonder what my tailor would say to that or Reuben Isaac Melchisedec? I've more than one creditor; they are a prolific and, I am sorry to say, a long-lived race."

"I hope Mrs. Purling may live to be a hundred years at least—"

"I don't. I'd rather she was choked by one of those pills you tell me she takes every morning and night."

There was something in his tone which made Phillipa look at him hard. Was it possible that he contemplated any terrible wickedness? The mere apprehension made her blood run cold.

"O Gilly, swear to me that you will not harbour evil thoughts, that you will put aside the devil who is prompting and luring you to some awful crime!"

"Psha, Phillipa, you ought to have gone into the Church. Moderate your transports—here comes one of the footmen."

"A person to see you, sir," said the servant. "He 'aven't got any card, but his business is very particular."

"I can't see him; send him away. If he won't go call the police."

"Says his name, sir, is Shubenacady."

"Take him to the library; I'll come."

Jillingham's face was rather pale, and his lips were set firm when he met his visitor.

"What the mischief do you want?"

"Five thou—ten—what you please. I know of a splendid investment."

"In soap?"

He was the dirtiest creature that ever was seen. He wore a full suit of black, but the coat and trousers were white with age and dust-stains; an open waistcoat, exposing an embroidered shirt which could not have been washed for months; his hat was napless, and had a limp brim; no gloves, and the grimiest of hands. But he was decorated, and wore a ribbon, probably of St. Lucifer.

"In soap, or shavings, or shoddy; what does it matter to you? When can I have the money?"

"Never; not another sixpence."

"Then I shall publish all I know."

"No one will believe you."

"I have proofs."

"Which are forged. I tell you I'm too strong for you: you will find yourself in the wrong box. I am sick of this; and I mean to put an end to your extortion."

"You dare me. You know the consequences."

"The first consequence will be that I shall give you in charge. Be off!"

"You shall have a week to think better of it."

Gilly rang the bell.

"Shall I send for a policeman, or will you go?"

He went, muttering imprecations intermixed with threats; but Gilly Jillingham, quite proud of his courage, seemed for the moment callous to both. He little dreamt how soon the latter would be put into effect.

Within a few days of this interview the greatest event of Mrs. Purling's whole social career was due; she was to entertain royalty beneath her own roof. This crowning of the edifice of her ambition filled her with solemn awe; the preparations for the coming ball were stupendous, her own magnificent costume seemed made up of diamonds and bullion and five-pound notes.

Long before the hour of reception she might have been seen pacing to and fro with stately splendour, contemplating the daïs erected for royalty at one end of the room, and thinking with a glow of satisfaction that the representative of the Purlings had at last come to her own. At this supreme moment she was grateful to dear Phillipa and to Gilbert little less dear.

Then guests began to pour in. Where was Phillipa? Very late; she might have dressed earlier. A servant was sent to call her, and Phillipa, hurrying down, met Gilly on the upper floor coming out of Mrs. Purling's bedroom.

"What have you been doing there?" she asked.

"Mrs. Purling wanted a fan," said Gilly readily.

She might want one fan, but hardly two; and had Phillipa been less flurried she might have noticed that Mrs. Purling had one already in her hand. But then their Royal Highnesses arrived; the heiress made her curtsey for the first time in her life, was graciously received, and the hour of her apotheosis had actually come. Presently the crowd became so dense that every inch of space was covered; people overflowed on to the landings, and sat four or five deep upon the stairs. Dancing was simply impossible; however, hundreds of couples went through the form. Phillipa, as in duty bound, remained in the thick of the *mêlée*, but Gilly had very early disappeared. He preferred the card-room; his waltzing days were over, he said. He was playing; it was not very good taste, but there were some men who preferred a quiet rubber to looking at princes or the antics of boys and girls, and he wished to oblige his friends.

"Can you give me a moment, Le Grice?" said Lord Camberwell, coming into the card-room. "I have had a most extraordinary letter. It accuses Gilly Jillingham—"

"God bless my soul," cried old Colonel Le Grice, "a letter of the same sort has been sent to me!"

"Have you had any suspicion that he played unfairly?"

"Not the slightest; I know he always holds the most surprising hands, that he plays for very high stakes, that he nearly always wins—"

"Is he winning now?"

Of course. Mr. Jillingham's luck never deserted him. He was trying now perhaps to make at one coup sufficient to silence for a further space his enemy's tongue; the bets upon the odd trick alone amounted to a thousand or more. But he was too late. His hour had come.

Suddenly Lord Camberwell spoke in a loud peremptory voice:

"Stop! Mr. Jillingham is cheating. He does it in the deal. I have watched him now for three rounds."

"And so have I," added Colonel Le Grice.

Gilly sprang to his feet. For a moment he seemed disposed to brazen it out; then he read his sentence in the face of those who had detected and now judged him. There was no appeal: he was doomed. From henceforth he was socially and morally dead, and, without a word, he slunk away from the house.

The buzz of the ball-room soon caught up the ugly scandal, and tossed it wildly from lip to lip. "Mr. Jillingham caught cheating at cards!" Everyone said, of course, they had suspected it all along; now every one knew it as a fact, except those most nearly concerned. To them it came last. To Phillipa, whose heart it stabbed as with a knife, cut through and through; then to Mrs. Purling, who, a little taken aback by the sudden exodus of her guests, asked innocently what it meant, upon which some one, without knowing who she was, told her the exact truth.

Quite stunned by the terrible shock, dazed, terrified, was the heiress, scarcely capable of comprehending what had occurred. Then with a sad, scared face, motioning Phillipa on one side, who, equally white and grief-stricken, would have helped her, she crept slowly upstairs, feeling that at one blow the whole fabric of her social repute was tumbled in the dust.

The lights were out, the play was over, the house still and silent, when, with loud shrieks, Mrs. Purling's maid rushed to Phillipa's room.

"Mrs. Purling, ma'am!—my mistress, she is dying! Come to her! She is nearly gone!"

In truth, the poor old woman was in the extremest agony; it was quite terrible to see her. She gasped as if for air; her whole frame jerked and twitched with the violence of her convulsions; gradually her body was drawn in a curve, like that of a tensely-strung bow.

The spasms abated, then recommenced; abated, then raged with increased fury. But through it all she was conscious; she had even the power of speech, and cried aloud again and again, with a bitter heart-wrung cry, for "Harold! Harold!" the absent much-wronged son.

"The symptoms are those of tetanus," said the nearest medical practitioner, who had been called in. He seemed fairly puzzled. "Tetanus or—" He did not finish the sentence, because the single word that was on his lips formed a serious charge against a person or persons unknown. "But there is nothing to explain lock-jaw; while the abatement of the symptoms points to—" Again he paused.

The muscles of the mouth, which had been the last attacked, gradually resumed their normal condition. The patient appeared altogether more easy, the writhings subsided; presently, as if utterly exhausted, she sank off to sleep.

Harold Purling had come up post-haste from Harbridge; and when the mother opened her eyes they rested upon her son.

A hurried consultation passed in whispers between the two doctors. Phillipa was present; she and the maid had not left Mrs. Purling all night.

"Mother," said Harold, "you are out of all danger. Tell me—do you recollect taking anything likely to make you ill?"

"Only the pills." She pointed to the family medicine—a box of which stood always by her bedside. She had some curious notion that it was her duty to show belief in the Primeval Pills, and she made a practice of swallowing two morning and night.

Harold opened the box; examined the pills; finally put one into his mouth and bit it through. Bitter as gall.

"They have been tampered with," he said. "These contain strychnia. You have had a narrow escape of being poisoned, dearest mother—poisoned by your own Pills!"

He half smiled at the conceit.

"There has been foul play, I swear. It shall be sifted to the bottom, and the guilty called to serious account."

But the mystery was never solved. If Phillipa had in her heart misgivings, she kept her suspicions to herself; no one accused her; there seemed explanation for her cowed and trembling manner in Gilly's downfall and disgrace. The man himself never reappeared openly; only now and again he swooped down and robbed Phillipa of all she, possessed—the thrift of her allowance from Mrs. Purling.

As for the heiress, surrounded by the real love and warm hearts of her lineal descendants, she was satisfied to eschew all further acquaintance with people of the Blue Blood.